Psychic Blind

PREQUEL TO THE OTHER HALF

By

Kimberly Atwood Balser

"Don't worry about what might not happen. Life changes in a heartbeat.

Live for today."

-KJ

Many thanks to Myrna D'Ambrosio for being my cheerleader, helping to edit and give constructive feedback on what turned out to be a very complex project.

Avery Atwood-1948-2017. There was so many times I thought of you during the writing of this book; I'd like to believe that I'm 'psychic blind'; that you're sending me signals. I miss you, dad.

Mary Sabina Koch Thomas- 1921-2015. I can still hear your laugh, Grammy.

Prologue

Maria had no idea how she'd gotten here, but the car she was in was on backroads and there were no streetlights and they were in the middle of a thunderstorm. The huge drops of rain pounding on the windshield were making it almost impossible to see anything, and she could feel the wind shaking the car. The car was going too fast and was fishtailing as the tires hit puddles of water. Maria was in the back seat in between two little girls in car seats. "You need to slow down!" She yelled to the man, but he kept driving as if she were invisible.

"Frank, I had such a good time this weekend. Even if it was tough with the girls." A young blonde woman was sitting in the passenger seat. She told him she was nervous about the rain. The man driving looked over at her. "Don't worry, sweetheart" he said and patted her on her leg. She didn't know why they couldn't hear her! She screamed in his ear, but he still couldn't hear her. It was as if she were invisible. "I did too, Margo. We need to start getting out more often." Margo grasped his hand and they were humming along to a song on the radio. The two little girls were adorably identical with beautiful blond hair, and matching blue and green dresses. Maria tried to wake them up by touching their chubby cheeks and squeezing their little hands, but they never woke up.

Frank and Margo continued talking when she noticed headlights from a car coming straight toward them. "Slow down! Get out of the way!" She screamed at them, hoping they could hear her. Frank suddenly noticed, "What the hell!" and swerved to avoid the car that was headed straight for them. Their car hit the gravel on the side of the road and as the driver tried to get the car back on the road, it hit a puddle of water and spun out of control. Margo suddenly screamed "Frank! Stop!" Maria was gripping the sides of the car seats, as the little girls woke up and began to cry. Maria tried to calm them. "It's okay, it'll be okay." She kept repeating over and over.

As the car was spinning around in circles, everyone in the car was screaming including Maria. The car flipped over and skidded toward the woods that surrounded the road. When it came to a stop, Maria could see flames coming from the back of the car. She could feel the heat, as both Frank and Margo got out of the car and ran to the back seat to get the little girls out. Maria tried to unfasten the clips on their car seat, but the clasps wouldn't budge. "Help, help!" She screamed even though she knew they couldn't hear her. Frank managed to get one of the girls out of her car seat and pulled her out, but the other girl next to her was stuck. Maria could see the flames getting closer and closer and the little girl next to her was crying. "Someone help us!" She screamed hoping that someone could hear them. She could hear voices outside; "get her out, get her out!" The car suddenly exploded in a ball of flames, glass and metal flying in all different directions.

She woke up screaming and was sitting straight up in bed when her babysitter, Megan came running in. "Maria? What's the matter?"

"There was an accident. An explosion! A man and woman that looked just like my mom and dad. They even had the same names. But there were two little girls in the car; I didn't know them." Megan looked relieved. "Maria, you had a bad dream, that's all. Want me to sit with you while you go back to sleep?"

Maria actually would have, but she knew she'd complained to her parents about having a babysitter at age 11 when most girls were actual babysitters, so she shook her head. "No, I'm okay." She managed although she was shivering underneath her comforter.

"Okay, let me know if you want me to come back." Megan gave her a slight hug and left the room. "Can you leave the door open though?" Maria asked as she started to close it. It was a compromise between what she needed to still maintain her 11- year- old dignity. 'It's just a dream, I can go back to sleep,' Maria kept saying to herself over and over. But something wasn't right. She just couldn't understand why she felt as though something had happened or was about to happen.

7 Years Later~William and Maria

William Carson was shocked that he'd been accepted by the University of Rhode Island when he got the letter in the mail. His grades had always been below average, mainly because he hated school and studying subjects that he had no interest in. He'd secretly been hoping to go to New England Tech for auto repair, but he knew his father wouldn't approve. "William, you need to get a good education! I've worked hard my whole life so that you and your sister can go to college and get a good job!" Jack Carson was tough on William especially. Jack had spent long hours as a mechanic right out of high school and he wanted nothing more than his son to get a college education so that he wouldn't have to struggle.

William agreed to attend URI and claimed business management as his major as his father wanted. He was dreading it but at the same time, he'd at least be out from underneath his father's thumb. Jack worked hard all day, just to come home and drown his sorrows in glasses of whiskey. William and his sister Barbara learned early on not to bother him after 6:00. On more than one occasion, Jack had taken his frustrations out at the dinner table when William's mother, Sara, would serve something that he didn't like. William remembered it clearly when his mother served chicken instead of steak and his father sent the entire plate of chicken flying across the table, nearly hitting him in the head. There were other times when Jack was upset with him for his grades and he got whipped with a belt until he couldn't sit down without pain for days. Barbara was spared the belt, because his mother and William sent her to her room while Jack was out of control.

William was moving his belongings into the dorm a few days before classes. He was carrying a huge basket that he could barely see over through the doors when he ran into someone. "Hey, watch it!" A female voice yelled at him. He was ready to yell back that his hands were full when he peered over the basket and immediately dropped it at his feet. The girl in front of him was scowling at him, but she was stunning. Her cerulean blue eyes would stand out in a crowd and her long blonde hair cascaded over her shoulders. She was petite, probably only a little over 5 feet tall, and her figure was amazing in her shorts and simple t-shirt. William was at a loss for words for a moment.

"Well, don't you have anything to say?" She snapped at him, as she stood with her hands on her hips.

"I'm so sorry, um. I didn't see you." William was stumbling over his words. 'Get it together, Carson!' He told himself.

"Well, watch where you're going next time!" She stormed off before he could say another word. But he was mesmerized as he watched her walk away. Her shorts showed off her tanned and toned legs. William had a few girlfriends in high school, but no one had ever had this impact on him before. She was beautiful, but there was something else about her that he knew he wouldn't forget. He could tell that she was feisty and independent. She probably hated him, but it didn't stop him from thinking about her.

William's dorm roommate was already setting up when he made it upstairs. "Hey! I'm Josh!" His roommate was a tall but muscular guy with a crew cut, dressed in running shorts and a tank top. 'Oh, no, not one of those jocks as a roommate,' William thought to himself as he piled his stuff on his mattress.

"Nice to meet you. I'm William, but everyone calls me Bill." He was less than optimistic about his ability to get along with this guy who clearly was fraternity material, but he was stuck with him until Josh pledged. William despised fraternities. He considered them a bunch of rich guys with parents who paid their tuition so they could party their way through school.

As it turned out Josh wasn't the frat boy that William thought he was as he spent the next couple of hours getting moved in. He was a sophomore transfer from Boston College, majoring in criminal justice. Josh wasn't arrogant, despite his good looks. He was friendly, outgoing and seemed genuine. When William mentioned the blonde girl that he'd run into, Josh was the first to give him information. "Her name's Maria Evans. She's a sophomore and just started dating Dan Ahearn. He's a football player of course, and kind of a jerk to her. I'm surprised she hasn't dumped him by now!" Josh said. "She's gorgeous. But she doesn't give anyone else the time of day, except Dan. Hopefully, she'll change her mind about him!"

William nodded. "I hope so! She deserves better." He didn't say anything more, but Josh did. "Uh oh, you're already into her, I can tell." He nodded. "Don't worry, my girl isn't far away. She's in Boston, but I see her every weekend. So, this place is yours on the weekends." Josh admitted that he'd partied too much in his freshman year in Boston and his parents gave him the ultimatum that he needed to switch to URI and keep the costs down or drop out.

William laughed. "I seriously doubt that Maria will be dumping him for me. If looks could kill, she just did me in when I almost knocked her over when I came in the door earlier!" He told Josh about his encounter with her.

"Hey, don't worry about it. There's plenty of good-looking girls to go around here!" Josh said. "Trust me, when you start classes tomorrow, you'll forget all about her!"

William hoped that was the case, but there was something about Maria that made him want to get to know her better, even if just as friends. When he went to his first class of the semester which was Intro to Business Management, he was pleasantly surprised to see Maria sitting in the front row when he arrived. Luckily there was a seat right next to her and he took advantage of it. She looked especially pretty that day, wearing a white skirt and a sky-blue top that made her blue eyes stand out even more. Her blonde hair was swept back in a long ponytail. She had an effect on him that no other girl had before.

He was suddenly nervous to talk to her, but knew that this might be his only chance, especially after his run-in with her the other day. She was fiddling with her purse and he figured this was a good time to strike up a conversation. "Hey, there. You look familiar." He said, hoping that she'd forgotten her irritation with him from a few days ago.

She turned in her seat to face him and she frowned. "Aren't you that guy that tried to run me over outside the dorm the other day?"

"I wish I hadn't but, yeah, it's me." William said apologetically. Clearly he'd made a really bad first impression! "I'm really sorry about that. My hands were full and I didn't see you. I'm William. William Carson." He decided to introduce himself, regardless of how awkward this was becoming. He waited for her to either tell him to get lost or just get up and move to another seat across the room.

"I'm Maria Evans." Her face softened a little. "Sorry if I was rude, but it's not the first time that guys have pulled stunts like that. But since you apologized, you're forgiven." She smiled at him and he was glad that he hadn't chickened out on talking to her. Her smile lit up her whole face and he knew that he was not going to ever forget about this girl. "It's nice to meet you, Maria Evans. Are you a business major?" William took the opportunity to ask her more questions before class started.

"No, I'm actually a psychology major, but I thought that taking this class might help me decide if I wanted to open my own practice someday." Maria admitted. "Are you a business major?"

"That's the goal. I'd like to own a business someday. Not sure what area yet, but here I am." William said honestly.

"Good for you. At least you have an idea of what you want. I haven't met too many guys that have a clue what they want to do. It seems like they're just partying and don't have any plan," Maria said, as a tall muscular dark haired guy came out of nowhere and put his arms around her neck. "Guess who?"

"Dan! Stop it! We're in class!" Maria sounded annoyed as she pushed his arms away from her. William's first impression of Maria's current boyfriend was as accurate as Josh's description. Total muscle head, arrogant and had no interest in learning. This was just a free ride for him while he played sports. Dan didn't seem to get the obvious hint as he sat next to her and moved the seat over to put his arm around her again. He glanced over at William. "Hey, she's taken." He said with an arrogant grin on his face. Maria moved his arm again. "Dan, stop it!"

William knew it was time to stand up for Maria despite only talking to her for five minutes. How dare this creep treat her this way? He was reminded of how his father treated his mom and he went into protective mode. "Hey, she said stop it! Do you understand English?" William said.

Dan turned to him with a smug grin on his face. "Yeah? What are *you* gonna do about it?" He stood up and faced William with his 6'2" frame. William was 6', and didn't have nearly the muscle to take on this guy. But something about the way he was treating Maria didn't sit right with him and he wasn't backing down, even if it meant getting his ass kicked! William was getting ready to tell him to bring it on when the professor walked in and took over the class. "Alright, people, take a seat!" Professor Samuels had a reputation for getting to the point and had no problem kicking students out of his class. He was older with graying hair and glasses, but he was tough. William sat back down and Dan continued standing, glaring at William.

"Excuse me, what's your name?" Professor Samuels asked Dan. Dan finally looked uncomfortable.

"Dan Ahearn." He finally answered.

"Well, Dan Ahearn, I suggest you take a seat or leave. You have 5 seconds to decide." Professor Samuels' voice let him know that there was no other option. Dan walked to the back of the room and sat down. Maria gave William a grateful smile and whispered, "Thank you, William Carson." William felt a tingle go through him as he saw her face.

9

"You're very welcome. It's the least I can do after I almost ran you over." William joked with her. He only hoped that she'd agree to go out with him and dump that loser of a boyfriend!

It didn't take Maria long to break up with Dan Ahearn. Only a few days to be exact and William wasted no time in pursuing her before someone else came into the picture. They began spending most of their time together after classes and on the weekends. They took weekend trips to Newport and spent time walking on the Cliff Walk or touring the mansions.

Maria was from a tiny town in Vermont called Orwell and had never been to the ocean before. Her face lit up the first time she went to the ocean, so they would spend hours walking at Matunuck beach in South Kingstown. William began to have a whole new perspective about his home state through Maria's eyes, as he watched her skimming her feet in the waves and watching the seagulls take flight after picking at beach-goers left overs. She was completely different from anyone he'd ever known and he knew that he wanted to spend the rest of his life with her. During the next few months, they became inseparable.

By the time the Christmas break came along, William and Maria were discussing their plans. "I think I'm just going to stay here and study." Maria told William. William wasn't especially looking forward to going home even though it was only a 45 -minute drive to Providence. In the end, he agreed to spend Christmas eve and day with his family, but insisted that Maria come with him. Maria finally agreed, although she knew that William wasn't excited about seeing his family. He'd told her the details about his father and she wasn't sure that she'd fit in, but it was important to him. And she loved him. She could hear her mother's voice in her head telling her that it would be okay and she believed her. So far, everything she'd told her had been accurate.

Maria

Maria never expected to meet anyone like William. She had always met guys that were asking her out in high school but never any that really seemed to care. She'd never really had more than a casual boyfriend and after she never gave them what they wanted, the 'relationship' ended quickly. She could tell he was different. And she'd gotten her mother's 'approval'.

Maria's experience as an only child was unique. Her parents had been killed in a car accident when she was 11 years old, and she was sent to live with her maternal Aunt Sylvia who lived in Middlebury. Sylvia didn't have any maternal instincts. She was divorced and had a teenaged son, Lucas. Maria had met her once or twice while her mother was alive and after meeting her again, she could understand why her mother didn't spend much time with her sister. From the first day Maria moved in, her aunt made it clear that she was 'only doing this because it's part of the inheritance', and Sylvia treated Maria as though she were just a guest in her home until she graduated from high school. Maria's mother, Margo had taken out a $500,000 insurance policy in case of her death to be overseen by her sister. Sylvia didn't have a problem spending the money, but it never included Maria. It had always bothered her that her aunt never once talked about her mother or even made an attempt to comfort her as a teenager that had just lost both of her parents.

However, Maria never felt far away from her parents, especially her mother. Just hours after the accident, Maria could still see her mother. The police had already notified them and there were several family members hovering around. Maria would continue to see her mother and father moving around their house in the weeks following, before moving in with Aunt Sylvia. Seeing them never frightened her. Maria had always seen shadows of relatives that she'd never met even as a young child and just assumed that most people could see them as well. She tried to tell her aunt about seeing her, but Sylvia brushed it off. "Your mother's gone! There's no way you could see her now." She told her the first time. The next time Maria mentioned it, her aunt became upset. "For god sakes! Stop with this! What is wrong with you, Maria? Margo is gone, she's just gone!" She started crying and from then on, Maria knew better than to mention her mother's presence.

Life in Aunt Sylvia's house was a different world than being at home. There were only two bedrooms, so she was stuck bunking up with her 13 -year -old cousin, Lucas, which was extremely awkward and becoming more so by the day. She missed her own room, in her own home with her parents that actually talked to her. Her cousin rarely spoke to her. Although on occasion, Lucas would make crude comments when they were both in his room about how they could become 'kissing cousins' if she wanted to. Maria immediately started sleeping on the couch from that night on. Aunt Sylvia woke her up in the morning the next day. "Why are you sleeping out here, Maria?" She looked surprised. Maria thought about telling her, but knew she wouldn't care or change the sleeping arrangements. She gave an excuse that she couldn't sleep and wanted to watch TV. Aunt Sylvia gave one of her disapproving looks so Maria knew that she'd have to start sleeping on the couch and setting an alarm before everyone else woke up.

The only constant in her life now was that she was able to stay in the Middlebury school district and that her mother continued to 'visit' her often, and once in a while, her father would also make an appearance. Maria had grown used to the fact that her mother appeared as a shadow, and occasionally give her advice. Her father's presence was rare. She was never as close to him, so she assumed that was why. She never mentioned seeing her parents to Aunt Sylvia again because she knew she'd probably be sent to a mental hospital.

Maria felt fortunate that she still had that connection with them. It was as if they were still with her, only she couldn't make any physical contact with them. It kept her going throughout her high school years when Lucas became even more obnoxious. By the time he was 18 and getting ready to graduate from high school, he would come home at 2:00 in the morning. Maria only knew this because she was still on the couch and she would pretend to be asleep while he was drunkenly bringing one of his many 'girlfriends' up to his room. She'd gotten a Walkman with headphones for a gift that past Christmas so she put it on in order to avoid listening to whatever Lucas was doing to those girls. How her aunt never heard him made her think that she was probably in a drug-induced sleep herself. Her aunt was probably one of the most miserable people she'd ever met. She never talked to friends on the phone or did anything with friends. She went to her job as a secretary at a local bank, came home and sat in front on the TV the rest of the night. At precisely 10 pm, she took her usual 'pills' and went to bed.

By the time Maria was a senior in high school, she was determined to go to college and get out of the home that felt like a prison to her all these years. She'd always been a straight A student; not because schoolwork was easy for her, but because she had nothing else to do except study. She knew that if she expected to get into college, she'd have to get scholarships in order to afford it. The inheritance that her parents left behind was gone, spent by Aunt Sylvia within a year after they died. The one thing that Maria had left was her mother's gold vintage jewelry box that had been passed down for generations. She wasn't sure of the monetary value, but saw how her aunt had been jealous when she received it. She kept it in a safe place in case Aunt Sylvia came across it. She was greedy and would probably try to sell it. It was an heirloom that Maria would not part with for all the money in the world.

Maria wanted to be as far away as possible from Vermont, so when her guidance counselor encouraged her to apply to the University of Rhode Island because they had a good psychology program with scholarships, Maria didn't hesitate. Besides, she'd never been to the ocean and was excited to go to school in the Ocean state where she could spend time at the beach. When she received her acceptance letter and several scholarships that would help her at least through the first year of classes, she was ecstatic.

She was surprised by her aunt's suggestion that she stay and go to Middlebury College, but she had no interest in sticking around, even if she didn't have to pay for dorm fees. Besides, the school was more expensive and even scholarships wouldn't make a dent in the cost. As soon as Maria mentioned the cost, her aunt quickly changed her tune.

15

Probably because she didn't want Maria to ask questions about the inheritance money that she'd already spent.

The night before Maria was going to drive her little Datsun that her aunt had given her to 'use' to go to school, she was having trouble sleeping as she tossed and turned on the small couch that had become her bed over the past several years. Just after midnight, she was finally drifting off when she heard the front door open and Lucas came stumbling in. He was still living at home, and supposedly working, but Maria knew he was probably just out smoking pot and drinking all day.

She tried to ignore the noise and go back to sleep, but then she heard him coming over toward the couch. "Hey, there Maria, room for one more?" He said in a slurred voice as he pulled off her blanket and tried to lie next to her. Maria was wide awake now and kicking him off of her.

"Lucas! Get out of here and leave me alone! You're drunk as usual!" Maria stood up. Luckily, she was wearing a full nightgown that covered her entire body. Lucas didn't seem to care and came toward her again, grabbing at her breasts. "Now that's something that I could get used to." He tried to push her back down on the couch, but Maria managed to move fast enough and grabbed a heavy lamp that was close to her on the side table. She held it like a baseball bat.

"Come any closer and I'll hit you!" She warned him. Lucas was either too drunk to realize that she was serious or he didn't care. He lunged toward her and she swung at him with the lamp, hitting him in the head and knocking him to the floor. He seemed to be unconscious and Maria was immediately worried that she'd killed him. "Oh, no! Lucas? Are you okay?" She started to panic as she felt for his pulse on his neck. He was still alive. She sighed in relief. He was just knocked out and would probably have a nasty headache when he woke up.

"What's all the noise down here?" Aunt Sylvia came down the stairs sleepily but saw Lucas lying near the couch. "What happened to him? What did you do?" She began screaming at Maria as she knelt down next to him.

"He was coming after me. He wanted to ….he wanted to rape me, Sylvia! I had to defend myself and he was drunk! He'll be fine." Maria was shaking, knowing that her aunt wasn't going to believe anything she just told her. She was right.

"I can't believe that this is how you treat me and my family after we took you in! Look what you did! I'm calling an ambulance and the police! I hope they arrest you for what you did!" Sylvia went to the kitchen and dialed the phone. Maria was glad that her car was packed and ready to go. She checked the back seat to make sure her mother's jewelry box was there. She decided that whatever else she left behind wasn't worth getting as she grabbed her purse, keys and ran out the door. She jumped into the little Datsun and floored it. She wasn't sticking around for police questions and potentially spending a night in jail because she was defending herself! She could see Aunt Sylvia in the driveway yelling as she drove away. "Goodbye Aunt Sylvia. I hope I never see you again!" Maria said out loud. She was still afraid that the police might be looking for her, so Maria kept driving for several hours until she found a rest stop in Massachusetts near a Boston suburb. It was close to 4am and she was exhausted. As she was drifting off, she felt a slight pressure on her hand. She opened her eyes to see her mother sitting in the passenger seat, holding her hand. "It'll be okay. They won't come for you. You're safe. Get some sleep now." Her mother's gentle voice always helped her.

"I miss you, mom. Please stay with me." Maria said softly as she finally went to sleep. When she woke up a few hours later, the highway was full of traffic and she looked at her map to find a way around Boston. She wasn't used to driving in a big city and it terrified her. After finally finding a route around Boston and driving for several more hours, she made it to the URI campus. "I'm here, mom. I made it." She said out loud. She finally relaxed after the past seven years of living at her aunt's house. It was time for a new start.

William

William felt nervous as he drove to Providence with Maria to visit his family for the Christmas holidays. He'd already warned her that his father drank heavily on a daily basis and that his mother did her best to tiptoe around him. His sister Barbara was still in high school, so she'd obviously be there. His paternal grandmother, 'Gram Laura' would also be there and he was looking forward to seeing her. She was probably the most level-headed person in his father's family and also one of the only people he was looking forward to spending time with during this visit. His mother's parents refused to come because they hated the way his father treated his mother. "William, just come and visit us afterwards. I can't be around that!" His grandmother was honest with him. He kept that plan in the back of his head because he was pretty sure this visit was going to be stressful, but he made a promise to Maria that if things didn't go well, they'd leave and either stay with his grandmother or go back to the dorms at URI.

"Bill, don't worry so much! I know what to expect. Trust me, I understand family problems!" Maria put her hand on his and gave it a squeeze. He loved that she had heard all the horror stories that he'd told her about his childhood and didn't see him as defective or someone that would eventually let her down. William felt like he could walk through fire if Maria was by his side. She'd told him about her parents being killed and growing up with an aunt who was just as bad as his father who was abusive.

19

As they drove up to the modest small home on Hope Street, William took a deep breath as he parallel parked the car in one of the designated spots. "You ready for this, sweetheart?" He asked Maria. She looked especially beautiful with her long blonde hair in curls and her petite frame accentuated by a pretty red sweater dress and black boots. He knew she was nervous too, but she kissed him on the cheek, "Let's do this!" As William rang the doorbell, he stomped the snow off his shoes and Maria did too.

His mother answered the door looking festive with her bright red Christmas sweater and green pants. Sara Carson 's light brown hair was in a bob-cut that suited her. Her brown eyes lit up when she saw him. "Hi, mom!" William was glad to see her as he gave her a big hug. She seemed so much more frail than he remembered. "You look great!" Although on further inspection, he could tell that his mother looked much thinner than 4 months ago. His sister, Barbara ran into the kitchen just then. "Bill! So good to see you!" She gave him a hug. Barbara was the opposite of William; vivacious and outgoing. She had pretty light brown hair and brown eyes and was petite like Maria.

"Mom, Barbara, this is Maria Evans." He introduced Maria as she stood next to him looking adorably nervous.

"Maria! How nice to meet you, you're prettier than how William described you!" His mother gave her a hug and Maria hugged her back. Barbara did the same. "Maria, my brother sure does like you a lot if he brought you here for Christmas!" William winced as his sister had no filter with her comments. "It's so nice to meet both of you!" Maria replied calmly.

He knew that she was uncomfortable with hugging strangers which made him love her even more. "Do I dare ask where dad is?" He asked his mother quietly as she took Maria's coat. Barbara was busy talking with Maria about college life; how it was to live in the dorm and how exciting it must be. Maria smiled and answered his sister's incessant questions patiently.

"Now, William. He's excited to meet your new girlfriend. He's been watching the football games all day." She hadn't changed a bit, still covering up for him. "Jack! William and his girlfriend are here!"

"Okay! I heard them come in, I'm not deaf you know!" William heard his father's voice booming from the living room. It was only 3:00 and he sounded drunk already. He grabbed Maria's hand and squeezed it again as if to get the anger that was building under control. "Dad's doing his usual." Barbara announced and was getting ready to launch into her literal explanation when the phone rang. Barbara ran to answer it and proceeded to take it in the other room. William was grateful that his sister was preoccupied so that she wouldn't state the obvious.

"He's just watching the game." His mom explained more to Maria than to him. She led them into the small but homey kitchen. His mother had finally gotten her way and the kitchen was updated with more cabinet space and a small breakfast bar that she'd always wanted. The furniture was the same; old and mismatched chairs around the Formica table. "It smells amazing in here, Mrs. Carson!" Maria commented. It did smell good. His mother always made lasagna and homemade rolls on Christmas Eve and William was glad she didn't deviate from her usual spread.

"It does, Mom!" William echoed Maria's sentiments. "Just the usual sausage lasagna that we have every year, sweetheart!" Sara Carson said as she went to the oven to check on it. "Needs a few more minutes to brown." She said as she pulled off the tin foil and put the casserole back in. "Not quite ready yet!" She announced. "How about some wine? I know you two aren't twenty-one yet, but hey, it's Christmas! I won't tell anyone." She joked.

"Like they don't drink at college, mom! Seriously." Barbara managed to throw out her comment, despite being on the phone.

"Some white, please." Maria said, blushing at Barbara's comment. William knew she wasn't much of a drinker, but maybe a glass would help her relax. William poured Maria a glass of pinot grigio and himself a glass of cabernet and took a gulp, knowing that he was going to have to deal with his father eventually.

"William, get in here!" His father's gruff voice came from the living room. He groaned inwardly knowing that he was probably on his 12th beer by now and he was expecting the worst. "Coming, dad!" He tried to put on a good face because Maria was here, but it was a struggle. His mother grabbed his arm before he headed into the living room. "Honey, just bear with him. He's a little 'tipsy' now. But he knew Maria was coming, so he promised to be on his best behavior." She said to him in a low voice.

"Thanks for the warning, mom. I'm just warning you that if he starts up with anything, Maria and I are leaving. I won't put her through any of that." William said in a low voice. Sara Carson nodded. "I understand. She's very pretty and seems so nice. I really like her." She told him.

"I love her, mom. I really think that she's the one for me. I just hope that dad is behaving himself today so that she doesn't run away from me." She nodded. "Gram Laura is on her way from Rumford, so maybe that will help."

William took Maria's hand. "Let me introduce you to my father." He hoped that he sounded more excited than he felt. His father was parked in his old rickety green recliner that he'd had since William was a child and yelling at the TV. "Dad." His father didn't hear him so he came over in front of him. "Dad?"

"Get out of the way! Give me a minute!" Jack Carson was watching the Patriots game. William moved to the side knowing that if he didn't, his father would just yell louder. "Sorry, he's into football." He told Maria. He was grateful when she smiled at him. "Bill, you already told me about him. It's okay." He loved that she was so understanding.

Finally, a commercial interrupted the game and William took advantage of it. "Dad, this my girlfriend, Maria." His father reached out his hand to her and made an attempt to stand up, but sat back down in his seat. "It's verrrrry nice to meet you, Maria! You're a very pretty young lady." Jack was starting to stammer his words. Maria didn't flinch as she grasped his hand. "It's nice to meet you, Mr. Carson. Thank you." She was so poised and acted as if his father's behavior was normal. He continued his grasp on her hand until she had to pull it away.

The football game returned just then and William took that opportunity to usher Maria out of the room as his father was preoccupied again. "I'm so sorry." He knew that she was uncomfortable. "We can leave if you want to."

Maria was flushed as if she were embarrassed. "We can stay. I'd just rather not have to shake your dad's hand again." She giggled, trying to make light of the situation, but William knew she was upset. He gave her a kiss on the cheek. "Let's go back in the kitchen. My grandmother should be here soon. As soon as the words were out of his mouth, the doorbell rang and his mother ran to the door.

"Merry Christmas, Laura!" William's mother greeted her mother-in-law. They'd always managed to get along despite Jack's drinking and verbal abuse. Probably because his grandmother knew far more what was going on than she would ever say. Gram Laura always stood up for *his* mother; it was one of the reasons he still had a relationship with her. She came with a huge box of gifts and a bottle of red wine.

"Merry Christmas, Sara. My goodness, are you eating? You look like you've lost weight! Well, I've brought my chocolate cheesecake! That should help!" She laughed as she hugged his mother. "Now, where's my favorite grandson?" William came into the room to greet his grandmother with a hug. "It's so nice to see you, Gram!" William told her. She didn't look her age and her blonde hair was always perfectly coiffed. She had a vivacious personality and tons of friends that kept her company since his grandfather had passed three years ago.

"William, you get more handsome every day! And who is this beautiful young lady?" His grandmother turned her attention to Maria.

"Gram, this is my girlfriend, Maria. Maria, this is my Gram Laura." William introduced them. He watched as his grandmother hugged Maria. He'd warned her ahead of time that his family were 'huggers'. Maria seemed less awkward about his grandmother's hug. "Well, aren't you just the prettiest girl ever!" Gram Laura was gushing as Maria's cheeks flushed. "William, you are a lucky boy!"

"It's so nice to meet you. Bill has told me so many nice things about you." Maria said. Gram Laura narrowed her eyes for a moment. "Bill? Oh, yes! We always call him William, but he's always insisted on 'Bill' with his friends." She said, laughing. "You're so adorable, you call him whatever he wants!" Gram Laura said good naturedly.

Williams' sister, Barbara suddenly made her appearance and Gram Laura turned her attention immediately to her. "Dinner's ready!" Sara Carson announced just then. She seemed to have a sense of when a distraction was needed. William was almost sure his mother had planned it that way.

They all sat down to the small dining room table and were enjoying the meal until William's father started to make comments about the lasagna not being well-done and that the bread was cold. "Sara, heat up this bread! This isn't even warm!" He was talking loudly, almost shouting. William could see the look of horror on Maria's face and decided to speak up.

"If you can't appreciate all this cooking that mom did for you, then you get back to the living room! I'm tired of your complaining!" William replied to him.

Jack stood up and began yelling at William. "You think you're better than all of us now, huh? Useless! That's what you are!" He slammed his fist down on the table so hard that several salad dishes fell and broke into piece on the floor. William stood up, ready to pounce on his father if he stepped one foot toward his mother or anyone else in the room.

"Don't do it, dad! I won't let you ruin this day by having one of your tantrums! Sit down and let's finish our meal." William said in a calm but firm voice. Barbara spoke up. "Yeah, dad. I think it's time to just have a nice meal together. Sit down. There's no need to get so upset." She glanced at William. He was grateful that his sister was helping him out. She usually just took off when he was drunk and acting up. Gram Laura gave him one of her best 'Sit down now!' looks and Jack begrudgingly sat down. "Well, now! We should have a toast! Sara, where's that wine I brought? Open it up!" She jumped up and got out the wine glasses, as William's mom opened up the wine. It was a good distraction and for now, Jack was behaving himself. Even though Barbara was underage, she was allowed a small glass of wine to toast. Gram Laura stood up and made her toast. "I'm so glad that we're all here today. William is in school and brought his lovely girlfriend, Maria! Barbara is close to graduating and we're all healthy. Merry Christmas Eve everyone!" Everyone including Jack raised their glasses and took a sip. "Does anyone need their lasagna or bread heated up?" Sara asked. She grabbed Jack's plate and put the lasagna in the microwave, and the bread in the oven to warm it up. Everyone else declined but at least Jack seemed to be content. At least for now. William breathed a sigh of relief and grabbed Maria's hand under the table. Maria squeezed it back. "I'm fine." She whispered to him.

The rest of the meal was thankfully uneventful; Jack finished his meal and went back into the living room with his drink to watch more football. Maria helped out clearing the table and with the dishes which endeared her more to his mother and Gram Laura. Barbara went back to her room to talk on the phone with her friends. William decided to sit in the living room but not in his father's view so he could watch the game and still be present so that Maria wouldn't feel like he'd deserted her. He could overhear Gram Laura asking her about her family and Maria informing her that her parents had passed away. William decided to walk back into the kitchen. Gram Laura was apologizing to Maria about her parents. "Gram Laura, really it's okay. It was a long time ago." Maria said softly.

"How about we take a walk? It's dark, but it's not too cold yet." William suggested to Maria. "I'd like to take you around, show you some of the shops and restaurants around here." He knew he was on borrowed time with his father's ability to be civil and lucid.

Maria agreed and they were just putting on their coats to go out when he could hear the drama beginning to unfold from the living room. A part of him wanted to walk out the door and pretend it wasn't happening, but with him being the only other man in the house it wasn't a good idea. "Babe, just stay in the kitchen for a few minutes. I need to deal with this." William did his best not to sound as mad as he was feeling as he walked into the living room that was about to become a lion's den within a matter of seconds.

Maria

She had been nervous going to Williams' house for Christmas, but she knew she didn't want to go back to Vermont, back to Aunt Sylvia's house. There wasn't anywhere else to go and William had become such an important part of her life, that she'd agreed, despite his warnings about his father and how he 'acted up' when he'd been drinking, which apparently he did every day. She wasn't much of a social butterfly and meeting new people made her anxious. William had warned her that his mother and grandmother were affectionate and liked to hug when greeting people, even people they'd never met, so when his mother swooped in to give her a hug, she was prepared and did her best not to shrink back. His Gram Laura was everything she wished that she could be; outgoing and the life of the party and she immediately liked her as well as his mother. It was nice to be part of a family gathering that wasn't full of gloom and doom like Aunt Sylvia's.

His father, Jack, was the only uncomfortable part of this trip, but she admired how William took charge when he started yelling at his mother at the dinner table and did his best to protect his mother and grandmother, as well as diffuse the situation. That is until they were getting ready to take a walk. William told her to stay in the kitchen, so she figured that wasn't a good sign. William told his mother and grandmother to stay with her. "Maria, would you like some coffee?" Sara asked her.

"Yes, I'd love some." She wished that William didn't have to be the gatekeeper today, but there wasn't anyone else. She could hear his father's voice above the TV in the living room and William trying to stay calm. "Hey, I brought dessert! How about some homemade apple pie? It's my mother's recipe." Gram Laura chimed in just in time. It was almost as if it was rehearsed, as if this was the scene every year.

"I love apple pie! Thank you, I'd love some!" Maria told her. Her mother wasn't much of a baker but she did make an amazing apple pie and she found herself getting misty-eyed when she thought about her own family holidays. It was the one time of year that her mother went all out; baking her apple pie and a turkey dinner.

Gram Laura saw her eyes watering and grabbed her hand from across the table. "Maria, we're so happy to have you here. You're the first girl he's brought to a family gathering, so you are someone very special to him." Maria couldn't help but let a few tears through as she said that and she quickly wiped them away. "Thank you so much. Being here with you all makes me feel like I have a family again." Gram Laura handed her a tissue to wipe her face and lowered her voice to a whisper. "My son, he's just lost, but William; he's a good person, he's always helped his mom and sister. He's a good man."

"I know he is, Gram Laura. I'm not going anywhere." Maria surprised herself with her statement. She wasn't normally that forward with people she'd barely met. Williams' mother was just bringing over the coffee and slices of pie when she heard a loud thud from the living room. They all jumped up and rushed to the living room. Jack Carson was lying on the floor, grabbing his chest and William was trying to help him up. "Jack, oh my god! William, what happened?" Sara Carson was frantic and hovering over Jack, then looked up at William. "What did you do?" She sounded angry.

"Mom! I didn't do anything! We were arguing and he suddenly grabbed his chest and fell over. Call 911! I think he might be having a heart attack!" William yelled at her. Gram Laura picked up the phone in the kitchen and dialed, giving them the information and address. "They're on their way!" Gram Laura took over. "Jack, can you hear me?" He was still lying on the floor with his eyes closed. His face was sweaty and taking on a grayish cast.

"We should get him face up. I know CPR." Maria said suddenly. She'd taken a course in her senior year in high school and hoped that she remembered it. If he was having a heart attack, which all the symptoms pointed to, she knew it wouldn't hurt to try. William, Sara and Gram Laura all worked to turn Jack over on his back gently, while Maria grabbed a pillow for his head. She bent down over him and instructed William how to do the chest compressions after she gave him breaths.

"You ready?" She began giving Jack mouth to mouth breaths with William giving compressions when she stopped. It seemed like eternity, but was probably only 5 minutes when the paramedics were knocking on the door and took over.

Maria and William stepped aside as they swooped in with a defibrillator. They took his pulse and hooked him up to a small monitor to measure his heart rate. "Seems like he's still breathing. Let's keep up with the CPR to stabilize." One of the male EMTs said. "What's his name?"

"His name is Jack. Jack Carson." William told him.

"Jack? Can you hear me? My name is Ethan. I'm a paramedic. I'm here to help you. Can you squeeze my hand?" Ethan asked him. He nodded as Jack was able to do so. "Folks, I know you're all concerned, but we need some room. Could you all go to the kitchen area while we help Jack?"

They all nodded, still in shock and made their way back to the kitchen. Maria suddenly felt anxious as she realized what had just happened. "Is he okay? Did I do the wrong thing?" She began chattering nervously as William hugged her.

"Sweetheart, no! You probably saved his life! You were wonderful." He assured her. Sara and Gram Laura crowded around Maria as she sat down.

"Maria, I can't thank you enough. Thank god you were here!" Sara was praising her. Gram Laura hugged her as she said, "I'm so glad you're here with us!" She looked at William who was shaking. "William, dear, sit down. I'll make us some coffee. How about a piece of pie?" Maria couldn't help but smile at her suggestion of pie at a time like this. It would be exactly what her grandmother would've said to change the subject, distract, or just have a moment of peace. Gram Laura made both Maria and William sit while she busied herself making a fresh pot of coffee and warming up the slices of pie from earlier. Sara was pacing back and forth on the porch just off the kitchen with her hand on her pale face.

Maria remembered from years ago how hard it was to wait and went to talk to William's mother. "Did they say anything? How is he?" Sara thought there was news.

"We don't know yet. I just wanted to see if you need anything. I know how hard it is." Maria said softly. Sara sat down on a wicker chair and put her hands over her face as she cried. "I know he drinks too much. I've tried to tell him, but he doesn't listen…." Her voice trailed off. Maria put an arm around her. "They're doing all they can. I'm sure he's going to be fine." Maria said, as her mother's shadow appeared. She was nodding to her, telling her it was going to be okay. Then she was gone. 'Mom, come back,' she thought to herself, hoping that she could see her again. Just then Ethan, the EMT came out on the porch. "Mrs. Carson, your husband is stable for now, but we're going to transport him to Rhode Island Hospital and have him evaluated. Do you want to ride in the ambulance with him?"

Sara Carson lifted her head up. "Really? He's going to be okay? Oh, yes, of course I'll go with him." She watched nervously as they wheeled him out of the house on a gurney and followed them. William, Barbara, Maria and Gram Laura all gave her a hug. "Please just stay here for now and I'll keep you updated everyone." Sara told them while she was waiting for them to put Jack in the back of the ambulance. He had an oxygen mask over his face and still looked very pale. "Mom, call me if you need me to come down!" William pleaded with her. Sara nodded as the EMT's closed the doors. The ambulance took off, sirens wailing as they headed to Rhode Island Hospital.

Everyone was suddenly quiet as they heard the sirens now in the distance. Maria remembered only too well what that sound meant; it was what she'd heard the night her parents were killed. She'd been home and her neighbor's older daughter, Megan had been there 'babysitting.' Maria had been upset when her parents insisted that 16-

year-old Megan was there to babysit! "Mom! Seriously! I'm 11 years old, I'm not a baby! If something happens, I know how to dial a phone! I know how to make myself something to eat and I know when to go to bed!"

Still, her mom always being overprotective, insisted. "Honey, I know you're capable of taking care of yourself. I'd just feel more comfortable if someone that was a little older was here. What if you hurt yourself and needed to go to the hospital? You can't drive!" Her mom was always bringing up the worst scenarios.

"Then, I'd call 911 and they'd come help me." Maria told her. Even her father was in her corner on that response, but her mom wouldn't budge. "This is the last time I'll have Megan stay with you. Next time, I promise I won't ask someone to sit with you. Okay?" Maria agreed and was looking forward to staying home alone. It would make her feel more grown up, like her friends who never had a babysitter at her age!

As it turned out, it was the last time she'd seen her parents alive. They were on their way home when they were hit head on, killing them almost instantly. She had just been going back to sleep after a nightmare about a car crash when she heard the sound of sirens racing by her house. 'I hope it's not serious,' Maria thought to herself. Hours later when her parents didn't return home, Megan was starting to worry. Maria overheard her on the phone with her parents. "They aren't home yet. They were supposed to be home two hours ago. What should I do?"

Megan's mother came over and began making some phone calls when there was knock at the door. When Megan's mother opened the door, it was a police officer that informed her that her parents had been killed in a car accident. Maria remembered how hysterical Megan and her mother had been, while she remained quiet. Megan had stared at Maria as if she were frightened of her. "Maria, your dream!" Megan whispered.

"He's lying. They're just fine!" Maria told her. "I just saw my mom walk through the door." Megan's mother just stared at her for a moment, then gave her a hug. "Oh, sweetheart, you're just in shock." She told her. Maria shook her head. "No, she's right here! Can't you see her?"

Megan's mother looked stunned as she embraced her. "I know you think you can. She'll always be with you, dear. You poor thing."

Maria kept insisting that she could see her mother walk in the door behind the officers. No one else noticed except her. "Maria, I'll always be with you," her mother had told her and then disappeared. "Mom! Don't go!" Maria had cried out. Megan's mother looked distraught as she tried to comfort her. "What happened to the little girls?" Maria had asked, remembering them from her dream.

"There were no children in the car, Maria. I can promise you that." One of the officers had told her. Maria knew then that the nightmare she'd had was a warning.

Suddenly, she felt someone shaking her shoulder. "Maria? Are you okay?" Gram Laura was asking her. "I was thinking that you could stay in the guest room and William agreed to sleep here on the sofa bed. Are you okay? You looked like you were somewhere else."

"Huh? Oh, right!" Maria tried to shake off the flashback, snapping back into the present. "I can sleep either way." Maria told her. She knew that William's family wouldn't let them stay in the same room, even though they'd already been intimate. William had already warned her about that.

William

William could tell that Maria was not herself after the ambulance left. She was standing in the kitchen staring out the window with a blank look on her face.

William brought her out to the porch to talk. "Are you okay? You seemed deep in thought and Gram Laura was talking to you but you were just looking straight ahead."

"Bill, I'm fine. Just worried about how your dad is doing and your mom seems very upset. Have you heard from her?" She seemed more relaxed, more like herself.

"It's been less than an hour. I doubt we'll hear anything for a while. If you're tired, you can go on up and go to bed." William was such a good person, always thinking of her.

"No, I'm fine. I was just.....remembering. That's all. Let's go have some of that pie." She grabbed his hand and led him back into the kitchen where Gram Laura was trying to distract the rest of them with the dessert. "Maria, here's a piece that I just heated up. Would you like some whipped cream?" She asked her.

"No, I like it just as it is. I'm sure it's delicious!" Maria told her. William could tell she was upset, but he'd let it go for now. At least she was talking to his grandmother. He knew that this situation was bringing back all the trauma with her parent's accident. She'd never told him in detail about it, but he knew that it was always hard for her.

After they sat down to eat dessert, Barbara began chattering on about senior year and her friends which was a welcome distraction for everyone. When the phone rang, everyone stopped talking and William grabbed the phone. "Hello? Hi, mom. How is he doing?" He wasn't sure what to expect. He hadn't been at the hospital very long and he crossed his fingers that his father was still with them.

"We're waiting on the cardiologist to evaluate him. They're running a stress test on his heart right now. I think he's doing okay." He could tell his mother was just needing to talk. "How's everyone doing there? I'm so sorry I'm not there, it's Christmas Eve after all." It was just like his mother to be concerned about that. "Mom, we're fine. Just having some dessert and now watching some TV. Maria and I will be staying. If you need me to come there tonight, just let me know." William was starting to think he should go to the hospital just to check on her.

"I'm fine for now. I'll call again later. Thank Maria again for all she did for your father."

"I will. Call us with any more news or if you want me to come there. Love you, mom. Give my love to dad." William hung up and immediately turned around to Maria, Gram Laura and Barbara right behind him. "What's this? I guess I'm popular tonight!" He joked. "It was mom. They think he's stable, but running tests right now. Gram, do you think I should go down there and sit with mom?"

"It's up to you. If you feel like you need to then go. I'll stay here with Barbara and Maria." Gram Laura said. He groaned inwardly, wishing she'd just told him to go. He did want to, but he didn't want to leave Maria. And he didn't want Maria to go with him. He knew it would bring up memories for her. In the end, he decided he should go, just to support his mother. "Bill, I'll come with you." Maria told him.

"No, I don't want you to deal with that tonight. You should stay here and get some sleep." William insisted.

"I wouldn't sleep anyway. I'll be okay as long as I'm there with you." Maria gave him a kiss on the cheek. "Don't worry about me."

"I'm not going to try and talk you out of it again, because I know I can't. But thank you for being there for me. You're an amazing person Maria Evans. I'm just glad you chose me over all the other options out there." He kidded with her.

The drive to the hospital was only 10 minutes and after several questions, they were able to find Jacks' room on the cardiac unit. He found himself more concerned about Maria than anything as they walked through the hospital to the nurse's desk. He was surprised that his mother wasn't in the waiting room. "We're here to see Jack Carson." He told the young-looking nurse.

"I'm sorry, he's only allowed one visitor at a time right now. Besides, he is still with radiology doing some stress tests. He should be back anytime now." William nodded. He and Maria went back to the waiting area. Maria started to drift off as she lay her head on his shoulder and he cradled her head, trying to make her more comfortable. "Get some sleep, babe. It's going to be a long night." He whispered to her as he glanced at the clock. It was now after 11:00pm. One hour to Christmas Day. It definitely wasn't going the way he expected, but then again, he didn't have high hopes anyway.

As the clock ticked by, William started to doze off himself when Maria began talking in her sleep. "Mom! Come back! Please!" She began moving around and William grabbed her legs to prevent her from falling off the small sofa. "Bill?" She said in a small child-like voice.

"Yes, sweetheart. Sorry, I must have woken you up. You were having a dream and I kept you from falling on the floor. It's okay, go back to sleep. There's no word yet." He assured her. He was shocked to see that it was now 1:00am. What was taking so long? He decided he needed to check with the nurse. "Maria, I need to see what's going on. I'm going to move, so just lay down, okay? I'll be right back." She seemed still half-asleep and nodded so he got up and moved a pillow for her head.

He went up to the nurse at the front desk. "I'm sorry to bother you, but I haven't heard any news about Jack Carson. Is everything okay? My mother is in there with him and I haven't seen her yet. I've been here for a couple hours now."

"What relation are you to Mr. Carson?" The nurse asked.

"I'm his son." William was starting to get irritated.

"I'm sorry for asking. We had a shift change just after 11, so I wasn't here. Oh, yes, I see, he was brought in for a heart condition. Let me check with the doctor. Wait right here." She left as he was really starting to worry. Why wouldn't they have given any updates? Where was his mother?

After what seemed like hours, she finally returned. "You can go to room 2013. It's just down the hall. The doctor would like to speak with you. Your mother is in there as well." The look on her face wasn't encouraging and William started bracing himself for the worst. He glanced over at Maria who seemed to be asleep again. "Could you do me a favor? If that woman over there wakes up, please let her know I'm in seeing my father and I'll be back." He asked.

"Of course." The nurse smiled. "My name's Hilary by the way." She gave him a wink and if he wasn't so tired, he'd think she was trying to flirt with him. He just nodded and went past the front desk toward Room 2013. As he neared the room, his mother was just leaving the room, crying. "Mom! What's going on? I've been here for hours!" William was blindsided as his mother grabbed him in the hall before he reached the room. She was hysterical. His heart started racing. What was going on?

The doctor was right behind his mother. He looked fairly young to be a doctor, but what concerned William more was the somber look on his face as he came toward them and his heart started pounding. I'm Dr. Staples. You must be William." Dr. Staples confirmed as his mother was clinging to him.

"Yes. What's going on doctor? I've been here for over two hours waiting for some news. What's happening with my father?" William felt himself holding his breath. "Is he.....?" He couldn't say the word 'dead'.

Dr. Staples shook his head, as he seemed to know what William was thinking. "He's resting. But I'm afraid your father has a serious condition called an aortic aneurysm. There's swelling around his aorta which is the main artery in the body that's causing a blockage to move the blood properly from the heart to the rest of the body. He'll need surgery in order to prevent internal bleeding. His heart is also showing signs of arrhythmia, which is also a concern especially with this surgery."

"William, they want to operate first thing in the morning." His mother said to him, as she dissolved into tears again. William was too stunned to say anything for a moment and he looked up at the clock. "It is morning. You mean this morning?" He was trying to comprehend everything he'd just heard.

"Well, later this morning. Probably around 10:30." Dr. Staples confirmed. "I've gone over the risks of this surgery with your mother, but I wanted to talk with you as well. There's a significant risk with this surgery, especially with your father's heart condition."

"Why so soon?" William asked. "I mean can the surgery wait a week or so?" He was thinking of his mother and the Christmas holiday. His mother loved Christmas and this was already going to be so hard for her.

"I'm afraid not, William." Dr. Staples said immediately. "This condition is serious, especially with the testing we've done on the aneurysm. It could burst at any time and if that happens, it will be fatal within seconds. That's why we need to operate as soon as possible." William hugged his mother as she burst into more tears during the doctor's explanation. He felt too numb to do anything at that point. "Can I see him?" William managed to ask.

"Of course. He is on some pain medication to help him rest, but he may wake up enough to talk to you." Dr. Staples said kindly. "I'm really very sorry for this news, especially on Christmas. Please take your time, but also make sure you get some rest. It's important that you all take care of yourselves emotionally and physically." Dr. Staples advised. "Why don't you go home and get some sleep. If anything comes up, someone will call you, Mrs. Carson."

His mother nodded and followed William into the room. His father who was just yelling at dinner a few hours earlier was now lying in a hospital bed. He looked pale, and almost unrecognizable to him. The many monitors that Jack was attached to were continuously making noise which put him on edge. "Can he hear me?" He asked in a quiet voice.

"I believe that he can. He's under some sedation to help him rest, but he may respond to you." Dr. Staples was still standing at the door of Jack's room. William nodded as his mother sat down in the chair near Jack's bedside.

"Dad, I'm so sorry that we argued. I didn't mean anything I said to you. You're going to get better, I know it. We're all here with you." The lump in Williams' throat that had been there since his father was taken by ambulance finally gave way to a flood of tears that he suddenly couldn't control anymore. He grasped his father's hand as he cried uncontrollably for several minutes. William suddenly felt a squeeze of his father's hand which was encouraging. "He squeezed my hand, mom." Sara moved closer to William and put her arm around his shoulders. "He loves you William, even if he doesn't show it much of the time." She brushed away tears.

"I love you, dad. You can make it through this." William said to a shadow of his father lying in the hospital bed. He managed to give him a hug despite all the IV's and monitors that he was attached to. "We should go home and get some sleep, mom. We'll have to be up early."

William was especially worried about her. She looked 10 years older suddenly than 5 hours ago. Her red-rimmed eyes were set in her pale face and she looked exhausted. Sara Carson nodded and gave his father a kiss on the cheek. "We'll be back soon, Jack. I love you." She allowed William to usher her out of the room. Dr. Staples nodded as they walked back to the waiting room. "Mrs. Carson, we'll keep you updated. Please get some rest."

Maria

Maria hated hospitals more than any other place, but even though William had insisted she stay at his parent's hous, she went without hesitation. It was time that she faced her fears. It just brought up so many memories, but she could handle it now. It was so hard to see him distraught. He kept talking about it being "his fault" and regretting getting upset while his father while they were in the waiting room that was getting to her. It was hard for her to see him so stressed out. He was completely out of his usual 'in control' element that helped her feel safe. But he was still taking care of her. "Are you sure you want to stay here? I can bring you back to the house, it's not far." William asked more than once.

She'd considered it, but the thought of being at the house without him made her more uncomfortable. "No, I'll stay with you." Maria insisted. Even if it wasn't the Christmas vacation she'd anticipated, at least they were together. As the minutes clicked by, she leaned her head on William's shoulder, struggling to stay awake.

She could see a shadowy figure in the distance down the hall calling to her. "Maria....follow me." It was her mother's voice. "Mom? I can't leave him now. I have to stay here." She tried to tell her. "You need to follow me." Her mother's voice insisted. Maria got up and began following, despite the fear. "I'm coming. Where are you?" She kept following the voice down the hall that was now endless and dark. "Maria, you need to see." Maria continued down the hall to an elevator.

"I'm coming, mom." She pressed the down arrow and the elevator brought her down to the basement. Her heart was pounding as she followed her mother's shadow when she finally stopped at a small room at the end of the hall. "Maria, come and look. You need to see." Her mother's voice prompted her forward. Maria crept toward the room, not wanting to see what was inside, but her mother's voice kept insisting. She stood outside the dark room and suddenly she could see a car in flames burning and she could hear screams coming from the car. "Come back, mom, please come back!" She screamed and rushed up to the car that was burning. She saw her mother walk away from the fire. "Be careful." Maria suddenly woke up, almost rolling off the couch in the waiting room. William wasn't there. "Bill?" She called out. She still felt so disoriented by the dream that it took her a minute to remember why she was here. "I'm right here. It's okay, go back to sleep. There's no word yet." He hugged her and put a pillow underneath her head. William said something about going to check on what was going on with his father and she closed her eyes again, hoping that she would see her mother again.

But now she was wide-awake and worried about Bill, so she decided to take a walk outside just to get some fresh air and try to shake off the lingering anxiety from her dream. As she walked through the sliding doors, she braced herself for the cold wind. It was snowing again.

Maria suddenly realized it was Christmas Day and although she wasn't a fan of cold weather, the snow made it more festive despite the fact that she was at a hospital. She stood outside, breathing in the cold air and lifting her face up to the snowflakes falling down. Suddenly, she saw a man that was walking slowly through the snow toward her. He was limping and as he came closer, he appeared to have severe burns. She ran out to help him. "Sir, can I help? You look hurt!" She had just reached him when he looked at her and realized it was her father. "Dad? Is that you?" He continued to walk as if he couldn't see her. "Dad!" She followed him, even though she was terrified. Was she dreaming again? 'I must have fallen back to sleep,' Maria said out loud.

"You're too good for him, Maria. I wish you would understand." Her father was in front of her now.

"Dad? I don't understand. How did you get here? Bill? No, he's been wonderful to me." Maria didn't even realize she was crying until she felt the wetness run down her cheeks, splashing onto her arm.

"His father is controlling everything right now. I can see him and he's not a good person. It's only a matter of time before he will be here." He started walking away from the hospital and she tried to follow him, but as suddenly as he appeared he was gone. "Dad? Are you there?" Maria cried out. She must be asleep and this was one of her dreams. She started willing herself to wake up as she walked back toward the hospital entrance and walked back through the sliding doors. When she saw William looking for her, she ran toward him. "William! You're here! Your real!"

Williams face was tear-stained as he hugged her. "Of course I'm here, I'm real. Where have you been? I've been looking for you!"

Maria thought about telling him about seeing her father outside, but maybe she'd just been sleep-walking again. "How's your dad doing?"

Williams' smile suddenly left his face as he had to tell her about his dad and the upcoming surgery that would happen later that morning. "We should get home and get some sleep. The surgery is scheduled for 10:30." Maria looked up at the clock. It was 2:30am. She knew she couldn't tell him about her dreams now. Especially about her father's warning that 'it's only a matter of time before he'll be here.' Clearly, she hadn't been dreaming. Now she was really frightened, but she didn't want to tell William. He was under enough stress as his mother met them in the visiting area. She was pale underneath the puffiness from crying. Maria gave her a hug. "I'm so sorry, Mrs. Carson. We'll be here on time so you can talk to him before the surgery." Sara Carson only nodded, too tired to talk. William ushered them to his car in the parking lot and they headed home to get some sleep before Jack's surgery in a few hours.

They arrived back to the house and William helped his distraught mother upstairs. Maria could hear him talking to his mother; she could hear her crying softly and William trying to comfort her. She lay down on the sofa and tried to sleep, but she could still hear his mother crying. She was just drifting off to sleep, when she heard her father's voice. "His father isn't here anymore, he's crossed over." "You're not real, it's just a dream." She told him.

"Open your eyes, Maria. You're not dreaming." Her father insisted. She opened her eyes and was startled by the image of her father for the second time that morning. She quickly closed her eyes, hoping that he wouldn't be there if she opened them again. 'Please be gone' she thought to herself as she opened her eyes again. She was relieved that he was gone; if he had even really been there at all. Maria was starting to wonder if the stress of school and then being here with William and family drama was getting to her. William crept down the stairs after his mother was finally settled. "Hey, babe, you're still awake? I was just coming to check on you. My mom's finally asleep."

Maria was again tempted to tell him about what she'd seen, but decided against it. She'd already seen her father outside the hospital and then sounded crazy enough, when she'd asked William if he was real. "I'm just worried about you and your family, that's all." William hugged her and she held onto him fervently hoping that the message her father had given her was just a dream, a fluke. William broke out of their embrace. "I'm so sorry that this didn't go the way I'd hoped. But my family really likes you and enjoyed spending time with you. I know my dad's a lot to take sometimes, but…." His voice drifted off, and he brushed his hand over his eyes. Maria could tell he was trying to hold back tears. "Bill, I loved meeting your family. I know your dad's got his problems, but he's still family and you've done the best you can."

"I love you, Maria." William gave her another hug, just as the phone rang. He sat up straight with a look of terror in his eyes. It was just after 4:00 in the morning. He knew it wasn't good news. Maria hoped that the message from her father wasn't true, but after William picked up the phone and the look on his face, she knew that it was. 'Oh, god no!'

"Are you sure there's nothing else you can do?" William asked, tears flowing down his face. He shook his head. "We will be there soon." He hung up and silently walked back to the sofa. "He's gone. My father's gone!" William said as he put his head in his hands and sobbed in Maria's arms.

William

As William picked up his end of his father's casket, he was still trying to grasp what had happened in the past week. It didn't even seem real. He'd come to visit his parents for Christmas, introduce them to his new girlfriend and within hours his father was in the hospital and died. It had been a fairly warm winter in Rhode Island. Despite the snow on Christmas Eve, it had disappeared and the ground wasn't frozen, unlike some winters the burial wouldn't have to wait until spring.

After he'd received the phone call, it was on his shoulders to deliver the news that his father was gone. Sara Carson had become a shell of herself from the minute she was told Jack had passed. It had taken several prescriptions called in by her doctor to get her to calm down enough to get out of bed, and now as they were preparing to take his father to the hearse, he wasn't sure how she was going to get through this. William had become numb as he glanced around at the other five men around them. They were his cousins that he barely remembered and two uncles. It left him feeling disheartened about how his family had become so distant that he didn't know any of them very well.

The one constant support was Maria. She was there for him and his family; helping his mother, his grandmother and his sister planning the services, writing the obituary. She was there during the funeral, sitting between him and his mother in the front row during the entire service and gripping his hand the whole time. William had been asked to deliver a eulogy so he stood up, determined to get through what few paragraphs he'd managed to write. He could feel eyes staring him down as he began to speak.

"My father, Jack Carson, was an amazing father, husband, uncle and friend to us. He worked hard every day so that we'd have food on the table, a roof over our heads and instill the values of caring about each other." William could feel the lump in his throat growing and without warning, the tears came and he struggled to continue. "He….His… ability to….. " William stopped suddenly. His Uncle Stuart helped him out and came up to finish while William sat back down, head in his hands. The guilt he felt was starting to eat away at him. 'If only I hadn't argued with him, maybe he would still be here,' he kept thinking as they carried the casket for the gravesite services. His mother seemed to be avoiding him ever since he'd told her that he'd died.

As he watched his mother put a red rose on top of his father's casket along with a photo of them at their wedding, he could feel the lump in his throat growing. Sara Carson began crying as Barbara and Gram Laura helped comfort her. Out of all the people that he thought would be devastated and needing support, Gram Laura held her own. Even after he let her know that horrible Christmas morning, she was upset, but she simply said, "It's his time. He's with his father now." She seemed to know, more than anyone, how much Jack really struggled with the depression that he'd tried to drink away through the years.

As everyone moved away from the gravesite, William was still standing there with Maria by his side, trying to still grasp that his father was gone, when Gram Laura came up next to him. "William, you were a good son to him. He always loved you; he was just pushing you and he didn't always have the right words." She looked sad for a moment, but then turned to Maria and smiled. "This young lady is who you should spend your energy on. She loves you, William. You can't do any better." She glanced over to Maria who was holding his hand. "The two of you need to go finish school and move on with your life! I'll help your mom out and Barbara's here until she goes off to school in the fall."

"Mom's mad at me isn't she, Gram?" William couldn't help but ask.

"No, sweetheart. She's grieving and she's lost right now. Your father died because he didn't take care of himself. He had a drinking problem, along with a heart condition and who knows what came first, but your argument with him didn't cause him to die, William. You must believe that." Gram Laura enveloped him in a hug. She turned to Maria who had been a silent presence during the funeral. "Maria, my dear, you are the best person for my William. Thank you for all you've done over the past couple of weeks. I do hope that I'll be seeing you again very soon." She came close to her and slipped a piece of paper into her pocket. "This is my number. Please call me if you need to. I think my grandson is going to struggle and I'm here if you need to talk." She whispered to Maria

"Thank you, Gram Laura. I'm so glad to get to know you all." Maria gave her a big hug. Gram Laura hugged her back, then reverted back to her vivacious self again. "Now, you both get your suitcases packed and head back down to school!" She playfully pushed them toward William's old 1975 Maverick that he'd bought from his dad when he graduated from high school.

They got in the car and William took a last look at his father's grave. He made a promise to himself that he would never treat his children the way he'd been treated by him. Despite Gram Laura's insistence that his dad loved him, he still didn't believe it.

Maria

Watching William going through the death of his father was just as hard as losing her parents at a young age. What made it so much more difficult is that she'd been told ahead by her father that it had happened before he ever got the phone call. She knew she couldn't tell him about it because either he wouldn't believe her and think that she was crazy or that she should have told him. There was no win with either situation. She was thankful for William's Gram Laura that somehow managed to keep everyone cordial and sane after Jack's death.

At least she hadn't had anymore dreams that involved either of her parents and was hoping that maybe she was just working through some of the trauma from when she was younger. After all, she'd never been in counseling after her parents died and she lived in a household with her aunt that never provided her with any stability or a feeling of safety.

As they headed back to URI, Maria couldn't help notice the change in William. He was more subdued, quiet and kept to himself. He barely said a word in the car all the way back to campus. "Hey, are you okay?" She finally broke the silence after half an hour in the car. She tried to keep quiet after the services, but now it was feeling awkward to her.

"I'm sorry, babe. I'm just thinking." He tried to sound casual but came across as stiff, almost forced. She could tell from his expression that he was deep in thought and that he was close to really breaking down, so she stopped talking and stared out the window. When they arrived at the URI dorms, she felt like she could finally breathe and go to her own dorm.

"Here we are, babe. What'd you say we go out to eat tonight and then settle in with a movie?" William seemed to have a burst of energy. Maria didn't have the same energy. In fact, she felt the opposite. She felt emotionally and physically exhausted.

"Maybe. I'm going to unpack, maybe do some laundry and try to relax. Give me a call in an hour." Maria said quietly. She knew that he was dealing with a lot right now and wanted to help him, but she needed a breather from the drama over the holidays. William looked over at her before she got out of the car. "Thank you for being there for me, babe. I'm not sure how I would have gotten through the past week without you."

"I wouldn't have it any other way. I just need to unpack and unwind for a few." Maria gave him a kiss before she got out of the car. William nodded, as a shadow of sadness crossed his face again. "I understand. I'll give you some time. Call me when you're ready okay?"

Maria went back up to the driver's side window to kiss him again. She suddenly realized this would be the first time he'd be alone since his father died. "Give me an hour or so." She smiled and ruffled his hair before she turned and walked toward the nearly empty dorms. Her booted footsteps echoed through the stairwell as she walked up to the third floor and down the hall to her dorm room. She'd been lucky to have her own room this year, thanks to her excellent grades that won her another scholarship to cover the cost. Her previous freshman year had been a roommate disaster from hell.

Her first encounter with URI's dorm experience was with Becca Dalton. The moment she met her, Maria knew that she was in for a rough year. Becca was beautiful and she knew it as she tossed her long dark hair and flashed her blue eyes at everyone. She couldn't wait to tell Maria how popular she'd been at her high school in South Carolina. While Becca had a cute southern accent, she did not possess the southern charm. She's always bragging about her family's money and it was clear that Becca needed to be the center of attention at all times. Becca made the cheerleading squad and quickly set her sights on Dan Ahearn, who was a quarterback for the URI Rams football team. So when Becca had practically dragged her to a party, Dan met Maria and paid more attention to her than Becca. Maria suddenly became her instant enemy. Maria and Becca tolerated each other until a few days later when Dan chose to ask Maria out instead of Becca. Then Becca's claws came out. She began torturing Maria by inviting people over late at night, while Maria was trying to study and spreading rumors that 'Dan must know an easy lay when he sees one' around campus.

Dan was handsome and in the first few weeks attentive and respectful that she was a virgin. That didn't last long and pretty soon he was pressuring her every time they went out. One night, he'd plied her with drinks at a party and she'd been completely drunk. She could barely remember what happened, but she knew when she woke up the next morning that Dan had taken advantage of her. Maria had been angry as hell and didn't talk to him for several weeks, but later gave in because she missed having someone in her life. But he'd shattered her trust and she'd started avoiding Dan as much as possible.

Maria was thankful for the end of the spring semester and found out she had qualified for a housing scholarship. She'd had enough torture during her teen years. She wouldn't take a chance for another roommate. She'd gotten a nanny position for a family on Cape Cod for the summer and enjoyed her time away from school and Dan. She only saw him a couple of times during the summer, but when school started again, he treated her as though she was still his girlfriend despite rumors that he'd been seen with multiple girls over the summer at his parent's home on Long Island.

When William came along, it was almost as if her parents had stepped in and forced her to make a decision. She had vivid dreams that involved her mother telling her to 'free herself' from a person that didn't really care. And Dan never really did. He just wanted her because she was pretty and he got to be her 'first' as she found out later after she'd told him it was over.

She had just reached her room and opened the door when she heard someone coming up the stairs. Probably just another girl whose Christmas break didn't work out, so she shut the door and began unpacking and sorting her laundry. A sudden knock on the door startled her as she was putting her shoes back in her closet. "Who is it?" She was always careful. Especially since no one else was around.

"It's Dan. Maria, can I come in for a minute?" Her hand froze on the sweater she was getting ready to throw in the laundry.

"Um, Dan I'm kind of busy and William will be coming over soon. Maybe we can talk later." Maria was shocked that he was even still at the dorms and why would he be knocking on her door? The hair stood up on her neck.

"Please? It'll just take a minute. I just want to talk." Dan pleaded from the other side of the door. Maria realized that she hadn't locked the door behind her and was unsure of what to do. She could hear her mother's voice in her head, "Don't open the door. He's not here to be friends." She crept over to the door to secure the lock when Dan flung the door open. "So, you won't open the door for me, but you'll let that Bill guy in here all the time!" Dan's eyes were bloodshot and she could smell the booze on him.

"Dan! What are you doing? Get out of here!" Maria knew by the look on his face that she was in trouble. She looked around for any object she could find that she could use as a weapon. His dark eyes were cold with spite and hate as he made his way toward her, charging like an uncaged bull. Maria managed to dodge out of his reach as he crashed into her small bookcase, sending the books flying and the cheap plywood book case broke in half.

"You know we were supposed to be together! And you dumped me for that loser Carson! How dare you! I'm going to make you wish you hadn't dumped me when I'm done with you!" Dan's face was bright red, his eyes were raging and now she was caught between the bed and getting to the door. "Dan! I broke up with you! You seemed okay with it! Why are you doing this?" She screamed at him as she glanced at the phone that was on her nightstand next to the bed and thought about trying to dial 911. Dan saw her and grabbed the phone, pulling it out of the phone jack and throwing the phone against the wall.

Maria grabbed a candle off the nightstand and threw it at him. It missed and shattered into pieces on the floor. Within seconds, Dan had her pinned down to the bed and was trying to pull off her jeans as she struggled. "Help! Help! Someone help me!!" She screamed as loud as she could as she tried to fight him off of her.

"No one is going to hear you." Dan said sadistically as he ripped her shirt off and pulled down her jeans and underwear. "Little miss virgin queen. Well, let's see how much Carson is into you after I'm done with you!" He pulled down his pants and forced himself into her. Maria felt as though her screams were coming from somewhere else. The pain he was inflicting was brutal and she tried several times to roll him off of her but he was too strong. After what seemed like hours, he made an animalistic noise and rolled off of her. Maria grabbed her clothes and ran to the closet, and found her tennis racket holding it like a sword. "Get the fuck out of here! Now! I'm calling the police, just know that. You won't get away with this!"

Dan pulled on his jeans and laughed. "You think anyone's going to listen to you? I'm royalty here! Good luck with that!" He stopped at the mirror to fix his hair as he walked out the door. Maria was left holding the tennis racket, too stunned to even scream, cry or run out of the dorm and ask for help. She managed to pull up her underwear and jeans; went to the phone that had been thrown and plugged it back into the jack praying that it would work. She was relieved when there was dial tone and dialed the first person that she needed by her side. William. He picked up on the first ring and hearing his voice made her dissolve into tears. "Bill, I need you..."

"I'm coming right now!" Bill told her. Maria knew that she had to make a decision about what she was going to tell him. She knew that she couldn't bear to tell him the truth; that Dan had raped her. It would tear them apart and Maria knew Dan was right. It was her word against his. She'd have to go to the hospital, be examined and humiliated and tell the person she loved most in this world that she was raped because she was too careless to lock the door.

William

He'd dreaded dropping Maria off at her dorm, but he knew that she needed a break from all the gloom that had surrounded them both during the holiday. He was suddenly afraid to be by himself with his thoughts after having Maria and his family by his side during the past week. He'd just gotten to his room and luckily his roommate wouldn't be back for a few more days.

He'd just unpacked, which meant throwing all the clothes in his suitcase into a laundry basket. He was just settling down to watch TV when the phone rang. It was Maria and she was crying so hard it was hard to understand her. He jumped up and grabbed his keys. "Maria! I'm on my way! I'll be there in two minutes!" He dropped the phone and ran down the stairs, jumped into his car and floored it. He forgot to put it in park as he pulled into a parking spot in front of her dorm. "Oh, shit!" He grumbled as the car started to roll away when he opened the door. He put the would-be runaway car in park and ran up to her dorm room. He turned the knob to find it locked. "Maria! Open the door! It's locked!" William shouted frantically.

He could hear her coming toward the door and opened the lock. He immediately pushed the door open to see her tearstained face as she ran and hugged him, hanging on to him as if he were a life jacket. "Bill! Thank god! Dan came in here and was threatening me!" Maria could barely speak between sobs.

"Babe, slow down. Dan? You mean Dan Ahearn?" He tried to keep his voice low and quiet, but he could feel his anger rising already.

"It....was Dan! He knocked on the door and it wasn't locked. He was knocking on the door and as I went to lock it, he barged in!" Maria was almost hysterical again. William looked over at the shattered glass from the candle in the corner, and all the books and the broken bookcase that were all over the floor. "Maria! What did he do to you?" William insisted. "You need to tell me!"

"He......he .....he was angry that I'd broken up with him!" Maria sat down on her bed and hid her face in her arms. Her sobs shook her as William held her while his anger began to spill over. "He came in hoping that I'd go back with him and when I refused he got angry and started tearing up my room." Maria knew from his reaction that if she told him what really happened he'd go off the deep end, especially with his recent loss.

William cupped her face in his hands " Are you hurt? Did he hit you? He's going to pay! Did you call the police?" His fists were clenched and he was so angry he was ready to go chase Dan down and kill him.

"N-no. You're the first one I called. I'm not hurt, he didn't do anything to me." Maria managed to lie. William knew he needed to stay calm enough for her but inside he was enraged. "Maria, we need to call the police!"

"It....won't do...any good." Maria said. "They won't do anything to him. Its....mmmy word against his. I forgot to lock the door." She rested her head on his shoulder, trying to relax and be somewhat coherent.

"I'm calling the police!" William told her. "You just lie down and try to relax." Despite Maria's pleas to leave it alone, William called and within 15 minutes, the police arrived. She explained that he'd come into her room and was angry with her because she refused to stop seeing William. He took his anger out on her bookcase and threatened her. The two male officers took her statement, but the female officer that was there pulled Maria to the side. She was blond, petite and very attractive and Maria had a feeling that she'd dealt with many male co-workers that tried to take advantage of her. "Ms. Evans, I feel like there's something missing here."

"What would be missing? I told you what happened." Maria insisted.

"Of course. Except that the comforter is very rumbled and there's some spotting on the comforter." She pointed out. Maria's eyes started to fill up with tears again. "Nothing happened. He just came in. He didn't hurt me." She insisted.

"If you ever want to talk to me further or press charges, here's my card. My name's Elyse Wincott." She pressed a card into Maria's hand. Maria took it quickly and hid it in her pocket as the other two officers approached her.

"Ms. Evans, we'll be filing charges against Mr. Ahearn and issuing a warrant for his arrest." The young dark-haired officer told her.

"But..I didn't want to file charges." Maria wished she'd never called Bill. Now this was never going to go away. William had enough and stepped in. "Of course. He should be arrested! He broke into her dorm room whether the door was locked or not!" He was still livid that

Ahearn still had the nerve to bother Maria. Maybe his cheerleaders were tired of what a narcissist he really was!

"Ms. Evans, we'll have to file charges since the report was made. You'll get a copy of the summons for Mr. Ahearn to appear in court. You don't need to appear, but there will be a summons for him regardless." William nodded his head in agreement and gave Maria a hug. "You'll be safe from him from now on, sweetheart. I'll never let anything like this happen to you again. I promise." He was beside himself that he hadn't been here. 'If I'd been here, this never would've happened.' He felt responsible for what happened and he was angry. He felt as though he couldn't do anything right! His argument with his father ended with his death. Now Maria could have been hurt because he should've walked her to her room. "No one will hurt you again." He whispered in her ear.

Maria

January brought more snow to Rhode Island as the new semester started. She'd tried to put what happened with Dan out of her head, although she still had nightmares about him coming into her room and forcing himself on her. On the weekends, Bill would sometimes stay overnight in her room and would wake her up, telling her that she was thrashing around and yelling. She hated keeping that secret from him, but she also knew that it would probably destroy him. William was still struggling with his father's death and after her 'incident', she noticed that he'd started drinking more than usual. Usually they would go out to eat or a party after classes. Now, it was hard to get him to leave campus. When he used to have a beer a few times a week, now had turned into a six-pack every other night. The other night, he was grabbing his third beer when she'd tried to casually mention it, "Bill, you seem to be drinking quite a bit lately."

"What are you, my mom now?" William became irritated. Maria knew she was walking the line. "No, of course not. I'm just worried about you, that's all." She said quietly. She knew that his mother called him every day 'just to talk' and although he loved her, she could tell that it was getting to him. A constant reminder of his father.

He hugged her. "I'm sorry if I snapped at you. I'm just stressed. You're right. I need to stop drinking so much. In fact, I won't even drink this one." He got up and dumped the beer out and Maria hoped that he was starting to realize the pattern that was going on. She resisted talking to his mother about it, when Sara always insisted on talking with her after checking in on her son.

After classes started back up, she overheard someone in her Abnormal Psych class talking about Dan. "Did you hear? They kicked him out of school. Dan Ahearn got arrested for breaking into someone's dorm over the holidays." Maria had been sitting five feet away and luckily class was ending so she left. She was just thankful they didn't mention whose room was broken into. She was shocked to hear that Dan had actually been kicked out of school, but then again, she'd never forget what he'd done to her. She'd kept Elyse Wincott's business card in her jewelry box. She wasn't sure why, but somehow it made her feel better that at least someone understood.

"Maria, isn't Dan your ex? Can you believe it?" Marlene Sanders asked her. She sat next to her in class but that was the extent of her relationship with her. Marlene was a known gossip, so Maria just shrugged her shoulders. "Kind of surprising, but then again, if he's breaking into dorms I'd say he shouldn't be here." She put on her best poker face and nodded nonchalantly. Maria was glad that the professor had just walked in so she had an excuse to stop talking to Marlene. She was finally able to relax a little, knowing that Dan was gone. Maybe this meant she could sleep without the light on from now on!

January dragged into February and Maria was just starting to feel more like herself emotionally when she woke up one morning nauseated, causing her to push William to the side and run to the bathroom. 'Maybe it was just something I ate,' she tried to convince herself. But when she realized that her period was about 3 weeks late, she knew that this wasn't a night of partying (which she rarely did anyway) or food poisoning. Right after her first class, she bought a pregnancy test at the store, her hands shaking as she gave the cashier the money. The cashier was an older woman, probably in her 50s and said, "Good luck, honey. I hope the results are what you want them to be." Maria just smiled as she felt the tears forming and grabbed the bag. She was thankful that the cashier had put it in a paper bag and she shoved it into her purse as she hurried out of the store.

Now she needed to think about the dates if it was positive. She and William had been together several times around the same time that Dan had broken into her room. She was on birth control. However, she knew she'd been forgetful about taking it, especially around the holidays. This was when Maria yearned for a close friend at the school. She had a few friends but they were just acquaintances. William was the person she spent most of her time with and she certainly couldn't talk to him right now. At least until she was sure.

She arrived back at the dorm at 11:00 and had about an hour before her next class. She remembered that Gram Laura's phone number was written down on a piece of paper in her jacket pocket. She went to her closet and felt around in the pockets. Thankfully, it hadn't fallen out and it was there. Maria thought about calling but then put it in her jewelry box, along with the officer's number. Hopefully, she wouldn't need either one.

She looked at the test sitting on her desk next to her books, trying to get up the courage to actually do it. She sat down on her bed for a moment, closed her eyes and took a deep breath. When she opened her eyes, her mother was standing in front of her. She appeared so real that Maria stood up to hug her but when she did, her mother had disappeared. "I must be crazy!" Maria said out loud as she went and got the test out of the paper bag. "Here goes nothing, mom!"

After 20 minutes, Maria willed herself to look at the stick lying on the bathroom vanity, praying that it wouldn't confirm what she already knew. It had a pink positive sign. She was pregnant. She wasn't sure what to think or how to tell William. And was it really his child? Keeping the truth from William about what really happened in her dorm had been relatively easy. Until now. Her mother's voice was in her head again. "You need him to get through this. He loves you. He will support you." Maria nodded. "I hope so, mom. I'm not sure who's baby this is and there's no way I can tell Bill about what happened now." She had Gram Laura's number in front of her. How would she explain all of this to her? Or maybe she didn't need to. She could just ask her advice....'for a friend'

William

The bright sun shining through the window woke him up and he winced as he looked at the clock. It was 10 am and he'd missed his first class of the morning. It wouldn't have been a big deal except that he'd missed it twice in the past month. It was his intermediate business class and the professor had already warned him about missing classes. "Mr. Carson, you really need to be in class. If you keep missing, you're going to have to drop it and take it either over the summer or in the fall, which will just make your course load more difficult."

His thoughts turned to Maria and how distant she'd been lately. Or maybe it was him. He knew he'd been drinking more than usual and needed to slow down. His mother had called him several times since he came back and he'd dodged her calls, not wanting to be reminded of his father's death. He suddenly felt the need to talk to Gram Laura. She always seemed to make sense when he couldn't. He dialed but surprisingly, her line was busy. He tried again a few minutes later, but it was still busy. "Guess she didn't get 'call-waiting'. William decided to get something to eat and then call Maria. She'd been upset with him lately about him drinking so much and he knew she was right. Without realizing it, he was becoming just like his father and he hated that. Josh always had a good selection of goodies so he rummaged through his stash and found some strawberry pop-tarts to snack on.

He took a shower and got ready to go to his 12:30 class. He called Maria, but her line was busy. He'd see her later on this afternoon. As he headed into his accounting class, he ran into Josh. "William! How's it going? Missed you in class this morning." He commented. William and Josh were in the same business class at 9:00.

"Yeah, just tired, that's all." William tried to brush it off.

"You and Maria doing okay? Hey, I heard that Ahearn was kicked out of school! Guess he broke into someone's dorm and the cops arrested him. His dad is some big shot out in Hollywood, so word has it he 'took care' of the legal stuff and moved him out there. It must be nice to have family that has money, huh?"

William's hands immediately clenched when he heard Dan's name mentioned. He was glad that it hadn't gotten out that it was Maria's room he'd broken into but just the fact that he was off in California now, living off his father pissed him off. "Yeah, I heard something about that break in." He tried to sound casual and keep his face from looking as angry as he felt.

"Yeah, I guess his dad got him a part in a movie that he's directing. Ahearn was always bragging about his father being a director and how his twin brother was already starring in some TV shows. Some people live a charmed life." Josh sounded wistfully envious. "If I was kicked out of here, I'd be working for my dad's landscaping business and hating every minute of it!" He laughed. "But that's why I don't do dumb shit like Ahearn. I can't afford to!"

"Neither can I." William agreed. "Hey, I gotta get to class. Catch up with you later?"

"I'll be headed out to Boston this afternoon to spend the weekend with Kasey, so guess I'll see you on Monday!" Josh said.

"See ya." William was tired of hearing the rumors about Dan, but was glad to know he wasn't going to deal with him again. He managed to make it to class on time, and tried to pay attention but his focus was still off. It had been since his father died. When class let out, he knew he needed to call his mother this afternoon before Maria came over. He'd been avoiding her long enough.

He had just gotten back to his room and picked up the phone to call his mom when there was a knock at the door. He was surprised to see Maria standing at his door, since she usually was in class until 2:30.

"Babe, what's going on? Don't you have class until 2:30?" William asked her as she walked in.

She was unusually quiet for a minute. "I usually do, but I needed to talk to you now." Her eyes filled with tears as she sat down on the bed.

William suddenly felt panicked. What if she found out she had some horrible disease, what if she were being kicked out of school? What if?" His mind went to the worst scenario.

"What is it, babe? Just tell me and we'll deal with it!" William sat down and put his arm around her.

"I'm pregnant." She said softly.

Maria

After the test, she'd decided to make the call to Gram Laura. She wasn't even sure how she would respond to the news, but she felt like she could trust her and her opinion on how to handle the situation. She didn't bring in the situation with Dan because that was way too much to talk about…with anyone!

Gram Laura seemed happy to hear from her, and so after filling her in on how William was doing, Maria decided to ask her advice about a "friend" that found out she was pregnant unexpectedly with a guy that she'd been dating for about 6 months.

Gram Laura laughed when Maria asked her the question. "What's so funny?" Maria was starting to wonder if this was a bad idea.

"Dear girl, I'm assuming you're talking about yourself. Am I wrong?" How did she know? But then again, she was very insightful and seemed to pick up on things that it made Maria wonder if the woman was psychic.

"I…I am….talking about myself. I'm pregnant. I wasn't feeling well and nauseous, so I took a test today. I'm so sorry to call you, but I didn't know who else to talk to…." Maria was crying softly.

"Maria, listen to me. My grandson loves you. I know that he does and like I told you, I think you're the best thing that's happened to him. You just need to talk to him. I'm sure it will be happy news for him." Gram Laura insisted.

"Maybe, but what about finishing school? How could we possibly finish school?" Maria knew for a fact that there would be no financial support from Aunt Sylvia, her only family besides her retched cousin that she hated. Besides the fact that she only had the basic health insurance that she had with the school. She was pretty sure that didn't include ob-gyn appointments every month, along with a hospital bill when the baby was born. If she couldn't go to school during the time she needed for recovery, she'd never keep her scholarship either.

"Everything has a solution, Maria. Just tell him and then we'll talk more. I'm not without ideas and I'm excited to be a great-gram Laura!" She sounded excited, which made Maria feel better. At least she wasn't getting beat down for being 'careless' like Aunt Sylvia would have done.

"I'm just not sure how he'll take it. He's been doing a lot of....well, he's just been down since Jack died." Maria caught herself. She was going to say "drinking", but Gram Laura seemed to get it. "He's been drinking more hasn't he? William has always been his father's son. Maybe that contributed to some of their arguments, but William was always Jack's boy, his favorite; if he had to pick one that is." Gram Laura called it again!

"He has been. I think it's taking a toll on his everyday functioning too. He's been missing his morning classes pretty frequently. I'm afraid to tell him this news. I'm worried that it'll put him over the edge." Maria was grateful for Gram Laura's positivity, but she also hadn't seen him since they returned to school.

"Just talk to him about it. How about I plan to meet you two tomorrow night for dinner?" Gram Laura suggested.

"I'd love that! It'd be great to see you again and I know Bill would be happy too." The thought of seeing her was comforting. She was like the mom that she'd missed since she was 11 years old.

"Just give me a call tomorrow morning if you want me to come down. Have you been to a doctor yet?" Gram Laura asked. She had a good point.

"No. But I've been nauseous and haven't had my period in 8 weeks." Maria admitted.

"Talk to William, let him know what's going on. I'll meet you two for dinner tomorrow night, as long as you call me to let me know it's okay. I don't want to impose or anything." Gram Laura understood the boundaries, which just made Maria that much more comfortable with her.

Maria wished that she could tell her what was really going on, but she knew it would change everything. Besides, he was gone. Out of her life and if this was his baby, then he'd never know about it. It was so hard for her to keep this secret, but she knew she had no choice.

"Thanks so much for listening to me. I'll talk to him this afternoon and call you later. Where would you want to meet for dinner?" Maria asked.

"Trust me. It will work out. I'll plan on meeting you for dinner tomorrow. I was thinking Georges at Point Judith. I'll make reservations. But call me later, okay?" Gram Laura sounded firm about the place and reservations, yet Maria still had to check with William.

"I'm sure it will be fine, but I'll call you." Maria told her. She wasn't even sure what he would say, but she knew they had no choice about talking to Gram Laura.

William

Maria's statement of "I'm pregnant," when he was thinking the worst was almost a gift to him. He was instantly relieved that no one had died, she wasn't sick or breaking up with him and, they were going to have a baby! The terrified look on her face told him she was scared that he'd be upset with the news. He pulled her into his arms and hugged her. "Babe, you scared me! I thought you were going to tell me you were sick or that someone had died!" William was beyond relieved.

"So you're not upset? I'm on birth control, so I don't know how it happened, Bill. Honestly." Her lower lip quivered and she looked as though she were going to cry.

"Of course not! This wasn't planned, but is certainly not something to get you so upset! I love you and there's no one else I would want to start a family with than you!" William insisted.

Maria sat down on the recliner in his dorm as tears ran down her face. "You have no idea how scared I am right now, Bill. I mean we have decisions to make." She looked very serious.

"What do you mean, 'decisions'?" William questioned. Surely she wasn't thinking about abortion!

"I mean we have to think about how equipped we are to raise a child right now. Are we going to finish school? How is that going to work?" Maria brought up very good points that William didn't have answers for right now. He was still trying to adjust to the fact he was going to be a father at 20 years old.

"We'll figure it out. I definitely don't want to even think about abortion or someone else adopting our child!

"No! I don't either, Bill! I'm just saying that we need to come up with a plan." Maria said calmly. "Don't get mad, but I told your Gram Laura about the pregnancy."

"What? Why would you do that without telling me first?" William felt like he'd been punched in the chest. Now she'd tell his mother and his sister and they'd be involved.

"Because I initially talked to her about it as I was talking about a friend of mine. But she knew, Bill! I couldn't lie. Besides, I feel comfortable with her. I feel like I can talk to her like she's my mom. She won't tell your mother. I know she won't." Maria was confident about Gram Laura keeping her secret.

"She wants to meet us for dinner tomorrow night. I told her that I'd talk to you first though. She's in our corner, Bill! She even eluded to helping us financially if we needed her to." Maria was hopeful that he'd at least meet with her tomorrow.

"We can't just take money from her, Maria!" William's ego was coming out now.

"I didn't say we were going to take money from her! I don't even have a doctor yet! All I have is some nurse practitioner at the health care center who isn't an OBGYN doctor! I need to see one to confirm that the results are correct and have ongoing care." Maria was getting frustrated with him. Suddenly, she wasn't sure she wanted any of this at all! "Or better yet, let me just take care of it, because it seems like you're living in a dream world right now! We're both in school, no jobs and think we're going to raise a baby? Are you kidding me? We need to talk to your grandmother!" Maria was angry and yelling now.

William was shocked into silence for a few moments. He'd never seen her so upset before. "Okay, babe. We'll meet her tomorrow night. I'm sorry, I guess I'm just trying to process this news." He went over to her as she paced back and forth across the room. "Please. Sit down. Relax. We'll have dinner with her and talk. Okay?" Williams' voice softened. She was right though. How were they going to make it with a baby? They would definitely need some good advice and definitely some financial help.

Maria finally sat down and started to cry. William put his arms around her. "Babe, we'll get through this. I'm sorry, I need to listen and I definitely need to stop drinking. I'll start today!" He walked to his fridge, grabbed the beers and dumped out the six pack of beers into the sink one at a time. "See? I don't need to drink anymore. I want us to be a family."

Maria finally wiped her tears. "Thank you for doing that, Bill. I don't expect you to not drink at all, but you have been drinking too much lately. I think meeting with Gram Laura is the best thing to do to help figure things out. Besides, I do feel like she's a mom figure to me. I really connect with her and I think she has our best interests at heart."

William just nodded in agreement. He didn't want to tell her about the truth about his grandmother. Gram Laura meant well, but there wasn't ever a time that he could think of that she would offer to help if it didn't somehow benefit her. She always had a need to be in control of every situation. He had seen her do it many times with his parents; such as bailing them out financially when his father kept losing jobs because of his drinking. But there was always a price to pay. Usually in the way of guilt; convincing his mother not to call police on his father when he hit her, making excuses for his father's drinking and behaviors and showing up at their house unannounced when she saw fit.

Gram Laura had a way of convincing people that her way was best, regardless of what they actually wanted. He was just hoping that Maria wouldn't be one of those people.

"Ok, we'll meet with her for dinner. But I want you to think about what *you* want and for *us* to talk about what *we* want. Not what she wants. Okay?" William asked. He wouldn't get into the details about Gram Laura now. "Just remember, there's a price for everything." He kissed her softly.

"I know. I'll keep that in mind." Maria smiled. "Alright if I call her now?" She picked up the phone.

"Go ahead." William sighed as he watched her dial. He watched her as she chatted amicably with his grandmother, her smile lighting up her whole face. It was still hard for him to believe sometimes that this incredibly beautiful woman loved *him*! He made a promise to himself that he wasn't going to let anyone interfere with their relationship, including Gram Laura.

Maria got off the phone with a smile on her face. "She's made reservations at Georges in Galilee in Point Judith tomorrow night at

6:00." William didn't say anything, but given his distaste for seafood, it was clear to him what was going on. Of course she picked Georges! Gram Laura adored oysters, quahogs and all the other Rhode Island seafood fare that she knew he hated. He preferred pasta, which Gram Laura already knew. Besides, he was pretty sure Maria hadn't ever eaten a raw oyster. His guard was up.

William and Maria

As they drove to the restaurant, Maria commented on the beautiful view of the coastline, but wondered why Gram Laura would choose a seafood restaurant when she knew he didn't really care for it. William loved Italian food and the more pasta the better. "Why would she pick a restaurant that specializes in seafood when she knows you don't really like it?" Maria asked him directly.

"Maybe she wants you to try some new Rhode Island cuisine." William said simply, as he tried not to sound sarcastic. He was trying to keep an open mind, but he also knew how controlling Gram Laura could be.

"I'm kind of excited to try some new food." Maria said as they exited the car. She looked exceptional; her simple black jeans with a dressy blue sweater accented her eyes and her blonde hair was down in loose curls. She wore a red wool pea coat that she told him had belonged to her grandmother. It was a classic cut that never went out of style. Maria wore it well and her blonde hair contrasted with the red. "You look beautiful." He told her as they entered the restaurant. "You look handsome yourself." She seemed to glow as she gave him a kiss. He'd worn jeans, but dressed it up with a light blue shirt and a dark blue tie. He just hoped that he wouldn't get a scolding from Gram Laura for wearing jeans. He knew she wouldn't say anything to Maria about her jeans. But Gram was very old-fashioned and seemed to be stuck in the 50's when it came to the way men dressed.

At the door, William gave the name but Gram Laura was already there and waving him toward her table. He could tell that she'd already ordered some wine and a tray of oysters. William tried to hold back his disgust. Why had she ordered wine, when she knew that Maria was pregnant and that he was trying to stop drinking? He did his best to mask his feeling as he led Maria toward the table.

Gram Laura was dressed up in a green dress and heels, as though this was a five-star restaurant in New York. "William, Maria! Come sit!" William pulled out Maria's chair as he'd been taught. "Maria, here's some oysters fresh from Point Judith today! I asked the waiter." This was what William had been worried about. Gram Laura acting as though she had tons of money when he was sure she didn't.

Maria was suspicious about the slimy looking oysters in the shell. "They're a Rhode Island staple, Maria! Try them. They're best if you put hot sauce and some lemon on them!" Gram Laura insisted, as Maria gingerly picked one up and put a few drops of hot sauce and lemon on it. "Now, just put the shell to your mouth and eat the oyster." Gram Laura instructed. Maria did and the look on her face was priceless. William wanted to laugh as he saw his girlfriend's face turn to horror.

"What do you think? Do you like it?" Gram Laura was asking as Maria grabbed a glass of water to wash it down.

"It….it was interesting." She managed between gulps of water. She was afraid to say what she really thought. It tasted salty and slimy. Not something that she wanted to try again. "They'll grow on you." Gram Laura insisted. Maria was certain they would not. She'd have to fake her way through that course. She noticed that William wasn't eating any of them. "Bill, you're not eating them." She whispered to him when Gram Laura turned her head to look for the waiter.

"I don't like them." He said simply. "I'm guessing you don't either. There's other things on the menu, so order what you want. Not what she suggests." William gave his best advice.

Both of them ended up ordering a pasta dish, despite Gram Laura's insistence that they try the special that was a salmon dish. William could see the look on his grandmother's face when they both ordered. "I think you should try the salmon." He noticed that the wine hadn't been for himself or Maria. Gram Laura had poured her second glass since they'd sat down. He was just glad she wasn't insisting that they indulge.

"Gram, you know I don't like salmon. Please stop trying to order from me." William felt more than ever he needed to stand up to her. Maria just nodded.

"So I wanted to talk to the two of you about maybe moving in with me." Gram Laura didn't waste any time. "You'll have your own room and a room for the baby as well. What do you think?" She looked excited, as if they'd agreed to her proposal already.

Maria was stunned, not sure what to make of this and William was already shaking his head. "Gram, we can't let you do that. It's too much." Maria could tell he was being as polite as he could.

"It's really not! I've got this big house near the water. There's plenty of room." Gram Laura continued on talking about her house in South Kingstown; near the beach, there were 4 bedrooms, 2 bathrooms, a spacious kitchen, and a fenced-in yard. William could tell Maria was becoming interested and changed the subject. "How's my mom doing? I haven't heard from her."

"Oh, I checked in with her yesterday. Your mom's doing fine. Barbara's been having some struggles, but you know, teenagers these days." Gram Laura waved her hand, as if his sister's problems were unimportant. It was what he'd expected.

"William, I'll help with all of your expenses! Just think of it. You'll have a place to live, you both can finish school and I can help with the baby." Gram Laura continued on with her pitch. William knew it was a bad idea, but Maria kept nodding her head again. "That's so nice of you for offering, thank you." As usual, Gram Laura had pulled her in with her promises. William tried to keep himself calm throughout the meal, but as Gram Laura kept talking to Maria about everything that she could provide, he could tell that she was wavering.

At the end of the meal, William reached for his wallet, knowing that Gram Laura would be trying to pay for their meal. "No, I'll pay for ours." He insisted as she gave him a look. The look that said "You can't do this." Which made him insist. She finally gave in, although she did pay for her oyster tray and her expensive salmon dish that she'd tried to talk them into getting.

"Thank you so much for your offer, Gram Laura. We'll talk things over." Maria seemed enchanted with the woman that he knew wanted to control their every move if they gave in. Still, he wasn't sure how they were both going to continue to go to school and take care of a baby.

On the drive back to the dorms, William was quiet, trying to weigh out the pros and cons of staying at his grandmother's house. Maria was looking out the window. "Babe, what do you think? About what she said?"

"I think it might be the best idea. The dorms are fine now, but what about after the baby? We can't live there anymore! I'm not even sure if it's allowed." Maria brought up a good point. "I think we should talk about taking her up on her offer. Maybe not now, but when the time gets closer."

"I'll think about it. But first you need to see a doctor and check on how you and the baby are doing." William said. He knew that he didn't really have a leg to stand on at this point. The health center at URI wasn't a substitute for prenatal care. He sighed as he knew that he was probably going to be under Gram Laura's roof whether he wanted it or not!

William

After dinner with Gram Laura, William knew he needed to make some decisions and quickly. The last thing he wanted to do was move in with his grandmother and have to play by her rules. He'd finally found an ob gyn doctor in the South County area that would allow him to finance the expense of visits and Maria had actually liked Dr. Sheila Malone. She'd seen her once already to confirm the pregnancy and an ultrasound was performed to check on the baby. William had gone with her to the first visit and hearing the baby's heartbeat helped make it all worth the stress of worrying about what they were going to do. "You're about 9 weeks along, Maria. The baby's heartrate is good. It's too early to tell the gender yet though. Did you want to find out as you're further along?" Maria looked at William and he shook his head. She agreed. "No, we'd rather be surprised when the time comes." Maria said.

"Well, you seem to be in good health. Do you drink or smoke regularly?" Dr. Malone asked her.

Maria shook her head. "Neither one of us drinks or smokes, Dr. Malone." William emphasized, more for himself than his girlfriend. He hadn't had a drink since he'd poured out the beers two weeks ago. He had missed having some beers after class initially, but now he was committed to figuring out a plan for how they could make ends meet with finances and a baby without moving in with Gram Laura.

After the appointment, he told Maria to wait in the car. He knew he'd need to fill out financial forms for the doctor. After talking at length with the administrative assistant, he was able to set up a payment plan that would be affordable. That is, if he was working full-time.

As they left the doctor's office and stopped at Cumberland farms for gas and something to drink, he noticed a help-wanted sign. He asked for an application and was immediately asked to talk to the manager. "I've got my girlfriend waiting in the car. Will this take long?" William asked.

"No, he just wanted to talk to you for a minute." The cashier told him. He was ushered into the office where he was greeted by an overweight older man sitting at his computer, munching on a bag of Cheetos.

"Mr. Carson? You're looking for a job?" His graying beard had crumbs of cheese dust sticking to it and William tried to look at his eyes instead. "Can you work overnights?"

William hadn't considered the possibility, but it would definitely work with his school schedule. "Sure." He agreed.

"You're hired. By the way, my name is Scott Sanders. I'm the General Manager here. You can start tomorrow night. The hours are 11pm to 7am. Still want the job?" He brushed his short stubby fingers against his shirt to clean them off.

William agreed and was given instructions on being there 15 minutes prior to his shift so the cashier could 'show him the ropes' according to Mr. Cheetos Sanders. He knew he wouldn't be getting much sleep but at least he wouldn't be ruled by Gram Laura. 'It's better this way,' he thought to himself. Although he knew Maria wasn't going to like him being at work or school all the time. He decided to wait and tell her later about his new employment opportunity.

"Wow, what took you so long?" Maria asked when he got back in the car. William took a deep breath, knowing his news of a night shift job wasn't going to be well received.

Maria

When William finally told her about his new night shift job at Cumberland Farms, it was about an hour before he needed to start his 11-7 shift the next night. They had stayed in Maria's room that night. "Bill! What are you talking about?" She didn't even know what to say. "How can you get up and go to classes the next morning?"

"Babe, I'll sleep during the day. I've got classes at 9 and 11. After that I don't have class again until 2:30. I can sleep then." He insisted. But Maria knew him. He'd probably sleep through the alarm and miss his 9:00 class, maybe make his 11:00 but then go to sleep again and potentially miss his 2:30 class. She shook her head. "No, Bill. This isn't a good idea. You'll end up missing too many classes."

"I need to try, Maria. Trust me, we don't want to move in with Gram Laura unless there are no other options. Right now, I'm giving another option a try." He gave her a hug. "Please. I really want to see if we can do this on our own." Maria threw up her hands. "Ok, Bill! But when you're exhausted and can't make it to class, we'll need another plan."

William just gave her a kiss as he headed out for the overnight shift. "We'll see, sweetheart. I'll see you in the morning." He headed out the door as Maria sank down onto the bed. She was exhausted and the 'morning sickness' as they called it wasn't just in the morning; it was on and off every day. Even a whiff of something that usually smelled good to her, such as bacon which she usually loved, now sent her straight to the bathroom. Gram Laura had called this morning, and left a voice mail 'hoping that William will change his mind.' She'd listened to the message when Bill was in the shower, knowing that it would make him upset. She'd put in an application at the school book-store without telling him and hopefully she'd hear back from them soon. He wasn't the only one who could work!

Maria had fallen asleep finally around midnight and didn't wake up until Bill came in at around 8:00 in the morning. He looked so tired. "Wow, what a night. You wouldn't believe the drunk people that come into the store at 2:00am!" He talked about it for a few minutes as she nodded, half-listening and knowing that this wasn't going to work long-term.

She watched Bill as he changed into his sweatpants and t-shirt, gave her a kiss and fell fast asleep as she was getting ready for class. She gave him a kiss on the top of his head and finished getting ready to leave for her 9:30 class. "Get some sleep." She whispered to him and he murmured, "night, baby," as he turned over in the bed to face the opposite way.

She knew that she needed to tell him about the book store job, but now wasn't the time. The biggest guilt of all was that she wasn't sure that she was carrying his child. She wasn't showing yet, but she knew just as the child would grow, the guilt of telling him about what happened with Dan would as well.

She made it to her 9:30 history class just in time. She hated this class and always had a hard time staying awake, but more so today. She hadn't slept well last night between worrying about William and feeling nauseated from anything she ate or drank. Her morning coffee hadn't stayed down very long and she knew that there were so many changes she wasn't sure how to keep up any longer.

After class, she went back to Bill's dorm to make sure he was awake for his 11:00 class, but he was still sound asleep. It was already 10:45. "Bill, wake up, you have a class in 15 minutes." He turned his head and continued to sleep. Maria gave up. This clearly wasn't going to work, no matter how much he wanted it to. She gave up and kissed him on the cheek, knowing how exhausted he was, and also knowing that this night shift job wasn't going to work. She went to her next class at 12:30 and came back to him at 2:00 still sound asleep. She tried to wake him. "Go 'way'" He murmured and rolled over. She was really frustrated now, and knew that this wasn't going to work at all. She reached over and gently shook him. "Bill, you need to get up. Your class is at 2:30."

He finally woke up and sat straight up. "What?! Really? What time is it?" He seemed disoriented and jumped out of bed, starting to put on the same clothes he had on yesterday. "Babe, you wore those clothes yesterday. It's almost 2:00. Your class is at 2:30. You have time for a quick shower and I'll put out some clean clothes for you." Maria tried to stay calm, but she was getting angry with the whole situation. There was no way this would work. For even more than a few days.

He did get up and take a shower and put on the clothes she'd laid out in an almost robotic fashion. He ran out the door without grabbing his books, but she saw them and met him at the main door. "Thanks, babe." He gave her a quick kiss as he headed to class. At this rate, he'd be dropping out of most of his classes by March if he didn't show up. They would need to find another way.

Maria decided to take a quick shower before her next class at 4:00, hoping it would help her anxiety. She stepped into the hot shower and was lathering up when sudden cramps made her double over in pain. She took deep breaths and told herself it was just because her body was adjusting to the pregnancy. But the pain continued and she became frightened, got out of the shower and dressed in some old sweatpants and sweatshirt that she'd grabbed from her bottom drawer. She decided to lay down, hoping that she was just having some cramping that the doctor had said was normal from her uterus beginning to expand, but when she used the bathroom, there was blood. Not a lot, but more than a few spots. And suddenly, she knew this wasn't normal. She glanced over at the clock, it was only 2:35. Bill had hopefully just made it to class, but there was no way to get in touch with him unless she physically went there.

She was trying not to panic, but the pain was becoming worse and she couldn't help but cry out. Someone was knocking on the door. "Maria, are you okay in there?" Maria recognized her voice as Stephanie Martin. She was a nice enough person and always seemed busy. Maria didn't know her well, but was really glad to hear her voice now.

"No, I need help!" Maria said. "Please help me." She could hear Stephanie wrestling with the door to realize William had locked it from the inside. "It's locked, Steph, I'm coming." She managed to pull herself off the bed and unlock the door. The effort caused her to crumple to the floor in pain and Stephanie immediately called 911. "Maria, I called an ambulance, they'll be here real soon." Maria managed to make it back to the bed, as she huddled in a fetal position, as Stephanie sat with her. She'd never felt as much pain before and she knew that this might be a miscarriage. Although she wasn't sure this baby was Williams', she didn't want to lose this child.

As soon as the ambulance arrived, they checked her vitals. "Maria, your blood pressure's really low, we're going to take you over to South County hospital for further evaluation," one of the EMTs told her. Maria was in too much pain to argue despite not wanting to go. "Steph, could you please let William know I went to the hospital? He's at class right now. He'll be back here in about an hour." Stephanie nodded. "What class is he in? I can let him know now."

"Finance Management. It's in Woodward Hall, room 202, I think." Maria told her. "Thanks for helping me out, Steph. Please let him know where I'm going." Maria felt another cramp coming on and she was doubled over again as the EMT's put her on a gurney and sped off to the hospital. She was given some pain medication while in the ambulance and suddenly, she was starting to drift off. Her mother's face suddenly appeared. "Mom! What's happening? I need you." Maria told her.

"You need to be honest with William. Whose child is this?" Her mother was upset, she could tell. "You need to tell him." Her mother said again and then she disappeared. "I will, I promise. I will tell him." She said.

" Maria,who are you talking to?" One of the female EMT's asked her.

"My mother. She was talking to me." Maria told her. The woman glanced over at her co-worker. "I think she's had enough Ativan for now." She whispered. "I think she's hallucinating."

93

'But she was there!' Maria thought. She knew she'd seen her, talking to her. She was suddenly feeling tired and felt herself falling into a deep welcoming sleep.

William

He barely made it on time to his finance class, despite still being dead tired from the overnight shift. The professor had just started his lecture, when a girl from Maria's dorm quietly walked in and tapped him on the shoulder. "I need to talk to you. It's urgent." She whispered. William stood up and followed her out the door, his heart racing. 'Please don't let it be my mom', was the first thought that came to his mind.

"I'm Stephanie Martin, by the way. Sorry I had to bother you during class. But it's Maria. She's been taken to the hospital." Stephanie told him. She explained what had happened, and that everything seemed to be okay when she left, but they were taking her in for evaluation.

"Was she conscious? Oh my god, I'll leave right now. Where did they take her?" William tried not to think the worst, but his father's death was still fresh in his mind.

"South County Hospital. She was alert when she got in the ambulance, just very anxious. She told me where you were." Stephanie told him. "I'm sure she's going to be fine, don't worry." She patted his arm. William thanked her and ran to his car for the 10 -mile drive to the hospital. She *had* to be okay!

When he arrived, he was told that she was still in triage since she'd just arrived by ambulance and he'd have to wait until the doctor had seen her. He sat for what seemed like hours, but really was only about

30 minutes, when a tall, dark-haired nurse came out to get him. "William Carson?"

"Yes!" He jumped up anxiously, hoping that there was good news.

"You can see Maria now. Follow me." The nurse brought him down the hallway, as he rambled nervously. "What's going on? Is she okay?"

"She'll be just fine. The doctor will talk with you." The nurse smiled patiently, as she stopped at a small room just off the emergency room area with the curtain pulled around the bed for privacy.

Maria was sitting up with a light blue hospital gown on that matched her eyes. She looked tired and pale, but still as beautiful as always. "Maria! What happened? I was so worried!" William tried to hold back the tears that were threatening to spill out in relief that she was okay. He ran to her and hugged her.

"I had cramps and started bleeding. Not a lot, but it scared me. The door was locked and I was crying. Steph heard me and came in. But the doctor checked me out and said everything looks okay. I'm so glad you're here!" Maria clung to him, letting him know how scared she'd been.

"The baby's okay?" William asked nervously. Just then, the doctor came into the room. He was an older man, with a kind face that reminded me of his grandfather. "You must be William. I'm Dr. Scott." He shook William's hand.

"What happened?" William was still leery of her prognosis, especially in hospitals. The memory of his father's hospitalization and death was still fresh in his mind.

"Maria was having some cramping which is normal. The spotting isn't unusual, although I do recommend that going forward, she should be in a stress-free environment as much as possible."

"So the baby's fine?" William gripped Maria's hand.

"The baby is just fine. In fact, here's a picture from the sonogram that was done earlier." Dr. Scott handed him a print out. The baby was still so small they weren't able to tell the gender yet, but he could make out the shape of their child and his heart melted. He knew then that he'd need to forget about his feelings about Gram Laura and take her up on her offer to move in to help with finances. He wasn't going to take a chance on Maria's or the baby's health because he was too proud and worried about his grandmother's influence.

"Will I be able to leave today?" Maria asked.

"Absolutely. You just need to follow up with your doctor in the next few days, especially if you're having any problems." Dr. Scott told her. "I want you to limit your activities as far as exercising for the next couple of days, but I'm not going to put you on bed-rest. Check in with your doctor and make sure you're getting good nutrition. I'm prescribing some pre-natal vitamins for you." Dr. Scott assured her.

"Thank you, Dr. Scott." William was grateful that he was leaving with Maria. As soon as the doctor left, he approached Maria about contacting Gram Laura. "I'm going to call Gram Laura today and talk to her about her offer of having us live there." He wasn't sure if she would still agree with it.

"Really? You mean it?" Maria sounded relieved. " Bill, I think it'll be best for us. I know you're worried about her controlling everything, but just one overnight shift turned you into a zombie. We need to stay in school, and I'm not sure we can do that without her help." Maria was happier than he expected. That was one less mountain to climb. The next would be to talk to his grandmother and he knew he'd be swallowing much of his pride to do so.

Maria

It had been over three months since they'd moved in with Gram Laura in South Kingstown. Her house was a sprawling ranch style home that had been updated many times over the years, even since William remembered coming here as a kid. The wall to wall carpeting was a light tan color. The living room was decorated in muted tones of yellow and open to the kitchen area with a breakfast bar. There was a view of the ocean from the picture window with a seating area which Maria loved.

There were four bedrooms; one was Gram Laura's with a master bath. Down the hall was William and Maria's room, which was big enough for a king-sized bed, along with a desk and studying area and a private bathroom. Their bedroom was like her haven; sky-blue walls, long sheer curtains and nautical pictures on the walls. The bedroom next to theirs had already become Gram Laura's project to become the baby's room. She'd already started consulting with designers about the room.

"Are you going to find out the sex of the baby? It would just be so helpful if I knew so that I could move forward on the nursery?" She asked Maria from time to time. Maria and William had both agreed that they didn't want to know. Besides, there was no guarantee even with the sonograms. They weren't always accurate, according to Dr. Malone. Although Gram Laura had tried to get another obstetrician, Maria had liked Dr. Malone and insisted on keeping her. William hadn't been kidding when he said that Gram Laura was controlling. From the day they moved in, she was always making 'suggestions' starting with Maria's doctor. "I've never heard of Dr. Malone. Why don't you let me set you up with another doctor that's 'more established?'

It was a battle that Maria didn't want to have with Gram Laura, so she agreed to switch to Dr. Simon upon her insistence. She was an older woman, on time, and patient with Maria's questions. She turned out to be a good choice. But it was Gram's little nit-picky things, such as specific dinner times and making dinner that included foods that she knew William didn't like that were other annoying factors that Maria tried to ignore. She had to remind herself of how much better off they were.

Maria was now 5 months pregnant and went from not showing to not fitting into her clothes overnight. Gram Laura immediately went shopping while Maria was in class and bought her maternity clothing. While Maria appreciated the gesture, the clothing looked like it was made for a middle aged woman that may or may not have been pregnant. She modeled a dress that Gram Laura had bought for William one evening. It looked like a rainbow colored tent that was shapeless and was so long that it touched the floor. "What'd you think? Should I wear this at a Halloween party dressed as a tent?" Maria joked. "Or maybe Mrs. Roper from Three's Company."

"You look beautiful no matter what you wear." William told her, trying to suppress a laugh. But she knew she shouldn't stir the pot. William was already irritated with her controlling everything from his breakfast, to what he was wearing. Was he was getting good grades and was he on time to classes? But at least he was able to go to class. He'd immediately quit the overnight job at Cumberland Farms and found a part time job at Dunkin Donuts which allowed him to have hours that wouldn't interrupt his sleep as much. Maria was finishing up her sophomore year and had already signed up for summer classes because of the upcoming birth at the end of September.

Still her mother would appear to her at least weekly in her dreams or just as she was falling asleep. Sometimes just voice, or an apparition to remind her of what she promised; that she would tell William that she wasn't sure he was the father. There were some moments that she and William had together when she almost blurted out the truth about that horrible night when Dan raped her, but then she knew there was too much to lose. Her dignity. William. Really, everything. There was never a right time and when William felt her growing belly expand and talked to the baby, she knew that no matter what, he was their father. She wouldn't, couldn't tell him about what happened. It would only destroy what they had together. Besides, there wouldn't be any way to be sure until after the baby was born. If she told him now, she'd have nowhere to go if Gram Laura kicked her out and William rejected her and the baby. She'd be out of options then. No, the only way to make sure that the baby had a father was to keep her secret. If not just for her, but for the child's well-being.

As she was resting on the couch on a late Saturday afternoon, she felt the baby kick for the first time. William had just walked in the door from working. "Bill! I just felt her kick! Come here and feel it!" It just struck her at that moment how much she wanted this child and she would do anything to protect it. William's eyes lit up and he ran over to her, put his hand on her growing belly. "Give her a minute!" Maria told him.

"You keep calling the baby a 'her'. What if it's a boy?" William joked.

"I don't know. I guess I just have a feeling it's a girl, that's all. Maybe it's wishful thinking, but I'll be happy no matter what." Just then, William's eyes lit up.

"I just felt her kick!" He said excitedly.

"You just said 'her'," Maria giggled. William nodded. "I'll listen to your woman's intuition on this one." He laid his head on her belly and fell asleep after a long day.

William

He'd never been so tired of his grandmother in his life. It was the hardest decision to make in his life when he chose to move them into Gram Laura's home because he was worried about Maria and the baby. But it was now almost Labor Day and it had been a long 7 months of constant micromanagement of his and Maria's life. He was still in school, as was Maria, and working as many hours as possible at Dunkin Donuts, which was more motivation to finish his degree. He knew he needed to try to get as many school credits as possible before the baby came. He'd taken on the maximum school load of 12 credits during the summer. Maria went from not showing at all to suddenly not fitting into her clothes in the 5th month and since then could only fit into shirts and maternity stretch pants in the past few months.

Maria was sitting on their bed one night after his long shift at Dunkin at 9:30. "I never thought I'd be this big." She had a sad look on her face.

"Babe! You're pregnant! If your stomach wasn't growing that would be a problem! I think you look beautiful!" He kissed her and felt her belly. He wasn't just humoring her; if Maria wasn't facing him, no one would even think she was pregnant. He had been saving up for several months to surprise Maria and ask her to marry him, and he'd just found the right ring. He just needed the right time. He'd even included Gram Laura with his intent to propose to her and shown her the ring. Gram

Laura was excited and he almost wished he hadn't told her, fearing that she'd ruin the surprise and tell Maria.

He suddenly realized that there were perfect moments every time they were together. "I'm going downstairs for a snack. Do you want anything?" He asked her.

"No. I think I ate my weight in ice cream today." She laughed. Pistachio ice cream was the one thing she couldn't say no to during this pregnancy and Gram Laura went out of her way to have an endless supply in the freezer.

William headed downstairs into the living room where he'd hidden the ring in a now empty flour container in the kitchen where he knew Maria would never find it. As he pulled it from its box just to look at it again, he was hoping she'd love it just as much as he did. It was a one carat marquis- cut diamond with a plain gold band. It was simple, yet beautiful. It was exactly what he thought she would choose and Gram Laura agreed when she saw it. He took a deep breath as he walked back upstairs. Maria was lying on the bed, staring up at the ceiling when he came back in the room. "Babe, are you awake?" He asked.

"Yup, I am. Just tired." She said. He was starting to wonder if he should do this now, but he'd already gotten up the nerve, so he decided to go for it. "Maria, look at me."

She turned over with a tired smile on her face. "What's up?" Then she noticed him down on his knee next to the bed. "Are you okay?" She asked.

William had rehearsed what he'd wanted to say a hundred times, but suddenly couldn't remember any of it. "Maria, I love you. Will you marry me?" He managed to say as he pulled the ring out of the box.

She looked shocked for a moment, then began to cry. "Oh my god! Bill!" She couldn't stop crying as William put the ring on her left ring finger.

"Does that mean you'll marry me?" William kidded with her.

"Yes! Yes, of course I'll marry you!" Maria pulled him to her and gave him a long kiss. "This ring is so beautiful, but we can't afford this!" She insisted.

"It's yours. Don't worry about the cost. It's already paid for." William assured her. He knew she worried about their expenses. "I was able to save money. At least there's something positive that came from moving in with Gram, right?" He tried to sound like he was joking, but they were both at their wits end with the rules and control Gram Laura insisted on. William found it sad that his grandmother would put conditions on helping him. Right now, they weren't in a position to leave or protest. But he promised himself that one day soon, he would be able to get a good job to afford to move out into their own place. And as much as he loved her, he wouldn't be choosing a house near Gram Laura!

"I know that we could wait until after the baby is born, but was thinking maybe next week? I'd like us to be a family when the baby gets here." William had been thinking about it for a month, but he wasn't sure what Maria would think. Maybe she would want to wait and have a traditional wedding with the dress and the wedding party that would take months to plan. He knew that Gram Laura would go for that idea and start planning now. But he wanted them to be a family now. Make it official.

Maria was quiet for a few moments and he was doubting himself, almost ready to tell her that they would wait when she nodded her head. "I think I can't wait to be your wife. Let's do it!" She sounded excited about it, which made him know that she *really* was okay with the idea.

"Are you sure? I mean I know that most little girls dream about their weddings." William had to ask.

"What I want is for us to be a family. There's no one in my family I would want to invite anyway. Your family really has become my family." Maria assured him as she gave him a kiss. William had never been happier. Now it was real; they were getting married. He just needed to tell Gram Laura. He knew she wouldn't be happy with a small ceremony next week at the courthouse or at her house, but they'd make it work!

"Okay, then!" He was tempted to tell his grandmother now, but it was almost 11:00 at night and he knew she was usually in bed by 10:00. "We'll talk to her in the morning before class. I'm sure she'll be happy. She loves you just as much as I do." William added. He knew it was true. Gram Laura did love Maria. The problem was that she was overbearing and he knew it was getting to her. "You're my fiancé!" William loved the sound of that word.

"I love the sound of that!" Maria sounded as excited as he did. They were able to go to bed excited for the future, and William felt the baby kick again as they fell asleep.

Maria

It was almost surreal as she stood there in Gram Laura's back yard underneath a willow tree in a private wedding ceremony. William had never looked as handsome as he did today in his simple black suit and bowtie. She'd never seen him dressed up before, but it was a look that he wore well. He'd gotten a buzzed hair-cut that was much shorter than she had ever seen it, but it suited him. He was everything to her and she had never been more sure of anything than marrying him today.

It had been difficult to find the perfect dress, considering she was 8 ½ months pregnant, but she'd found the perfect dress in a consignment shop in East Greenwich that fit her with very few alterations. Maria didn't care about the dress being white, so she'd chosen a beautiful lilac colored dress that was a shift style so that it fit without being confining. The only alteration was the length because of Maria's petite 5'3" figure and it was taken up to hit below her knees. There were only a few people in attendance, which made her feel less self-conscious. Barbara, William's mother, Sara and a handful of his cousins were the only guests. She didn't bother inviting her Aunt Sylvia or anyone in her family. There was no point. It was a day that she desperately wished that her parents were still alive; to share in this moment.

As they said their vows, Maria noticed a transparent figure in the distance that was moving toward them. The minister announced them as man and wife and the few guests clapped and threw the rice, and

Maria headed into the garden area that Gram Laura had set up for the reception as she looked over her shoulder. The woman was nowhere in sight and she sighed in relief until she appeared in front of her again for a split-second. "I wish you happiness, dear daughter. We're still here with you." Her mother's voice was a whisper that no one else could hear, but it put tears in her eyes. A sudden flock of sparrows flew overhead and Maria knew it was a sign that her parents were watching over her. Her mother had always had a fascination with sparrows. She loved them because 'they symbolize empowerment and positivity.'

"What's the matter, Mrs. Carson?" William asked her, noticing her weepy eyes. "Having doubts already?"

Maria got her bearings and tried to refocus. "Well, it's a little late for that! Since we're already married, I'll see how it goes!" She joked and gave him a kiss, which brought on cheers from the guests. She winced as she felt a slight pain in her lower abdomen and hoped that it was just the Braxton-Hicks pains that the doctor had explained to her. "Are you okay, babe?" William asked. He had noticed.

"I'm fine. Probably just the baby wanting some attention right now." She said. She didn't want anything to interrupt their wedding day, especially since it was probably just the baby moving. The reception that Gram Laura had planned was beautiful; she had hired a decorator to turn her backyard into a romantic setting. Delicate strings of tiny white lights adorned the trees and small café style tables were set up for the guests. Bouquets of calla lilies with a splash of color from salmon colored roses were on every table. She'd even had the food catered by Twin Oaks, a well-known Italian restaurant in Cranston, and hired wait staff to serve the food. When she was told about their plan, Gram Laura had insisted on planning and paying for the reception, so she was happy that an Italian caterer was chosen. Gram Laura had made sure that the food selection included some of Williams' favorites; lasagna and spaghetti with Bolognese. As they sat at a table next to their guests, Maria felt herself begin to relax finally.

The finale was the cake that Gram Laura had made herself. Gram Laura admitted that she'd always loved baking and decorating, and while Maria was initially hesitant about her ability, she was shocked at how beautiful it turned out. It was a simple two tier vanilla cake, but the decorations of roses, lilies and greenery all done in sugar looked so amazing, it looked as though she'd hired someone to do it. As she and William were cutting the cake, she felt a sharp pain and tightening that caused her to bend over. "Maria! Are you okay?" William immediately put his arms around her.

She hoped that it was still the Braxton contractions, but just then there was another one that brought her to her knees. "I …I think the baby's coming…." She managed to tell him. The pain was much different. William helped her over to a chair as Gram Laura scurried over to her. "Maria, just do your breathing. I'm calling Dr. Simon right now." As the guests began to hover over her in concern, Maria was starting to feel claustrophobic. "Bill, please get me away from here. Just drive me to the hospital. It's only 5 miles away." She managed to tell him. He nodded and helped her up out of her chair. "I'm taking her over to the hospital now, Gram Laura. Please let Dr. Simon know we'll be there." She began to protest but William interrupted. "I think our little blessing is about to arrive just as we've tied the knot. Thank you so much for being here!" William announced to the guests that were hovered around. Gram Laura looked shocked. "William! Dr. Simon isn't on call tonight!"

"Well, the baby apparently didn't know that, so we'll have to go with whoever is." William was matter of fact about the situation. Maria was grateful to her new husband for taking over, because the pains were so intense and every few minutes, she wasn't able to speak. He hurried her to the car as Gram Laura came out with a packed suitcase. "You'll need this!" She gave it to him as he helped her into the car and sped away toward the hospital.

Maria struggled through the contractions that seemed to be coming stronger every few minutes as William drove as fast as he could. She could tell that he was stressed by the sweat rolling down his face and onto his already drenched white collared shirt that he'd worn along with the suit that Gram Laura had rented for him. He'd shed the suit jacket already and taken off the tie. She could feel another contraction coming and gripped the arm rest on the passenger door and his leg as she tried to breathe. "Bill, it hurts." She managed to tell him between breaths.

"Hang in there, babe, we're almost there! Just keep breathing like they said in the birth classes. In and out, very slowly." She could tell he was trying to stay calm for her and she tried to remember the breaths that they had learned in the few birth classes that they'd managed to attend.

By the time they arrived at South County hospital, Maria's contractions were coming more frequently and as she struggled to get out of the car, William ran over to assist her. Apparently, Gram Laura had called ahead because several staff members met them at the door with a wheelchair and took Maria straight in, much to her relief. She wasn't sure she'd be able to walk in and then wait to be admitted. She was immediately wheeled up to Labor and Delivery where a young nurse was waiting to take her vitals and help her into a room. Maria's contractions continued to be every 2 minutes and her blood pressure was up.

"Maria, my name's Mary. I'm going to be assisting Dr. Taylor who's on call tonight for Dr. Simon. When did your contractions start?" She asked. She looked very young, not much older than Maria, but she had a good bedside manner and at this point that was all Maria cared about. She was feeling very unprepared and overwhelmed.

"About 45 minutes ago. During my wedding ceremony." Maria told her, suddenly laughing because she realized how crazy this sounded. Mary laughed along with her. "No worries there. Babies don't care about a timeline, right?"

"I guess not! Not this one anyway!" Maria tried to relax but knew that the next wave of contractions would be coming. "Where's my husband? William Carson is his name." Maria kept looking for him now that she was in a hospital bed and being hooked up to all the fetal and vital monitors.

"He's just working on the admitting paperwork. He'll be here real soon." Mary assured her, just as an older gray-haired man who appeared to be in his 60s walked into the room. "Maria Evans? I'm Dr. Taylor." He said.

"Actually, I just became Maria Carson about an hour ago, Dr. Taylor, but yes I'm the same person." Maria joked with him, just as another contraction was building and she groaned in pain. The tightening in her lower abdomen made her feel as though she might split in half at any moment. Mary had just hooked up the fetal monitor that showed the fetal heart rate, which Dr. Taylor quickly inspected. "Ok, Maria Carson!" He winked at her, acknowledging her new name. "The baby's heart rate is a little high, so I'm going to check and see how far you're dilated. Maria nodded and was grateful that Mary was by her side as the doctor checked. "You're about 7 centimeters already! Only 3 to go." Dr. Taylor announced. "Young lady, I do believe you're going to have this baby soon. Unfortunately, I really can't give you anything for the pain at this point. It will only slow things down." He patted Maria's hand.

"Is the baby okay? You said the heart rate is a little high." Maria managed to ask as the contraction began to subside again.

"The baby is fine, but just as a precaution, Mary is going to stay and monitor." Dr. Taylor smiled. "Don't worry. The heart rate is within a safe range." Maria nodded as she felt another contraction starting. "Bill! Where's my husband?" She cried out. She was scared and she needed him.

Dr. Taylor went out the door to ask the nursing desk, when he suddenly returned with William next to him. "Guess who I found out here?" Dr. Taylor said as William rushed to her side and kissed her.

"Hi, Mrs. Carson. I guess our wedding anniversary will also be our baby's birthday!" William said. "Are you okay? Is the baby okay?" Maria nodded as she grimaced with another contraction that made her cry out. William did his best to help her breath through it. "Guess we should've finished those birth classes," he said to Maria, who wasn't laughing right now. In fact, she was trying not to scream as the contractions became more intense. Dr. Taylor came back into the room to check her progress. Maria felt beyond any privacy and didn't care, but William turned toward Maria. "Babe, does that hurt when he's checking you?"

Maria suddenly started laughing despite the pain. "Bill! Seriously? I'm about to give birth; I'm having contractions and I'm about to squeeze a baby out of my body! I think it's safe to say no, it doesn't"

"We're going to need to move you to the delivery room, Maria. You're 10 centimeters dilated. Several nurses came in and moved Maria onto a gurney. "I'm sorry, but you'll have to stay in the waiting room, Mr. Carson. We'll keep you updated.

Maria had never felt so scared and excited at the same time in her life. She gave him a kiss as they wheeled her into the delivery room.

William

Watching Maria being wheeled into the delivery room scared him. It reminded him of his father when he'd been in the hospital and he tried to remind himself that this was different; she was having a baby. But sometimes that was dangerous, wasn't it? He tried to read the latest Providence Journal that was sitting on the waiting room table, but as he flipped through it, he knew he needed to talk to someone. He reached into his pocket and headed for the pay phone that was near the elevator. Gram Laura wasn't the first person he wanted to talk to, but he knew that she was waiting for his call.

She picked up on the first ring. "William! How's she doing? Has she had the baby yet?" Her voice was excited, firing questions at him all at once.

"She just went into the delivery room. I'm gonna be a dad, Gram, can you believe it?" William suddenly felt like confiding in her, despite his animosity about her trying to control him. "Did you call my mom?" He suddenly realized that instead of calling his mother, he'd called his grandmother. She had been at the wedding, but he hadn't had much time to talk to her or his sister.

"She's still here, waiting for news. I'll let her know. We'll come and wait with you." Gram Laura decided. "We'll see you in about 20 minutes." Gram Laura hung up before William could check with the nursing desk to see if other visitors were allowed. But then again, it *was* a waiting room. He hung up the phone and wandered back over to the mustard-yellow vinyl couch. He could hear Maria's screams from the delivery room that made him want to run into the room and comfort her, but scared him at the same time.

It seemed like hours, although it was only 15 minutes, when Gram Laura, his mother and sister arrived in the waiting room. He'd never been so glad to see his family. "Any word yet?" Gram Laura asked, as his mother gave him a hug and sat next to him. William shook his head. Gram Laura immediately headed for the nurse's desk. "Excuse me, is there any word on how Maria Carson is doing? She's in the delivery room." William rolled his eyes as he heard her. "Gram, I'm sure they'll come out as soon as they can with news." The nurse nodded and pointed to him. "Ma'am, yes, that's accurate. Someone will come out and give you an update."

William was too anxious to sit down, so he continued to pace back and forth within the waiting room, while his Gram Laura and his mother patiently sat, calmly reading the latest issue of Good Housekeeping. His sister, Barbara, was at the hospital gift shop looking around because she had been bored sitting with them. 'How in the world are they so calm?' He couldn't help thinking.

A nurse came out of the delivery room, but her facial expression wasn't one he wanted to see. Above her masked nose and mouth, her eyes looked worried. "What's going on? Is everything okay?" William felt his heart racing, knowing that it wasn't.

"Mr. Carson, your wife is having complications. She's dilated but the baby is not moving through the birth canal and we'll have to do a C-section which will need to be done quickly due to the baby's heart rate dropping. Your wife's blood pressure and heart rate is extremely high. We're doing all we can." The nurse gave him all this information with a grave look, telling William all he needed to know. "Is she going to be okay?" William felt tears sliding in streams down his face.

"We're doing all we can, Mr. Carson." The nurse repeated in a gentle tone. William just nodded as he sat down next to his mother, grandmother and sister who'd just returned from the gift shop with a teddy bear in tow 'for the baby.' They'd already overheard and now there was a quiet tension in the air.

"Can I see her? Please? I know that it's not policy, but we were just married an hour ago…." William knew he couldn't bear it if something happened to Maria and he couldn't at least see her face.

The nurse was clearly sympathetic. "Let me check with the doctor and I'll be right back." She told him. She went back behind the doors and William waited for what seemed like hours, but was only a few minutes.

"I'm sorry. Your wife is under anesthesia now and the doctor is preparing for a cesarean." She saw the despair on William's face. "I'll give you updates every step of the way, Mr. Carson." He just nodded and sat down next to his mother who gave him a hug. "She's in good hands, William."

William could hear the words, but he wouldn't believe them until he saw his wife and child, alive and well.

Maria

It was almost as if she were in a dream, as she was in the delivery room; her contractions were coming quickly now and it was hard to catch her breath. She could hear the doctor and nurses around her and her feet were up and she was feeling as though she needed to push. The nurse near her head and the doctor that was monitoring the baby's progress kept telling her to push, but she was out of energy and suddenly she felt as though she couldn't breathe. She struggled to get air, while the nurse shouted something to the doctor, machines were making noise and then Maria felt herself relax and suddenly she could see everything. She could see the doctors and nurses and wait! Was that her on the table?

'What's going on here?' She thought to herself. "Hey! What's going on? Is my baby okay?" She tried to talk to the people below her, but they just put a machine up to her chest with paddles and kept pushing a button. "We've got to save the baby; she's in cardiac arrest. Keep working on her while we get this baby out!" She could hear one of the doctors saying.

"I'm right here!" Maria tried to tell them, but they still didn't seem to hear her. But she could hear another voice. "Maria, we're here with you." It was her mother's voice that echoed through the sound of their voices and the scene that was below her began to fade further away.

"Mom? Can you hear me?" She suddenly felt weightless and enveloped in a warmth that was as comforting as her mother's voice. She didn't feel any more pain and there were bright colors all around her with a light brighter than the sun high above.

"Yes, Maria. I'd hoped that this wouldn't happen, but it's up to you now. Those little baby girls will need you. It's always easier on this side, except for the few of us that can communicate with our loved ones from time to time."

"I want to stay with you and dad." Maria felt the pull to just stay in this peaceful place with her parents.

"You can't stay here now. I will always be here when the time comes. But it's not now. You need to go back to your husband and your daughters."

"Daughters?" Maria asked. "Mom? Can you hear me?" But already, the bright sunlight had disappeared and the colors were fading. She could see the hospital room again and suddenly she was aware of a nurse beside her and someone pushing on her chest. She could hear a machine beeping and heard a voice say "She's back!" She found herself looking at a sheet over her mid-section and someone saying, "it's a girl!" There were a few seconds and she could hear a baby's cry. She felt no pain from the waist down and she felt herself tearing up as she heard her daughter's cry.

The doctor made another announcement, "I can't believe this, here's baby number two! Did anyone know that this woman was pregnant with twins?" A few moments later, she heard another cry. Twins? There was never any suggestion, but it must be true because as the nurses took the aspiration mask off of her face and checked her vitals, the nurse closest to her said, "You have twin daughters, Mrs. Carson. I'm so glad that you're back with us. You gave us quite a scare."

"Are they okay? Can I see them?" Maria was overwhelmed, not sure what was real anymore after the experience she'd had. Gave them a scare? She was the one watching them from above!

"We're just going to make sure you're stabilized before you hold them, but here they are!" Another nurse brought them up to Maria's head so that she could see them. They were so tiny, but appeared to be in perfect health. "They're perfectly fine, Maria. We're just going to clean them up and get them wrapped up. Your husband is right outside along with the rest of the family. You can see them soon. We just need to finish your sutures."

Everything went dark again and when she woke up, she was in a regular hospital room with William, Sara and Gram Laura all in the room along with the babies who were in their bassinets. "Hi, sweetheart, you're awake!" William moved toward her bed and gave her a kiss. "Can you believe that we have twins! Two perfect little girls!" He'd never looked so excited. It took her a moment to remember, but now she couldn't wait to hold her daughters. They'd talked about breast-feeding and Maria had felt squeamish about it at first, but now the maternal instinct was kicking in. Mary, the nurse that had been with Maria from the beginning came in just then to check on her vital signs. "Everything looks really good here. Would you like to hold your daughters?" Mary smiled. "Congratulations, mom and dad!"

Maria couldn't help but cry tears of happiness as Mary and William helped place a baby in each of her arms. They both had small patches of blonde hair and were completely identical. "You're going to have to mark their booties or dress them differently for a little while to tell them apart."

But Maria could tell the moment she held them that they were individuals. The baby on her right was already looking up at her with inquisitive blue eyes and the baby on her left was dozing. "They need names, Bill. I know we decided on Karen for a girl, but now we have two." Then Maria remembered a girl that she'd known from grade school who'd been her friend; her name was Krista and she'd always loved her name. "What about Krista? I know it's the same letter as Karen and kind of cliché for twins, but I love both of the names."

William nodded. "I love them too. They'd talked about using either "Ann" which was Gram Laura's middle name or her mother's middle name "Marie" along with Karen when they'd discussed girl's names. Now they could use both. "How about Karen Ann and Krista Marie?"

Maria nodded, glad that he'd remembered that Marie was her mother's middle name. "Sounds perfect to me." She could still hardly believe that she was a mother to not one but two babies now, but already she felt as though she was where she was supposed to be. It was a moment to be cherished and remember, because in the back of her mind, Maria already knew that there was little chance they'd be able to get a place of their own anytime soon with two babies. She only wished her parents could've have been here for this moment, but then again, she was sure that her mother had been. She didn't know the details about what had happened to her during the time she could see herself on the delivery table from above, but she was sure that seeing her mother and talking to her was real.

William

When the nurse had come out to tell him there were problems with Maria, he had no idea how serious the situation was, until the nurse came out to let them know that Maria had gone into cardiac arrest and they were working to revive her. "What? What do you mean? Cardiac arrest? She's a healthy 20-year-old woman! I need to see her!" William was yelling now. He was beside himself with this update and tried to push past the nurse to get to the delivery room. He couldn't not be with her now! "Mr. Carson! You can't go in there! Please let the doctors help her. They're doing everything they can." The nurse nodded to the tall, muscular security guard that appeared out of nowhere and blocked his way toward the doors as the nurse went through them.

"Mr. Carson, please have a seat. I know this is a difficult time for you, but if you won't calm down, I'll have to escort you out of the hospital." The security guard said to him. William retreated, and tried to calm down. "Sorry, I just wanted to see my wife. We just got married an hour ago." His eyes filled with tears as he went back to sit with his family. Gram Laura and his mother both hugged him as he sat down crying uncontrollably. "She's young and strong. She'll get through this," His mother insisted. "Sometimes there are cardiac issues that come up during a delivery, but I'm sure they are doing everything they can." His grandmother tried to assure him. Barbara had gone for a walk outside after William became upset. "Maybe you should take a walk, honey, it might help you feel better." His mother suggested quietly.

William just shook his head. "I can't. I need to be here when they come back out!" He insisted. The ghostly-white hospital walls felt like they were closing in on him and he felt almost paralyzed with fear that he wouldn't get to see his wife of a few hours again.

They all waited for what seemed like a lifetime, but after 30 minutes, he thought he could hear a baby crying from the room. He ran near the door and peered through the small windows in hopes that he could see something. He could see one of the nurses headed toward the door and he quickly retreated to the vinyl couch. He sat between Gram Laura and his mother as the nurse came out to give them news.

"Congratulations, Mr. Carson. You're a father of two beautiful twin girls!"

William almost fell off the couch in shock. "Twins? Really?" There was never any indication from Dr. Simon that Maria was having twins! He was beyond happy that the babies and Maria were okay.

"Yes, it wasn't detected on any ultra-sounds, but here they are! Maria is recovering and will be fine, but we'll be monitoring her for a little while." The nurse smiled. "We'll have the babies brought to the nursery and Maria over to recovery soon and you can see them soon."

He immediately ran to Maria when he was finally allowed in the room and hugged her. "Hi, sweetheart, you're awake! Can you believe that we have twins! Two perfect little girls!" Tears were running down his face as he saw the babies for the first time. He was still trying to believe that not only was he a father, but a father to twins! They'd decided on naming them Karen and Krista and he made a promise that he would do whatever it took to get through school and work hard to provide for them. It would mean at least another year at Gram Laura's but it was a sacrifice he was willing to make for his new family.

Maria

It had been an adjustment over the past 2 years with Karen and Krista. William was still working and attending as many classes as he could so that he could get his degree, which was only a semester away. Maria still attended classes, but her maternal instincts had kicked in and she missed a few semesters after they were born. She was due to finish her degree at the same time as William. But her focus was on the girls. They were identical in appearance; blonde hair just like her own, blue eyes and identical in every way. But it was easy to tell them apart from the beginning. Krista was adventurous and outgoing, and Karen was quiet and subdued. She often would follow Krista's lead, even if it was just a toy that Krista was interested in, Karen would let her check it out first. It was always Krista that crawled first, then began walking at about 10 months. Karen was right behind her, walking a few weeks later. Maria even checked with the doctor, concerned that Karen might have some delays in functioning, but the pediatrician assured her that Karen was on track. "This sometimes happens with twins; there is a definite difference in personalities and also milestones."

Even living with Gram Laura turned out to be the best thing for them and the twins. Gram Laura adored them and they her. As soon as they could walk, they would immediately head her way if they heard her voice. 'Gam Ora', they would say as soon as they saw her. And Gram Laura took care of them, which allowed Maria and William to finish school and go to work.

William was always exhausted when he arrived home, but his daughters brought out the energy in him. Maria still couldn't help but wonder if their daughters were actually his, but it didn't matter now. He was their father and he did his best to spend as much time with them as he could. Williams' mother and his sister came over often, but the twins were attached to Gram Laura.

It was a Sunday afternoon on the rare occasion when both William and Maria were home. It was beautiful day in late August; no humidity and clear sunny skies, when Gram Laura hosted a cook-out for the family. William was working the grill and Maria was enjoying catching up with a few friends that she had from school, Stephanie Martin, who'd helped her back on that frightening day when she was in her first trimester and Andrea Whitcomb. William's mother and sister, along with a few aunts and uncles that Maria didn't know well also attended. Karen and Krista were running around in the backyard, along with some of their cousins, when Karen suddenly stopped what she was doing and ran into the house. Maria didn't think much of it at first; the twins were potty-trained early on, and at 2 ½ years old, she wasn't worried that Karen would need assistance. Besides, Gram Laura was in the house. But after a couple of minutes, Karen hadn't returned and Maria went in to check on her. "Karen? Where are you?" She looked in the downstairs bathroom, and all around the kitchen and dining room area. "Karen! Where are you? Gram Laura?" Maria was starting to worry and ran upstairs.

Just as she headed toward the twin's room, she saw Gram Laura sprawled face down on the floor with Karen beside her saying, "Gam Ora, Gam Ora, wake up!," in her squeaky 2- year -old voice. "Mommy, she no wake up!" Maria scooped Karen up into her arms and screamed for William as she ran down the stairs. "Bill! Call 911! Somethings happened to Gram Laura!" William, and several other guests ran up the stairs, while someone called an ambulance. The ambulance arrived within minutes and the EMTs took over.

Karen was completely distraught and clung to Maria, while Krista seemed confused. "Daddy, what's wrong with Gam Ora?"

"I don't know sweetheart. She'll be fine, don't worry." William told Krista, while Karen clung to Maria. "Karen, did you see what happened to Gam?" He asked her.

"She told me to come see her, daddy."

Maria shook her head. "Bill, there's no way she could've heard her from the yard. She was outside, then she was suddenly gone inside. I thought she had to use the bathroom."

"Daddy, I heard Gam Ora. I outside. She said 'come see me.'" Karen insisted.

"What happened then?" William asked.

"Gam Ora fell down. She won't get up." Karen said "Okay, sweetheart. Gram will be fine." Maria assured her, although the paramedics were using a defibrillator on her now and it didn't look good. As they put Gram Laura on a gurney, her face already had taken on an ashy gray cast while the EMT's were doing chest compressions. They rushed her downstairs and into the ambulance. "She's in cardiac arrest and we need to get her to the hospital. She still doesn't have a pulse." One of the paramedics informed William. "Does she have a heart condition that you're aware of?"

"No! My grandmother's never said anything to me. We've lived with her for several years and she's been fine." William told them.

"She did tell me once that she was taking medication after a doctors' visit several months ago." Maria told them. William looked at her as if she'd betrayed him.

"What? You never told me?" He was almost yelling at her.

"Bill! She told me she was taking care of it! I assumed she told you. Besides, she acted like it wasn't a big deal!" Maria was upset now that he seemed to be blaming her. She grabbed Krista and Karen's hands and headed outside to the backyard to get some space from the drama. It was almost too much for her. It triggered flashbacks from her own parent's tragic deaths.

"Mommy, Gam Ora's gone." Karen said with tears running down her chubby cheeks.

"Sweetheart, we don't know that. She wasn't feeling well and she went to the hospital, that's all." Maria tried to sugarcoat the situation for her daughter, but Karen kept shaking her head.

"No, mommy. She gone. I saw her go." Karen insisted.

"No, you didn't!" Krista said suddenly. "Gam is okay! You don't know, it all, Kawyn!" Krista had always been outspoken, but usually protective of Karen. It was the first time that Maria had seen Krista get this upset with her twin.

"Girls, Gram will be fine. It's almost time for bed! Let's head upstairs and get into your jammies. I'll read to you, okay?" Maria's voice was shaking with worry. Losing Gram would be like losing her mother. She couldn't help but wonder about Karen's insistence that she'd seen Gram Laura. Was it the same as seeing her own mother? 'No absolutely not the same.' She told herself. 'Karen's just a little girl, she probably imagined it.' Maria didn't want to believe that her daughter would have any of the same bizarre experiences she had.

Maria headed back inside with the twins in tow, while William met her in the hallway. "I'm headed to the hospital with mom and Barbara." He looked completely devastated. "I don't want to lose her!"

"I don't either. She'll pull through, sweetheart. I'm going to stay here with the girls. Karen is especially upset. I don't want to leave them with a sitter tonight. Are you going to be okay?" Maria hugged him close to her.

"Mom and Barbara are going to drive me there. I'll be fine. I'll keep you updated." William kissed her, then bent down to hug Krista and Karen. "Daddy's going to check on Gam. I'll be back soon. You be good for your mom, okay?"

"Okay, daddy!" Krista told him as she hugged him.

"But, Gam said she's gone." Karen said. "I told her bye." She looked confused. William shook his head and hugged her. "Gam will be fine, Karen. Daddy will see you later."

Karen buried her face in Maria's hip. "Ok, daddy." She was crying and Maria picked her up and took Krista's hand, leading them to their room. She was so sad, because she knew that Karen was right. Karen knew somehow that she was gone. It was going to be a tough night for all of them. Maria now knew what set Karen apart from her twin; she had the same intuition to see and hear the dying and the deceased.

William

As his mother drove to the hospital, his sister was riding shotgun and William was quiet in the back seat, trying to get himself together. "I think she'll be fine, but I had no idea that she had any heart condition, mom. Did you?" He knew he was rambling, but he needed to fill the silence somehow.

"She'd mentioned it once, but she never made a big deal about it, William. You know she liked to keep these things to herself." His mother reminded him.

"She just always seemed healthy, always helping with the twins. Maybe we shouldn't have asked her to watch them every day. Maybe it was too much for her." William knew he was repeating himself. Barbara cut him off as she turned around in the front seat. "Bill! Stop it! She did what she wanted to do and that was to take care of her great granddaughters!" Her blue eyes were blazing and her sharp tone caught him off guard but it made sense. She did insist on everything; there was no stopping what his grandmother wanted.

When they arrived at the emergency room, they were sent to a waiting area. William felt like he would lose his mind if he had to sit and wait, so he took a walk around the building for a few minutes. When he got back, he noticed his mother and sister were gone. He went to the ER nursing desk and asked about his grandmother. "Oh, your mother and sister just went in to see her. You must be William,

130

they told me to send you back. It's through these doors and the second room on your left." She instructed, giving no indication of what was going on, or what he would find.

As he walked into the room, he saw his mother and sister in tears, along with a priest who was standing over his grandmother. She was barely recognizable with tubes coming out of her nose. "Mom?" He asked.

"William, she's gone. She just passed a few minutes ago." She whispered. "She did ask for you." She added as William sat down in a chair next to the bed. "I just had to go for a walk, didn't I?" William felt numb as he realized that he hadn't been there. He said nothing as the priest did his rituals, as was part of Gram Laura's request. Before they left, William asked for a moment alone with her. "Gram, you were the best ever. Thank you so much for being there for me, for Maria and the girls. We all loved you. I hope you know that. Not having you with us is going to be very hard." William grasped her cold hand. "I'm so sorry that I wasn't here to say goodbye."

His mother dropped him back off at the house an hour later where Maria was waiting. The girls were sound asleep upstairs. She could tell by the look on his face what had happened. "Oh, no! No, Bill!" She started to cry softly as she hugged him. "How did Karen know?" She asked him.

"What? What do you mean?" William stared at her. "Bill, Karen kept saying that she was gone before she ever left the house in the ambulance. It was so hard to get her to sleep. She kept talking about how she could still see Gram. I tried to convince her otherwise, but she insisted that she could see her." Maria wiped her eyes.

"I don't understand anything anymore, babe. I really don't." He was exhausted and collapsed on the couch. "I just need to be alone for a little while. We'll have to figure something out with the twins, but let's just get through the next few days. I'll be helping with the funeral arrangements." Maria nodded and kissed him. "I'm here to help. I'll take the next few days off from class. We'll work it out, Bill." She sat with him for a few minutes, almost falling asleep on his shoulder.

"Maria, get up and go to bed. I'll be okay. I just need a few minutes by myself alright?" William assured her. She nodded and headed upstairs. He sat for a few minutes, then headed for the liquor cabinet. There it was; a full bottle of Jim Beam whiskey that his grandfather had never opened. He hesitated as he took out a glass and filled it with ice and then broke the seal on the bottle. "Here's to you, Gram Laura." He poured several shots worth into the glass and gulped it down. He instantly felt buzzed as he hadn't had anything to drink since he quit drinking when Maria had found out she was pregnant. Now, it seemed the only solution at the time and he quickly poured himself another shot and another until he was unable to sit up and passed out on the couch.

He awoke to his wife shaking him and calling his name. "Bill! Wake up!" She wasn't yelling, but he had a splitting headache and her voice was causing his head to feel as though it were exploding. He opened one of his eyes and immediately shut it as the sunlight glared through the sliding glass door through the living room to the deck. Maria stood over him, angry and had the bottle of whiskey in her hand. "Really, Bill? Are we headed back to this again? You passed out last night. I know it's hard that your grandmother's gone! I miss her too! But this can't continue!" She stomped over to the kitchen sink and proceeded to pour what was left of the whiskey down the drain.

"Maria, I'm so sorry. I only meant to have one drink. It was my grandfather's that he'd saved. I was just upset....I don't know what came over me." William realized he never should've taken that first drink. "I promise. It won't happen again." He sat up, putting his hand up to shade his eyes from the sunlight that made his headache a million times worse.

"I hope not, because if it does, I'm out of here and I'm taking the girls with me!" Maria's blue eyes blazed with anger. He knew she meant it too. Maria was usually tolerant; she did her best to avoid drama, so he knew that she wasn't just making idle threats. Even if it seemed she had nowhere to go, he knew Maria was resourceful; she'd find a way.

William stood up, immediately got dizzy and grabbed the couch arm for stability. Just then the twins ran downstairs and started yelling, "Daddy, daddy!" while grabbing each leg. He sat back down. "Hey, my pretty girls!" His head was throbbing, but he pulled Karen and Krista onto his lap. He kissed each on the forehead and hugged them. He knew he needed to pull it together for them and for his wife now. There was no Gram Laura to save the day and no amount of whiskey was going to bring her back.

"Let's see if we can help mommy with breakfast, and then we'll do something fun today!" William told them as he set them down and they ran into the kitchen. He managed to get up without falling over and walked over to his wife who was making eggs and bacon. He wrapped his arms around her, and was glad when she didn't shrug him off. "Bill, you're forgiven this time. There won't be a next time. We've got a lot to do in the next week; funeral arrangements, going through Gram's things, her will, this house. We've got an appointment with her attorney today at 1:00.

"I know. I'm going up to take a shower and then we'll deal with all of this together. I'm so sorry, Maria." He knew he was starting to sound like a broken record, but he meant what he said. He was determined not to lose his family because he chose to act like his father.

Maria

Seeing William passed out on the couch at 7:00 in the morning was almost more than she could stand. Putting the girls to bed was difficult enough; especially because Karen kept talking about seeing her grandmother. As they were finally settled, she couldn't help but hover over Karen and wonder how she herself had this 'insight' and passed it on to her daughter. "Mommy, Gam Ora is here now." Karen said sleepily. Maria was startled for a minute, thinking she was asleep. She glanced over at Krista who was sound asleep, in the bed next to Karen.

"Is she sweetheart? Is she saying something to you?" Maria suddenly felt a chill come over her.

"She says I see her soon." Karen murmured.

"Karen, what do you mean?" Maria felt the hair on her neck stand up suddenly. But Karen didn't answer and appeared to be sound asleep again. She shook her head. 'Maybe I'm just tired; too much has been going on.' She thought to herself. Maria changed into pajamas, washed her face and headed down to see if William was coming upstairs. But he was passed out on the couch and she noticed the bottle of Jim Beam on the coffee table. Her sadness turned to anger and she headed back upstairs. There was a lot to do in the morning and he was going to help with it, regardless of his hangover!

She had no mercy in the morning when she woke her husband up at 7:00. He knew it too. While she knew that he was grieving his

135

grandmother, it wasn't an excuse now. Maria missed her, despite her controlling tendencies. Over the past several years, Gram Laura had been a mother to her that she didn't really have and her sudden death felt almost like losing her mother all over again.

William was his usual apologetic self, promising to never drink himself into oblivion again, but she threatened him with leaving him and taking the twins. She had no idea how she'd actually do it, but she knew she wasn't going to put up with his drinking because he was sad and didn't know how to deal with it. In the meantime, the girls were up and wanting his attention. One thing she never had to worry about is how much he loved them. "Hey, pretty girls!" He greeted them, even though she knew he felt like shit, but he still gave them loving hugs at all times.

It was times like this that made her feel even more guilty about the secret that she'd held tight onto all these years. Dan, the rape and not being certain about who the twins' father really was. She hoped she never had to actually face that day! They had an appointment with Gram Laura's attorney today at 1:00 to go over her will and discuss funeral arrangements if she requested anything specific.

William headed upstairs to shower, as Maria prepped the girls for spending the day with Grandma Sara and Aunt Barbara. It was going to be a long day and Maria wasn't looking forward to it. But both girls loved spending time with them, so when she explained, they seemed happy enough. Until Krista asked "What about Gam Ora? She can watch us." Krista asked. She'd tried to explain to the twins about death on their level, but last night had been hard.

"Kris, Gam Ora is gone. She's watching you from all around now." Maria told her, and teared up as her daughter started actually looking for her.

"Kista, Gam told me bye." Karen chimed in. Maria gave them both a hug before bringing them out to the car, just as William came downstairs.

"Girls, no arguing now! Yes, Gam is gone, but you can still talk to her. You just can't see her now." Maria was getting frustrated that William was taking his time as she put the girls in their car seats. When he finally appeared, he looked freshly shaven and handsome, like his usual self. "Sorry, babe." He jumped into the passenger seat and gave her a kiss on the cheek. Maria took off and dropped the girls off, reminding Sara that Karen was still talking about seeing her great grandmother passing. "Just entertain her and go with it." She advised.

As they sat in front of Gram Laura's attorney, Jack Turner, they were surprised at how much money she really had. Besides owning the house in South Kingstown where they currently lived, she also owned a property on Block Island that she rented out during the summer season. William nodded. He remembered when his grandfather died seven years ago, that Gram Laura never went to that house on Block Island, except at the beginning of the summer season to make sure it was suitable for guests. She left the rest of the upkeep to the maintenance staff. William vaguely remembered several summers at the house beginning at age 10, right after his grandfather bought it. He didn't remember much except that there was a huge cliff that dropped off to the ocean and that he always heard noises at night that scared him. After a couple of years, his parents stopped going there during the summer and after his grandfather died, Gram Laura began renting it out.

She had requested that she be cremated and that her ashes were scattered over her estate on Block Island. There were no specifics about the ash spreading ceremony, but her will indicated that her South Kingstown house would be left to William and Maria and that her Block Island property to be up for sale.

Even Jack Taylor looked at them with surprise about the Block Island property. "It really shocks me that she wouldn't want to keep that in the family. But then again, I'm just the messenger." He waited for them to argue with them, but Maria knew how mysterious Gram Laura could be and nodded in response. "I'm not surprised, actually."

"You're not?" William asked her. "She adored you and the twins! Why wouldn't she want to leave this to us?" He was suddenly feeling blindsided. He knew she didn't reside there, but why not keep it in the family?

"I remember her mentioning the Block Island house to me before, but when I suggested that maybe we could go there for a weekend in the summer, she always seemed to have an excuse. She must have had her reasons. Besides, the house we live in is ours, so it isn't going to be up for sale." Maria was being practical. William had to admit she was right. They never went there, so maybe it was for the best.

They finished up their meeting and discussed the scheduling of the ceremony at Block Island that Gram Laura had requested. The next available weekend when it wasn't rented out was on the twin's birthday in September, and Maria absolutely refused. "No! I will not have this on their birthday. Out of the question!" William agreed.

So they finally settled on the second week of October where they would spread the ashes and have the ceremony. It was exhausting and Maria felt like she'd need to sleep for 16 hours straight just to get through this nightmare she was living.

The next week was especially stressful with Gram Laura's cremation and the twins' third birthday celebration coming up that weekend. Maria couldn't help thinking how ironic that she died a week before their birthday. Sara and Barbara, along with a handful of cousins and relatives that Maria hadn't even met were invited to their small get together, along with several neighborhood kids that Karen and Krista had met before.

William seemed to be doing okay, except he was secretive at times. He was spending more time with his mother, which Maria considered a good thing. What bothered her is when she came near him and Sara, they'd immediately start talking about something else. It was clear that there was something going on, but when she asked both of them separately, they innocently said, "No, we were just talking." Maria noticed that William had stopped talking about his grandmother as well, and if the twins talked about her, especially Karen, William would change the subject.

As she was setting up for the party, William came down after keeping the twins occupied. "Maria, Karen keeps talking about Gram being here with us."

"Well, I've told you the strange things she said when Gram died. She said she could see her saying goodbye. I'm not surprised." Maria continued setting up the party decorations.

"Do you think she's okay?" William asked.

Maria stopped hanging streamers for a moment. "Honestly, Bill. I hope that she is, but she has been acting strange. Krista told me the other day that she was just sitting in their room, staring out the window. Karen told her that she was watching 'Gam Ora outside the window.' 'Maybe it's her way of dealing with this, but we've got a lot to deal with now. Can you help me hang this streamer?" Maria knew all too well her daughter's preoccupation with Gram Laura's death, and wasn't sure what to do about it. She only hoped their 3rd birthday party would go well. William nodded and helped her hang the streamers.

The party seemed to be a success. Krista was especially happy to be the center of attention, while Karen as usual, held back. But they had a good time. William surprised her and them with necklaces that were half-hearts, one for each twin. They were beautiful 24 karat gold with gold chains. The girls loved them and felt very grown up as Maria fastened them on their necks. "Bill, what a beautiful thing to get for them that they can cherish the rest of their lives." She gave a him a hug. He seemed to be getting back to himself and focusing on his family again. For that, she was grateful.

"It's something that will keep them connected, even after they grow up." William said. "I just want them to be close."

"They are and they will be always." Maria said. She was glad the party was a happy day for them. Gram Laura's memorial was the following weekend. She was just thankful that she wasn't organizing that event. William and Uncle Stuart had hired someone to take care of the details. "I can't believe we never got to visit the house." Maria said quietly. She was actually looking forward to seeing the house that she'd heard so much about in the past two weeks. Gram's attorney described it as a mansion. She remembered Gram Laura talking about it in passing but always changed the subject when Maria brought up visiting the property with the twins during the summer.

William

He tried to keep himself calm as he got ready for Gram Laura's service that morning. It was going to be more casual, so he was dressed in a pair of dress pants with a button down shirt and some flat brown loafers that would be practical for the ferry ride over to Block Island. He tried not to think about the long day ahead. Karen's behavior and, her constant talking about his grandmother was also starting to concern him. He agreed with Maria that she was overly preoccupied with Gram Laura lately. Just this morning, she'd been staring out the window when Maria came in to help them get dressed.

"Mommy, Gam Ora says I should wear this dress." Karen pointed to an old dress in the closet that was pink and white checks with roses around the neck. It was a dress that no longer fit and Maria hadn't had the time to put it in the donation bag yet. As Maria tried to explain this to Karen, she realized that it was a dress that Gram Laura had bought for both Karen and Krista over a year ago for their last birthday. Gram Laura always loved having the girls dressed alike, whereas Maria preferred them to dress in what they wanted to wear. Krista was the one to argue with Karen that the dress was 'itchy and yucky' and she didn't want to wear it. Krista won the argument, but it worried both William and Maria. The girls finally agreed to wearing identical blue dresses with ribbons along the bottom hem that Gram Laura had given them a couple of months before.

A few hours later, they'd managed the ferry ride on a relatively calm day on the ocean over to the island. It had been chartered, rather than the regular ferry so there was more privacy. The mansion could be clearly seen from a mile away, as the cliffs appeared. It was situated only a few hundred yards away from the steep, reddish clay cliffs called Mohegan Bluffs that were a landmark for Block Island and a tourist attraction.

William felt chills as he saw it again. It loomed above the cliffs. The exterior of dark stone and off-white siding that had been added over the years made it seem less intimidating. The veranda-style porch that encircled the front of the mansion had been updated and painted to match the siding. Yet he remembered when he'd visited as a kid that he didn't like staying there. It was almost maze-like on the inside. He could remember getting lost after walking up the giant staircase, and there was something stagnant and cold that he didn't like about it. He vaguely remembered having nightmares when he slept there and begged his mother to go home.

The twins were fascinated with the view of the bluffs and the house. They couldn't wait to run around the grounds and look inside the house. Maria warned them as they went up the stairs from the dock. "Girls, you need to stay with me and Daddy, okay? There's a steep cliff there and I don't want you getting close to it, understand?" Both girls nodded, but Karen seemed to be intrigued by the cliffs. "Can't we go over there, please mommy?" She pointed toward a clearing where the cliffs seemed to meet the ocean. "We can later, sweetheart. I promise. We'll even have our picture taken there, okay? But you need to wait."

Maria told her firmly. Karen nodded, although she kept looking back as they walked toward the mansion.

William immediately felt the same eerie sensation that he had as a child as he walked into the foyer and saw the sprawling renaissance-era staircase ahead, with red-carpeting and the sculpted banister. "God, this place still gives me the creeps," He whispered to his wife. Maria nodded in agreement. "It's beautiful, but there's something scary about it as well." She whispered back. He grabbed her hand and squeezed it as they moved toward the living area where relatives and other friends had gathered to remember Gram Laura. Maria looked beautiful in her simple black dress with a single-pearl necklace that he'd given her on their first anniversary. "You look gorgeous by the way." Maria just gave him her half smile. She turned to the twins who were behind them. "Girls, please come up here and hold my hands." She told them. William knew she was worried about them running off into the yard, especially Karen.

There was a gathering with appetizers and drinks and then they moved out toward the lawn to have the ceremony and spreading of the ashes. Krista was fidgeting most of the time, while Karen continued to focus on the cliff edge that she'd seen earlier. William kept an eye on her, and as they went to spread the ashes over the cliff, they all moved over the place that Karen wanted to visit. The priest invited all of them to repeat the prayer as he spread the ashes out over the ocean. William and Maria both held the girls' hands as the ceremony was finished and guests began giving final condolences to them and heading back to the house. Karen was reluctant to leave, staring out toward where the ocean met the cliffs. "Daddy, Gam Ora is here. I want to talk to her." William kneeled down next to her.

"She is here, because we're thinking of her. She'll always be here in our memory, Karen." William said softly, but Karen was still staring out toward the cliff as if she didn't hear him." Maria came over, still gripping Krista's hand. "Bill, what's going on?" She whispered in his ear.

"Mommy, Gam Ora says you look really pretty today." Karen said suddenly turning toward her mother. Maria was speechless for a moment. "Really? That's nice of her." She was curious, waiting to hear anything else Karen had to say.

"She says that pearl necklace looks nice with your dress." Karen told her. Both William and Maria looked at each other in shock and immediately began pulling Karen back. "Well, thank Gram Laura for me and tell her that you'll talk to her later." Maria tried to sound calm.

Karen nodded, "Gam Ora, Mommy says I gotta go." She waited a few seconds and then nodded. "Okay, mommy. I can go now."

Maria grasped her hand while William followed her with Krista, who seemed frustrated with her sister that she was keeping her from seeing the pool. "Want to see the pool, daddy!" Krista kept telling him. They indulged the girls in seeing the pool area even though it was too cold to go in the water, as the sun began to set early and the temperature dropping.

After the chilly trip home on the ferry, William and Maria talked to Karen and Krista about the services while tucking them into bed. William sat on the edge of Karen's bed as she held his hand.

"Sweetheart, you do understand that your Gram is gone. She isn't coming back."

Karen shook her head. "No, daddy. She talks to me. I see her. She's wearing a blue shirt with birds on it." William tried to compose himself as he remembered that was what his grandmother was wearing that day. She'd been wearing a blue shirt with a white pattern that looked like birds.

"What does she say to you?" He tried to keep his voice calm although now his daughter was scaring him.

"She says that she'll see me soon." Karen told him. William's hair stood up on the back of his neck just then.

Maria was sitting reading to Krista to distract her, but Krista overhead them. "Kawyn, I don't see her! Gam Ora loved me too and I don't see her!" She began crying in anger. Maria picked her up and hugged her. "Kris, Gram did love both of you. Your sister is just using her imagination. Maybe it's better that we don't talk about her for a few days." Krista nodded. "I miss her too, Mommy. Tired of Kawyn talking to her all the time." Krista's eyes looked droopy and Maria knew she was overtired. She kissed her and tucked her in. "Night Kris, I love you."

" Love you too, mommy, love you daddy." Krista said to William as he came over to kiss her good night.

"Love you too, sweetheart." He told her. He went over to kiss Karen good night, but she appeared to be asleep. He and Maria kissed her on the forehead. "Good night sweetheart. Mommy and Daddy love you."
"

"Gam Ora says good night." Karen said sleepily. Her eyes were still closed and she moved her head away. They looked at each other with the same concerned look.

"Night Gram Laura." They said in unison. As Karen closed her eyes, William and Maria turned off the lamps and left the twins night light on.

"What is going on?" William asked his wife as they headed back downstairs. Maria shook her head. "It must be the same for her." She said more to herself that William.

"What? What do you mean?" William asked. What the hell was she talking about? "Honey, what are you talking about? 'It must be the same for her.'"

Maria sighed. "I guess I should explain some things that I've never told you." She sat down in the recliner and tilted her head back.

"What do you mean by that Maria? What haven't you told me?" William suddenly felt tempted to grab that bottle of whiskey that he'd hidden from his wife in order to hear this. What was it? A million things were going through his head now of what 'I never told you' meant.

Maria

Maria had never explained to William about her ability to hear and see her parents since they passed away. The only person she had mentioned it to was her Aunt Sylvia, who thought she was making it up. Maria knew it wasn't something that other people could do, and worried other people, including William, would think she was crazy if she told them about it.

Now, it was clear to her that Karen had inherited her ability to see and communicate with people that were gone. She took a deep breath, as she tried to explain it to William after they'd put the girls to bed. "Bill, I know this is going to sound extraordinary, because it is. But I've been able to communicate with my parents since they died. Especially my mother." When she said it out loud, it even sounded impossible to her. But it was true. William started to say something, but Maria cut him off. "Just hear me out. Even since they died, my mother has been around from time to time, giving me advice. Usually by just a voice, but sometimes I can see her."

"So how often do you see her? Is she here now?" William was surprisingly not telling her she was being ridiculous.

"No. I don't see her all the time, but I did when she died. I also saw her when I was in cardiac arrest when I was in the delivery room. I didn't say anything about it before. I didn't want to scare you, but I saw my mother and I wanted to stay. My mother sent me back."

William was suddenly at a loss for words. He stared at her for a moment. "You mean you were.....dead?"

"I'm not sure, but I could see myself on the table and doctors working on me, so maybe you could say I was 'almost dead?'" Maria tried to joke, but William was upset now.

"Why didn't you tell me until now?" William had to know.

"Because of the way you're reacting to it right now. It had no bearing on our life until now. I only told you because of what's going on with Karen. She really does see Gram Laura and if we tell her otherwise, it'll just make her upset. I'm telling you this because it will get better. Eventually, Karen will grow and Gram Laura will be someone that maybe is in her mind, but not the focus. That's the way it's been for me with my mother. I rarely get any contact from her especially since the girls were born, because I'm in a place where I'm focused on them."

William looked like a deer in headlights. "So you're saying that you think Karen really can communicate with Gram Laura. You know that sounds completely impossible, right babe?"

Maria shook her head, knowing that he still didn't believe her. "How do explain Karen telling me that Gram Laura liked my *pearl* necklace? That was specific! Karen wouldn't have an idea of what kind of necklace I had on. Or that she was completely focused on the cliff and talking to her as if she were there?"

William seemed to be trying to come up with an explanation, but he finally shook his head. "You're right. I know it doesn't make any sense, but Karen has been so different since Gram died. Krista has been complaining about her and you know how close they are."

Maria sat down next to him on the couch and put her arms around him. "Bill, I'm not trying to scare you. I'm just telling you what I know and have been through myself. Karen is the one with whatever this 'gift' is, if you can call it that. Just because they're twins doesn't mean they're the same person. Karen seems to be sensitive to people that she was close to that have passed."

He hugged her close to him and Maria felt better that he was at least not thinking that she was out of her mind with her confession about her past. "I think we should take Karen to a psychologist and have her evaluated."

William sat up immediately. "I'm not taking our daughter to a psychic!"

Maria shook her head. "I said a psychologist. A child psychologist. Maybe she can help Karen with her grieving. Because I do believe she really is so sad. She and Gram Laura were close. Krista loved Gram, but Karen was really close to her. Probably because of that 'gift' that they have."

"Gift?" William asked. "Oh, you mean the 'gift' of seeing people that are dead? I don't really see that as a gift, babe."

"It *is* a gift, even if it doesn't seem that way to you right now." Maria said quietly. "It really helped me through some tough times after my parents died. I'm trying to remember that. It seems like a curse to me now."

"I'm sorry. I'm glad that it helped you. It's just so strange to me right now." William told her. "You're right, Karen should see someone. She just seems different. Krista has been fine during this, but Karen's behaviors are starting to scare me." He admitted. "If you think that would help her, then I'm all for it."

Maria nodded. It was first on her list to do in the morning before her first class. She only had one final semester to graduate and she wanted to make sure that she didn't miss any classes that she didn't have to. She'd taken a year off after the girls were born and was taking less credits to do her internship at a local mental health center.

The next day she went to class as usual, but afterwards spent time looking up different psychologists in the phone book in the library. She'd called several, but none seem to be specialized in child therapy. Just as she was ready to give up, she heard a familiar voice. "Maria? Maria Evans?" She turned around to see Stephanie Martin. She was suddenly embarrassed that she hadn't been in touch, but glad to see her. Steph was still very recognizable; tall, thin and the same brown hair cut in a shorter bob style. The only change that Maria could see was that she wasn't wearing her thick glasses. 'She must have decided to get contacts finally.' Maria thought to herself. Stephanie's eyes were very pretty, which the glasses had been hiding all those years.

"Steph! It's so good to see you!" Maria stood up and gave her a hug. She really missed female friendships lately. Her life had been school, work and the twins for the past three years. It was hard to believe that much time had passed.

"Maria, you look great! How are you doing? I heard that you had those beautiful babies and married that handsome William Carson."

Stephanie always came across as genuine and still did now. Maria had learned early on after she and William were married and the twins were born that there were certain people that just liked to find out information to gossip. She knew Steph wasn't one of them.

"I'm great! Bill and the girls are doing well." Maria admired Stephanie. She was smart and had graduated early with honors. She was already almost finished with her master's degree in psychology at URI and interning with Dr. Santos who was a respected professor at URI and had his own private practice in Wakefield, just outside of South Kingstown.

"I'm sorry to hear about Bill's grandmother." Stephanie expressed her condolences.

"Thanks, Steph. It's been hard on Bill, but especially on the twins. Well, the youngest twin actually." Maria suddenly was talking about her personal business which she rarely did. She was just frustrated that after searching for two hours, she couldn't find a psychologist in the area that worked with children. "That's why I'm here, looking for someone that can work with Karen. She's having some....well....grieving issues. She was especially close to her great - grandmother." She stopped before mentioning Karen's seeming abilities to communicate with Gram Laura.

Stephanie nodded. "I know there aren't many, but I can give you the name of someone you might want to call. She's in the same building as Dr. Santos' practice. Her name is Dr. Janine Welch. I've heard good things about her."

"Do you have her number? I've been looking everywhere through the yellow pages. That name doesn't sound familiar." Maria was skeptical.

"It's probably because she just started her practice within the past few months. Here, I've got her number with me." Steph pulled out a mini address book out of her purse and flipped to the W's. "Here it is." She wrote it down for Maria.

"Thanks so much!" Maria was relieved to have at least one person that might be able to help.

"We should get together sometime! I live over near Point Judith with my boyfriend. We should try and get together sometime. Bring Bill and the twins along! I'd love to catch up with you."

Maria was glad for the invitation. She hadn't had a close friend in several years, just acquaintances that occasionally invited her over to be polite. They also had small children at the time, and they never seemed to have anything in common with her. Especially since she was still completing her degree.

Maria smiled. "I'd love to!" She thought about asking for her number, but then decided to let Steph make the first move. "Here's my number. Give me a call. I'm usually free on the weekends, as long as you don't mind me bringing the girls with me." She knew people that didn't have kids didn't always want them around.

"Absolutely! I'd love to. I'll give you a call soon, okay?" Steph said. "Give Dr. Welch a call."

"I will. Thanks again, Steph!" Maria smiled. Even if this Dr. Welch wouldn't take Karen as a client, it was worth checking out. She called and was surprised to get an appointment for the following week. She was worried about Bill's reaction, but he'd agreed to give it a try.

William hadn't been exactly happy about Karen seeing a psychologist, but he knew that she needed help. In the end, he was able to go for the initial appointment. Maria thought it would be a good idea to bring Krista as well and Dr. Welch included her in the session with Karen. Dr. Welch gave the girls access to the therapy play room where she observed them for a few minutes before going back in to talk with them. Dr. Welch had been in the field for 25 years and was open to all their questions. In a way, she reminded Maria of her mother, if she'd lived to be her age; probably around late 50s. She had the same calming effect on Maria, and in a way looked like her; with her shoulder length blonde hair with streaks of gray and her blue eyes. After she met with both Karen and Krista, she asked her assistant to watch the girls in the play room while she met with Maria and William.

"I'm not overly concerned about Karen. She was very attached to her great-grandmother, but she's only exhibiting signs of grief and working through them. Krista seems to be the independent, kind of 'backbone' for them both. She is very strong-willed and obviously the more outgoing twin. I did notice several times that Karen insisted that 'Gam Ora' was there, while Krista kept saying she was making it up. It seems to upset Karen very much. I'd advise on talking to Krista about letting Karen talk about her. It seems to be causing a lot of friction between the two of them." Dr. Welch said.

"That's going to be hard; they share a room, Dr. Welch." Maria told her.

"If you have the room, maybe it's time for them to have their own space. If not, then just watching out for conflict with the two of them." Dr. Welch suggested.

After they got home, Maria and William had to decide what to do. "We could move into Gram Laura's bedroom and that would leave our room open for either Karen or Krista. What do you think?" Maria asked him. William didn't like the idea of them being in different bedrooms, but agreed to try it.

"But if it makes things worse and they still aren't getting along, we'll have to discuss this again." William warned. The next day, they began the task of clearing out Gram Laura's bedroom and moving their things in. All the while, Karen seemed to be upset, while Krista was just curious. "Why you moving Gam's things?" Krista asked.

"Honey, we thought that you could have your own room and Karen can have hers. What do you think?" Krista smiled and jumped up and down.

"I'm glad!" She said. "Kawyn talks to Gam too much. She keeps me up at night." She ran off to tell her sister about the new plans. Karen didn't seem to mind either. "Kista gets mad, cause I talk to Gam Ora."

So after a huge amount of rearranging rooms, putting Gram Laura's things in storage and the girls settling into their 'own' rooms, it seemed that Dr. Welch had a good idea. Both girls seemed to be getting along better and both weren't too tired to get up when Grandma Sara arrived in the morning while Maria and William went to school and work.

Both were hopeful that this would help Karen adjust to Gram Laura's death so that she could enjoy being a little girl again.

William

Eight months had gone by since Gram Laura had left them. They'd finally gotten through the paperwork on the house that was now in their name which was a huge relief. William was graduating with his Business Management degree next week, and Maria was graduating with her Bachelors in Psychology.

The girls seemed to be thriving in their own separate rooms, although William was still worried that it would affect their twin-connection. It seemed to do the opposite and William had to admit that Dr. Welch and Maria were right. There was less conflict between the two of them, and he had to be honest; it was hard for him to hear Karen talking about his grandmother as if she were still there. Karen having her own room seemed to help her adjust and although he knew Maria got the brunt of the discussions about 'Gam Ora' from her, she was more understanding because of her experience with her own mother.

Both he and Maria's graduations were bittersweet. He would have loved his grandmother to be there after helping them all those years and with the twins, but he knew she'd be proud. Maria had said the same thing, although his mother, Barbara and Uncle Stuart, with his wife Jenna, along with the twins were there as they got their degrees. The girls had accompanied Sara to the graduation and then Barbara agreed to sit for them so they could go out to celebrate.

Stuart was a smart man and had been successful over the years, but there was always relationship drama. He'd married his high school sweetheart, Beth, when they were twenty-two. Thirty-three years later, he was still recovering from a disastrous divorce after Beth found out he'd been having an affair with his secretary for over five years. It took two years to finalize the divorce and before the ink dried, Stuart married Jenna. Jenna was nice enough, but she was ten years younger and had the insight to know that people in Stuart's circle knew that she'd been the 'other woman.'

As they settled down to dinner at The Black Pearl in Newport, Stuart who had been named executor over Gram Laura's estate announced that they had a potential buyer for the Block Island property.

"Really?" William was surprised. It had been a couple of months since it had been up for sale, but the asking price was close to $750,000. Whoever it was, definitely wasn't in the local work force.

"Yeah, some new hot shot from Hollywood. I guess he's decided to start spending his money quickly instead of saving." Stuart said sarcastically. Stuart had little tolerance for celebrities and their 'wasteful' lifestyles. He had a successful construction business. He'd worked hard for years to build up the business and had no respect for 'someone that walked onto a set, said some lines and suddenly made millions', as he put it.

"Well, at least it's not going to just sit there. It's such a beautiful place, it would be a shame to have it sit empty for several more years." Maria said diplomatically. Stuart nodded his head. "You're absolutely right, Maria! We should go out there this weekend and spend some time there. After all, none of us really have over the years." Stuart looked at William.

William squirmed, knowing that Stuart was insinuating that he hadn't wanted to visit, and his mother caught his eye across the table. "I don't think it's a matter of not going there, Stuart. We just weren't invited." Sara offered her opinion, which was unlike her. William wanted to jump up and kiss his mother for sticking up for him just then. She knew just how uncomfortable and scared he'd been when he'd been there when he was a young boy. "The last time we went to visit. A little girl fell off that cliff right near the house. Bill, you saw her fall." William had been taking a drink and choked on it, and started coughing as Maria patted him on the back. He glared at his mother for bringing up something that he hadn't thought about since he was 10 years old.

William decided he'd had enough discussion. "Okay, lets decide on dessert. Anyone?" He changed the subject and Maria took over, acting like she was deciding on a selection. "Should we have the cheesecake or the crème Brule? I think I'll have the cheesecake. It's my favorite. You should get it too, William, it's always been your favorite!" She nudged him with her elbow.

"That sounds good to me." William put an arm around Maria. She knew him so well. She managed not to appear rattled at all, despite the fact that she'd never heard about that incident from William's past. After the desserts were ordered, the uncomfortable silence seemed to envelope the table.

"Well, since someone might be buying the property, maybe we could go out there this coming weekend?" Sara broke the silence after dropping her bombshell of a comment.

"We're pretty busy this weekend; we had plans to take the girls over to Roger Williams Zoo. It's supposed to be nice out." William was quick to respond as he glanced at Maria, hoping she'd agree to the impromptu plan. "Yes, the girls are excited to go!" Maria agreed.

"William, this is the last weekend we can go there. Once the buyer makes up his mind and makes an offer, we won't be allowed any longer." Stuart was pushing it now.

William didn't know what to say, but Maria spoke up. "Stuart, we'll talk it over and let you know. After all, it's next weekend. How about we let you know mid-week?" She said smoothly.

"Sounds good. Let us know as soon as you can. It would just be Saturday and Sunday. We could enjoy the house and the pool if the weather is good." Stuart said.

"I think it would be nice for us to spend some time together." Sara added. "I hope you two will come and bring the girls. I'd love to spend time with them there." She seemed to have forgotten her comment about William's past that was the elephant in the room now.

After dinner, it was a quiet drive home. "Do you want to tell me about what happened back then, Bill?" Maria asked softly.

"I guess so. Until my mom brought it up, I'd forgotten about it. That's why I didn't mention it to you, honey. I wasn't hiding it from you, I promise." William told her.

"It's okay. I'm listening now if you want to tell me about it." Maria said.

"We were there that summer with my grandparents, mom and dad, my sister and cousins for a week in July. I was probably about 9 or 10. We had a good week. There were kids in the neighborhood that came to play around in the yard every day. We played kick ball, hide and seek, tag. You name all the fun games that kids can play, we played them. There were two kids from next door that spent all summer there. Carrie and Spencer Malone were their names. Carrie was about my age, probably 10, and Spencer was 13. We always had so much fun. I remember I had a little crush on Carrie; she was a cute blonde girl with pigtails and a daredevil. I was infatuated with her at the time and would do anything to gain her respect. Do you really want to hear about this, babe?" William asked, as he took the exit toward home.

"Of course. Go on, I'm listening." Maria said softly.

"So we were out playing a game called 'chicken' one day with a couple of the other kids that were over every day. Carrie, Spencer and I were on one team and the other neighbor kids were on another team. The dare was to see how close we could run toward the cliff and then stop without going over the edge. The team that got closer was the winner. So the other team did pretty well, one of the kids stopped short of going over the cliff. Spencer went first and he seemed scared, so he didn't come close to the mark. I went next and I got scared, so I stopped at least 5 feet from the edge. Carrie was always so competitive, always wanted to win. She turned to me and said, "I'm gonna win this for us, Bill!" She ran as fast as she could. And she stopped right at the top of the cliff, by far the closest." William stopped and took a deep breath.

They were in the driveway and William suddenly found himself tearing up.

"Bill, it's okay. You don't have to tell me the rest." Maria put her hand on his.

"Yes, I do. Because you're the only person that's really heard this." He closed his eyes for a moment as he shut off the engine to the car. He could picture the scene in front of him; he and the other kids shouting and yelling that Carrie had done the best and then without warning, the edge of the cliff had given way.

"Bill? Are you okay?" Maria was shaking his shoulder.

"Oh, I'm sorry. Where was I? Oh, yes, Carrie had won and Spencer and I were jumping up and down and saying that we won. Then Carrie disappeared. She was screaming for a second and then there was nothing. We all ran to the edge and saw Carrie lying in a pool of blood on the rocks below." William suddenly shivered as he talked. "The soft ground where she'd been standing had given way and she fell. I don't remember much after seeing her lying there. I was so scared and so sad. I looked up to her." William's eyes were watering with tears now.

"Oh my god. Bill, now I can understand why your mother didn't take you there anymore." Maria hugged him. "That must have been so hard for you."

"It was. I don't remember much about what happened afterwards, except that the Coast Guard and police were there and she was eventually taken out on a stretcher with something covering her. They said she died instantly."

"Bill, we don't have to go this weekend. Really, we don't. We can just say that we can't change our plans." Maria could tell he was still experiencing anxiety from this tragedy from almost 13 years ago.

Just then, Barbara came out of the house. "Hey, you guys are back! I thought I saw headlights." She was wearing pajama bottoms and a light tee shirt. "I was just going to call you. Karen's been acting strange tonight and I can't get her to sleep." Barbara looked upset.

Both William and Maria quickly headed into the house as Barbara tried to explain further. "She kept talking about some girl that fell off a cliff."

"So she wasn't dreaming?" William asked, as they both got out of the car and ran into the house.

"Well, no. I don't know how she could have. Karen wouldn't go to sleep so I read to her. When I was done and getting ready to turn off the light, she got this strange look on her face and was looking around her. That's when she starting talking about this 'Carrie' person falling off a cliff." Barbara said, looking scared. "I'm sorry, William. Both girls were fine all night up until a few minutes ago when Karen started talking about this." Barbara looked shaken up.

"Thanks for watching the girls, Barb. We can take care of it. Just go ahead home, okay?" William told her. His sister went inside to grab her purse and was back out to her car in 5 seconds flat. "I hope she's okay, William. I'm kind of worried about her. Call me tomorrow, okay?" Barbara said before jumping into her little red Camaro that she'd bought with her share of Gram Laura's inheritance money. William just nodded, hoping that his sister wasn't overspending.

William looked at Maria. "I really can't believe what I'm hearing right now! I've never told anyone except you, honey. I swear to God."

Maria nodded. "But Gram Laura knew about it." She said. "This has really gotten out of control. I'm not sure what to do anymore." She said more to herself than him. As they headed upstairs, Maria put a finger to her mouth, "Let's just listen for a minute." She told William

"Gam, I don't want to fall off cliff", they overheard her saying. Then, "Gam, I wanna see you, but I don't wanna leave mommy and daddy."

Both William and Maria looked at each other and knew it was time to open the door and find out who she was talking to. Karen was sitting on her bed, facing the open window. She turned around, surprised to see them.

"Mommy, daddy!" She immediately ran over to them and gave them hugs. "Karen, who were you talking to sweetheart?" William asked her. He was trying to be calm, but listening to her talk to his grandmother was unnerving. And he had to even admit to himself. He was scared.

"I was talking to Gam Ora. She showed me that little girl Carrie that fell off the cliff. She's with her now." Karen said.

"How did she 'show' you?" William was feeling the hairs on his neck stand up. Karen looked confused. Maria stepped in. "Baby, how did Gam Ora show you?"

"Gam was here and she showed me, mommy. She shows me lots of things." Karen said. "Sometimes, scary things. I don't want to fall off a cliff, mommy!" Karen started crying and buried her face in her neck as Maria picked her up to comfort her.

"Honey, nothing can happen to you. Gam Ora is just a memory now, up here in your head. Besides she loved you. She doesn't want you to fall off a cliff." Maria glanced at William, nodding toward Krista's door. 'Please go check on Kris.' She mouthed to him. He nodded, glad to get away for a moment.

He went across the hall to Krista's room. Krista was sound asleep. Her blonde hair was spread around her pillow and she looked so angelic and peaceful, he couldn't help but give her a quick kiss on the cheek before he went back to Karen's room. 'At least one of them isn't affected by whatever this is!' He thought to himself.

He braced himself to go back into Karen's room. Thankfully, she was lying in bed with her eyes closed and Maria was singing a lullaby to her. "Twinkle twinkle, little star, how I wonder where you are. Up above the world so high…" Maria's voice faded as she saw William at the door and mouthed 'I think she's finally asleep.' William nodded and left the door cracked as he waited for his wife to leave the room.

As Maria quietly moved out of the room and met William in the hallway, she motioned him to move downstairs. "I don't want her to wake up." She whispered as they moved toward the kitchen.

William didn't realize he'd been holding his breath until they were away from Karen's room. "What is going on here? Maria, you need to call Dr. Welch. This is beyond anything she was talking about!"

Maria

After last night's discovery from William about the cliff incident and Karen's knowledge of the information, Maria knew without a doubt that Karen had inherited her abilities to see and hear people that had died. She wasn't sure how to approach this with Dr. Welch, but knew that she needed to know what was going on and called her first thing the next morning. Her receptionist said that she was with clients all morning, but could call her later and talk with her about the situation. Maria thanked her and said she would try to be available. William had a job interview with a local real estate firm and was headed out the door as she hung up.

"Good luck today, sweetheart! You'll do great!" Maria didn't want to bring up Karen or last night's discussion about the tragedy that he'd never told her about. He really wanted this job and needed it. Although the house was in their name, the mortgage and taxes weren't cheap. She had a few interviews lined up that week as well. They were up in the air about asking Sara to babysit the twins while they weren't in preschool a few days a week. Sara loved spending time with them, but with Karen's increasing preoccupation with Gram Laura and 'weird stuff' as Krista worded it, she seemed to back off with her babysitting offers.

William grabbed a coffee cup and downed half of it on the way out the door before giving her a kiss. "Thanks, babe! I hope so! We've got some savings, but I really need to get a good income. Roberts & Sons is a great agency for real estate, so we'll see."

She waved as he headed out, just as the twins came wandering downstairs. Krista ran to William as he was headed out the door. "Daddy!" He scooped her up and gave her a hug and kiss. "Daddy's gotta go, but I'll be home later. Be good for your mom, okay?"

"K, daddy. Bye." Krista and her father had a special connection that Maria recognized early on even when Krista and Karen were babies. Krista seemed to feel more comforted when William was in the room, while Karen craved her attention. Karen followed Krista, but didn't run after William. She seemed mopey and was sucking her thumb (a habit that Maria thought they'd gotten through months ago) and carrying her blankie that was raggedy and falling apart. "Karen, daddy's leaving, come give me a hug, sweetheart!" William said to her as he stood in the doorway. Maria knew he put out an extra effort with Karen because of the latest difficulties since Gram Laura died.

Karen just waved to him from her chair at the table. "Bye, daddy." She seemed more interested in the glass of orange juice that Maria had set in front of her. Maria glanced at William who looked disappointed. She went to him and gave him a hug. "She's okay. She had a rough night, honey. Go nail this interview!"

As he drove away, Maria knew that there was more she needed to know about Gram Laura. She fed the twins and as they played, she brought down a few boxes that belonged to her. There were photo albums and she flipped through trying to find anything that would give her an idea of what she was really like. At the bottom of the second box, there was a journal with a rose on it. She flipped through it and toward the end, there were several entries that caught her eye.

'Karen seems to understand me and that I connect with her on a level that's beyond this world. Even though she's only a year old, I can tell. She knows.'

Maria kept looking through entries that were only a month before her death. *'I don't want to leave Karen, so I'm hoping that Janice was right; that she's going to follow me soon after I'm gone.'*

'Who the hell is 'Janice'?' Maria wondered. She didn't find any other entries in the journal, but she found a card at the bottom of the box that must have fallen from the journal itself. It read 'Janice Suran-Medium/Psychic' with a phone number on the second line. She gave the girls their cereal and turned on their favorite cartoons to keep them occupied for a few minutes. She dialed the number on the card expecting either no answer or an answering machine to pick up. So when a woman answered, she was surprised. "Uh, hello, could I speak to Janice please?" Maria found herself unprepared for what she wanted to say.

"This is Janice. How can I help you?" The woman sounded friendly enough. Maria was trying to decide between saying 'wrong number' and hanging up, or talk to her, but not sure what she would ask. "Hello?" Janice asked again, as Maria tried to figure out what she wanted to say.

Maria recovered quickly, determined to find out why Gram Laura had this number in her journal. "Hi, Janice, I was wondering if you were still doing psychic readings. One of my friends recommended you

168

and I wanted to schedule an appointment." Maria hoped her voice didn't sound as shaky as she felt.

"Well, of course you can! I'm glad to know that someone recommended me. When would you like to come in?" Janice said. Her response was welcoming. Maria was intrigued. Anything she'd heard about psychics was that they were frauds and a waste of time, which is why she was shocked to see that Gram Laura had seen her in the first place!

"Do you have any openings for today?" Maria crossed her fingers. 'Why not, I might as well see her as soon as possible.'

"I have some time at 1:00. Would that work for you?" Janice offered.

Maria was surprised and now wondered how she would be able to make her 2:30 interview that she had today. "Where are you located?" She stalled. If she were close enough, she'd be able to make it.

"I'm in North Kingstown. I'm located in Wickford Village right on Main Street." Janice told her.

Maria's interview was in North Kingstown, only a few miles away from Wickford Village at Wellbeing, a private mental health agency. "Yes, Janice. That works for me. What is the charge for the visit?" She didn't have much cash on her and she didn't want William to know that she was going, so she didn't want it to show up on the bank statement and write a check.

"Twenty-five dollars for 30 minutes." Janice said. "I only take cash."

"Fine. I'll see you at 1:00." Maria told her. She had enough cash on her.

"Could I have your first name? Just for the appointment book." Janie asked.

"Maria." She was surprised that Janice didn't ask for her full name. At least she couldn't look her up in the phone book or see her relation to Gram Laura.

"See you at 1:00, Maria." Janice said warmly. As Maria hung up, she wondered what the hell she was doing. Dr. Welch was supposed to call about Karen this afternoon. But then again, Dr. Welch probably wouldn't be able to explain what happened last night. She was a psychiatrist, not a psychic. Just then, William came back from his interview. He looked happy. "I think it went well!" He told her before she could ask. "I've got another interview in a few hours so I'll watch the girls and then take them to my mom's on my way to the interview.

"That's great that it went well. I need to go over a few things to prepare for my interview at 2:30. I'll need to leave around 12:30 to run a few errands." Maria told him. She was careful not to mention her appointment with Janice. Maria knew that William wouldn't be happy about it. He'd always said that he thought people that claimed to be psychics were 'ripping people off' with their 'predictions.' But at the same time, Gram Laura obviously cared about their advice because she talked about Janice and her card was there. Karen didn't mention anything about Gram Laura or Carrie this morning, but Maria knew that Gram Laura spent many hours with Karen. She'd said so in her journal about her 'connection with Karen.'

She was busy for the next hour preparing for her interview with Wellbeing, while William spent time with the girls and made lunch for them. The position that they'd posted was fairly vague and somewhat tailored to her skills, it was only a case management position. She knew when she went into psychology, it was likely she'd need to get her Master's degree. It had seemed possible at the time, but now that was light years away. She was just glad that Karen hadn't mentioned 'Gam Ora' or 'Carrie' again today and hoped that she wouldn't when she was at Sara's house later on.

At 12:30,after kissing the twins and William goodbye, she headed out to see Janice Suran. She almost felt guilty about lying to William about seeing a psychic, but she knew it was something she had to do for herself. It would just unnecessarily create an argument if she told him. She felt a sudden sense of renewed hope as she drove toward Janice's office. Maybe she didn't have anything to offer, but at least she could say she checked it out for herself. She followed the directions that Janice gave her and she pulled up in front of a small shop that was tucked away in a corner of Wickford village that she would have missed without Janice giving her directions.

She walked up the few rickety wooden steps to the bright blue door opened it and a bell rang. The inside was small and very much what she'd expect; the woody scent of incense was heavy in the air and various angels, stars and luminaries decorated the space. There was a small desk toward the back, although no one was sitting there.

"Hello? Janice?" Maria called out. It was 1:00 on the dot. There was no answer, so she waited for a few minutes and was ready to leave when a petite older woman, no taller than 5 feet tall appeared. She had a bright colored green outfit on that looked like pajamas, eccentric make up around her eyes, and her graying hair was piled on top of her head in a bun. She looked every bit like what Maria envisioned a psychic would look like. She just hoped that she was helpful.

"Maria? I'm so sorry. I was doing my meditation after my lunch." Janice's high voice matched her diminutive stature. Maria nodded. "No problem. I was just here a minute or two."

Janice walked to the small desk and turned on the small Tiffany-style lamp. "Please have a seat." She pointed to the chair in front of the desk. Maria sat down. Janice closed her eyes for a few moments and Maria was ready to ask her if she was okay when she opened them again.

"Maria, you have some abilities to hear from those that have passed. One of your daughters also has this ability as well." She said suddenly. Maria was shocked. How could she know this?

"I can tell just from the aura surrounding you that you have these abilities." Janice told her as she opened her mouth to ask how she knew this. "Your mother and your husband's grandmother also had this ability."

"How do you know all this?" Maria was astounded and the hair on the back of her neck was standing up now. She'd been amazed that she could feel *her* energy, but Laura and her mother were gone and Karen was alive and well at home. Maybe this was worth her time after all.

"Maria, I remember Laura Carson well. She came here often. I heard about her passing. I'm very sorry." Janice began. "Laura used to come and see me fairly often, especially in the last few months before her death. She wasn't feeling well, although I suspect that she didn't tell anyone. She was so fond of you and especially her great granddaughters."

"Yes, she was." Maria confirmed this, but was cautious not to give too much information.

"Laura also had the gift of seeing beyond, a gift she didn't realize until later, but then discussed with me on several occasions." Janice disclosed.

"What 'gift'?" Maria asked.

"The ability to be able to communicate with those that have passed, hear their voices, and occasionally see them. You wouldn't be here if you didn't know, Maria." Janice said softly. "Would you?"

Maria had been skeptical, but Janice was right. William and Krista couldn't see what was happening either. Only she could see these things, although she tried to pretend that she didn't. She nodded. "I'd call it more a curse than a gift, but yes, it's true." Maria admitted.

"It's absolutely a gift. Because there are only a select few in this world that can see and hear those that have passed." Janice insisted. "What is troubling you that brought you here today?"

"My daughter, who is an identical twin, just turned three was very close to Laura. She even knew before we did that she was gone. Laura had a heart attack in the house at a party and passed suddenly. Karen said that she could 'hear' her and went to her. She just knew. Now, it's been months and Karen has been talking to Laura as if she's in the room. She even mentioned a little girl that died years ago that my husband witnessed when he was a boy shortly after we were discussing the incident. She's mentioned that Laura wants her to come with her. Frankly, I'm here because I'm afraid that Laura wants Karen to be with her. I'm afraid that ... maybe, she could make things happen that could cause Karen's death. Karen has told me that her great- grandmother wants to be with her." Maria felt the tears rolling down her face as she talked. She hadn't realized how stressed she'd been until now.

Janice looked solemn for a moment and took several deep breaths. "Give me a moment, Maria." She whispered. She seemed to disassociate for a few moments as her eyes became glossed over and she didn't blink. Just when Maria was about to ask her if she was okay, she seemed to come out of the trance. "I'm here again. I was trying to connect with Laura, but she wasn't receptive."

"What do you mean, she wasn't 'receptive'?" Maria was getting irritated with this whole process. Maybe this was a huge mistake.

"I mean that I was trying to reach out to her in the spirit world and she was deliberately blocking me. It happens sometimes." Janice said. "I wanted you to be able to talk to her about her influence on your daughter."

"So she's not receptive. Now what? What do I do?" Maria was upset now. Her husband's grandmother was ruining their lives, despite the fact that she died months ago!

"Maria, please give me another chance to connect." Janice whispered. "I can feel that she's here now." Her eyes suddenly went vacant and she stopped talking as her hands gripped the table. Her whole body became rigid for a moment.

Maria had to admit she felt a chill in the air and suddenly the scent of Gram Laura's perfume that smelled like roses filled the air. She shivered as she watched Janice's face. Janice suddenly smiled.

"Hello, Maria. It seems you, the girls and my grandson are doing well. I'm so glad that you both have graduated. He'll get that job that he interviewed for this morning; I'm sure of it." It was strange looking at Janice's face, but her voice was definitely Gram Laura's. She was suddenly scared and unsure of what to say.

"You're worried about Karen. That's why you're here." She said. Maria suddenly felt anger toward her. Who did she think she was, talking to Karen and disrupting their lives?

"Why do you keep talking to her? It's not healthy, Laura! Telling her that you want her to come see you! Why are you trying to take my . daughter away from me?" Maria felt her anger rising about this disruption.

"I love Karen. I would never deliberately want her to cross over. There are others here that might be trying to deceive her. She has the ability just as you to hear and see souls that have passed. I believe that there is someone that's trying to deceive her, to lead her to believe that she's talking to me." The voice coming from Janice sounded sincere. "Karen is simply using her gift, but isn't sure how it works. There are others here that might be interfering. Please be careful."

Maria wasn't sure if she believed her, but what choice did she have? "What can we do to help her?" She felt even more helpless now.

"You need to stand firm as a family. I'm only an entity now. The most I can do is observe, although I wish I could do more." Gram Laura's voice said.

"I miss all of you, especially my grandson. The Block Island property is being sold for a reason. If you go there this weekend, please be careful! There's someone else….." Her voice started to fade out then.

"Laura! What do you mean?" Maria asked, but it was too late. Janice's head was down for a few minutes and when she lifted it again, Laura was gone. "You're back." Maria could see the difference in the posture and attitude immediately.

"I am. I could hear the conversation. I think she's sincere, I really don't think she's trying to create a situation for Karen to cross over." Janice told her.

"She said something about being 'careful' if we went this weekend to her Block Island property that's being sold. That there's 'someone else'. Is there any way to find out what she meant?" Maria was worried now.

"I'll try to connect with her again." Janice sat still again and closed her eyes. She nodded a few times, then said, "I understand. I'll tell her." She opened her eyes again.

"Laura wasn't able to make a good connection but I could feel that she wants you to be careful in the next few weeks." Janice said. "There is someone that's trying to gain Karen's trust. Karen is vulnerable and needs to be protected."

"How can we do that? Protect her?" Maria was beside herself. First she thought it was Laura, but now she was warning her about other 'spirits' that required Karen to be protected from?

"Maria, calm down. Karen is fine. She's vulnerable, but she has you and her family. Whoever she needs protection from isn't able to reach her now. She's safe now. You just need to keep her busy and distracted, that's all. Her great-grandmother is also a protector. Give her a few weeks and she will be less sensitive to the other side once she has processed her grandmother's passing." Janice said quietly.

"I really hope so." Maria wasn't sure what to believe, but she didn't have anything else to go on at this point. "This has been really helpful, Janice." Maria looked down at her watch. It was almost 2:00 and she needed to head to her interview. "I need to get going." She gave her cash along with a tip.

"Anytime, Maria. Please don't hesitate to come back when you need to" Janice advised, as Maria headed out the door. Maria just waved as she got into her car and sat for a moment to digest what had just happened. It surprised her that Gram Laura had actually come through. She wasn't sure what she was talking about others that might interfere. What was shocking was that her own mother did not. Surely she wasn't talking about her mother! She spent the drive to her interview with no more answers to her questions about Karen's behavior, except that Gram Laura wasn't responsible. So who was? Was it her mother? Suddenly she remembered Carrie, the girl that had fallen off the cliff. Maybe she was the one trying to lure Karen?

The interview was a blur to Maria as they went through the questions and she'd answered them, but she knew that she wasn't focused and she was sure they could tell. It didn't matter. The job was basically driving clients around and making sure they were taking their medications. She didn't go to school to be a taxi driver and had no interest in the position. She knew that they needed an income, so she let them know that she was interested. They assured her that she would be able to move forward as a therapist eventually. It wasn't her dream job, but it was worth taking it just to get some experience.

She headed home as her mind went over everything Janice had said and 'Gram Laura' had said through her. She was beginning to wonder that if Gram Laura hadn't been talking to Karen the whole time. Maybe it was her mother, or someone else. Whatever was going on, she wasn't sure that anyone could help them anymore.

William

He was certain that his interview with Roberts & Sons agency had gone well, but he had another lined up at 2:00 with another real estate agency in Warwick in an hour. The twins were playing in Krista's room, when he announced they were going to Gram Sara's house for a visit. Krista quickly got up and headed for the door. Karen seemed to take her time and when William insisted she hurry up, she said, "Daddy, I wanna visit Gam Ora."

William wasn't sure what to say, but decided to use Maria's words instead. "Gam Ora is far away. You can't visit her now." Karen nodded and went downstairs and got herself into the car. He just hoped she wouldn't scare his mother with her commentary about seeing her great-grandmother while she was there.

His mother was happy to see them and gave both of the girls a big hug. Krista was excited and ran in to pet his mother's elderly beagle, named Butch. Karen was more hesitant, but gave his mother a quick hug but hung around near the door. "Maria had an interview at 2:30, and might pick them up, but I've gotta go or I'll be late. Thanks, mom!" He kissed her on the cheek before leaving.

He only hoped that Karen wouldn't start acting as though she were talking to his grandmother again while he was gone. He was early for the interview with Remax that he'd heard good things about. Within the hour long interview, he knew that he wanted the position and that he was hoping they felt the same about him. They were willing to work with him to get his real estate license if hired. The future was looking good and he stopped by a pay phone to call home to tell Maria. But she wasn't home and the answering machine picked up. He didn't bother leaving a message, figuring she was picking up the twins.

He headed home and Maria's car was in the driveway. He walked in, expecting the girls to be running up to him. "Babe, where are the girls? I thought you were going to pick them up from my mom's house after your interview."

Maria looked at him as if she had no idea what he was talking about. "I thought you were going to pick them up." She sounded distressed, almost disoriented.

"Never mind. I'll go pick them up. Come with me." Something about her demeanor was off and he didn't want to leave her alone. As William passed by the dining room table, he noticed a business card and picked it up. 'Janice Suran-Medium/Psychic' it read. He suddenly had a feeling what was going on. There was a reason this was here; Maria had found it, probably saw her today, if he had to guess. He thought about confronting his wife about it now, but decided to wait. But he felt like he was about to burst with building anger that she'd contacted this person without talking to him.

"Okay." Her voice sounded almost emotionless, but she agreed and got into the car. She was silent most of the way, although he asked her how her interview went. All she would say is 'fine' and didn't elaborate. "Babe, what's going on with you?" He asked, tampering down the anger about the card he'd found.

"I'm just worried about Karen." She told him as she was staring out the window.

"By the way, Dr. Welch called and left a message. She said you'd called this morning." William tried to engage her in some kind of conversation.

"I did call her this morning, but she didn't have anything available. Karen has an appointment in a few days." Maria was still being evasive. Suddenly, William had enough and pulled the car over on a side road. He turned toward her as she looked surprised that he'd stopped.

"Maria, look at me. What's going on?" William asked her directly. "You've been acting strange since you got home. Was it the interview? Or did something else happen?" He was getting frustrated, but tried to keep his voice from sounding too angry. She was quiet, but turned to him.

"I'm sorry, Bill. I think I did well at the interview, but the salary wasn't great. Not what I expected. But I think it's worth me taking it, at least for now. As long as your mom would be able to watch the girls a few days a week." She was close to tears now. She'd had higher expectations about what kind of job she'd get with her degree.

"Honey, don't get upset. I think you should take it at least for a reference for other jobs. Don't worry about the salary. I had two great interviews today, but I'm really hoping I get the one with Remax. It's a great opportunity."

"I'm really glad, and I'm sorry I didn't remember if you were picking up the girls or not." Maria started to sound like herself again and they got back on the road. William was just crossing his fingers that Karen wasn't talking about Gram Laura or acting odd today.

As they pulled up to Sara's house, he could see her waiting at the door. 'Not a good sign', he thought to himself. Hoping he was wrong, he and Maria met her at the door. "Is everything okay?" He asked. He could tell by the look on his mother's face that something was going on.

"It's been fine, I guess. But Karen has been out of sorts today." Sara said simply. William knew there was much more to that statement.

"She's just been quiet and looking out the window. Krista's been fine. In fact, Krista got upset with Karen earlier because she wouldn't play tag with her." Sara told him. William nodded. "Karen's still struggling with Gram Laura being gone, I guess." He tried to sound casual, but he knew that it was an on-going issue.

His mother nodded. "I know you both are doing what you can." Her voice was quiet, but William could tell that she was upset. He wasn't sure what else to do anymore. Maria went in to let the twins know they were ready to go. Krista came running as soon as she saw her. "Mommy!" She was excited to see her.

"Hi, sweetheart. Where's your sister?" Maria asked.

"I don't know. Probwy looking out the window. She used to talk about Gam Ora, but now she's been talks to some other girl named Carrie. It's weird, mommy. She don't talk to me." Krista told her. "Grammy asked her who she was looking at today because she was staring out the window and she told her 'Carrie'. Who's Carrie, Mommy?"

Maria was stunned for a moment. "Carrie's just a little girl." She tried to keep it simple, hoping that Krista would drop it.

"I know. She's a little girl that died. Kawyn told me." Krista didn't miss anything.

"Sweetheart, your sister has a good imagination. She must have heard daddy and his family talking about her, so she decided to pretend that she can talk to her." Maria looked around for William.

He had gone upstairs to get Karen and found her staring out the window. "Karen, what are you doing?"

"Just looking outside. I can see them waving at me." Karen told him. William sat next to her. There wasn't anyone outside.

"Okay, I don't see anyone now. It's time to go downstairs now so we can go home." William tried to sound calm, although he wasn't sure what was happening with his daughter. She was seeing people that weren't there waving at her? Karen turned to him. "Don't you see them too, daddy? They're waving to you too."

"No, sweetheart. I don't see anyone. Let's go downstairs and say goodbye to your grandma." William grabbed Karen's hand. He'd had enough of whatever was going on now and he wasn't going to entertain her imagination any longer. Karen followed him downstairs although she kept looking back and waving.

As they drove home, Karen was quiet, but Krista was the opposite, talking about how she and Grammy went outside on the swing, and made cookies. Maria was silent, because Sara had already expressed her concerns to her while she was downstairs; Karen had no interest in whatever she and Krista were doing. She did come down while they were making cookies, but kept staring out the window and seemed uninterested.

"I think it's good that she has an appointment with Dr. Welch in a few days." William said to his wife as they pulled into the driveway.

"I'm not sure that's going to help, but it couldn't hurt." Maria said, then realized that she'd said too much.

"What does that mean?" William had shut the car off and they were getting the twins out of the car.

"I mean, it hasn't really helped so far, but maybe this time it will make a difference." She said vaguely.

William looked at her for a moment. "I saw the business card, Maria. You left it near the phone. You went to see this Janice Suran." He was tired of stewing about it for the past hour. "Why didn't you tell me about it?" He could hear the anger in his own voice despite trying to tamp it down.

Maria looked surprised. "I was going to tell you later. Let's get the girls in the house and get them some dinner. We can talk when they're in bed, okay?" Her voice sounded tired, defeated.

William bit back his initial impulse to yell at her, but knew the girls shouldn't overhear the conversation. "We'll talk after then. But we're not going to bed until you can explain this to me, Maria."

She nodded as they led the twins into the house. It was going to be a long night for both of them.

Maria

It was only after a long night of getting the twins to bed later that she had to face her husband with her explanation of Janice. Her visit to see Janice and what she had told her. As she explained it to William in detail, she could tell that he was becoming more upset and worried. "The card fell out of Gram Laura's journal, Bill. That's how I found it." She felt the need to remind him before he launched into his tirade of seeing a psychic, which she was sure was coming.

"Maria, I know you told me about how you're able to communicate with your mom and that's hard for me to understand. But now you're claiming this woman can actually talk for my grandmother? And that Karen is being stalked by someone else, maybe that girl, Carrie? Sorry, I'm having a hard time believing all of this." William told her in a calm voice. She was glad that he wasn't yelling at her as she'd expected.

"I know it sounds impossible, but how do you explain Karen talking about Carrie? You said that you never talked about her before." Maria asked.

"I don't know, but there's got to be a logical explanation. I mean, besides Karen talking to a girl that's been dead for twenty years!" William insisted. "I think she needs to go to her appointment with Dr. Welch in a few days. You can talk to her about it and see what she thinks."

"I don't think Dr. Welch can help her, Bill." Maria said softly.

"And you think this Janice person can?" William retorted. "Really, Maria, I'm surprised at you! You just finished your psych degree and now you think a psychologist can't help our daughter because she's got imaginary friends?" He was almost yelling now.

Maria knew now whatever she told him would fall on deaf ears, so she agreed to take Karen to Dr. Welch. There was no use arguing with him now. "But I don't think we should go to that reunion on Block Island this weekend." She went on to explain what Janice had said about needing to be careful, but William just became more upset.

"So now we're just supposed to do whatever this psychic says? NO! We're going and that's it! All of us! I don't want to hear about it again! The girls will be fine; they won't be wandering around the cliffs because *we* will be watching them!" William was almost shouting at her now.

Maria felt the tears coming and without another word, headed into the master bathroom to get away from him for a few minutes. She could feel the sobs in the back of her throat that were reminiscent of her teenage days at Aunt Sylvia's when she was overwhelmed and suddenly she was crying so hard that it was hard to breathe.

Suddenly, William's arms were around her pulling her close to him and he was holding her. "Babe, I'm sorry. This isn't your fault at all. I'm sorry I yelled. We'll figure this out together, okay?" After a few minutes, Maria was able to pull herself together and got back into bed. "We'll talk about this later tomorrow, okay?" William asked.

Maria just nodded, exhausted after her emotional breakdown. She knew that he wouldn't understand tomorrow or maybe ever. She just had to hope that between the two of them, and perhaps some help from Dr. Welch that they could protect Karen from what was going on.

Over the next two days, Maria felt like she was treading on eggshells with her husband. Karen saw Dr. Welch for her appointment, and as Maria suspected, she was not welcoming to the potential of any paranormal explanations for Karen's behaviors. Maria tried to give her an abridged version of Karen's behaviors, along with her own observations while omitting that she'd seen a psychic herself. Dr. Welch was open to suggestions, but Maria didn't want to find herself sent to a psychiatric facility because she knew that it sounded impossible.

"Karen did mention a girl named Carrie to me while I was talking with her and observing her in the playroom, but I think she's still struggling with her great-grandmother's death and creating these imaginary characters as a way to cope, Maria." Dr. Welch gave her assessment.

Maria just nodded. "So do you think we should go to the family reunion on Block Island this weekend? I'm just worried that it will upset Karen." She fervently hoped that Dr. Welch would agree, but she did not.

"Actually, I think that it would be good for Karen to go there. She would get a chance to see where Laura spent her time in the summers. Besides, Block Island is a great place to visit. It would be a short getaway for all of you as a family." Dr. Welch's words came from a good place, Maria knew. But Dr. Welch also had no idea about the reality of what was happening. And there was no way to explain it without sounding as though she were delusional.

Maria nodded, knowing that this trip was inevitable. William had told her that if Dr. Welch agreed that it was okay that they would be going. He was in the waiting room with Krista as they came out of Dr. Welch's office and when she told him her assessment of the problem, William agreed. "Thank you so much, Dr. Welch. This is a huge relief." Maria felt the exact opposite and defeated as she scheduled Karen's appointment for next week, but she knew there was no point in arguing.

Early Saturday morning, they were headed out on the ferry from Point Judith to Block Island. Maria tried not to let her anxiety about the weekend show, especially to the girls. After all, it was a beautiful house and location; anyone that loved being near the ocean would have paid top dollar to stay at this house. Maria knew this because William kept reminding her over the past few days. Maria had resigned herself to going, but she had told William several times about the strict rules regarding the girls and their safety.

"If they're outside, someone needs to be watching them at all times, Bill." Maria had said one too many times until William had finally snapped at her.

"Maria! Enough! Between all of us adults, there will be someone watching them outside at all times! Please stop with this so we can relax and have a good time!" He gave her a hug to make up for his harshness with her.

Krista and Karen loved the ferry ride and wanted to stand near the railing on the top deck. Maria felt nervous as they wanted to climb onto the second rail to see over and insisted that William help them. "Mommy, I can do this myself!" Krista told her at one point and she knew she needed to relax. She did want to have a good time at the house with the family and reminded herself that she was being overly protective.

Once they reached the main land, Uncle Stuart picked them up. Barbara and Sara were at the house to greet them as they had arrived the night before. The house was amazing and so huge it was easy to get lost in. Krista and Karen had already picked out different rooms that they wanted to stay in. One was a cute pink bedroom that had a twin bed with a pink and purple comforter. The walls were painted pale pink as well and had a small pink chaise lounge along with white furnishings. "I want this room, Mommy!" Krista insisted as soon as she saw it.

"Okay, you've got it! Put your stuff down on the bed to reserve it." Maria told her trying to relax finally.

They checked out the next room that overlooked the pool. The walls were a pale mint green color. There was a twin-sized bed, with a green comforter and white furnishings as well. Karen inspected the view from the window and Maria almost expected her to say she saw someone, but instead she jumped onto the bed. "I like this room, Mommy!" Maria was glad that Karen hadn't mentioned anything about 'Gam Ora' or 'Carrie' in the past couple of days. Maybe getting away had been a good idea after all. Maria was still skeptical.

"Ok. Just like your sister, put your stuff on the bed to reserve it!" Karen put her little pink backpack down. Maria breathed a sigh of relief that the girls were having fun.

That night, Sara cooked a special dinner of seafood; lobster, crab cakes, scallops and clams. She'd made some macaroni and cheese for the girls in case they didn't like the seafood options, but both Karen and Krista loved the lobster and crab cakes. "Mommy, this is good!" Karen told her as she dunked a piece of lobster in a ramekin of melted butter. Krista loved the crab cakes and ate two of them, plus some of Sara's homemade macaroni and cheese. After dinner everyone went out to the front deck to enjoy the ocean view and relax. William sat down with a glass of his favorite; whiskey on the rocks. Maria eyed the glass as he whispered in her ear, "I'm only having one." She nodded and decided to have a glass of pinot noir which she rarely did. The girls were outside with them on the deck with their dolls, sitting at a small children's table. Karen was animated and talking to her doll, while Krista who loved books was 'reading' to hers. Sara had brought her camera and was running around taking pictures of everyone, especially the twins. Maria was finally feeling as though she could stop worrying for a few minutes.

As the sun started to set and the ocean breeze picked up, it became chilly so they all went back in and the girls were sleepy so Maria decided it was bedtime, even though it was only 7:30. "They've had a long day." She said pointedly at William who was deep in conversation with Stuart about real estate and investments.

"I'll go with you to tuck them in." William excused himself and followed Maria with the twin's upstairs. Maria turned around and mouthed 'thank you' as they arrived at Krista's bedroom. Krista loved her room and as long as she had a nightlight on, she was fine. Maria had made sure to buy small nightlights for the girls "Mommy, please read with me." She had her favorite book; Raggedy Ann and the Cookie Snatcher' which Maria read to her before bed at night. Krista knew it so well that Maria would just start reading and then Krista took over. Tonight, Krista got through a few pages and then started dozing off and it was on as they shut the door, leaving it open just a few inches.

William brought Karen to her bedroom, along with her stuffed worn floppy-eared bunny that she'd had since she was a baby. "Good night, sweetheart. See you in the morning." He made sure to plug in the nightlight that Maria had given him. Just as he was closing the door, Karen said, "Daddy, do you see her?"

William stopped and came back in the room. "See who, sweetheart?"

"The little girl that's standing near the window, over there." She pointed to the corner near the big picture window with the cliff view. Maria poked her head in just then. "Good night, Karen." Then she noticed that Karen and William were both looking toward the window. "Everything okay in here?" She felt a chill run down her spine as she could tell that it was not.

"Mommy I saw that little girl over there. She's gone now." Karen said, clutching her stuffed rabbit. Maria knew William had good intentions to bring her here, but knew that this was likely to happen. She came and sat next to her on the bed. "Honey, that little girl isn't real. She's a girl that lived a long time ago and she can't hurt you. I want you to close your eyes and think about how much fun we'll have tomorrow okay?" Maria tried to keep her voice steady and calm. Because inside, she wasn't sure what else to do. William sat down on the end of the bed next to Maria. "Mommy and Daddy will be right next door if you need us, okay?" They'd shown the twins their room ahead of time which was literally 10 feet from Karen's room.

Karen snuggled down with her bunny. "Okay. Night mommy, night daddy." She closed her eyes. William tiptoed out the door, while Maria waited a few minutes to make sure Karen was asleep. Finally, she left the room with the door cracked open a few inches. William was waiting outside the room. "Babe, stop worrying. We're right next door. She'll be fine." He assured her.

Maria nodded, wanting to believe him. But she could feel the presence of someone else, not unlike when her mother would appear. And this was not her mother, she was sure of it.

William

He'd wished Maria hadn't come into Karen's room, or at least waited until after her 'episode' as he started referring to them had passed. He knew he was probably in for a lecture beginning with 'I told you we shouldn't have come here.' But surprisingly, she didn't. Instead she gave him a hug. "You handled that well, Bill. We just need to keep our cool, even though it's scary. If we acted afraid, it'll only make it worse." He was glad for the sentiment. "Thanks for coming in and saving me! I wasn't sure what to say next!" He joked, but he was starting to understand that this wasn't something that was going to go away with counseling.

"Let's try and relax for a little while before we go to bed. I'll keep an ear out." Maria said, taking his hand. They went back downstairs to finish up their evening, although William found himself on edge now.

"Everything okay?" Sara asked. She knew how troubling some of Karen's statements could be.

"The girls are asleep. So, who's up for a few games of poker?" William asked. Stuart pulled out his poker chips and cards. William felt himself finally starting to relax as they played a few practice hands for beginners like Maria, then started playing for money. They all had fun playing for the next several hours. He was surprised that Maria had done well at the game and won the entire pot at the end. "Nice job, sweetheart! William told her. She looked happy; it just hit him that it had been so long since she'd laughed or had fun that he couldn't even remember. It reminded him of when they'd first started dating, before his father's death, marriage, twins and Gram Laura's death and now Karen's 'imagination' as he liked to refer to it. He realized how much time Maria had spent helping Gram Laura and the twins all these years and suddenly felt so grateful. This woman deserved much more than what she had now. He needed that job with Remax or Roberts & sons to get back to him as soon as possible. He needed to be able to provide for them so that Maria could take care of them. He made a promise to himself that he would do whatever it took to take care of them.

William found himself unable to sleep that night. He and Maria had left their bedroom door open in case Karen began to talk or see things or worse; walk outside in her sleep. He fell asleep finally, but every time he heard a noise, even if it was just a branch being blown across the window, he was alert. He was glad they were only here one more night after tonight. It brought back his own fears from childhood and although he wasn't completely on-board with Maria's insistence that Karen could communicate with the dead, he wasn't ruling it out either.

The next thing he knew, the sun was shining through the window and when he reached over for his wife, she wasn't there. "Maria?" He called out.

She emerged from the master bathroom, completely dressed in a cute light pink sweater and jeans. Her blonde hair was back in a low ponytail that made her look even more youthful and beautiful than he remembered. "Hi, sweetheart. I let you sleep in today." Her smile was contagious and he promised to remember this moment on days when they were arguing. He fell in love with her all over again in that moment.

"You look so beautiful! I wish I had my camera with me right now!" William said. He actually had brought his camera. "Where is my Nikon by the way? I need to use it now!" His camera wasn't a higher end brand, but he did like to take pictures and Maria had bought him his Nikon last year for Christmas as a surprise.

"It's in your bag, over there." She pointed to the top of the dresser where he'd put his backpack.

He got out the camera and snapped a few candid pictures of Maria posing. Suddenly, he could hear Krista and Karen downstairs. "Daddy! Mommy!" They were in unison. Maria giggled. "They went down to have breakfast with your mother this morning so you could sleep. But I guess your time has run out!"

"So it has, but thanks for letting me sleep, babe." William still felt groggy because he probably only got about 4 hours of sleep, but not waking up at 6:30 with the girls was a gift! He got up showered and got downstairs before everyone starting heading out to Ballard's beach for the day. "William, good to see you could join us! Ready for a day at the beach?" Stuart greeted him as he poured himself a cup of black coffee. William glanced at Maria who raised her arms as if to say, 'it wasn't my plan'.

"Actually, I'd like to take Maria and the girls around the island this morning, take some pictures, that kind of thing." William told him casually. Ballard's was usually full of young spring-break types that were drinking heavily and it was always crowded.

Stuart didn't seem to mind, although his mother wasn't happy. "William, please. We're only here for one more full day. I'd like to spend more time with the girls."

"Mom, this house is on Mohegan Bluffs. There's a beach about 500 yards from here. Why don't you all just go there if you want to spend time with us?" William was starting to get annoyed with his mother. It was almost as if she were trying to make things more difficult than they needed to be.

"Oh, William, that beach is so rocky, not really a beach if you ask me. But never mind. We'll just meet up with you later." Sara said casually, although her tone indicated that she was upset that he'd made a different plan. Normally, William would just concede and go with what his mother wanted to do. But this was his vacation too and the last thing he wanted was to hang out on a loud crowded beach today. Maria gave him a look of gratitude. He knew she wanted time away by themselves today. "Ok, mom, we'll see you later this afternoon." William told her. She looked surprised, but headed out with Barbara, Stuart and his wife to the car.

"Now, ladies, we need to get ready to head out and do some sightseeing; maybe go to the Mohegan Beach?" William announced to Maria and the twins. Krista and Karen were ready to go; dressed in their look alike pink one-piece bathing suits with pink terry cloth cover ups on. "Maria, you might want to dress them in shorts and t shirts and bring along sweatshirts too. We're doing some sightseeing too."

"Beach, daddy!" Krista said loudly. She loved the ocean and was fearless when it came to running into the waves. Karen was more fearful and preferred to run back when the waves came in, but both girls loved the beach.

"We will, I promise, but first I wanted to take a walk over to one of the lighthouses." William assured her.

"Don't houses all have lights daddy?" Krista asked. "Yes, daddy, lights are in all houses." Karen echoed. Maria couldn't help but giggle at their comments. Krista was always so precocious and Karen followed her lead. "They've got a good point, Bill." She tried not to laugh as William struggled to answer so that his 3- year- old daughters would understand.

"This is a different kind of house, girls. I'll tell you more about them when we get there." William said to simplify. He winked at his wife, and went to tickle her underarm for putting him on the spot. "Are we ready yet?"

Krista and Karen jumped up and down. "We've been ready forever!" Karen complained. Maria nodded in agreement. "These two have been up since 7:00am. They've been ready to go for three hours!"

"Well, let's go! We got everything?" William turned to Maria who grabbed a big beach bag with a blanket, towels and the twins beach toys, along with a small cooler. William eyed his backpack which was also filled to the brim with his camera, sunscreen and whatever Maria couldn't fit into the beach bag. "Geez, I guess we're not walking too far! I hope you know you'll be carrying at least one of these bags!" He told his wife.

" I'll carry the cooler. You get the backpack and beach bag." Maria told him with a smile. William agreed and grabbed everything. The backpack was pretty heavy, thanks to his heavy sweatshirt that took up too much room. "Don't want to get cold!" He joked. "Are we ready? Let's go!"

They headed out toward the Southeast Lighthouse that was less than a half mile from the bluffs. It was a humid, hot August day but the island breeze was blowing, cooling them off. There was very little traffic and they allowed the girls to run ahead. As the brick lighthouse came into view, Krista yelled. "Daddy is that the house that has lights?" William and Maria both laughed.

"Yes, sweetheart!" They jogged to catch up with them. As they reached the Southeast light house, they grabbed the twins' hands and took in the view. It was only a couple hundred feet from the bluffs that dropped to the ocean below. Its tower was overlooking the ocean and the house that was built connecting it was fairly extensive. "Daddy do people live here?" Karen asked as she stared up at the 52 -foot tower.

"Someone does live there. They're called 'lighthouse keepers'. They live here and watch over the ocean for ships and shine a light from that tower that lets them know that they are close to rocks especially during storms. There's a horn that sounds out if a ship is too close to warn them." William said. He loved reading about lighthouses and the history behind them.

"So they sleep here too?" Krista asked as she looked around the area. "I don't see any toys. What do their kids do?" William burst out laughing. "I don't think they bring their families here to live." Although the connecting house area appeared quite livable. It resembled a typical house aside from the light tower connected to it.

"Daddy, can we go inside?" Karen asked. William shook his head. "No, sweetheart, but we can walk around outside and look." He was waiting for the inevitable question 'why' and was surprised when she didn't ask it. She seemed fascinated by the lighthouse, much more so than Krista who was complaining that she was hot and hungry. "Wanna go to the beach!" She was throwing a typical three –year- old tantrum.

"Kris, we'll go to the beach in a few minutes!" Maria told her. Krista pouted as Karen continued to look up at the tower, mesmerized. "Daddy, I see someone up there." She pointed to the tower.

William was curious and wondered if the keeper was actually there. He couldn't see from that far away, so he pulled out his camera and used the zoom lens to get a closer look. He couldn't see anyone or any movement. "I don't see anyone, Karen."

"He's right there! He's moving!" Karen insisted. "He's got white hair and a beard."

"Ok, Karen, I believe you, I just don't see him." William gave Maria a worried glance. Was she actually seeing someone or was it another 'special' sighting that only Karen could witness?

Just before Maria could answer, an older man with graying hair and a beard appeared on the front porch of the house. He seemed to be stumbling around as if he were intoxicated. "See! I told you!" Karen said.

"You're right, there is someone there. I just didn't see him." William felt relief wash over him.

"Can we go talk to him, daddy?" Krista was asking, suddenly interested now.

"I thought you were hot and wanted to go swimming, Kris." Maria reminded her.

"But I want to see the inside of the tower. Maybe he would show us." Krista and Karen were both asking to go see the inside of the tower. Just then, the man went back inside. William was glad that he did, so that he wouldn't have to directly disappoint his daughters. But the man looked as though he needed to sleep off the booze for the next 2 years.

"No. He went back inside and I thought the two of you wanted to see the ocean!" William tried to distract them. It worked. "Want to go to the ocean!" Both of them said at once.

"Okay, let's go! It's this way." William pointed toward the way they had come. They took off running and Maria dropped the small cooler to go chasing after them. The cliffs were dangerously close and she was still worried about Karen and 'Carrie' from the cliff.

Before long they reached the stairs that would lead them down the 200-foot drop from the bluffs to the beach below. Luckily there was a railing to hold onto, but Maria gave William the cooler so that she could hang onto their hands going down the wooden stairs. When they reached the beach, it was pretty rocky, so they walked a little while until they found a good spot that had enough sand between them and the waves splashing up. They decided to park and set up the blanket and towels for the twins and get out the snacks that Maria had brought.

The twins ate the bologna sandwiches that Maria had made and were anxious to go play in the waves. "Please stay near us. Don't go out further than your knees, girls." She had the look of an anxious mother as she watched them run toward that waves. "Babe, we're right here, watching. You know that Karen won't go past her ankles, and I doubt that Krista will go much further." They laid the blanket in the sand, ate some cheese and crackers that Maria had packed while they watched the girls run back and forth with the waves. William finally felt like he could relax for a few minutes.

"It's nice here, Bill. I'm glad you insisted on coming here, to this island. It's really beautiful here." Maria said as she leaned against him, her eyes closed. He was glad to hear her say that. If he had known how stressful this 'reunion' was going to be, he probably would have agreed with Maria and stayed home. But today had been a better day. As long as there were no more incidents with Karen and seeing 'ghosts', everything seemed to go well.

After an hour, the twins came back to grab their towels and get dried off. "Hey, babe let's get some great family pictures while we're here." William didn't want to miss a chance to use his camera today. He took several pictures of Maria and the twins on the blanket, then had them move to a nearby rock that was large enough for all three of them to sit on. "That's perfect, don't move!" William instructed as he snapped several shots of them. The background and lighting couldn't be more perfect. He knew this particular picture was a keeper. "Best picture of you and the girls ever!"

"Now, let me take some of all of you." Maria insisted. She grabbed the camera and after some instruction from William, she managed to take a few that 'might make it to the photo album,' as she joked with William. She practiced taking some more pictures but she could tell the twins were tired. They were complaining about being hungry. "I guess this is our cue to pack it up and go back to the house." Maria advised.

"I'm right behind you. Let's get going. I'm so glad we're not far from the house." William was glad they'd chosen this beach. Both of the girls were tired and walking up the stairs was a chore for all of them and luckily they only had a few hundred yards to go to be back at the house. When they got back, Maria immediately brought the twins to the bathroom and got them into the tub to wash up. The rest of the family wasn't back yet so William decided to make himself a Canadian Club and ginger ale drink and sit on the back deck to relax. He was starting to doze off when he heard the rest of the family coming back from Ballard's Beach. From the sound of them, they'd had their fair share of liquid amusement. His sister, Barbara was particularly loud and complaining about 'why did I have to leave?'

'Guess relaxation is over.' William thought to himself and got up to go meet them. Maria had just finished with the twin's bath and everyone seemed to be in a good mood, except Barbara who made plans with a boy she'd met on the beach.

The rest of the night was a combination of his mother and Stuart's wife, Jenna making dinner, Barbara complaining about needing to leave soon, and the twins getting grouchy from their long day. Their dinner of salmon, with some rice and asparagus was delicious to the adults, but the twins turned up their noses and Maria ended up making some boxed macaroni and cheese for them. By the time 8:30 rolled around, the twins were falling asleep on the love seat in front of the TV that adjoined the dining room. "Time for bed, girls." William announced, as he picked each twin up in his arms and carried them upstairs. Neither one protested, and he saw that as a good sign. "Daddy, can we go visit that lighthouse man again tomorrow?" Karen asked.

"Maybe, sweetheart." He wasn't sure what the plan was tomorrow, except that they were going back home. He couldn't see the moonlight anymore and he could hear the wind picking up. It sounded like a storm coming in.

Maria joined him outside in the hallway after tucking in Krista. "It looks like a storm is headed here. We should think about leaving early tomorrow if we can."

"We'll leave as soon as we can." William told her. He wasn't prepared to stay up another night to make sure Karen didn't wander off.

Maria

They had just put the twins to bed and stayed up to play some more poker with Stuart, Jenna and Sara. Barbara had gone back to meet up with a guy she'd met at the beach. Sara kept talking about it, but thankfully William had cut her off. "Mom, give her a break! After all, she is 20 years old and an adult!" Sara surprisingly nodded and didn't say anything more.

"The wind's picking up out there. Guess there's a storm headed our way." Stuart observed from staring out the window as they finished their last hand of cards. As they turned the TV to the news, there was a storm headed their way. The meteorologist announced that it was part of a tropical storm that was headed up the Atlantic. "High winds and surf as well as some rain is expected on Block Island." The news continued on.

"Well, as long as we can get back home tomorrow." Maria said, although now as she said it, she was starting to worry. What if they couldn't go home? What if they were stuck there for days and days? William grabbed her hand just then. "Babe, we'll be able to get home. Ok?" He knew her so well; he knew when she was stressed and she never had to say it.

"Ok." Maria squeezed his hand. She knew she could trust him.

"I'm sure the ocean will be calm enough for the ferry to go tomorrow." Stuart also offered his positive insight. "It's only supposed to be overnight." They could hear the wind starting to blow huge gusts with one of the tree branches hitting the living room window that startled Maria for a moment, as she jumped up to look around outside.

"I guess the storm is arriving." William observed, putting an arm around his wife. She laughed nervously. She'd never liked storms and being in a strange house made her feel more anxious. "I'm okay." But during the next hand, Maria kept looking outside as the sheets of rain appeared out of nowhere. Something made her want to check on the twins. "I'm going to go check on the girls; just to make sure the storm didn't wake them up." She told them and headed upstairs. The girls were always a little nervous during a thunderstorm, but she was especially worried about Karen. She quickly checked on Krista, who was sound asleep. She smiled at her sweet little face, and quickly headed to Karen's room. Karen wasn't in her bed. She felt herself starting to panic and flipped on the light. "Karen? Where are you?" She looked under the bed and in the small closet, but she wasn't there. "Karen!" She called out loudly. When there was no response, she headed back downstairs when William met her at the top of the stairs. "What's wrong?"

"Karen's not in her room!" Maria was panicking and starting to look everywhere. "Did she come downstairs? Maybe she's hiding in the bathroom!" She immediately went to check the hallway bathroom. She wasn't in there.

"Maria. Calm down. She couldn't have gone far! I'll let the rest of the family know and we'll go look for her." William knew how to talk her off the ledge and for that she was grateful. But she wouldn't be able to be at peace until they found her. William went back into Karen's bedroom and searched again, with no luck. He called downstairs. "We need to go find Karen. She's not in her room!" He could hear the rest of the family scrambling around, looking and calling her name.

Maria was frantically looking around the other bedrooms when she peered outside and could see a small figure standing outside about 50 feet from the cliff. A flash of lightening illumined her blonde hair and she knew immediately that it was Karen. She opened the window and yelled out "Karen!"

Karen didn't turn around, but Maria immediately alerted the others. "I think Karen's outside, near the cliff" as she headed downstairs as fast as she could without falling down the stairs and ran outside. William and Sara were right behind her as she felt the rain pelting down in sheets, soaking her immediately.

As she got closer, she knew it definitely was Karen! "Karen! Karen!" She finally reached her and picked her up. Karen's eyes were open, but she wasn't responding to her mother's voice. Maria held her close and whispered to her "Karen, wake up!" Karen seemed to respond and said "Mommy? Why am I all wet?" She was soaked and shaking from head to toe. Maria knew she was probably sleep-walking. "It's okay, sweetheart, we're going to get you warm. Mommy and daddy are here!" William grabbed her from Maria and they ran into the house to get her out of the rain and warm her up. Karen's lips were almost blue and she was shaking as Sara grabbed several blankets and helped wrap her up. "What on earth was she doing out there?" She sounded almost angry as if she were blaming them.

"Karen must have been sleepwalking. She's only done it one other time." Maria replied, in an equally angry voice. She wasn't in the mood for her mother-in-law's dramatics tonight. Karen was waking up and confused. "Mommy, I'm cold!" She turned to Sara. "Would you mind running a warm bath for her?" She figured if Sara was going to be there, she might as well help out.

"Oh, of course!" Her mother-in-law headed to the bathroom to run the water, while William and Maria both hugged her close to them to give her some body heat.

"I know sweetheart, we're warming you up and we'll get you into a warm bath." Maria told her. William looked scared. "I guess this isn't going away is it?" He whispered quietly. "What do we do?" He asked his wife.

"I don't know. We'll watch her tonight obviously. But we need to get home tomorrow. I hope we can get there with this storm!" Maria was worried about not being able to take the ferry home in the morning.

"We'll figure that out in the morning." William assured her. Karen was starting to be more coherent now and as she was in the bath, she became more aware of her surroundings. "Daddy, I was dreaming about that girl that fell off the cliff. She was calling to me." She said. William looked at Maria, unsure of what to say to her.

"Karen, you were just dreaming and you walked in your sleep, that's all. Are you feeling warm now?" Maria said soothingly. She could tell she was warming up, she just hoped that she didn't catch a cold being out there. She was just glad she was able to find her.

"I'm tired." Karen had warmed up enough and Maria got her into some warm pajamas. "I'm going to put her in our bed tonight, Bill." She didn't care what he thought, but her husband nodded and agreed.

"Definitely. Don't worry, we'll get home tomorrow." He promised Maria. "Even if I have to charter a boat, we'll get home." She could tell that he was regretting coming here now. It wasn't anyone's fault, but suddenly Maria felt as though she should have been more convincing to stay home especially after her experience with Janice.

The rest of the family checked in with Karen who was back to sleep in Maria and Williams' room. "She's resting, but we really should get home as soon as we can tomorrow." William announced to them. His mother looked disappointed, and started to talk about their plans tomorrow before they left. "But, William, we had…." She stopped. "I understand completely. Poor thing." She kissed Karen on the cheek before she left the bedroom. Barbara had finally arrived from her night out and ran up to see what was going on. When William told her, she nodded and didn't seem surprised. "Yeah, she seemed pretty focused on her. What's up with this?"

"Let's not talk about it now, Barb. We'll talk later, okay?" William said gently. Barbara nodded. "K. Good night, sweetie." She kissed Karen on her forehead. By now it was almost midnight and everyone was headed to bed. Maria went to check on Krista again, who was still surprisingly sound asleep, despite all the commotion. "I swear this girl could sleep through an earthquake!" She told William as they got ready for bed.

"Babe, I'm sorry that we came here. I know you didn't want to." William was apologizing, but Maria shook her head. "Bill, we had a good day. This is just something that she's going through and maybe she would have done this at home. We'll get through this. But, I am ready to go home tomorrow." She added.

"We'll get there, storm or no storm." William promised her. With Karen between them, they both drifted off into restless sleep.

William

He laid awake for what seemed an eternity, as he listened to the sound of the downpour of rain being whipped against the windows by the force of the wind. He tried not to think about why his daughter had been sleepwalking, but he was starting to believe what Maria said was true. As much as he didn't want to admit it, maybe Carrie was somehow connected to Karen. Karen, luckily wasn't tossing and turning, probably because she'd worn herself out with her venture out in the rain and the aftermath of everyone fussing over her. He was trying to make a plan for how to get off the island tomorrow if this storm kept up, but exhaustion took over from not sleeping the night before and he fell asleep.

When he woke up, Karen and Maria were no longer next to him and it was light outside, although the wind and rain was still present. He glanced at the clock next to the bed. 8:45. He usually never slept past seven, so he figured he needed it. The smell of bacon and coffee was enough to get up and head downstairs. On his way, he peeked into Krista's room. She was just waking up and opening her eyes. "Hi, daddy!" She said as she jumped out of bed and ran over to him. William picked her up to hug her. "How'd you sleep sweetheart?" He was worried that she might have woken up last night because of the scare with Karen.

"Good, daddy. I had a nightmare though, but then it went away." Krista told him. William put her down and helped her pick out an outfit. He was curious about what she'd said.

"What do you mean, the nightmare went away, Kris?" He asked as he went through her suitcase and picked up a rainbow colored sundress. She shook her head. "No, daddy, I don't want that one!" She insisted. She picked up a pink sweatshirt and little jeans. "This is what I want!" William laughed. "Ok, good choice! Kris, how did the nightmare just go away?"

She looked thoughtful for a moment. "I was scared in my nightmare and I woke up and then I felt someone holding me and I went back to sleep." She started to pull her nightgown off and get dressed. He offered to help, but she said, "No, daddy, I can do it myself!" Always the stubborn one, she managed it herself.

"Do you remember who was holding you?" William asked her.

"It felt like Gram Ora's hugs. I know she's not here anymore, but it felt like her. She smelled like flowers." Krista said impatiently. "I'm hungry, daddy!"

William nodded. "Of course. Let's go have some breakfast, it smells good!" But his mind was focused on what she'd told him. She'd obviously been protected by his grandmother, but why not Karen? He wasn't sure if he should tell Maria about it. 'Maybe later,' he thought to himself as they met everyone down at the breakfast table. There was a feast that his mother and Jenna had cooked up; omelets, bacon, pancakes and hash browns along with coffee.

"Nice spread! Thank you for this!" William said as he kissed his wife and gave Karen a hug. "How'd you sleep sweetheart?"

"I liked it in you and mommy's bed, daddy." Karen told him, which set Krista off. "She got to sleep in your bed daddy? That's not fair!" She turned away from him and sat next to Maria, stewing until her stack of pancakes came, then she seemed to forget for the moment. "Just let it go, she'll forget about it, Bill", Maria whispered to him.

As they finished up breakfast, William checked the weather report. It called for rain, but the storm surge was not a problem and the wind had died down. "Looks like you all can head out today." Stuart advised as he came up behind William.

"Good thing. I wasn't sure after last night!" William said. He didn't want to get into a discussion about last night with him. Or anyone else, including his mother. He called the Block Island transportation number to find out the ferry schedule that day. The woman on the phone advised that ferries weren't running until the afternoon; the first ferry would be at 2:30, weather permitting. "What does that mean?" William asked.

"There's still some more weather that's supposed to come in later today, much like last night's storm. If that happens, we'll have to cancel that trip." She told him. "But if it's cancelled, you'll get credit for the tickets on the next ferry."

"Thank you. I need four one way, two adults, two children for the 2:30 ferry." William booked them with his credit card over the phone. He'd been hoping to leave earlier, but hopefully the weather would hold out and they could leave at 2:30.

When he let Maria know, she just nodded. "Karen's been so quiet this morning. More than usual. I just hope we can get on the 2:30 ferry." She said. He could tell that she was worried. It was still grey and raining outside so they focused on indoor activities to entertain the girls and themselves until it was time to head to the ferry.

Sara and Barbara spent the late morning with the twins playing games, while Maria and William packed up to get ready to leave. "How was Karen this morning when she got up? Did she remember anything?" William asked his wife. He wanted to get off the island before anything else could happen, including Karen seeing someone near the cliff.

"No. She was surprised that she was in our bed because it doesn't happen often, but I just told her it was because she wanted to be there. She didn't say anything else." Maria told him as she packed up the twins' suitcases. "Did Krista say anything?"

William nodded. "I poked my head in and she was just waking up. She said something about having a nightmare, but then someone 'gave her a hug' and made her feel better. She said she thought it was Gram Laura. She smelled her perfume, Maria." Maria turned pale all of a sudden. "I don't know what's going on, but we can't get off this island fast enough!" She looked panicked.

"Babe, it's fine. Calm down. We'll be leaving, don't worry. They said as long as the weather isn't too bad, the ferry will be running." William said the words and at the same time hoped the same as his wife.

Luckily the ferry was still running that afternoon despite the intermittent showers. "It might be a rough ride folks, so please stay inside during the trip." The captain of the ferry made the announcement. There were very few people on the ferry and they were able to sit comfortably inside and the twins were actually able to lie down across seats and take a nap. The captain of the ferry wasn't wrong. It was a rough ride the entire way and he could tell Maria was feeling queasy from the waves. She laid her head down in his lap midway through the trip. He was drinking a beer, hoping it would relax him after the weekend. It did take the edge off but he couldn't wait to get to their car once they were docked.

Finally, they arrived back at Point Judith and headed to their car in the adjacent parking lot with the girls still groggy from their nap. "Just get the girls in their car seats and I'll get the suitcases and put them in the trunk." William told Maria. By now, it was raining again. Not just drizzling, but a downpour. "Ahhh!" Maria was getting soaked from the rain putting the twins in the car, as William made his couple of trips with the suitcases. When they finally settled into the old Maverick, they were soaking wet from head to toe. Maria was frantically trying to fix her wet hair that had become a rat's nest on her head. William was wiping his face from the raindrops that were still running down his face. He looked at her and suddenly burst out laughing. "Some vacation, huh? I know how to pick em!"

Maria stopped messing with her hair and suddenly started laughing along with him. "Well, it was nice there, Bill. The house was amazing and we had a good time yesterday with the girls." "It was fun there, daddy! Can we go back again?" Karen asked. "Yeah, I liked it there!" Krista echoed her sister.

"We'll see." William said vaguely, knowing that the house was sold and glad that they wouldn't have to go back for any reason. The rain continued during the 30- minute drive home. He finally pulled up to the house, breathing a sigh of relief that they'd made it home in one piece. Hopefully, Karen would get back in her usual routine at home and they wouldn't be worrying all the time. "Welcome home, girls!" Maria smiled and gave him a hug. "Thank you for coming home early."

"We needed to and I'm glad we did!" William hugged her as they unpacked the car and into the safe haven of home. Just after they walked in the door, the phone range and William dropped the suitcases to answer it. He was glad that he'd gotten to the phone because it was Roberts & Sons calling to offer him a job. The salary was more than he expected and he would be working directly under the VP in the company as an accounts manager. There were also opportunities to get his real estate license and he couldn't believe his luck! The girls had gone upstairs, but Maria was waiting right next to him.

"Guess what, honey? I'm the new accounting manager for Roberts & Sons!" He swept her up in his arms and swung her around, giddy with excitement and relief. "I guess there's a reason for everything, right? I mean, if I wasn't home, I would have missed that call!"

Maria

Maria was glad that William was finally employed after the endless interviews he'd gone on in the past month. She couldn't help but think about what the psychic had told her before their trip about William getting the job offer from the first interview. The next few weeks were busy with William starting his new job; getting up early and working late.

She'd taken the job as a case manager, although she wasn't feeling challenged. The twins were in pre-school a few days a week. William always had something to talk about when he came home at the end of the day, while she felt dull, with the exception of taking care of the girls and shuffling them to pre-school. Whatever had been happening with Karen at the Block Island house suddenly stopped as soon as they got home.

"I guess I should feel happy that everything isn't drama lately, but I feel so, well bored!" Maria mentioned to Steph Martin who'd called to invite her to her housewarming party the following weekend. She was moving into an oceanfront home in South Kingstown. Maria couldn't help but be envious of her, but she knew that Stephanie had worked hard to get there.

"So you'll come? I'm excited to see you and please bring the twins! I can't wait to meet them!" Steph was insistent that it was a family gathering and there would be other children there as well.

"I'll check with Bill's work's schedule, but it's on a Sunday, so the agency is closed that day!" Maria said jokingly. But it was true. Since he'd started this job, he was gone from dawn until dark, Monday through Saturday!

"Okay, so we'll see you next Sunday then?" Steph asked her as William came walking in the door at 7:15. Maria waved at him as she answered. "Yes! I definitely need to get out!" William waved back and made motions 'who are you talking to?'

She mouthed back 'Steph Martin, housewarming party on Sunday. We're going.' He shook his head, but Maria took down the address and the time before she hung up.

"What? Housewarming party? Who is Steph Martin?" William was tired and she decided to not argue with him now, but she knew she wanted to go.

"She's a friend of mine from URI that is having a housewarming party. She and her husband just bought a house in South Kingstown and invited us. We're going." She told him.

William just shook his head. "Okay. Is my mom watching the girls?"

"No, she said we could bring them. Actually she wants to meet them, so they're going. She said other kids would be there as well. Maybe they'll make some new friends, it'll be fun." Maria tried to sound enthusiastic. She could tell that he was tired, so she didn't say anything more and he didn't either. It was as if they were living in different universes right now; she was at home most of the time while he was at work 12 hours a day.

"Sounds like fun." Her husband sounded less than happy about it, but it was settled and she wasn't going to mention it again until next Saturday night, when she'd probably have to remind him.

The next week flew by uneventfully, until Saturday night when William arrived home late; almost 9:00 and Maria could tell that he had been drinking. He was stumbling in the door and Maria was surprised and upset that he'd driven home. "Where have you been?" She was angry and he knew it. "I'm sorry. I went out with Pete Roberts and some colleagues after work for a few drinks. I know I'm late."

"A phone call would have been nice!" Maria wanted to scream at him, but then knew it would fall on deaf ears now. He practically fell into bed and she was wide awake when she heard Karen screaming from her room. She ran into her room and she was sitting up in bed screaming, "No, Carrie, No!" Her eyes were wide open, yet she seemed to look right through her as she tried to comfort her. "Karen, it's okay, mommy's here!" She held her in her arms until Karen finally calmed down. "Mommy, I had a bad dream. Carrie was trying to push me off the cliff into the fire."

"It's just a dream, sweetheart, go back to sleep." Maria reassured her as Karen finally closed her eyes again. She quietly left her and checked on Krista who was sound asleep. She returned to her bedroom, feeling more than annoyed that William was completely passed out. She lay awake for another hour, listening and worrying about Karen and how she'd hoped that everything would fall into place once William started working. She was still waiting.

Maria didn't sleep well, but was used to waking up around 7am with the girls, even on the weekends. William was still asleep and she'd hoped that she'd feel less angry about his drinking and coming home late, but she didn't. She could hear the twins waking up and headed downstairs and went to get them breakfast.

William got up then and came down, reaching out to give her a kiss, but she moved away. "Hey, now. Are you mad at me?" William seemed oblivious to him coming home last night and passing out.

"I was. Now, I'm just getting over it. It's done with. But I do expect you to be ready to go." She snapped at him.

"Ready for what?" William asked. Maria glared at him for a moment. "You don't remember? My friend's housewarming party this afternoon. I told you about it a week ago!" She was suddenly fuming again. She left the kitchen then and William followed her. "Honey, I'm sorry. It won't happen again. I'm just trying to fit in there and.."

"I don't care, Bill! I'm glad that you have a job that you like, but I feel like I'm overwhelmed here! I'm working at a place that I don't like and taking care of the girls myself because you're never home!" She sat down and started to cry. William sat down and put his arm around her. "Maria, we have that party to attend. Let's get my mother to watch the twins and we'll just go to the party by ourselves."

She thought about it for a moment. It would be nice to go by themselves, but she was worried about leaving Karen, especially after last night. Besides, Steph had wanted to meet them, and she had already told her they were coming. *And,* there were going to be other families there, maybe the twins would make some friends. She was hoping they would. Krista did well with the other kids at pre-school, but the teacher mentioned more than once that Karen 'seemed shy' and 'didn't want to do activities with the other children.'

"No, Steph wanted to meet them and they'll be fine. Besides, we probably won't stay that long. I just want to catch up with her." William nodded but she could tell he wished the girls weren't going. It was as if his new job was taking over; he rarely came home before 7pm and then was on the phone most of the night. He was often working on Saturdays as well and receiving work calls even on Sundays. The job that she thought would save them financially had done so, but at a price. She wasn't sure how much longer their marriage would stand up to the strain.

Maria brushed off Bill's attitude and they didn't talk most of the morning and early afternoon until it was time to leave for the party. The girls didn't want any part of dressing alike, although Maria thought it would be cute.

"Mommy, I want that blue dress!" Krista insisted, while Karen wanted a multi-colored sundress. At the end, she threw up her hands. "They'll dress how they want to dress!" She finished getting ready, dressing in a pair of dark jeans and a flowing blue blouse that matched her eyes.

"Bill, are you ready to go? It's almost 3:00, we're supposed to be there around 3:30." Maria called out to him. He came downstairs, dressed in his jeans and button-down light blue shirt. "Does this meet your approval?" He asked, jokingly.

"Yes, you look great!" Maria had to admit, he did. She just wished they could spend more time together and have time to themselves without the girls. Today wasn't the day though. Steph did want to meet them and she had a suspicion that it was the reason she'd been invited in the first place.

"Thanks, babe, so do you!" William looked at her appreciatively. "Wait till we get home tonight." He winked at her and she smiled, kissing him on the cheek. "We'll see." She winked back at him.

"Well let's get going before this gets outta hand!" William winked at her as they piled into the Maverick. William kept talking about buying a new car, but he was waiting for a good deal and didn't want to jinx their financial situation which was just getting to where they could put money in savings again.

Stephanie's new house was nothing short of amazing. It was literally a few steps away from the ocean, near Matunuck Beach, but on a cul-de-sac so that they didn't have the beach traffic that came with living near the beach. The house itself was fairly new and a modern design; smaller than Maria thought it would be. But then, Steph and her husband Tony, didn't have children so the three bedroom house suited them.

The kitchen was an open space to the living area and there was a breakfast bar that they had set up as an actual bar with beer and wine selections. The front of the house had a sliding glass door that led out to a good-sized deck that was large enough for a grill, along with a patio table and chairs that seated eight people. The stairs to the deck led straight out to the beach and there was a huge picture window from the kitchen with an ocean view. The off-white furniture in the living area and pale-blue walls gave the room a beachy feel. Maria felt a tinge of jealousy that her friend had completed her Master's degree and could afford what she considered a luxurious home on the beach. "Wow, this place is great!" Bill whispered to her.

Steph was excited to meet the twins. "Oh my god! Your girls are adorable!" She gushed as she gave her a hug. "This is my husband, Tony." Tony was very tall, and clearly worked out. His biceps were visible as he shook William and Maria's hands. He could have easily passed for a movie star with his dark hair, chiseled face and clear, blue eyes. But he was an investment finance manager at a bank in Boston and Maria could tell that William and Tony had a lot in common. Maybe this party was a good way to get out and meet new people.

"This is Krista", Maria introduced them. "And this is Karen." It was easy to tell them apart from their outfits and the fact that Karen clung to her leg, while Krista said "Hi! Are there any other kids here?" Stephanie laughed. "Hi, Krista! There sure are! My niece, Sabrina is right outside there, with my nephew Kyle. Sabrina is five, so you're right around her age!" Steph pointed out toward the beach where a dark-haired little girl and boy were throwing a beach ball back and forth. Krista looked interested. "Mommy, can I go meet them and play ball?" Maria nodded.

"Of course you can, but please stay out of the water, okay? Stay where I can see you. Take your sister with you." She nudged Karen who was reluctant, but Krista grabbed her hand and Karen followed her outside. Maria felt nervous about them being close to the water, and Steph seemed to understand.

"Don't worry Maria. Sabrina and Kyle have been here several times. Kyle's eight and very responsible. He looks out for his sister and any younger kids. They're my sister's kids. The girls are so beautiful; they look just like you!" Stephanie told her.

"Good thing!" William said jokingly. "They did get their mother's looks!"

Stephanie laughed. "Let me introduce you to everyone." Maria and William met Stephanie's sister, Samantha and brother-in-law, Jeff, as well as a few of her friends that had arrived.

The afternoon turned out to be fun; William was in deep conversation with Tony and several of his friends, Steve and Steph's brother-in-law, Jeff about business and real estate. Maria was enjoying some girl-talk with Stephanie, Samantha and her friend, Janet. Maria started to wish that maybe she should have left the twins at home, because she felt herself worrying and checking on them. Steph noticed and finally said "Maria, they're fine. Don't worry, they're having fun!" And they were. Even Karen seemed to come out of her shell and was running, having fun on the beach with the other kids and her sister.

They enjoyed an informal dinner on the deck with a seafood buffet that Stephanie had catered. Even the twins found something to eat and William whispered to Maria; "Guess I should follow Tony for employment advice!" She noticed he'd been drinking quite a bit during the day and he'd just uncapped another Narragansett beer that Tony handed him.

"You think you need that?" She said in a low voice. She could tell that he was feeling pretty buzzed.

"I'm fine, honey. It's my last one, I promise. I'm having a good time!" William told her. She decided not to bug him anymore, but she made sure not to have another glass of wine in case she needed to drive home. As the evening wore on, it started to get dark and the twins were starting to get cranky. "Mommy, I'm tired." Karen complained, and Krista for once agreed with her twin. "Me too, mommy." Sabrina and Kyle were seated in the living area one on each side of their father, Jeff. All of the men were watching the Patriots game and as Maria motioned to William, he didn't move from his seat as the Patriots scored and all of them stood up to clap and yell at the players on TV. "Yes! We've got this game in the bag!" Tony and William gave each other a high five.

"Looks like those two may have found each other!" Steph said to Maria with a smile. "I'm glad Tony is having a good time. Ever since he left Boston to move here, he hasn't had time to make new friends. He spends so much time commuting during the week and works long hours, we don't get a chance to get out and meet new people."

Maria nodded. "I know what you mean. Bill is the same; works till 7pm and then falls into bed after dinner."

Samantha arrived at the kitchen table at the end of Maria's comment. "Maria, all three of us should get together again soon! Sabrina and Kyle had a great time with the twins today. They're all worn out!" Samantha and Jeff lived a few blocks away.

"Definitely! We only live a few miles away." Maria was glad she came. Krista wandered up to her as she was talking. "Mommy, I'm tired. Kawen is talking about Gam Ora again. Can we go home?"

Maria had hoped they'd get through a night without Karen's 'episodes' but clearly it was time to go. Besides it was past 8:00 and they were used to being in bed around 9:00. "Time to round up Bill and head home! Thanks so much for inviting us, Steph! We should get together again soon!" Maria gave Steph a hug and Samantha as well after getting her phone number so that they could plan to get together soon. "Now to get Bill to leave the party!" She glanced at him with the guys on the couch. She motioned to him, but he didn't see her until she went up to him and said "We need to go. The girls are getting tired." He took another swig of his beer and stood up. "Guess it's time to go, guys. The wife has spoken!" He joked. He wobbled a little as he stood up.

Maria giggled a little as the guys started razzing him about being a 'light-weight," but as they rounded up the twins, and put them in their car seats, she insisted that she drive. "Bill, you drank too much. I've a had two glasses of wine over about 6 hours. Just let me drive." It had started raining and there was a loud clap of thunder.

William became upset. "Babe, I told you, I only had a few beers. I'm fine to drive! Trust me, I wouldn't if I weren't sure! Especially with my precious cargo here." He nodded to her and pointed to the girls in the back.

Maria opened her mouth to argue further, but the girls were complaining in the back seat. "I wanna go home!" Krista was whining and Karen echoed her sister as usual.

"Okay. Just get us home safe." Maria knew that he wouldn't budge, and the more time spent trying to convince him that she should drive, the more time they'd still be sitting in the driveway.

William

The rain turned into a downpour as soon as they left the party and he was starting to regret his insistence on driving home. Maybe he'd overestimated his ability to drive tonight. Despite the windshield wipers on full blast, it was hard for him to see, but he always hated to admit that he was wrong.

"Bill, put on some music. It will help us all relax." Maria commented, her hands clenched nervously in her lap. William nodded and put on a local station. "Midnight Confessions" came on. Soon, he and Maria were singing along as the girls quieted down and fell asleep. "Nothing like oldies to get the little ones to sleep, right?" He glanced over at his wife who was singing along with the radio. He joined in, "Midnight confessions, when I tell all the world that I love you!" He glanced over and pointed at Maria when she suddenly screamed, "Bill! Look out! That car is coming right toward us!" He immediately faced forward to realize that the car headed toward them was in their lane.

"What the hell? What are they doing?!" William pulled the car to the right hoping that he was far enough over to avoid the oncoming vehicle. But the headlights kept coming their way. "What are they doing? What's going on??" William pulled the car further to the right, with the right front and rear tires off the pavement, hoping to avoid a head on collision.

"Bill! He's headed right for us!" Maria was panicking now.

"I know! I'm trying to get out of their way! What is wrong with this guy!" William was starting to panic now as he glanced in the rear view mirror at his toddler girls now sleeping in their car seats.

" He's going to hit us!" Maria screamed just before the oncoming car hit the drivers' side of the car, causing it to flip over several times. It happened so fast, but being turned upside down in the car several times seemed to go in slow motion at the same time. All he could hear was screaming; Maria, the twins and himself. He blacked out for what seemed a few seconds and discovered the Maverick came to rest right side up. William sat still for a moment trying to take it all in. He was still alive. He frantically reached for his wife in the passenger seat. She seemed to be fading in and out of consciousness; her eyes were open and then closed again. He undid her seatbelt, thankful that they'd been wearing them. There was smoke coming from the engine that was billowing up into the sky and he knew they needed to get out.

"Maria! Wake up! C'mon, we've gotta get out of here!" He shook her and she woke up and automatically, reached for the door handle, pushing hard. "It's stuck!" She was holding her arm in a strange way. "I can't move my arm, Bill!" He looked her over to make sure she wasn't bleeding. "I'm going to get you out!" He pushed on his door and was thankful that he was able to open his door.

William could feel the blood trickling down his forehead as he hurried to the passenger side to get his wife out. Once she was out of the car, Maria held her right arm to her side and immediately tried to open the back doors to get the girls out with her left arm. But the door handle to Karen's side was mangled from the roll over and she couldn't open it. "Bill! The door won't open!" She continued pulling as hard as she could on the right passenger door, as William rushed to the left back door. It was smashed in as well. "We've got to get them out from the front of the car!" William shouted to his wife. The smoke pouring from the engine was so thick it was filling the car and he knew it was only a matter of time before the car would be on fire. He needed to get the girls out! "Maria, run, get away from the car!" He yelled to her.

"But, Bill! We have to get them out!" She was panicking now. William nodded, "I will! Just get away from the car! I'll get them out!" He gave up working on the crushed door handles of the rear doors and started crawling through the smoke-filled car to unstrap Krista from her car seat behind the driver's side. "Krista! Karen! It's daddy! Can you hear me?"

"Daddy...it's smoky!" Krista whimpered. She was struggling, trying to unbuckle herself. But she couldn't reach the release button on the straps.

"Daddy's gonna get you out of here! Hang on, Krista!" "Karen, Karen!" William was yelling out to his other daughter. She didn't make a sound and as he came closer, her eyes were closed. He could tell that she was unconscious despite the smoke that was filling the interior of the car. "Karen! Wake up!" He reached toward her to touch her face, wake her up, but he couldn't reach her.

He could hear someone behind him. "Hey, are you all okay? Do you need help?" It was a man's voice and when he looked behind him, he saw a man about his age with a deep cut above his forehead. It was the driver of the car that had hit them. As he came closer, William thought he'd met him before, he looked so familiar. And his breath reeked of alcohol.

There were a million thoughts going through his head including 'why were you driving down the middle of the road!" But he just said, "Yes! My daughters are in here! We need to get them out!" The man ran over to the other side of the car where Karen was and pulled on the handle. "It's stuck!"

Suddenly, there were flames shooting out of the engine and William finished unbuckling Krista who was crying and he was able to grab her and pull her through the front seats and out the driver's door. "Hurry! Go through the front!" He yelled to the man who was still struggling with the back door, as he carried Krista over to Maria who held onto her with her left arm.

"Get Karen! Get Karen!" She screamed at him as he headed back toward the car that was now in flames. The other man was struggling with the front passenger side door and William dove in through the driver's side door and began wrestling with Karen's car seat fastening button that wouldn't budge. "Come on!" William yelled as he could feel the flames coming toward him in the front seat. He attempted to unlatch the car seat from the seat belts, but they were starting to melt because of the heat of the flames. "Karen! Karen!" He screamed at her, but she was still unconscious. The driver of the other car tried to pull the other back door open to help him, and William pushed on the door, but it wouldn't budge. "NO!" William started to realize that there was no way to get his daughter out of this burning car and it was killing him; emotionally and literally as the flames got hold of his shirt as he was still pulling at the car seat with Karen in it.

The other man grabbed him from behind and pulled him out of the burning car, and threw him on the ground, rolling him around to put out the flames on his shirt. He couldn't feel any pain now. "It's going to explode, man! There's nothing else we can do!" The driver of the other car yelled at him as William got up from the ground and tried to go toward the car that was engulfed in flames now. Just as the man grabbed him, the car exploded and the shards of flying metal and debris from the car flew toward them.

"NO!!!!!" William screamed as he realized that Karen was still in there; she was gone. He couldn't save her and it was as if everything went into slow motion now as the fire trucks, police cars and ambulances arrived on the scene. But not soon enough. Not soon enough to save Karen. He remained on the ground, until EMTs picked him up and put him on a gurney to the ambulance. He'd heard about people that had out of body experiences and thought they were ridiculous until now. He felt as though he were floating and watching what was happening from above. He could see Maria and Krista being checked over by EMTs near the ambulance. Maria was crying and bending over him, but he couldn't move or say anything. He still couldn't feel any pain and he was glad because from what he could see, his arm was burned pretty badly. He could hear his father's voice now. "William. You tried to save her. You need to fight to be there for your other daughter, for Maria now."

"I can't. I failed her!" William insisted. Then he could feel himself being lifted up and all he could see was a bright light that surrounded him. "It's not your time, William. You need to stay longer. I miss you and we will see each other soon enough." It was Gram Laura's voice. He could make out an image of woman but the light was too bright and he couldn't see her clearly. "Wait, Gram! Wait for me!" William called out to her, but the light was dimming and suddenly he was aware that he was lying down with an oxygen mask on his face; his arm was in excruciating pain, and there was an older nurse standing over him. "William? Can you hear me?"

He nodded, wondering if she was real. He nodded, "Yes." His voice was muffled by the oxygen mask. He was suddenly aware of the excruciating pain from his left arm. He reached over and found his upper arm covered in gauze. "William, you were in a car accident. Your arm has third degree burns. We're giving you some medicine for the pain now. He looked further down his arm to find an IV needle as the nurse added some liquid to the IV. "My wife, my daughters, are they okay?" He managed to ask as he became groggy from the pain medication.

"Your wife and your daughter are okay. Get some rest and someone will be in to talk to you shortly." The nurse told him as he faded off again. Only this time, he was present. Not floating outside his body, but he knew. He'd seen the car. He knew. Karen was in that car and he couldn't get her out in time. His drug induced dream recreated the explosion of the car and his anguish knowing he couldn't get her out and he was awake screaming out for his daughter, tearing off the oxygen mask on his face. "Karen! Karen!" The nurse and a doctor came running into his room as he was sitting up in bed yelling her name.

William stared at them as the monitors measuring his heart rate and blood pressure were making noise, announcing that all was not well with his vitals. "Please tell me. I need to know. Where are my daughters?"

The young doctor, probably not much older than himself sat down next to him in a chair. "Mr. Carson, I'm Dr. McDaniels. I've been treating you, your wife and your daughter since you came into the hospital this evening. Your wife and your daughter, Krista are fine. Maria has a sprained arm and a slight concussion and Krista had no injuries at all. They're both fine to leave the hospital today. You have third degree burns to your upper arm, but with some pain medication and perhaps some skin grafting, you'll be fine."

The doctor paused for a moment and William found himself holding his breath. "Your other daughter, Karen, unfortunately, did not survive." William knew now that he wasn't dreaming; this was real. He was hoping that he'd dreamt the whole thing; that Maria and the girls would be there next to him in the car as they were driving. But it was real.

Tears were streaming as he asked, "Can I see my wife? Is she well enough to come and see me? My daughter?" He suddenly felt faint and laid back on the pillow. The room was spinning around and he could hear a flurry of noise again and the noisy beeping of those monitors again. "I've gotta get through this! It's real, I need to face it!" He told himself and he managed to open his eyes again.

"Of course. Your daughter Krista is being discharged as we speak. However, your wife is still in shock and we'd like to keep her overnight. She does have a fracture of her left arm and she will be fine. However, her emotional state is very unstable right now. We're going to keep her and if there isn't an improvement, we may need to move her to our psychiatric unit for further observation and treatment. Your mother and sister are in the waiting room as well. Would you like to see them?" Dr. McDaniels informed him.

"Please…I need to see them!" William felt so tired and weak, but he needed someone familiar, he needed his Maria, his Krista. Dr. McDaniels opened the door and called to the nurse to bring them in. His mother, sister and daughter came rushing into the room all at once. "Daddy!" Krista came running to his side immediately. "Daddy, you okay?" She pointed to his left arm wrapped in gauze. He tried not to cry as he grabbed her with his good arm and gave her a hug. "Daddy's fine, sweetheart, just a boo-boo that's all!" He minimized. His mother's eyes were bloodshot and tears were streaming down her face as she hugged him. "Thank god you're okay. You're going to be just fine. We're going to get through this." She sounded as if she were trying to convince herself, but having his mother there was suddenly just what he needed at that moment. Barbara was teary- eyed as well and gave him a hug. "Looking good for a car accident, big brother." She joked with him. He couldn't help but laugh, but after a few minutes, it was becoming all too real that Karen was gone. It was what they weren't saying and they knew. He knew that they knew. "Mom, I'm not sure how long they'll keep me here. Hopefully I'll get out tomorrow, but the doctor told me that Maria…."

"William, please don't even think about this right now. I'll take Krista home with me and she'll be just fine." She pulled Krista to her as if she were worried about her disappearing and kissed her forehead. "She can stay with me as long as she needs to." Her eyes started to fill with tears again and she brushed them away. "You'll be home soon and so will Maria." She nodded as if that was the end of the discussion.

"I'll be home from school for break in a few weeks. I can help with anything you need, Bill. Really." Barbara said earnestly. Krista gravitated toward his sister and was holding her hand. "Daddy, are you coming home tonight?" Krista asked him. William was shocked and thankful that aside from a slight bruise on her cheek she had no other injuries.

"No, sweetheart. Mommy and daddy need to stay here overnight, but you'll get to spend some time with Auntie Barb and Grammy, okay?" William tried to keep himself from letting tears spill over while looking at his daughter. Did she know? She hadn't said one word about Karen.

"We'll go to grammys. That'll be fun! Won't it Kawyn?" Krista said, turning her head as if she were speaking to her twin. His mother glanced at William, unsure if she should say something, but William shook his head to her 'don't say anything yet.' He mouthed to his mother. He was concerned, but she seemed physically fine. "Daddy, Kawyn says she wants to go to grammy's with me. She can go can't she?" Krista asked again. William nodded, and decided to just go along with it.

"Sure, sweetheart, of course she can!" William tried to act as though everything was normal; that Karen was right there, as Krista seemed to believe that she was. "Give daddy a hug, and be good for your grammy, okay?" Krista gave him a hug and nodded. "Daddy, you need to give Karen a hug too!" She insisted. William reached out to an invisible Karen and pretended to hug her. "Be good for your grammy, Karen." He said softly with tears in his eyes. He motioned to Barbara to take Krista out of the room while he talked to his mother.

"Mom, she must be in some kind of shock. I'll give you Dr. Welch's number to schedule an appointment with her. Just let her know what's going on and hopefully you can get her in tomorrow. I doubt I'll be here more than a few days." William told her. He'd read about twins having a special connection and maybe that was what was happening now. He was still expecting Karen to come into the room with Krista and he was an adult that understood death.

His mother looked somewhat unnerved but nodded. "I'll call Dr. Welch when I get home. But I think you're right. We're all still trying to take this in. Barb and I will take good care of her. Just worry about getting healed." William gave his mother a hug. "I put you on the contact list to talk to staff about how Maria is doing, mom. I'll try to keep you updated, but they will be able to tell you if you call."

After his mother left, William shut his eyes and tried to rest. There was a knock at the door and he opened his eyes, expecting to see a nurse come in. Instead was a tall, dark-haired man with a slightly scruffy beard. It only took a moment to recognize him; he was the driver who'd caused the accident! William sat straight up and narrowed his eyes. "What are *you* doing here?" He asked suspiciously. Why wasn't this guy arrested last night? He didn't have much recollection after the car exploded, but he would never forget his face. It was the driver of the car that killed Karen.

Maria

It was as if she were watching a movie in slow motion. There was a sudden recognition of what was happening; she'd dreamed it long ago after her parents died. She'd been watching from the back seat what had happened. Now she was living it. And there was nothing she could do to stop it.

The accident, the struggle and panic to get out of the car, the pain in her arm. The sounds of her daughters screams as the smell of smoke filled the car. The relief that she felt when William brought Krista to her, and the terror building up as William and the other man struggled to get Karen out of the car as the flames grew. She thought she could see Karen headed toward her and was putting Krista down, ready to run to her when there was a thundering noise with flames shooting in every direction. There were loud screams coming from everywhere. Then she realized she was the one screaming. "Mommy! Mommy! I'm scared!" Krista was crying. Maria knew she needed to hold it together for her daughter and immediately stopped screaming as the tears poured down her cheeks. 'They got her out! I know they did!' she said out loud. She held Krista tight in her arms, "shhhh, sweetheart, it's okay! They got Karen out!" Maria pressed Krista's face into her shoulder and turned around so that Krista couldn't see the burning car. She kept waiting for them to bring Karen to her. She could hear the driver of the other car yell as he rolled William on the ground to put out the flames on his arm. Maria thought she was imagining the sound of sirens in the distance, but to her surprise, an ambulance pulled up seconds later and several EMT's jumped out.

One of the young men rushed over to her and Krista. "I'm Eddie. What's your name sweetheart?" He focused on Krista initially. "I'm Krista. My sister isn't okay, Eddie." She said pointedly. "Can you help her?" Eddie nodded at Krista. Maria motioned to him to speak to her outside of Krista's earshot. Eddie moved away from Krista for a moment. "I'm her mother, Maria Carson. We're okay. Really, right girls?" Maria turned to Krista. "Mommy! Kawyn's not here!" She insisted. Eddie looked confused, looking at them and then toward the burning car. "Mrs. Carson! Your daughter…"

Just as he started to tell Maria that her other daughter was still in the car, a man with dark hair came running up to them. Maria recognized him immediately. It was a face she'd never forget, the man who'd raped her back in college! Dan Ahearn was standing in front of her now! She felt her legs give out from underneath her and everything went dark. She awoke while being carried onto the ambulance on a gurney. "What is Dan doing here? Where's my husband? Where's my daughters?"

"Maria! Can you hear me? She remembered he was the EMT from the ambulance. Where was Dan? Was he coming to get her? She felt terrified! "Dan! He was there! I remember! What's he doing here?" Maria kept asking.

"Maria, stay with me. There's no one here named Dan. We're on the way to the hospital. Your husband and daughter are on their way as well." Eddie's voice was soothing and the next thing she knew she was being transferred into the emergency room at South County hospital. She was in the triage where she was in the middle of getting her vitals checked when she spotted Krista and then William going past into another room. Maria tried to sit up and started calling after them. "Krista! Bill! Karen!" She struggled to move as the nurse next to her assisted in holding her in place. "Maria, you need to be still right now. We'll give you updates on your daughter and husband shortly." Her voice was calm, but suddenly Maria asked where Karen was. "Where's Karen? Where's my other daughter? Surely she must be here!" She began struggling to get out of bed again and the nurse gave her an injection of Ativan to help calm her. "Maria, we're doing all we can for you and your family. I just gave you something to help you relax okay?"

Maria's mind flashed back to the accident. She remembered William struggling to get Karen out. Maybe the EMT's had helped her get out and she hadn't seen it happen. Yes, that must be and Karen was now in the hospital. She was starting to feel drowsy and fell back against the pillow. She was vaguely aware of the noise going on in the background, but it eventually faded and she could hear a child's voice. "Mommy, mommy, where are you?" Maria was standing in the hallway of the hospital and there was a misty fog that surrounded her and made it hard to see. "Karen? Is that you?" She kept looking but she couldn't see her.

"Mommy. I can't find you. I'm here!" She kept hearing her voice. "Baby, I'm trying to find you. Where are you?" She kept looking through the fog, and suddenly the fog started to dissipate and she could see Karen's small figure and her blonde hair. "I see you, Karen! Stay right there!" She began running toward her but suddenly Karen disappeared. "Karen! Where are you?" Maria was yelling now.

A familiar voice came through although Maria couldn't see her yet. "I'll take good care of her. Karen's with me now." It was Gram Laura's voice. "Gram Laura! Help her come back! Please!" Maria was begging now. She couldn't see her, but she could feel Laura's touch on her cheek. "She's already here. She can't come back but she's always looking out for you, William and especially Krista."

"No! She can't go yet! I didn't get to kiss her goodbye! She can't go yet!" Maria was screaming to Gram Laura. "I love you, mommy." Karen suddenly appeared in front of her kissed her on the cheek. Maria reached out to her, but she was gone. "Karen! Come back! Come back!" She kept calling.

"Maria? Mrs. Carson?" Someone was shaking her shoulder. She opened her eyes to see a stranger. Where was she again? The hospital? 'It must be the nurse,' she thought to herself.

"She was just here! Didn't you see her? Karen was just here!" Maria kept insisting. "I need to go find her! I feel fine, I just need to get up and go find her!" She struggled to get out of bed, but as she swung her right arm she cried out in shock at the sharp pain. " Maria, look at me. Focus. I'm Katharine, your nurse. You have a severe sprain that's why you're in pain. You won't be able to use that arm for at least a few days, but it should heal just fine." Katharine looked over at the other woman seated in a chair next to Maria's bed. "This is Sherry Myers. She's a social worker here at the hospital. Is it okay if I leave you here with her for a few minutes? She needs to speak with you." Maria nodded. "Is she going to tell me where Karen is?" She whispered.

"She's going to talk with you about Karen, yes." Katharine nodded, looking sad as she left the room. Sherry pulled her chair close to Maria's bedside. She was very petite with short blonde hair and a pretty face that probably looked even more so when she was smiling. But she wasn't now. "Maria, I need to talk with you about your daughter Karen. I know that you were at the accident when it happened, but sometimes when something traumatic happens, the brain goes into protective mode."

"What do you mean? I know that Karen got out! I saw her!" Maria insisted.

"You wanted to believe that she did, Maria. Like I said, trauma often tricks our brain into a different outcome or scenario because reality is too difficult to comprehend at that time.

"You don't know what you're talking about! I remember the accident. Me, Bill and the girls got out. We're all here at the hospital." Maria insisted. What was this woman talking about? She'd just seen Karen a few minutes ago! She was in the hallway!

"Maria, your daughter Krista and your husband are here. Your daughter Karen didn't make it. She died in the car." Sherry spoke softly. "I'm very sorry."

"No, she didn't!" Maria started raising her voice and a security guard poked his head in the door. "Everything okay in here?" He asked.

"Everything's fine, thanks" Sherry told him and put her hand on Maria's non-injured arm. The security guard nodded and closed the door behind him. "I'm sorry for the interruption, Maria. Go ahead with what you were saying."

"I was standing in the hallway and I saw her standing there. It was hard to see, there was some kind of foggy haze. She was…she was with Gram Laura…" Maria stopped. 'How could she be with Gram Laura? Gram Laura is dead,' she thought.

"Who's Gram Laura?" Sherry inquired. She could tell that Maria was starting to realize that Gram Laura wasn't physically there and she was probably dreaming.

"Gram Laura. She's my husband's grandmother. She died late last year. How could I have seen her and Karen though?" Maria suddenly remembered what Karen had been saying. 'Goodbye, Mommy.' And Gram Laura had said she'd take care of her. She hadn't been dreaming though. It was the way her mother had contacted her in the past, along with Gram Laura and her father on occasion. She realized she'd been really blind all this time. Psychic blind. She knew now that Karen was gone. "Oh my god. She was saying goodbye, just like my mom. Karen's really gone." She could feel the tears running down her face, but she felt like she was frozen, unable to move to brush them away.

"Maria, I'm so sorry. I know this is probably the hardest thing you've had to deal with in your life." Sherry began. 'She has no idea, but it's close.' Maria thought as she tried to think of how she was going to get through the rest of this day and the rest of her life without Karen. "Krista! How is Krista doing?" She was suddenly horrified by the thought that Krista had died as well.

"Krista is fine. She's actually being released tonight. Your husband will need to stay a few extra days, so we contacted your mother in law and sister in law to take care of Krista." Sherry was glad to be able to give her some good news.

241

"What about me? When can I leave?" Maria asked. She was starting to feel the panic rising again. What if she was here all alone? Being alone was one of the worst things she could think of right now.

"That's why I'm talking to you. We feel like you might need a few extra days just to adjust to what's happened." Sherry said quietly. The bottom line was they thought she needed observation given that she had been traumatized and her belief that her daughter was still alive all this time. She was going to be monitored overnight and then going to the psychiatric unit for observation. Sherry couldn't imagine going through what Maria had just witnessed, but based on what Maria had told her, she felt that it was better to keep her than have her go home and then fall apart.

"What do you mean? Adjust? Like I'm going to adjust in a few days to the fact that my daughter died!" Maria was getting angry now.

"We're just concerned that because of what's happened it would be better for you to start on some medications that would help you cope with the trauma." Sherry told her gently, although she knew that Maria wasn't going to make this easy.

Maria knew that she was going to be stuck here for at least a few days. She was exhausted and just wanted to sleep, too tired to argue any longer. "I just want to see my husband and daughter soon."

Sherry agreed. "We'll have them visit you as soon as they're able to, Maria." She assured her.

Maria just nodded and turned her head. She wanted to escape from the nightmare she seemed to be living in now. Sherry left and gave an update to Katharine. "I let her know she wouldn't be leaving tomorrow.

She seems very vulnerable right now. Her daughter and husband can visit once they are able to." Katharine just moved on to the next patient nodding her head as she left.

For the first time since she'd arrived at the hospital, she was awake and all alone. She wasn't sure if she welcomed the silence. She was grateful for not hearing doctors and nurses scurrying around her, but now she was alone with her thoughts and the realization that Karen was gone. It was too much to think about. She finally fell asleep from the medication and emotional exhaustion.

It seemed as though she'd just closed her eyes when the nurse knocked on the door and came in. Light was streaming in from the windows and she looked up at the clock. She was shocked to see it was 8:00 in the morning. "Good morning, I'm sorry to wake you, but I have some visitors that want to see you." The nurse came into the room. It wasn't Katharine and Maria was glad. She'd been nice enough, but there was something condescending about her that she didn't like. "Really?" Maria sat up, wondering who was here.

Her mother in law along with Barbara and Krista walked in the door. "Mommy!" Krista ran to her. She looked physically fine and Maria was amazed and grateful that she didn't have any injuries. "Maria, how're you feeling, dear?" Sara's eyes were puffy and red from crying. Maria felt another wave of tears just watching her mother-in-law.

"Okay, I guess. Hi, sweetheart!" Maria greeted Krista who immediately demanded to know what was wrong with her arm. "Mommy's arm needs some help right now, but she'll be better soon."

243

Sara gave a simple explanation that Krista seemed okay with for now. "Kawyn's here too, mommy." Krista told her.

Maria felt like the wind had been sucked out of her lungs and it took her a minute to regroup, while Sara shook her head at Krista. "Mommy, she's right here. Give her a hug too." Maria knew she had to help Krista and pretended to give a hug but then felt the tears coming again without warning. Sara motioned to the nurse outside and asked that she watch Krista for a moment so she could talk to Maria.

"Krista's still a little confused, honey. I'm going to take care of her until you and William can come home okay? Don't worry. She'll be fine." Sara assured her.

Maria started crying. "How is Bill doing? I wish I could talk to him! I just can't believe that she's gone. Is Krista okay?" She knew that Krista could probably still see her sister and that was what was helping her through this initial shock, but she knew it would probably continue.

"As you can see, she's still pretending Karen is here. We'll work through it." Sara tried not to cry in front of Maria, but a few stray tears broke through. "We'll take her to see Dr. Welch. Just focus on yourself now, sweetheart." Sara gave her a hug.

Maria was unable to hold back and began sobbing hysterically, while Sara just sat and hugged her. "I'll be home soon, I promise." Maria told her. Sara didn't say anything. Did she know something that Maria didn't know? "I'll let Krista come in and say her goodbyes. We'll visit soon." Sara seemed vague which made Maria start to question when they were going to discharge her. She opened her mouth to ask when Krista came back into the room and was hugging her. "Mommy, I want you to come home with us." She whined.

Maria tried to keep from crying. "Sweetheart, you'll see me tomorrow. You go have fun with grammy tonight!" She tried to infuse some enthusiasm into her voice. Sara gave her a hug before leaving.

As Sara left, Maria suddenly felt more alone and depressed than after her parents had died. "I don't know if I can do this." She said out loud.

William

The man who had caused the accident did not seem intimidated by William's animosity. "Mr. Carson, I can tell that you recognize who I am, so I won't state the obvious. My name is Stanley Ahearn. Let me start off by saying how truly sorry I am for your loss as well as your injuries." He paused a moment, as though he were expecting a response from William. The lump in William's throat grew and tears threatened to spill out so he bit back telling Stanley to get the hell out of there! He simply nodded.

"We both know that my careless driving was partly the cause of the accident," Stanley continued.

"Partly? How about THE cause of the accident! AND the fact that you had been drinking! Your breath reeked of alcohol! Don't even try to deny it!" William was unable to keep quiet any longer and his anger was fueled by the nerve of this stranger who showed up after killing his daughter.

"You're right. I had been drinking that night. I wasn't obliterated, but I definitely shouldn't have been behind the wheel." Stanley admitted calmly. His collected demeanor was making William suspicious. What was this guy up to?

"How is it that you aren't in jail right now?" William snapped at him. "Last time I checked, drunk driving is against the law!"

"I'm surprised by that myself, Mr. Carson. The police did talk to me at length after the accident. Apparently, they didn't suspect me of being under the influence. It is interesting that you're talking about drunk driving though. As I can recall, you had a few yourself." Stanley said pointedly.

"What do you mean? How dare you accuse me of drunk driving?" William began to protest, but he knew Stanley was right. He had quite a few drinks, too many to be driving. But it had been Stanley's car that had caused him to go off the road!

Stanley just smiled calmly and folded his arms across his chest. "You know exactly what I'm talking about, William. The breath smell test works both ways." He waited for William's response. William knew there was no point in arguing, so he just nodded.

"So why exactly are you here? I'm sure it wasn't just to give your condolences." William said snidely. Suddenly, he knew why Stanley seemed so familiar! He looked just like Maria's ex-boyfriend from college. What was his name? Dan! That was it! Dan Ahearn! Maybe this guy changed his name? "Before you answer that, tell me who you really are!" William insisted.

"I already did." Stanley looked amused.

"No, I recognize you from college. You went to the University of Rhode Island, Dan! Who do you think you're fooling? Isn't it a coincidence that you happened to hit our car? With Maria in it." William raised his voice, as his mind started to concoct scenarios about Dan trying to get Maria back.

"I did not go to that college and I've never met you. I live in California and am only here to close on some property that I bought in Rhode Island. My brother is Dan. He's my twin, in fact." Stanley informed him. "Dan did go to URI for a few years, but moved out to California. Anyway, I believe you wanted to know why I'm here."

William nodded, surprised by the information. So this Dan had a twin. How fitting! It explained why he recognized Stan at least. "Go on."

"The police will be investigating this accident and definitely be interviewing you, sooner than later. The last thing I need is to have you telling police I'd been drinking or that I caused the accident. I came here to see if there was some kind of arrangement we could work out. That will benefit both of us. For example, I'm guessing that coming into some money is something that would benefit you."

"What makes you think that? You don't know me!" William said, suddenly feeling defensive about his financial status.

"The car you were driving for one thing. I doubt you left the BMW at home." Stanley said mockingly.

William felt his face flush. "Okay, so I wouldn't say no to some extra income. Not many would! What's your point? I suppose you're going to buy my silence, right?" William laughed. "Sorry, writing me a check for a couple hundred bucks isn't worth keeping quiet for what happened!"

Stanley gave him a strange look. "I think you don't have any idea who I am, do you?"

"I don't know you, except that you caused an accident that led to my daughter's death. Why, are you famous or something? Never heard of you, except that you look like your scumbag twin brother that assaulted my wife back at school before he was kicked out!"

Stanley started to laugh. "Apparently you don't watch movies very often. I'm a director of several movies that have come out in the last few years that have done very well in theaters." His tone sounded condescending now and it pissed William off even more. "I am sorry that my brother assaulted your wife. Believe me, I'm not a fan of his actions then, or now for that matter."

"Ok, Mr. Hollywood, so you're here to pay for my silence? What are these supposed movies that you've 'directed'?"

"Let's see, my latest was "Dark Hall" and "When the Wind Blows", not that I would expect that you would know of them. It seems like you don't get out much." Stanley was just playing games now. Of course William had heard of them! He'd seen both of them with Maria and had liked them. The lead actress, Anna Arquin, was one of his favorites. He was genuinely impressed and had to ask questions.

"Is Anna Arquin really like her character as a person? I really liked her performance in Dark Hall." Dark Hall was a thriller and the character Anna played was a quiet, feminine woman but took on a tougher persona toward the end that William really appreciated.

Stanley suddenly stopped with his power play for a moment to answer. He always liked it when people asked him specific questions about his movies. "She actually is more bad-ass than she is at the beginning of the movie. She had to work on being the passive housewife." He told William.

William found himself getting drawn in and had to regroup suddenly. "So you came here to obviously propose some kind of deal? What's your offer?"

"If you agree to keep quiet about the drinking, and you agree not to file any lawsuits, press charges or talk to the press, I will help you out financially with whatever you need." Stanley said without blinking an eye.

"So basically, you're buying my silence about the fact that you caused the accident. You don't want to be blacklisted in Hollywood." William summarized for him in layman's terms.

Stanley cracked a smile. "I didn't want to put it that way, but basically, yes. Whatever you need for you and your family. I assume you think I'm an uncaring person, but that's not the case. If you recall, I did pull you from that car and rolled you on the ground so you didn't go up in flames along with it. I made a huge mistake by being on the road and I'd give anything to make a different choice now, but I can't. It's not just my reputation that I'm concerned about either. I really want to help you out. I can't imagine losing a child." Stanley sounded genuine for the first time.

"Do you have children, Stanley?" William was curious.

"I do. I have two daughters that are just slightly older than your children." Stanley said quietly.

William was caught between wanting him to pay for causing the accident by being charged with drunk driving and penalized, and the opportunity to finally start his own realty business that he knew he could make successful. After all, he'd been drinking as well. Stanley knew that and could easily give that information to police which would only make his financial situation worse than it already was. His job at Roberts & Sons was paying the bills but with Karen gone and Maria being in a fragile mental state, he wasn't sure what he was going to do. He knew that Stanley's deal would be off the table if it was up to Maria, but he knew that this guy owed him and it could make or break their lives together emotionally and financially.

"So if I were to make an agreement with you, would you be opposed to setting me up with my own real estate agency, with no debt?" William had an idea, but he needed to know if Stanley would only be floating him a loan.

"If that's what you are requesting, then it would be done. No loan, no debt and I would not even be an investor, unless you wanted me to be." Stanley said evenly. He looked surprised that William wasn't looking for a multi- million-dollar pay-out.

"And I would own it. Debt free. Not an investor either. It would be mine. Just like that?" William laughed. "Am I on candid camera?"

"I mean what I say, William. I didn't get successful by bullshitting people. Hollywood is full of creepy cheaters, but only keeping your word is how respect is earned. Even in Hollywood." Stanley was candid. It was true that the world he lived in now was full of that kind of people and he knew that William thought he was a liar. The questions William was asking made him question his own integrity and he liked that. It showed good character.

"I'm interested." William nodded. "What I would want is enough money to open my own realty office, along with start-up costs including utilities, hiring a few employees and business equipment that I would need. I won't be able to afford a lease up front, so either the office space is payed for or leased, your choice. You said that you won't be an investor and I'd want that as part of the deal. I certainly don't want you looking over my shoulder." William said, knowing that he should talk to his wife, but she was not in the right frame of mind and maybe he wasn't either. But this opportunity wasn't one he was going to let pass.

"Done. I'll start looking at properties now that would be suitable and we'll go from there." Stanley replied as casually as though he was going to check out a restaurant to have lunch the next day. "I'll bring the pictures and layout of the space to you if you're in here much longer." He offered.

William was shocked that he had the resources to make this happen. "I doubt that I'll be here longer than a day or so." It was all he could manage to say after Stanley agreed without question.

"Then do we have a deal, William?" Stanley asked.

William knew that he shouldn't be doing this deal without talking to Maria. At the same time, he knew Karen wasn't coming back, but maybe he could make the best out of a horrible tragedy to get back on their feet financially in order to provide the best life for his wife and Krista.

"We do. As long as all my requirements are in place and this will end your involvement in my life, then yes." William said.

"Done. I'll have my attorneys draw up the paperwork in the next few days and get to work looking for potential property." Stanley stood up and headed toward the door. "Just remember, William. Any word to the press, police, or any hospital staff about the accident will immediately cancel anything we discussed today. So when the police come to talk to you, you'd better come up with a plan."

William nodded. "Yeah, I understand." He'd just given away any justice for Karen. He wasn't proud of himself, but he hoped that Maria would eventually understand that something positive for their family would come out of this deal. Stanley going to jail wouldn't bring Karen back.

As if on cue, the police contacted him and wanted him to give information about the accident later that day. He'd just been cleared to be discharged from the hospital when a police officer knocked on the door before entering. "Mr. Carson, I'd like to ask you a few questions about the accident. I'm Detective Sumner. We haven't had a chance to talk to Mr. Ahearn, the driver of the other vehicle, but if you can give us any recollection about the accident, it would be helpful."

"No problem." William agreed. He gave Sumner what he remembered about the accident, leaving out the part about the alcohol on Ahearn's breath and also the fact that he himself had been drinking. It wasn't difficult for him to be vague on details, because he didn't really remember anything except for his injury that happened right before the explosion and then the screams from the car.

"Do you know who hit you?" Detective Sumner asked.

"No, I don't. It was some man that saved me from more severe burns, so whoever it was, I'd thank him for that." William said, hoping that the detective didn't know he'd already talked to Stanley.

"He's Dan Ahearn. Apparently, he was in some trouble back around 5 or 6 years ago, got kicked out of school for assault at URI. I read in the file there was some suspicion that there was rape involved, but the victim denied the charges and they were dropped." Detective Sumner told him.

William had to remember not to correct the detective about the identity, although he wanted to. He wanted to tell him everything, but he knew that at the end of the day, Stanley would have the money for lawyers if needed to protect himself. He had barely enough money to support his family and keep a roof over their head. Suddenly the word 'rape' resonated with him. He knew that Dan had broken into Maria's room and injured her, but what was with the rape accusations? Maria had never said anything about rape. He tried to forget about it, but it was something that was in the back of his mind.

Maria~3 Days Later

Maria's days and nights were starting to blend into each other. Between the medication that she was taking and the vivid dreams, she wasn't sure what was real anymore. Some of the dreams were of Karen who seemed very much alive, others with her mother and Gram Laura all combined to make her feel even more exhausted the next day when the nurse came in to check her vitals.

"Is my husband going to be able to visit me today?" It was the first thing Maria wanted to know every day. William had been there every day since he'd been discharged, the day after the accident. She really needed him now. She could remember that he visited but he'd been very quiet when she'd asked about how everything was going at home.

"You know he'll be coming by around 11:00, Maria. You're being discharged today. You're going home. Remember, the doctor told you this morning." The young nurse named Kate told her. Time seemed to stand still and her memory seemed very foggy lately. The psychiatrist that met with her on a daily basis told her that the new medication she was on was going to help with her depression and cope with the trauma of losing her daughter. But all it really did was was make her feel like a zombie. She was tired most of the time when she was awake. When she was sleeping was when reality came in the form of nightmares

The phone next to her bed rang just then. It was her mother-in-law Sara who put Krista on the phone. Sara had been keeping Krista with her while William was dealing with the funeral services. "She wants to hear your voice." Sara told her and Maria felt a moment of joy followed by guilt for not being able to be there. "Hi, sweetheart! Are you being good for grammy?"

"I am. So is Kawyn. We're being the goodest girls, mommy!" Krista told her. Maria's heart jumped when she heard her say Karen's name. She wanted to ask about why she was mentioning Karen, but she didn't want to bring her name up again because it sent her into an uncontrollable wave of tears. She was probably just dealing with the trauma in her own way.

"I'm glad that you are. Mommy misses you. They told me I'm coming home today!" Maria felt so numb that it was still hard for her to be happy about coming home. "Love you too, mommy." Krista's tiny voice sounded so sweet as Sara got back on the phone. "She keeps acting as though Karen is here, Maria. I'm not sure what to say to her." Sara sounded upset.

"She's probably just adjusting to what's happened." Maria said, trying to remain calm about the situation. "She has an appointment with Dr. Welch coming up."

"Maria. She had her appointment with Dr. Welch. I told you that two days ago." Sara reminded her gently. Maria was silent, feeling foolish that she couldn't recall the conversation. "Oh, yes, that's right." Maria was vague, trying to sound as though she remembered.

"Dr. Welch says she's fine. Krista's just adjusting. She was also a twin and Dr. Welch said that it's normal for twins to have that special connection from the womb." Sara recapped the conversation from yesterday. But to Maria, none of it was familiar. "Is Krista going to come visit with Bill today?" Maria was anxious to see her.

"Maria, we're all going to come today. You're leaving the hospital. Don't you remember?" Sara sounded concerned.

"Oh, yes, that's right. I'll see you all later then." Maria tried to sound happy, but upset that her memory was failing her once again. "Sorry, it must be these medications they've been giving me." Maria felt like she'd been making the same excuses over the last few days. The truth was that she didn't feel much emotion at all. She had hoped that she would hear from Karen, Gram Laura or her mother while she was sleeping which happened when she was stressed. But now there was nothing. Although it scared her at times, she was now wishing for her mother to appear to her. What she really wanted was to see Karen, but with the exception of the night of the accident, she never dreamed or saw her again.

"We'll see you soon, sweetheart! Just be glad you're coming home." Sara tried to sound encouraging but at the same time, she wasn't sure if Maria was ready to come home. The funeral for Karen was tomorrow. Although the doctors had told her and William that she needed to be there, she wasn't so sure she was ready to leave the hospital. She was still in denial.

When William came into her room, Maria was excited to see him. "Bill!" He was smiling, but despite her medicated haze, she could tell that all of this was wearing on him. He had bags under his eyes and had lost at least 10 pounds in the past few days. "Hi, sweetheart, all ready to go?" He gave her a hug, but she could tell that he was tired and just done emotionally. Some of the fog from the medication started to lift and she was starting to feel the emotional weight of what was just beginning for them. "Where's Krista?" She missed her.

"My mother kept her so that we could have some time together alone now that you're 'being sprung'." William said jokingly, but Maria didn't crack a smile. "What's that supposed to mean?" She snapped at him. "Like I wanted to be here, right?" She turned away from him and suddenly the tears were overflowing. 'What is wrong with me?' She was starting to wonder if maybe a longer stay here was warranted. She turned back to William. "I'm so sorry, Bill. I don't know what came over me." He pulled her in for a hug.

"Sweetheart, it's fine. We both need to adjust. We just need to be honest with each other about how we're feeling. Dr. Welch suggested that we do some counseling sessions as a couple and with Krista to help with the adjustment."

After all the individual and group sessions she'd been to in the past few days, the last thing she wanted to do is to do more therapy sessions. But she just wanted to get home. "Mmm hmm. Yeah, we can talk about it later, Bill. Let's just go home."

William nodded. "Agreed. Let's go home. No more talk about this, promise." Maria thanked some of the nurses and doctors on as she headed down the hall and outside without any hospital staff for the first time in four days. As she got into the car that William had borrowed from his mother until they could get a new one, she felt as close to feeling like herself as she could, given the circumstances. She knew that tomorrow was Karen's funeral services and immediately started to feel panicky and feeling as though she was having trouble breathing. She remembered one of her counselors telling her to take deep breaths when she was having a panic attack. She began taking deep long breaths and focusing on her hands in front of her.

William noticed her taking deep breaths and fighting tears. "Honey, we will get through this. Tomorrow is going to be the hardest day that we'll probably ever have, but we just need to take it minute by minute. We need to lean on each other now and be there for Krista." He reached over to hug her. She hugged him back, knowing that there wasn't any way out of feeling devastated, but unlike when she was a young girl, she had people that she could count on.

William

He knew that as hard as it was for him to come home without Karen, it was going to be the hardest for Maria. The funeral was small, but still overwhelming. William had dealt with the arrangements. Stanley Ahearn also agreed to cover the expenses, so she was buried next to Gram Laura and his father. The half-heart necklace that William had given Karen was retrieved and he'd cleaned it off and gave it to Maria at the gravesite. She'd held it to her heart and then gripped it in her hand as if she were afraid that someone would take it from her.

The only other person that wasn't family was her friend, Stephanie Martin. Maria had taken medication to relax her so she was able to manage throughout the ceremony, but then went directly to bed afterwards and stayed there. Krista was quiet and subdued during the gravesite ceremony, but perked up at the house afterwards. William caught her talking out loud with no one else in the room a couple of times, but figured she was just using her imagination. Maria managed to get through the visitation at home afterwards, but after a few minutes went upstairs to take another sedative and she slept the rest of the afternoon and into the night.

Over the next few days, they'd settled back in with Maria and Krista at home. William noticed that Maria began spending hours in Karen's bedroom. William didn't want to pry and ask what she was doing. Sometimes, she said she was 'going to put away some of her things' and then she would come out hours later. When William looked in the room later on, nothing in the room had been touched. But he did notice an indentation in her pink comforter that covered the bed. She barely ate anything and when she wasn't in Karen's bedroom, she was sleeping. She rarely spent any time with Krista and luckily his mother was helping him with taking her to pre-school and watching her in the afternoon while he worked. Maria attended her weekly counseling appointments with Dr. Sanchez to monitor her moods and medication. He wanted to call Dr. Sanchez, but he knew that Maria would resent him for it. He also knew Dr. Sanchez wouldn't talk to him about Maria unless she agreed to it. He knew she probably wouldn't.

After a week of this, he needed to know what she was doing. He spied on her and found her lying down on Karen's bed with her eyes shut. Krista came into the room and climbed onto the bed with her. Krista whispered in her ear and Maria looked stunned for a moment, gave her a slight hug and then went back to staring up at the ceiling. Krista left the room and came to find him. "Daddy, does mommy still love me?" She started to cry as William scooped her up in his arms.

"Sweetheart, mommy loves you so much. She just misses Karen right now." He felt tears forming as he realized that in the midst of this tragedy, Krista was left out. Karen was her twin and here they were worrying about themselves.

"But Kawyn's right here! I see her every day, daddy!" Krista told him. "She tells me to tell mommy not to be sad but mommy doesn't talk to me anymore."

"You see Karen? Where?" William figured she was using her imagination, pretending. Dr. Welch had told them that it was Krista's way of dealing with the loss of her twin.

"She's here with me all the time, daddy. She helps me get to sleep at night." Krista told him.

William was at loss for words. He just gave her a hug, "Mommy and daddy do miss Karen. Make sure you tell her that, okay? But we love you very much. How about we do something special tomorrow? Just the two of us?" Krista's blue eyes lit up and she was excited. "Can mommy come too?"

William decided it was time to address the problem with his wife and knocked as he came into Karen's room. "Babe, what are you doing?" He asked softly. She was dressed in the same raggedy t- shirt and sweatpants from the day before and her long blonde hair was dull and lifeless. She opened her eyes slowly and glared at him as if he'd just committed a crime. "I'm resting. What does it look like I'm doing?" She snapped at him in a tone that she'd only used with him once or twice during their marriage.

William didn't know what to say so he shut the door just as the phone was ringing. "William, Stan Ahearn here. I have a property selected for your business and I need you to come look at it." It wasn't a request. It was a command. William bit back his impulse to tell him he couldn't be ordered around. But at the same time, Stanley Ahearn was providing him with a financial opportunity that he couldn't refuse.

"Sure. Where is it?" William tried to mask his irritation. Now was not the time to argue with the guy who had the keys to his future.

"It's in Warwick. I know it's a little bit of a drive for you, but the location is phenomenal and right off Route 2 near the mall." Stanley sounded certain about it. William agreed to meet him and brought Krista over to his mother's house with a brief explanation. His mother loved having her there, but said, "William, maybe she needs to go back to the hospital! This isn't good for any of you, especially Krista!" William agreed, but he needed to finish up this business deal with Stanley. Their future was depending on it.

William was initially apprehensive about it but when he met him at the property later that afternoon, he changed his mind. The office space was 2000 square feet and ready to go with office equipment included. There was a parking lot and the location was right on the main road that would make it very visible. "This is amazing, Stan!" He told him.

"I do think you can make a go of it here, William. You can succeed at anything if you're willing to work for it." Stanley told him. Usually Stan's words were only to discuss their 'deal' or to 'keep this to themselves' so it gave William the extra motivation to make this business work. Although he had no idea how he was ever going to explain all of this to Maria. She was struggling just to get up in the morning and he wasn't ready to tell her that he'd obtained his own business courtesy of the driver that caused the accident and killed their child.

"I can make this work! This space is perfect!" William tried to focus on the one thing he could control right now.

"Then it's yours. I'll go through the paperwork with the realtor tomorrow and you'll need to be available in the next few days to sign once it's settled." Stanley told him. "Just keep your end of the bargain; not a word to police or anyone about the details. I don't care what you tell them about this property deal, but don't mention me or my involvement. Are we clear on that?" Stanley demanded to know.

William tried to forget about Maria's face if he were to tell her about this. He needed to do this for them, for their marriage and for Krista. "Yes, we're clear. It's an investment that I made on my own." William parroted back to him. They shook hands and as he watched Stanley walk out the doors and into his limo, he hoped he'd never have to deal with him again. He'd made a deal with the devil and he knew eventually he'd have to tell his wife the truth. And sooner than later. He was going to work on getting staff hired and getting ready to open the business, so even though she seemed to be distracted most of the time, she deserved to know.

A week later, William felt he was ready to start out on a new challenge and prepare to open Carson Realty in the next month. He'd gotten all the utilities turned on in his name, ordering supplies, approval for his realty and business license, and putting out ads for hiring a couple of realtors that were tired of the corporate world and wanted a change. William was surprised that when he went to pay the bills for the utilities, they told him it had been taken care of. Stanley had already paid it, and although William knew they hadn't agreed on that, he was glad. Because his next step was to give notice at Roberts & Sons and tell Maria about the business. Neither was appealing, but necessary.

Maria

It had been almost a month since Karen had died and she still had trouble getting out of bed. Krista's 4th birthday had come and gone. It was a small family celebration with Sara, Barbara and her friend, Steph. Krista had insisted on setting a place for Karen and everything she did and said included her sister. It had been so hard for her to be present and pay attention, but she'd managed the afternoon until the end of the day when she found herself lying in bed after a healthy dose of Ativan. Maria's psychiatrist had prescribed the medication to help her with sleep, but warned her that she wasn't to take it except at night. But she did. She was taking it after she'd been in Karen's room, in the afternoon before Krista got home and at night just to stop her mother's overbearing presence that kept reminding her of what she'd been hiding from William all these years-that William might not be the father.

"Now is not the time, mom!" She finally shouted out at her just as William came into the bedroom. She was tired of drowning her mother's voice out with Ativan and knew she needed to get a good night's sleep. Her boss was expecting her back at work tomorrow. "What? Who are you talking to, Maria?" He snapped the light on and sat down next to her.

"No one, Bill. Really. I'm just tired and not myself." Maria tried to smooth it over, but she knew his patience was growing thin with her melancholy. William didn't say anything for what seemed an eternity and she was starting to wonder if he was going to tell her he was leaving her.

"I have something to tell you, sweetheart. Just hear me out before you say anything, okay?" William started out and she could feel her heart sinking as he said the words.

"You're leaving me, right?" Maria blurted out suddenly.

"What? No, Maria! I'd never leave you! I needed to talk to you about something. Something that's been in the works for quite some time now. I feel guilty for not telling you about it. He slid into bed next to her. "Do you remember the driver of the car that led to the crash?"

Maria shut her eyes for a moment and got a flashback from that moment when she'd seen his face. "Of course. I'll never forget! He looked just like Dan Ahearn, that guy that I was dating before I met you. The guy that rape—" She suddenly almost said the words she'd never meant to tell him. "That guy that assaulted me around Christmas when we were dating." She tried to cover it up, hoping he wouldn't notice.

"That guy that what? What were you going to say the first time, Maria?" William suddenly got out of bed. He'd started to hear the word rape, but she'd changed her wording. Why? He remembered something that Stanley had said about his brother and suspicion of rape. And he'd heard it from somewhere else too, the hospital? Suddenly it all made sense now. Maybe in a way, he'd always suspected it, but now he was certain it happened. And she never told him.

Maria shook her head. It was more than she'd expected tonight, but she was tired of carrying it around with her. Her deceased mother never stopped reminding her about it. She began telling him about what really happened; how he'd forced her down and raped her and how she tried to stop him. She was worried that William would leave her for not being honest with him, but as she told him she felt a weight being lifted. "I didn't tell you because I was afraid. Afraid for what people would say, what you would think and if you wouldn't believe me." Maria told him, bracing herself for his reaction.

William was trying to wrap his head around what his wife had just told him. He couldn't even say anything, got out of bed and headed downstairs. Maria was shaking, knowing that this might be what would break them apart. She knew she needed to make this right with her husband and forced herself to follow him downstairs.

"Bill, let me explain." Maria began, but he cut her off as he pulled a beer out of the fridge and began drinking it down quickly.

"I'm not sure what there is to explain, Maria. You've kept this from me for close to 5 years, before we were married, before the girls were born. Oh, wait. Were they ever my children? The fact that I have to question that now is a lot to take right now." He was shouting at her now. He finished his beer and grabbed a bottle of whiskey from underneath the sink cabinet. He'd stopped drinking it a few years ago when he stopped drinking all together, but now he was glad to have it. So what if she saw it? He was beyond caring at this point.

"Of course the girls are yours, Bill!" She had never been sure, but she sure as hell wasn't going to admit it now.

"And how the hell would you know that for sure? Did you do a paternity test with some hair off my brush when I wasn't looking? And then not tell me about it?" William demanded to know.

"No, I didn't." Maria admitted. "I wouldn't do that. What I do know is that you were there through the pregnancy and the birth. You've been there to raise them. You've been there after...." She felt herself tearing up. "After one of them is gone. You took care of everything. You are their father. But if you want to get a paternity test now, I'd understand." Maria went back upstairs to the bedroom. She felt surprisingly calm as she turned on her side and closed her eyes. She could hear her husband walking in circles downstairs, muttering to himself and she didn't blame him. Her mother had been right; she should've told him the truth when it happened. He'd proven over and over again that he loved her and she'd been too insecure to tell him the truth.

She'd fallen asleep until William finally came back into the bedroom a few hours later. "Babe, I'm trying to understamed." She could tell he was more than a little drunk. "I'm just.....ya know..surprised...by all this this." He was slurring his words and she didn't want to talk about this anymore tonight.

She turned toward him as he got into bed. "Bill, let's talk tomorrow. You've been drinking. Let's just go to bed." She hoped that he'd just go to sleep. But he wasn't done talking. "I was gonna tell you that the driver of the other car offered to set me up with a realty business. All expenses paid."

"Really? He offered to do that? Why?" Maria turned over to face her husband. He looked tired and he reeked of whiskey. She knew that this wasn't a conversation to have tonight. "On second thought, let's talk about this in the morning. It's late, we're both tired and I have a feeling I'll need to be prepared for this." Maria told him.

"But I wanna tell you now." William was clearly intoxicated and not listening to reason. He was trying to kiss her and climb on top of her. She became annoyed and got out of bed. "I told you tell me tomorrow! You're drunk and I'm sleeping on the couch!" She yelled at him and went to the closet to get a blanket and pillow to take to the couch.

"He wants me to be quiet about his drinking while he was driving that night." William blurted out. "He agreed to set me up with my own business and cash to buy supplies." He started talking more about this new business that she'd known nothing about. Until today.

"So in other words, he's not going to be questioned, go to court or jail where he belongs! Although it was his fault! Is that what you agreed to already? Without talking to me? What the hell is wrong with you!" Maria was furious. She picked up the pillow and blanket, slamming the bedroom door behind her. William was still talking even after she shut the door, but she knew that they'd come to a crossroad now. He'd allowed some rich guy to buy him off for his silence about the cause of Karen's death in exchange for a business, and he hadn't mentioned one word until now. And if she had to guess, he'd already signed the papers so it was not even a discussion now. Just when she couldn't feel more alone, she'd just hit rock bottom.

William

He'd woken up with a splitting headache and sprawled across the bed. The sun was shining through the windows and he squinted as he glanced at the clock on the nightstand. 9:30! He reached over for his wife, but she wasn't there. What the hell had happened last night? Then he remembered; she'd said something about that asshole Dan Ahearn raping her, him questioning whether the twins were his kids, then he started drinking. He vaguely remembered mentioning the reality business that Stan had set up for him in exchange for his silence about the cause of the accident. He didn't remember anything after that, except that he assumed that Maria was pissed and slept on the couch. As he stumbled down the stairs, he noticed the empty couch with a pillow and blanket still there and knew that he was right about that. He was also extremely late for work. Until he had everything up and running with his new business, he needed to stay off his boss' radar. He was planning to give his notice this week, so he didn't want to raise any suspicions.

First things first; he called work, claiming he was ill. "I'm so sorry, I was sick and slept through my alarm," he told his boss, John Roberts while feigning a cough for good measure.

"Okay, William. Feel better. Hope to see you in first thing in the morning." John sounded less than thrilled, but not as upset as he'd expected. He was grateful for anything positive today. "Maria? Krista?" He called out as he started making some much needed coffee. No answer. He went up and glanced in Krista's room. Her bed was made, so clearly wherever Maria was, Krista was with her.

He called his mother. She picked up on the second ring. "Mom, is Krista there?"

"Of course. Maria dropped her off at 8:00 this morning. I'm getting ready to take her to school. What's going on with you two, William? She was all upset and refused to tell me anything." She sounded upset.

"It's a long story, mom. I can't get into it now." William knew that the day of reckoning was coming soon with his family. He'd have to tell them about his new business, he just didn't want to talk about how he managed to finance a business on his own when he clearly didn't have many assets to start one.

"Well, you and Maria need to figure things out. Krista is constantly referring to Karen as if she's there next to her. She has another appointment with Dr. Welch on Friday. I think it would be a good idea for both of you to go to her appointment!" Sara insisted. She sounded angry, which was unusual for his mother.

"We will mom. Thanks for helping out." William was apologetic. He wasn't sure what they would have done in the past few years without her help.

"You know I'd do anything to help all of you. But Maria needs to get her head on straight and if you ask me, she's taking too much medication. She looked like a zombie this morning. Krista seems fine, but thinking that her dead sister is still following her around isn't normal, William." His mother was sugar-coating the mess they'd been in since Karen's death.

"I know." William sighed. There were no easy answers to Maria and Krista's issues but he was doing what he could to resolve their financial issues. "I'm working on it. I'm headed to work. Talk to you later." He hung up. He had a whole free day to figure out smaller details for getting the business up and running so he took an aspirin for his headache and pushed himself to move forward despite the bomb that Maria had dropped on him last night about Stan's brother, Dan. He tried to put it out of his mind as it did no good now, even though he was furious with the whole situation. Maybe when things calmed down, he'd address the paternity issue. For now, he forced himself to put it to the side. This business needed to succeed and he couldn't afford that distraction now.

He made a few calls about his reality license which was approved, and began looking over the resumes that had come in after putting out ads for real estate agents. He tried Maria at her office, but she wasn't answering. He decided to take a trip to his new office building just to see if everything was in place. When he arrived, he was surprised to find Stan Ahearn there.

"Everything okay, Stan?" William suddenly felt nervous, as though telling Maria last night about the deal had suddenly been leaked out. But he knew that was impossible. Or was it?

Stan eyed him closely. "All is fine here and ready to go, William. However, I don't need your wife going and stirring up the police department." He pulled him outside.

"What do you mean, Stan? I just told her what happened with the deal last night. After all, she is my wife. She'll know that I didn't magically come across all this money in a loan to start this business."

William's heart dropped. He couldn't believe that Maria had gone to the police. Now, there was going to be another hill to climb!

"You did what you needed to do. I understand that. However, she contacted police last night and they were at my doorstep first thing this morning, wanting more information. I told them it was ridiculous of course and that your wife is under the care of a psychiatrist, which I assume is the case." Stanley said calmly. "However, in the future discussions with her, you should probably not focus on our agreement. It's not sitting well with her and she seems to be a loose cannon. If this continues, I'll have to back out. This was the whole point of the agreement, so that things like this don't happen, get it?" He was smiling, but the tone of his voice was serious and William knew that Stan could pull the plug on this as fast as he made it happen.

As much as William wanted to punch Stanley Ahearn in the face for the accident, he knew he needed to continue to play along. "Of course, Stan. I get it. I did try to explain, but obviously that wasn't a good plan. If the police contact me, I'll let them know that my wife has been dealing with mental health issues just as you did. That should keep things straight."

"Good. I'm glad to hear that. I think you'll do well with this business. If you keep it all business and not let your emotions run it, William. Do your work and do it well and then go home and have a good cry. Love doesn't pay the bills, does it?" He smiled and patted him on the back. "Just make sure your wife isn't running around town telling everyone in the world about this, because that would pose another problem. I don't care what you have to tell her, but figure it out." Stan waved to his limousine driver that was waiting for him in the parking lot. "I've gotta go. You're all set here, William. The rest is up to you." He said as he climbed into the back of the limo.

"Yes, it is. I heard you today. No more problems." William said to him before his limo pulled out of the parking lot. He had to have a plan if police asked him more questions. He didn't want to use Maria's depression as an excuse, but it might have to come to that. He'd have to talk to her about it in a different way. That Stan had financed the money for him with a good rate? Yes, that was it. Stanley had felt guilty and financed the business with a good interest rate. No more mention about Stan's drinking. After all, she probably didn't know that until he'd said something last night. He was ready to start a new chapter and maybe he'd made a bad decision, but they were only a few paychecks away from losing everything so there wasn't much choice.

He spent the rest of the mid-morning going through resumes that he'd received and contacting applicants. He was intent on hiring two people to start and hopefully business would be good and he'd need to hire more. Stanley had also mentioned that he would be giving his name out to people he knew. William sat in his new office with the smell of fresh paint and took a deep breath. He felt guilty about the way that this opportunity had come to him, the cover up and minimizing the truth to his wife. But some success after all this tragedy was what he wanted for him and his family. He picked up his office phone and tried Maria again at work.

She picked up right away. "This is Maria." He could hear the stress in her voice.

"Hey, sweetheart. How's your day?" William tried to sound upbeat, even though he felt like he was tiptoeing through a field of dynamite.

"Hi." She responded quietly. "How was your day?" She asked him, telling him that she'd at least calmed down from last night's drama.

"It was okay, despite the hangover this morning. I'm sorry about drinking too much last night and what I said to you. Let's talk tonight when you get home over dinner. I'll order some pizza so you don't have to make anything." William offered. "I'll pick Krista up from school too."

"Sounds good. I'll see you around 5:30." Maria agreed. "I've gotta go, I'll see you soon. Love you." She told him.

"Love you too, sweetheart. See you soon." William was grateful that she had calmed down. He just needed to remember that they both had so much to overcome. He finished up at the new office and headed out to pick up his daughter. He needed to focus on them now and make things as best as they could be after losing Karen.

He arrived at Krista's school to pick her up and went inside promptly at 2:30. "Mr. Carson, could I talk to you for a moment outside?" Krista's teacher, Ms. Walker asked him as he came to the door. "Krista is finishing up a drawing. This will only take a minute." She came outside the classroom and shut the door.

"I just wanted to let you know first of all how sorry I am about Karen. She was just the sweetest girl. Krista is as well," Ms. Walker began. She was very young and seemed intimated. She had a rolled up piece of drawing paper in her hand.

"Thank you, Ms. Walker, it's been a difficult adjustment for all of us." William told her. "How has Krista been here at school?" He knew that her behavior at home had been more than strange and wouldn't be surprised if it was happening at school.

"Krista's been talking a lot as if Karen is there next to her." Ms. Walker began. "I know this sounds really strange, Mr. Carson, but it's almost as if she believes that Karen is there with her."

William nodded. "I'm aware of this, Ms. Walker. It happens at home all the time. She is seeing a therapist that's working with her. She says that it's pretty common for twins when they have that bond." William tried to summarize, even though he suspected there was more to it, especially now with his own unexplainable experience with Gram Laura after he'd been injured.

Ms. Walker looked relieved after he told her about Krista's psychiatrist. "If her doctor makes any suggestions, please let me know. I just want to help her. On a positive note, she is really creative and a joy to have in class. She gets along well with the other kids. I did want to show you a drawing that she did today though that was concerning." Ms. Walker rolled out the piece of paper in her hand. It was a drawing of a cliff with a person in mid-flight toward water. "This is Krista's drawing from this morning. She's drawn others of course, but this one was particularly concerning."

William looked at it and immediately thought about Carrie, his childhood friend. The picture was replicated based on what he remembered. He tried to keep his face from showing what he felt as he said. "As you said, Krista is creative. We did go on vacation this summer to a place that had cliffs like this. I can assure you, no one fell in." He tried to joke, but Ms. Walker's face told him she wasn't buying it.

"She told the class that this was the little girl that fell off the cliff years ago. She also mentioned that this is the little girl that wanted her sister to be with her." Ms. Walker told him.

William was suddenly taken back to that day for just a second; a flashback of when Carrie went over the cliff instead of stopping. Mr. Carson, are you okay?" Ms. Walker asked.

"Oh, yes. I'm sorry. I've been busy today. Yes, I can understand how this is concerning, but again, she is seeing a doctor to help her through these difficult times." He knew he sounded generic but he also knew he didn't have an explanation either.

Ms. Walker looked relieved. "I'm glad to know she's getting some help. She and Karen seemed so close. Karen was always with her; she seemed so shy, but Krista met some of the other kids and Karen seemed to warm up to them as long as her sister was there."

William felt suddenly anxious. "I really need to get going. Is there anything else I should know?" He was trying to be polite but aside from the cliff picture, he was used to Krista's constant references to Karen.

"I'm sorry I've been keeping you, Mr. Carson. I just thought you should know." Ms. Walker seemed flustered as she ushered him back into the classroom. "Krista, your dad is here to pick you up."

Krista looked up from her drawing and grabbed it, running to him. "Daddy!" She was excited to have him pick her up. Her blue eyes lit up when she saw him and he was grateful to have her.

"Hi, sweetheart!" William picked her up and hugged her close. "Ready to go home? Maybe we'll stop for ice cream on the way!" He couldn't help but spoil her. He missed Karen as much as Krista and Maria did, but he knew it was time to give his attention to Krista. She was excited for ice cream, but even more to show him her drawing that she'd brought with her. "Look, daddy! I drew Mommy and Kawyn at that house we went to. He could see the large house only a few yards from the cliff depicted in the background. Two figures were standing close to the cliff's edge with the water below. It bothered him in a way that he couldn't put his finger on. "I love it sweetheart. It's very nice, but where are you and I?" He asked her.

"She wouldn't let me put us there, daddy." Krista said. "I tried.

Maria

It had been a long day at work and William's call in the middle of the day helped to relieve some of her anxiety about the argument, but not about his decision to allow Mr. Ahearn to pay for his silence. She couldn't believe that William hadn't told her about this when Ahearn approached him. She knew that she hadn't been in the right mindset, but he'd had plenty of time to tell her about it. Just then she could hear her mother's voice in her head, 'You also didn't tell him about Dan until last night. Just remember, no one's perfect. We all have flaws. Are you any better than he is, considering?' She opened her mouth to react to her mother, but then thought about what she'd said. Her mother was right. She'd been hiding the rape from her husband, and yet he was still willing to overlook the possibility that the twins weren't his and accept what he had now.

She headed home, ready to face it. She was nervous, and was so caught up in her thoughts, she almost rear-ended another car at a stop light and stopped just in the nick of time. 'I really need to focus,' she said to herself. She managed to get home, unsure of what William was going to say to her. Maybe he'd insist on a paternity test, maybe he'd just leave her. Anything was possible. As she parked, she forced herself to take a deep breath. "You can do this, Maria!" She said out loud. She walked into the house, expecting to be hounded by questions.

Instead, she was greeted by William, Krista, and a pizza that had just been delivered. A glass of wine for her and sparkling grape juice for

William and Krista were waiting as well. Both Krista and William gave her a hug. "Hi, mommy. Daddy got pizza!" Maria felt tears come to her eyes. "Bill, I'm sorry about what I said to you. We have a lot we need to talk about." She hugged him close to her and then reached down to hug Krista. "I love you, sweetheart. I'm sorry mommy's been a little upset lately, but I'll be okay."

"It's okay mommy. It's okay to be sad. Dr. Welch says so." Krista said in a stoic-type voice that sounded so much like Dr. Welch that it made Maria and William laugh. It was a moment that she needed to feel like she'd joined the family again. Even if she felt like everything was coming apart. They had a nice evening eating the pizza and watching E.T. Krista loved the movie and afterwards when Maria was tucking her in she said "Mommy, if E.T. can phone home, why can't Kawyn?"

Maria initially laughed but saw that Krista was serious. "Why can't she call us? I can hear her and sometimes I see her but no one else can. Dr. Welch says she's a fig newton of my 'magination."

Maria had to suppress a giggle just then because of her wording. But the fact that she could see and hear her made her feel almost envious that she had very little contact. But she needed to try and explain. "Kris, sometimes people that are alive can still see people that most can't see anymore. You and Karen are twins; something very special. So remember that it's special that you can see her and hear her. Daddy and I can't do that."

Krista looked surprised. "You can't? She's sitting right here now. Can't you see her? She says she misses you." Maria felt the tears spring to her eyes and had to turn away for a moment. "No, sweetheart, I can't. But please tell her that we all miss her very much." Maria managed to say. She really wished that whatever connection she had with her parents would carry over to her daughter, but even when she tried to meditate, it just didn't happen. And it made it that much more difficult to hear about her from Krista.

Krista turned her head and seemed to be listening, then said "She misses you and daddy too."

"Let's read a story before bed, okay?" Maria wiped her eyes quickly as she grabbed the first book she could find. She tried to concentrate on 'Raggedy Ann and the Cookie Snatcher' but Krista knew most of the story and Maria was convinced she could read some of it.

Maria held back her emotions as she kissed Krista good-night but after she turned off the lamp and shut her door, she began to sob and ran down to the bathroom and stood over the toilet feeling as though she were going to be sick. She took some deep breaths and tried to control herself as William knocked on the door.

"Honey, you okay in there?"

"Uh, yeah, I'll be out in a minute. I just needed to wash my face. I'm fine. I'll be out in a minute. She stared at her reflection in the mirror and said out loud. "You're fine. Everything is fine. Krista's just grieving; it's fine!" She splashed some water on her face and opened the door.

William took one look at her face and enveloped her into a huge hug. "I'm so sorry that I didn't tell you about what Mr. Ahearn had asked. I should have, but I wasn't sure what else to do." Maria just hugged him back, but she knew that this empty feeling would never end. No amount of hugs or psychiatric drugs or anything would make this feeling go away. It didn't matter to her what deal William had made. She couldn't keep going this way any longer. A plan began forming in her mind and she knew that it would hurt William and Krista and maybe a few other people, but it would be best for all of them.

"I don't blame you Bill. I understand why you did it, although I wish you'd consulted with me. But you're right. Even if we said something to the police about his drinking, they would just ignore it. You said he's a celebrity of sorts so we'd go through a bunch of interviews that are difficult to do and so on." Maria knew it was true about Stan Ahearn, but it didn't stop her from being angry.

Maria knew she needed to address the elephant in the room; the rape and whether he was the father of his daughters. "Bill, if you want a paternity test, I can schedule that for you and Krista.

"I'll need to think about it. I don't think it matters to me now. They're my girls. I'd rather keep it that way, but I keep going back and forth. I just wish you'd told me when it happened. I understand from your point of view, but I would never think it was your fault. Never!" William told her.

"Thank you for being the best husband a woman could ask for." Maria told him. She meant it. She was going to miss these moments.

William

A few days later, William was nervous as he headed to work. Today was when he was giving his notice and he wasn't sure what to expect. He felt confident about the business that he was starting but he also didn't want his current boss to have bad feelings about him leaving, especially when he was going to be competition in the future. He'd managed to hire one realtor, Shane Chaswick who was 25, but had a degree in business and a realtor's license. He'd also hired a part-time billing/receptionist, Callie Billings that was a college student, but had experience with billing and scheduling. They both fit what he needed to begin his business and he just needed to go for it now.

He went straight to his boss's office and knocked on the door. "Hi, John, can we talk for a moment?" He was nervous and felt like all the moisture just drained out of his mouth.

"Sure, pull up a chair, Bill! What's going on?" John seemed so sincere that for a moment William considered chickening out altogether. But he knew that if he wanted to get his business going, he needed to start working it as soon as possible. The next two weeks would be a transitioning period for him.

John was quiet as William launched into what ended up being a very lengthy explanation before finally getting to the point, that he was giving his notice. "I do appreciate the opportunity that you gave me, John." William added when his boss didn't immediately respond. The uncomfortable silence caused him to keep talking. John sat back in his chair and sighed. "I'm sorry to hear that, Bill. You've done well here and our clients have nothing but good things to say about you."

For a moment, William thought he was just going to tell him to forget the notice and felt a rush of anxiety. He needed this job for the next two weeks, as he still had final details before opening the doors to Carson's Realty. "Thank you, that means a lot." He told John, hoping that he wasn't going to be asked to clear out his desk immediately.

"We'll be sad to see you go. Is there any way I can keep you here if I offered you a raise?" John offered. William hadn't even thought that he would be faced with this decision, but he knew that despite whatever John was going to offer, this was what he wanted. Besides, he was ready to go. There was no going back now.

"I'm sorry, John. I really appreciate that offer, but I'm committed to starting this new venture." William told him. John nodded, knowing that he probably wouldn't take it. Not when he was starting out on his own. They shook hands and William felt like a weight had lifted knowing that he was leaving on good terms.

The next two weeks were a whirlwind of William closing on a few clients and transferring existing clients that were still looking to buy. On his last day, they threw him a surprise going away party at work which brought him to tears. "Thank you so much everyone! I'll miss you all!" He told them as he left the office for the last time. Now, it was up to him to make his business work. When he arrived home, Krista came running up to him and gave him a hug. "Daddy! Mommy is sad." William put down his briefcase and took off his coat.

"Where is mommy, sweetheart? Is she okay?" Krista shook her head and led him upstairs. He opened the door to find his wife sobbing hysterically on the bed. William turned to Krista. "Honey, please go in your room so daddy can talk to mommy, okay?" Krista nodded, looking confused about what was going on but headed to her room. "Maria! What happened?" He pulled her up to face him. She was almost hyperventilating she was crying so hard. "Maria! Look at me!" She struggled to put her head back in the pillow, but William wouldn't let her.

"You need to calm down and tell me what's going on!" William told her more sharply than he meant to. But he needed to get her attention and luckily it worked. He'd even gotten the picture of her and the girls from Mohegan Bluffs at Block Island put in a frame which was still in his briefcase and he was going to give it to her tonight. Maybe it wasn't such a good idea now.

Maria tried to catch her breath as William forced her to sit up. She wiped her eyes and blew her nose as tears continued to pour down her face. "They let me go from my job today." She managed to tell him.

"What? Why?" William was upset now. Maria did a great job with that agency. She really cared about clients and was on time for work despite everything she'd gone through in the past few months. Maria finally was able to explain that they felt as though she wasn't 'present' enough with the clients and she seemed distant. She'd also forgotten to do some paperwork that needed to be done. "I know I should've gotten it done, but they didn't give me any warning." Maria told him in an irritable voice, her tears turning to anger.

"Babe, you've been through a lot in the past few months! If this agency wants to fire you over some paperwork and concerns about your 'presence' then you'll find another place to work." William tried to be supportive and he was angry that they hadn't even bothered to give her a warning. "At least you'll be able to apply for unemployment benefits." He offered a positive solution for now.

"I can try, but I wasn't there for very long especially with taking so much time off after the accident. They may deny it." Maria seemed as though she was becoming at least lucid and listening to reason now.

"We will figure it out, sweetheart. Just fill out the paperwork and we'll go from there." William was feeling the stress on himself more now to be successful, but he wouldn't put that on his wife. He could tell that she was hanging by a thread. He put a frozen pizza in the oven for dinner and decided to put in a call to Dr. Sanchez who was supposedly seeing Maria every few weeks. He called only to get voice-mail. He checked the clock; it was past five. He left a brief message about Maria and then forgot about it. He was sure he wouldn't hear back until the next day. He started rummaging through the kitchen drawers and came up with Janice Suran- Psychic business card. He laughed to himself for a moment, but then decided to call just to see if she answered.

"Hello?" The woman actually answered. William was shocked.

"Hello, is this Janice? Janice Suran?" He asked just to be sure.

"Yes, how can I help you?" Janice had a pleasant southern accent that was welcoming even on the phone. Just then Krista came downstairs. "Daddy, can I come down now?" She asked.

William motioned to her and moved his mouth away from the phone. 'Yes, sweetheart.' He uncovered his mouth and answered "I need. ….that is …can I make an appointment to talk to you?" William was feeling flustered now. What the hell was he doing calling this psychic lady anyhow?

"I can see you in the morning. How about 9:00?" She suggested. William knew he couldn't be late to work especially since giving his notice. "Can you do 4:00 instead tomorrow?" William was crossing his fingers.

"I can do that. I'll see you at 4:00 tomorrow. What's your first name?" She asked him.

"William." He said cautiously. He wasn't sure if this was a scam, but at this point he felt like he needed to find out what was going on with this wife. Dr. Sanchez just kept giving her medication that didn't seem to be helping, but maybe this psychic person that she met with might have some answers.

Krista had been hovering around in the background the whole time. "Who was that, daddy?" She was always asking questions, but this one time, he'd hoped she wouldn't.

"That was just someone daddy needs to talk with tomorrow." He said. "Let's see if this pizza is ready!" He opened the oven to a frozen pizza, then realized he'd forgotten to turn the oven on. "Daddy is pretty silly. I forgot to turn it on!" He had to laugh because everything was so upside down right now. "Hey, sweetheart, how about we order some pizza and go pick it up?"

"Yes! I like pepper a ronis, daddy!" Krista's favorite food was pizza. He placed the order and went upstairs to check on Maria before they left. Her face was in the pillow and he could tell that she was sound asleep. He decided to leave a note on the kitchen table instead in case she woke up and came downstairs. They'd be back in 20 minutes anyway. He took the picture of Maria and the girls that he'd framed and set it out on the counter so he'd remember to bring it upstairs and give it to her.

Krista looked at the picture. "We look happy, daddy." She told him.

"You all do. We'll be happy again soon, sweetheart." He said, but more to convince himself than his 4 -year -old daughter.

After he'd come home to his wife sound asleep and a bottle of medication next to her, he knew he was right about at least checking out what Janice Suran had to say. He and Krista had a pizza dinner in front of the TV and while he was grateful for time with his daughter, he hoped that Maria would become more consistent in participating in their lives.

He headed out to his new business and spent the day working with Shane and Callie, letting them know what he expected. Luckily, he'd already had help with his former clientele that he'd worked with that had put out the word that he was starting his own business. Stanley Ahearn had gone a step above what was promised and put out an ad in the newspaper announcing his new business. At 3:30, he headed out to see Janice in Wickford. He'd almost cancelled at the last minute, but knew that he'd spend too much time wondering what she had to say.

She was right on schedule and greeted him at the door. She was not what William expected; a small petite woman wearing a lime green sweat-suit and her gray hair in a bun on top of her head.

"Hello, William. It's nice to meet you." She ushered him into a small office space that smelled like incense with angels and star décor on the walls. She sat down behind a small desk with a Tiffany-style lamp and gestured for him to sit down in a vintage winged chair in front of the desk.

"I knew your grandmother, Laura Carson, very well. She came here often. She knows that you're here. You must be here because of Karen."

William was shocked. "How did you know that? I didn't tell you anything." He had to admit, he was less skeptical now.

Janice nodded. "Karen has passed. I'm so sorry that she went, but it was meant to be. All births and deaths have a plan, William."

"Do they? Because if they do, then it's not fair!" He was suddenly angry, not at Janice, but because no one could convince him that life was supposed to end at 3 years old for anyone.

"I'm here as the messenger, remember that William." Janice reminded him, "I'm just telling you what I know. And I agree with you; it isn't fair."

"I really want to know about my wife, Maria and my daughter that's alive. Karen's twin, Krista. Can you tell me what's going to happen? I just can't handle any more surprises." William suddenly felt scared. What the hell was he doing here? Did he really want to hear any of this?

But he knew he had to try. Maybe she could give some advice about Maria and Krista.

"William, I can't really tell you the future, but I can do a Tarot reading which will give some guidance. I can also try and see if Karen or someone that you know that has passed can give some insight. She had him shuffle some cards and then started her reading. "You've had some tragedy and you're struggling emotionally. Your wife and daughter are as well." She laid down a bunch of cards that made no sense to him, but she kept talking. "There's a little girl named Carrie that keeps coming up. She's talking to me. She says that it's your fault that she fell off the cliff."

"Carrie? She's here?" William looked around, suddenly creeped out.

"She's made her presence known. She blames you for why she fell off the cliff." Janice told him.

"It was just a game. Really. I didn't want her to fall off!" William insisted, starting to remember that day. He had been teasing her and telling her she was chicken. "But if she thinks that then I'm really sorry. I just want to know if she had anything to do with Karen's death." William felt himself start to tear up. Janice waited a moment and nodded before she spoke. "She had communicated with Karen before her death, but she insists that she does not have capacity to intervene in that way."

William wasn't sure why he believed her, but he felt a sense of clarity about Carrie's accident that he hadn't before.

Janice shuffled the cards again. "Your wife is struggling right now. So is Krista but for different reasons. Your wife is trying to decide if she wants to be with Karen or Krista right now and the choice is hard. Karen has the same gift as your wife, you know. She has the ability to communicate. She wants her mother back. Krista doesn't have the gift to communicate with others deceased. But because Karen was her twin, she is able to have some communication with her specifically. She may even be able to see her and talk to her as if she were there." Janice told him.

William nodded because it explained Krista referring to her sister as if she were there. "That's true. Krista's psychiatrist believes it's her imagination that's causing this. So what's she's seeing is real? She can really see her sister?" He couldn't believe that he was buying into this, but he didn't have any other explanation.

"It's real to her. Even if you can't see Karen, doesn't mean that Krista can't. As long as Krista continues to go about her usual activities and not focus all her time on her sister, Karen will likely stop appearing to her as often. I understand why her therapist would make the suggestion about Karen being 'imaginary'. After all, the rest of us can't see her, but the term 'imaginary' came from somewhere, didn't it?" Janice advised.

William had to agree with her. "What about Maria? Can you tell me more about her? Of course she's struggling, but I don't know how to help her. Janice shuffled her cards again and then had him cut the deck and pulled out a few more. "There's conflict with you and something that happened in the past that's become an issue. Are you aware of this?" She asked him pointedly as if she could see right into his mind.

"I am. We have many actually." William admitted.

Janice pulled out the final card which was a picture of a tower depicting several people falling to the ground. William hadn't really paid attention to the cards until this one. "That doesn't look good." He commented, hoping she would tell him otherwise.

"The Tower card represents some danger, conflict, but it can also be liberation from such." William could tell that Janice was probably sugar-coating it for him. The look on her face when she turned it over told him it wasn't good.

"Let's be honest. I've got a lot to worry about. What's your advice based on this reading for me to help my wife and daughter?" William was direct.

Janice put down the Tower card. "Honestly, I think you should just pay more attention to what's going on around you, and with them. How they're feeling and trying to communicate with them. I can assure you that Carrie or Karen is not causing them any harm physically. But Karen is present to Maria and Krista. It's important to keep together as a family." Janice advised.

"Well, thank you so much for your time, Janice. I think many things got resolved today." William suddenly felt as though they did. There was a sense of relief about being able to relay the message that he was sorry that Carrie died. He had a new perspective on Krista's 'talking to Karen' now as well. What Janice said did make sense. They were twins, they had that special connection.

He was still worried about Maria, because as much insight as Janice could give, there was no easy answer for what he could do. He just had to try and be there for her. He was starting to wonder if he'd made the right decision about taking Stanley's offer. But there was no turning back.

Maria

When she woke up from her medicated sleep, she looked at the clock and it was past noon. She felt drowsy and drugged, as she pulled herself out of bed to make her way to the shower. It was the one place that she felt content with the hot spray beating down on her body and she sat down in a fetal position, wishing she could stay that way forever.

But after about 20 minutes, the water started to run cold and she reluctantly got out and dried off. She sat in her bathrobe on the side of the bed crying for another 20 minutes. She drifted over to her mother's gold jewelry box and looked inside. There were locks of Karen's and Krista's first haircut, Karen's half-heart necklace, a sapphire gold ring that had belonged to her mother and her mother's engagement ring and both her parent's wedding rings inside. Treasures that she could never part with. She started to tear up again as she thought about Krista and William; she wasn't present for them now and wasn't sure if she would ever get back to being who she was when Karen was alive. She'd escaped tragedy with her parent's death and living with Aunt Sylvia and her horrible cousin. She'd survived Dan Ahearn's wrath and as a twist of fate, his brother was the one who was footing the cost for William's new business.

The phone rang and snapped her out of going down the rabbit hole of demons that was always waiting for her. She grabbed the phone on the nightstand table. "Hello?"

She could hear static and then a faint child's voice. "Hello? Is that you, mommy?"

"Who is this?" Maria could feel her heart pounding just hearing the voice.

She could hear more static, then it subsided. "Maria! It's Sara, who did you think it was?" She sounded upset.

Maria felt relieved, but still shaken from the first voice she'd heard. Was she starting to go crazy? Maybe she should stop taking that new medication Dr. Sanchez was prescribing!

"Sorry, the connection wasn't good at first. I could barely hear you." Maria made an excuse to her mother-in-law.

"I was calling to see if I could stop by this afternoon. I'm picking up Krista from school because William said he was working a little late." Sara asked carefully. Maria could tell she was tip-toeing around her, but she meant well.

"Of course! It'll be nice to catch up!" Maria did her best to infuse some enthusiasm into her voice, although she felt the opposite. She loved her mother-in-law dearly, but she wasn't in the mood to spend much time with anyone lately.

"Great! I'll see you around 3:30 then." Sara told her and hung up. Maria looked at the clock. How was it 2:30 already? She quickly wet her hair again, since she'd neglected to brush it after her shower and got herself together. She didn't want anyone, especially Sara to know how she was really feeling. She needed to stay strong for Krista and appear as though everything was fine. She looked at the medication bottle next to the bed and reached for it before putting it down. Maria knew that if she took it, she'd be tired in an hour, but she noticed that she was needing to take more than one to sleep at night now. 'I can wait until later,' she told herself, but she felt restless, so she began cleaning up the kitchen, doing some laundry and soon enough, Krista was running through the door with Sara behind her.

"Mommy!" Krista ran to her.

"Hi, sweetheart! How was your day at school?" Maria picked her up and hugged her. Sara smiled, glad to see that Maria seemed like she was feeling better.

"It was good mommy! I drew you a picture." Krista was excited to show her. Sara held her breath. She'd seen the picture and was worried about how Maria would react to it.

"Well, let's see it!" Maria insisted. Krista unzipped her backpack and pulled out a piece of paper with a picture of a house with four people in front of it. "That's you, daddy, me and Kawyn. Do you like it mommy?" Krista asked. Her bright blue eyes were eager for her approval. Maria felt tears coming to her eyes but managed to keep them in check.

"It's wonderful, honey! I love it!" She feigned excitement about the picture, even though she wanted to cry. But this was going to continue. Just because Karen was gone, didn't mean that Krista understood how reminders made mommy sad. They made Krista happy and Maria was grateful for that.

"Will you hang it up on the refrigerator?" Krista asked. Maria nodded and obliged by hanging it up with the fridge magnets on the bottom door. She was biting her lip to keep from crying but managed.

"Kris, can you go upstairs and put your backpack away? I need to talk to Grammy for a few minutes." Maria needed a minute to collect herself. Krista headed upstairs and Sara took a deep breath. "I'm sorry I didn't warn you, but she didn't show me until we got in the car on the way here." Sara told her. "Are you okay?" She reached out to give Maria a hug.

Maria hugged her back and let go of her tears for a minute. "I am now. This is just what I need to get used to, Sara. I'm going to *have* to be okay." She let go and shrugged her shoulders. "At least Bill is doing what he wants to do finally. He's excited about running his own business. I think it'll be a success don't you agree?" She needed to change the subject.

Sara had a look of doubt on her face. "I still don't know how he managed to get a loan for it, but I hope that he does well." Maria could tell she didn't want to talk about it, and glad that she wasn't with him when he mentioned it to her. William would never reveal to anyone else what he'd done to start his new business.

"How about some tea or coffee, Sara?" Maria needed to change topics or be forced to deal with his mother's negative thoughts about his business deal that he'd made with Stanley. She knew he'd made up a lie, telling family members that he'd saved money and gotten a loan. She could barely stand listening to him talk about it, just knowing the truth. It cost them way more than any amount of a loan. Their daughter's life had paid for it.

She spent another half hour with Sara talking about simple things over tea; the weather, the neighborhood, the holidays coming up in a few months. "So I was thinking that we could maybe go to a restaurant for Thanksgiving and do Christmas at my house." Sara was talking, but Maria's heart wasn't into even talking about holidays. As far as she were concerned, the holidays weren't even on her mind even though it was almost the end of October. Maria was thankful when William walked in at 5:00. It relieved some of the pressure of trying to pretend everything was okay, when it was anything but.

"William!" His mom greeted him and gave him a hug. He seemed very tired and less than happy to see his mother there, but he hugged her back. "What are you doing here?" He asked.

"Well, I dropped Krista off after school and then I stayed to talk with Maria. I hope that's okay." Sara could sense the coldness of his welcome.

"Sorry, mom. It's just been a long day." William took off his coat and sat down. "Want some tea, Bill?" Maria offered. But he was already headed to the fridge for a beer. "No, thanks. I'll have a beer." He waited for his wife to object. She gave him one of her disapproving looks but didn't say anything, since his mother was there. But he knew she wasn't happy. Screw it, he'd had a rough day. Janice's message was clear; communicate with his wife and his daughter.

"Where's Krista?" William realized he hadn't seen her yet.

"She's up in her room. Oh, Bill, can you go see what she's up to? She went upstairs about an hour ago." Maria just realized that she hadn't heard anything from Krista, which was unusual.

"I'm gonna go up and see what's she's up to. What's for dinner?" He asked. Maria realized she hadn't even thought about it and got up to look in the fridge for ideas. "I thawed out some ground beef, I think." She tried to sound as though she'd been planning, but she realized she'd spent the whole day doing nothing except being sad.

Sara took note of the dynamics, and didn't want to be involved. "Well, I'm headed out. I'll see you guys later this week. Good to see you, sweetheart." She gave William a hug before he went upstairs. She turned to Maria. "Please give me a call anytime you need anything, okay? I'm always here for all of you." Maria thanked her and hugged her as she left. Maria sank down in one of the kitchen chairs after she was gone; her energy was spent; she had her plan. It was just a matter of time.

William

"Hi, daddy!" Krista greeted him and he scooped her up in his arms. "What are you doing, Kris?" He asked. He noticed that she had her tea set and dishes set out on her child-sized table with four chairs set up. "What's for dinner here, Kris?" He joked.

"Karen is visiting with me. Do you want to sit with us and have some tea, daddy?" Krista asked him.

William remembered Janice's words. "Karen is still with them. You need to communicate with them as they see her." He managed to squash himself into one of the tiny toddler sized chairs in front of the tea cups and plates. "I'm ready for some tea, Kris!" He said.

"Kawyn is right next to you. She says she likes your new beard, daddy." Krista observed. William felt his face. He had grown some facial hair lately that he didn't have before. "Thank you, Karen." He said to the empty seat next to him.

"Kawyn isn't there daddy, she sitting on the other side of the table." Krista insisted. He gave his sentiments to the other empty chair on his left instead. "Is that where she is?" He asked his daughter.

"She says your welcome daddy. Yes. That's where she is." Krista continued on with her tea party experience, serving the pretend tea and appetizers. William went along with what she said, although it was real for him now. Although he couldn't see Karen, his perspective had changed and he found himself interacting with Krista and 'Karen' as if

300

she were there. According to Janice, Krista could really see her and if that was the case, he wanted to participate fully. He wasn't sure what to expect; maybe that Krista would start having long conversations with her sister, but that didn't happen. Krista just kept up the conversation between him and Karen; it really was like she had an imaginary friend. But now he knew different.

"Dinner's ready!" Maria called from downstairs about a half hour later. "We're coming!" William yelled back down to her. "Karen, we have to go downstairs, but I had fun!" He tried to keep the tone light, although he was struggling now emotionally. The tea party with 'Karen' had made him realize how out of touch he'd been with Krista since her death and how he had detached himself from it. Now he was feeling as though he was deserting her.

"Daddy, Kawyn says she's glad you came. She wants to give you a hug." Krista told him. His eyes teared up. "I'd love a hug from Karen." He told her. He reached out to where 'Karen' was sitting and pretended to hug her.

"She says she loves you and will see you later, daddy. She's gone." Krista informed him. She hugged the air where Karen was supposed to be. "She's gone now. We can go downstairs." Krista announced.

"That was the best tea party ever!" He picked up his daughter, her long blonde ponytail bouncing as they headed downstairs to dinner. "I think so too, daddy. Karen was glad that you came! She wants to invite mommy, but she's afraid she'd be too sad." Krista's bright blue eyes stared into his. He knew that she or Karen that whoever was making this observation was right on the mark. Because, it was definitely not something Maria could get through without getting overly emotional.

"I think Karen's right. Mommy's still sad that Karen isn't here so we all can see her like you do, sweetheart. But hopefully, she'll start feeling better and she'll be back to herself." William hoped that would be the case. But he wasn't so sure anymore.

"Mommy is always sad. I wish I could help her be happy again, daddy." Krista told him as they arrived at the dinner table. He could see the sadness behind those beautiful eyes that were so like Maria's and it tore him apart. Somehow, he needed to get Maria to start living in the present again.

Over the next three weeks, William continued to work hard on getting his business up and running. They already had several clients that he suspected Stanley had sent his way. They were extremely wealthy people that were seeking out vacation homes in Rhode Island and he found himself busier than ever, trying to get the right home for these clients that had high expectations. He checked in with his right hand, Shane, who was busy showing properties from 9am until almost 7pm.

"Wow, Bill! This has been great! I was never this busy before! And these people are actually buying, not just 'looking to buy.'" Shane was clearly a happy employee and William was glad to hear that. He knew it was true, because between showing homes and making sure to stay on top of the business end, he was working from the time he dropped Krista off at school at 8am and not getting home until after 7:00 at night. He was happy about how well the business was doing; at this rate, he'd be making twice the money he'd made at Roberts & Sons, but coming home to Maria's depression was worrying him. It wasn't what she said, but more what she didn't say to him that bothered him.

She used to be very expressive about her emotional feelings, sharing them with him. Now, she sat in a chair all day, staring out the window, but when he asked her what was wrong, she told him she was 'fine.' He'd reached out to Dr. Sanchez who was treating her supposedly on a weekly basis just today.

"Mr. Carson, I haven't seen your wife in over 3 weeks. My office has called to schedule an appointment with her, but she never called back." Dr. Sanchez informed him. "Is she doing better, I'm quite concerned." She said.

"So am I, Dr. Sanchez. I watch the woman that I love more than anything sit in a chair, wasting away because she can't get over our daughter's death." William was honest with her.

"I think the best you can do for her is encourage her to continue with counseling. Do you feel as though she's suicidal?" Dr. Sanchez asked.

"She's never mentioned that, so no, I don't think so. She just seems to be stuck in her own world right now. She's not doing much now and not looking for work." William told her, but suddenly he had an idea that might help. A vacation away! Get away from the house at least!

"Please let her know that unless she comes back in for an appointment, I won't be able to refill her medications." Dr. Sanchez reminded him.

"I'll have her make an appointment then." William assured her. After he got off the phone he approached his wife about seeing Dr. Sanchez again.

"Honey, when was the last time you saw Dr. Sanchez?" He mentioned it casually, while they were sitting in front of the TV, although he'd planned how to ask her since he'd talked to Dr. Sanchez.

"I don't know. A few weeks I guess." Maria answered nonchalantly. She was busy watching "Designing Women" and wasn't really paying attention to the conversation.

"You should make an appointment with her. Because I was thinking that we could book a vacation soon after New Year's. Maybe to the Caribbean, somewhere tropical?" It was the beginning of November in Rhode Island, getting cold already. He was hoping to lure her away and get her spirits up.

"I'd like a vacation, but I'd like to go back to Block Island. It was nice there." Maria said.

"It *is* nice there, Maria. When it's summer time! You do realize it's going to be really cold if we go there in January." William wasn't following her logic, but at the same time he was glad that she was willing to go *somewhere*!

Maria thought for a moment. It *was* going to be cold soon and he was right. Block Island was great in the summer. In the winter months, they'd be lucky to even be able to get there by ferry because of the weather. "You're right, Bill. How about planning us a trip to Florida or somewhere warm. Maybe in February when we're really tired of the weather here?" She agreed.

"How about Disneyworld in Florida? Krista would love it!" William suggested. Maria smiled. "That's a great idea! Let's do it!" She actually seemed more animated than she had in months. "But we can definitely plan a Block Island vacation in the summer. In the meantime, I'll contact a travel agent and set up a trip for Disney in February. How about that?" William was ready to do it today, since she seemed happy about it.

He contacted his friend, Josh from college. They'd stayed in touch here and there throughout the years and Josh's wife was a travel agent. She was able to get him a great deal for a week at Disneyworld, staying at the park, the flights and including all the park passes for much less than he would have gotten from any other travel agency. Josh had recently moved to Bristol in Rhode Island from Boston, so they agreed to get together sometime soon.

When he received the reservations and park passes in the mail a week later, he couldn't wait to surprise Maria and Krista. "Guess where we're going?" He came in the door after a long day at work. He could smell something on the stove that seemed to be burning. "Maria? Where are you? Somethings burning!" He noticed several pans on the gas stove with the flame off, but there was one that was still lit and the pan was smoking. He immediately turned it off, moved it and looked inside. It looked like it was supposed to be rice, but it was glued to the pan and brown now. Maria came in the kitchen just then, yawning as though she'd just woken up.

"Hi, honey. I was just lying down for a minute on the couch and I guess I fell asleep!" Then she noticed the burnt rice in the pan. "Oh, no! It's ruined!" She picked up the pan and ran some water in the pan to soak.

"Maria, what were you thinking leaving the stove on while you took a nap? What's going on here?" He'd started to wonder if she was drinking, but she didn't smell like alcohol and this had never happened before. "Where's Krista?" He looked around. Just then, she came down the stairs. "Here I am, daddy!" She ran to give him a hug and wrinkled up her nose. "Smells yucky in here!" She told him.

Maria stepped in. "Mommy accidentally burned something on the stove. But luckily everything else is still edible." She glanced at William who was clearly upset with her, but turned his attention to Krista. "Guess what, sweetheart? We are all going somewhere special in a few months. How would you like to go to Disneyworld?" He pulled out the information that included all the brochures of the hotel and the park in Florida.

"Yay! Get to see the princesses!" Krista started jumping up and down and hugging him. Maria stood back with a quiet smile on her face. "That sounds like fun, Bill! When is it?" She seemed less happy than he expected.

"The end of February. So we just need to get through the holidays and it'll be here before we know it!" William tried to focus on Krista's excitement about the trip and hoped that soon his wife would come around.

.

Maria

Maria tried to feel happy about the trip to Florida, but she felt as though she needed to go back to Block Island. It had been their last family vacation and what she remembered most when she thought of Karen. But Bill was right. It wasn't a good place to visit in the wintertime. She just needed to make it through the holidays, which she wasn't looking forward to. But she was going to do her best. Besides, it was Krista that was so excited about the trip. She could over hear her talking to her dolls in her room one afternoon after school. "We get to see the princesses; Cinderella and Snow White and also Mickey Mouse!" She talked incessantly to her dolls and an empty chair that she had always reserved for her sister.

Her days continued to be difficult; she had nightmares, sometimes she couldn't remember them and other times, she woke up with the smell of burning flesh in her nose from the fire that killed Karen.

It was the same dream that she'd had when she was 11 years old and she'd been an unknowing witness; a quiet passenger to what would eventually happen. The car spinning off the road, the two little girls in the back, and then the fire. It had been the same night that her parents had been killed, and it didn't occur to her until now that it was her parent's crash that happened while she was sleeping. She wished she'd heeded the warning that it was, but she hadn't understood at the time. Sometimes, she would wake up to a shadow over the bed, but when she whispered, "Karen" the shadow would disappear. There was nothing.

It was worse than seeing her from time to time; at least she knew that her energy was still here. But now it was gone.

Every morning, William would let her know he was leaving for work. Most days, he would take Krista to school and then arrange for Sara to pick her up and bring her home. The business that William had started was doing well and while Maria was grateful, she almost felt guilty about it. Her husband had a successful business, but it was given to him for his silence. To her, it was a trade-off. In the end, Stanley Ahearn was found not at fault and the case had been closed. But she couldn't talk to William about it. After all, she'd lost her job and now, her days were taken up by sleeping until late morning, then roaming around the house, looking for a purpose, a reason to stay. When Krista arrived home, it was the only bright spot in her day. Krista would talk about her new friends and then eventually refer to her sister. "Mommy, Karen wants to give you a hug." She would say and Maria would oblige with a hug in the air. But she couldn't see her anymore as Krista could. Karen just didn't appear to her at all anymore, even in dreams, as much as she wished for her.

Maria had started seeing Dr. Sanchez again at Williams' insistence and she was not prescribing the Valium as before, but an antidepressant that didn't seem to work. Dr. Sanchez had told her it would take up to three weeks for her to feel the difference, but did give her a week's worth of Valium to help her sleep 'as needed'. Unfortunately, Maria felt as needed meant every night and in a week they were gone. When she asked for more sleeping medication, Dr. Sanchez refused to prescribe more. "But why not?" Maria was on the phone with her two days before Thanksgiving. She felt desperate.

"Maria, you haven't been in to see me for counseling in over two months. Besides, you can't rely on that medication to go to sleep." Dr. Sanchez insisted.

"Ok, I'll schedule an appointment now. When's you're next available appointment? I'll come in tomorrow!" Maria was feeling frantic.

"I don't have any openings tomorrow, but I can work you in at 9:30am the day after, Maria. Can you make it in that early?" Dr. Sanchez knew that Maria had often missed earlier morning appointments.

"Yes, I can make it then. Thank you!" Maria struggled to make it through the next few nights.

She managed to get through that day and the next, trying to focus on looking for a job. William noticed her looking that evening after dinner. "Honey, the business is doing really well. Don't stress yourself out about finding a job." He'd told her.

"I need to find something to do. I just can't sit here anymore." Maria said, irritated. "We're supposed to go to your mother's for Thanksgiving in a few days. The last thing I want to talk about is how I sat around this house doing nothing." She snapped at him suddenly.

"You said you had an appointment with Dr. Sanchez tomorrow. Go and talk to her and get your medications straightened out and talk to her about how you're feeling, Maria." William's voice sounded strained. She knew that he was growing tired of her attitude and she couldn't blame him. She was tired of feeling this way too!

Her appointment with Dr. Sanchez went as expected. Dr. Sanchez insisted that she needed to keep taking the antidepressants, and gave her a two-week supply of Valium. She was a very small framed 40-something Latina woman, but she was very strong with her opinions. "Maria, I'm not going to give you anymore Valium after this. I have to be honest; I think you're using them more than you need to and it won't help you in the long run. The antidepressants don't work the same as the sleep aid. They help to increase the serotonin in your brain to help you feel better. The valium is just to help you sleep if you're having a hard time. Not for every night. Now tell me about what's happening with you."

"I'm just having dreams that wake me up and then I can't get back to sleep. I'm sad all the time and I feel like I can't be there for my daughter. I lost my job a few months ago and I just feel useless and have no energy to do anything anymore." Maria admitted. "My husband started a new business recently that seems to be going well." She looked down suddenly.

"That sounds like something positive. Why are you looking down when you talk about it, Maria?" Dr. Sanchez asked.

"Because the way my husband got the money to start the business bothers me." Maria was honest. She wasn't going to tell her everything, but since William wanted her to talk to Dr. Sanchez, she was going to tell her what was on her mind.

"Bothers you how?" Dr. Sanchez pressed her to continue.

"Let's just say that he didn't save the money himself or get a loan from a bank. It was deal he made and I'm having a hard time with it."

Maria wasn't going to go any further into it, but suddenly it made her feel a little better telling someone about it. Even if it wasn't the whole awful truth. She wasn't even sure she could tell anyone what William had done; it made her angry and embarrassed.

"Maria, you don't have to tell me anything you're not comfortable talking about. But it might help ease some of your anxiety." Dr. Sanchez told her. Maria thought about it and considered telling her what had happened, but she couldn't bring herself to talk about it. Not even to Dr. Sanchez.

"I don't want to discuss it." Maria said softly. "We are going on vacation in February." She told her to change the subject.

"How wonderful! I hope you're going somewhere warm!" Dr. Sanchez was glad she was at least willing to go somewhere.

"We're going to Disneyworld in Florida, so it'll definitely be warmer than here." Maria agreed without any enthusiasm that didn't go unnoticed by Dr. Sanchez.

"You don't seem very excited about it, Maria." Dr. Sanchez commented gently. "I know it's hard for you to feel some happiness right now, but maybe try to think of it as taking a vacation from your depression. The sun and activities will do you some good. Besides, I'll bet Krista is counting the days! As for you, try to enjoy your time with your daughter and husband. People go on vacation to take a break and relax." Dr. Sanchez reminded her.

"I think I am. It'll be nice to get out of here for a week. Bill won't be at work and Krista will love it. I feel as though I don't know her anymore. As if we're drifting away." Maria didn't even realize it until she had said the words, but it was true. She *did* feel disconnected from her daughter lately.

"Make sure to enjoy yourself!" Dr. Sanchez agreed and they scheduled another appointment for after the holidays. Maria suddenly felt a wave of fear come over her. "Dr. Sanchez, what if I can't sleep without the Valium?"

Dr. Sanchez gave her a knowing look. "If that is the case, Maria, then I think we might need to talk about that more." Maria knew what she was eluding to; that she was addicted to it. She knew that she wasn't, so she just nodded. "Of course. I'm sure I'll be fine. I was just wondering." But now she knew. She needed to figure this out on her own. There was one thing that she needed to find out, but she couldn't tell anyone. She needed to know who was the father of her daughters.

When she got home, William was already there with Krista, making dinner. William had cooked up ground beef with some pasta sauce and spaghetti. "Look at you, making dinner! I'm impressed!" Maria tried to put on a happy face, even though she knew what she was going to do behind Williams' back. "Just in time for you to come home, sweetheart! How was your appointment with Dr. Sanchez?" He piled some pasta with sauce onto plates as they sat down to dinner.

"It was fine." Maria didn't want to get into details. "She thought it was good to get away." "I'm glad we're going somewhere together as a family. I think you're going to have a good time. Just think of how excited Krista is about the trip." William told her.

"It will be." Maria agreed. She tried not to think about what she was going to do in the next 24 hours. After Krista was in bed and

William was downstairs watching TV, she looked through her jewelry box and found it. It was still here after over 6 years! The business card was starting to yellow around the edges but she could still read the name and number. 'She knew, but I wouldn't tell her,' Maria thought to herself. She picked up the card, and dialed the number, hoping that Elyse Wincott still worked there. When the dispatcher picked up, she asked for Elyse and was transferred to an extension. 'Well, good at least she still works there!' Maria got her voicemail, which she expected and left her a quick message with her name and number.

William

Maria seemed to be in a better mood lately. They got through the holidays with a few bad moments at Thanksgiving and Christmas eve, when Maria retreated to the bedroom or wherever she could go at the time, because they went to his mother's for both holidays. As their February trip to Disneyworld grew closer after New Year's. Maria seemed to be calm, although he'd caught her on the phone a few times and she'd acted as though she were talking to someone else. But he knew better.

It was right after New Year's in early January. Maria was getting dressed and ready to go to meet with Elyse Wincott. She'd said nothing to William about her interactions with Elyse who was helping her as a rape victim and finding out the true paternity of her daughters. But she decided it was better to not mention it to her husband. He'd said he didn't want to know. But she did.

"Where are you headed?" It was 4:00 and he happened to get home early that day. "What do you mean, Bill? I told you, I'm going to see Dr. Sanchez." She was dressed in some jeans and a blue turtleneck sweater that accentuated her eyes.

"You just saw her a few days ago." William observed. Maria's eyes looked down for a moment.

"Well, I wanted to see her again before we go on our trip." She told him, as she went into the closet to get a pair of boots. As she retrieved the boots, she turned around to find him standing in front of her and she jumped. "Geez Bill, you scared me!"

"Are you seeing someone else? I'd just like to know, Maria!" He'd been watching her through the holidays; she felt better, she was going out more, even meeting up with her friend Steph Martin a few times (so she said) and seeing Dr. Sanchez. Maybe he was being paranoid, but he couldn't help but feel that she was keeping something from him.

She stood straight up after putting on her boots. "What? Are you serious? Bill! Really, I know things have been tough, but now you're accusing of me of having an affair!" Her blue eyes flashed fire at him as she looked him in the face. "You've got a lot of nerve asking me that, after you've been working 12 hours a day! Hey, maybe you're having an affair, but guess what? I believe that you're working those hours because I trust you!" She finished lacing up her boots and stomped downstairs angrily.

He knew he'd messed up big time. He ran down the stairs after her. "Maria! I'm sorry! We just haven't been communicating as much! I'm trying to make this business work!" She was grabbing her coat to walk out the door when he grabbed her arm. She spun around with tears in her eyes. "I thought that you'd trusted me by now, Bill. After all we've gone through, you actually think that I'd spend the time to have an affair! You don't know me at all anymore!" She slammed the door and headed out to the car.

He stood in the driveway, watching her drive away. Krista was still at his mother's house. He was supposed to pick her up by 5:00. He ran inside and called his mother. "Mom, can you keep Kris for another hour or so? Something just came up." He didn't want to explain what was going on.

"Sure, she's busy anyway." His mother agreed to keep her for a little while longer. "Is everything okay?" She sounded worried.

"Everything's fine, I just need some time alone with Maria, that's all." He didn't want to get into what he feared might be going on. He hung up and jumped into his car. Maria had quite the head start on him, so he needed to hurry up. Fortunately, he knew where Dr. Sanchez' office was so as he came close to the medical building, he slowed down to see if he could spot Maria's car. Her car wasn't there. Where the hell was she? He thought about going into Dr. Sanchez' s office and asking but he knew she couldn't answer any questions for him anyway. He drove further down the road and happened to spot her car at the police department of all places. Did he dare walk in and find out what she was up to? He decided to wait and see if she came out in the next few minutes.

After 15 minutes, he started to feel like he was stalking, but then he saw Maria come out with a female officer. Maria hugged her, which he thought was strange. What could she possibly be doing here? But she got in her car and headed back toward the house. William was tempted to go in and find out why she'd been at the police station, but then he thought about his deal with Stanley and decided against it. Maybe she'd decided to tell the police about Stanley's deal? He shook his head at just the thought. After all, it wouldn't just ruin his life, but her and Krista's life as well. Still, he was suspicious. He followed her car from a distance so that she wouldn't know it was him, but he was starting to feel weird about following her. Clearly, she was headed home. She wasn't having an affair and he felt awful for his accusations and then following her. He decided to go to his mother's house and pick up Krista now. Hopefully his wife would tell him what she'd been doing there sooner than later.

A few minutes later he was pulling up into his mother's driveway and picked up Krista. "She already ate dinner, so she's fine." His mother advised him. He could tell that she wanted to talk but he wanted to get home to see if his wife had actually gone back there. "I've gotta go, mom. Thank you so much. I'll call you later." He put Krista in her car seat and headed out toward home, hoping that Maria was there by now. As he pulled into the driveway, her car wasn't there and his heart sank. Now, he didn't know what to think. He was tempted to try and find her, but with Krista in the car, he wouldn't. He would just go inside and wait.

Maria

She'd spent the last few weeks talking with Elyse Wincott about what had happened and needing to get paternity testing done. She needed to know for sure who was the father of the twins. She knew William had said that he didn't want to know, but she did. Elyse had helped so much and it required time when Maria had to lie to William to provide the hair samples for the testing and she felt awful. Especially today, since he'd accused her of having an affair, which made her cringe because she was the last person on earth that would cheat on her husband.

She wasn't sure if she should look at the results that Elyse had handed her, but then she knew she couldn't do it alone. And she definitely couldn't do it at home, with or without William there. So there was she was in a South Kingstown police office, with a police officer, opening the envelope that was giving her either the best or the worst news ever. It was very nerve wracking. "Can you do it for me?" Maria asked Elyse who was standing in front of her desk looking just as anxious as Maria.

"I can't do this for you, Maria." Elyse told her softly. "But I'm here with you, so you won't be alone." Elyse knew that it was a boundary she couldn't cross, even though her heart went out to this woman who'd struggled with the rape, her daughter passing away and now a paternity test. Maria nodded and slowly opened the envelope and pulled out the results. There were a bunch of lab testing results that she didn't understand and she sifted through them to the final page where it stated the conclusion with all of the lab results. It was confirmed that Dan Ahearn was 99.9% the father of Krista and Karen. Maria felt her legs giving out and Elyse immediately ran over to grab the chair from behind and grasped her shoulders to sit down.

Maria tried to rationalize that she'd suspected this all along which is why she'd done the test in the first place. "It's not like I didn't think it was possible. I just wanted it to be William." Maria said softly. But then she remembered that Dan was a twin, and she'd known that going in when she asked for the test. Maybe she needed to know to make a decision about what she was going to do.

Elyse kneeled down beside her. "Maria, you've told me that William has always been there; always provided and he even said he didn't want a test because he felt as though he was their father." She was starting to worry that Maria wouldn't be okay to drive back home after the news. "Should I call your husband or someone to come pick you up?" She wanted to mention that Maria could go after Dan Ahearn for child support, but this wasn't the time or the place. She knew Maria would never go for that anyway.

Maria suddenly realized that she'd made a mistake in finding out the truth, but there was nothing she could do now. Now, she knew. It suddenly made everything much easier in a way. She would never tell William, because he didn't want to know and she knew it would hurt him even though it wasn't her fault. It would hurt him as it was hurting her now; that he *was* their father in every other way, except genetically. And now she realized that it had been important to her because she wanted these little girls to carry on William's kind heart, his unique characteristics and now she was faced with the truth that it belonged to a man that she hated. The man that had raped her. But Krista still had a chance, and she knew she would never tell her or William. As long as William was there, Krista would be fine.

"No, I'm okay to drive. I'm going to go home to my family. I'll be okay." Maria told Elyse. She didn't want to worry her. "Thank you so much for helping me with this. It wasn't' the news I'd wanted, but it's what I thought I needed to know." She stood up to leave Elyse's office.

"If it's any consolation, I think your husband loves you and your daughter more than anyone in this world. If you told him tonight, he would still love all of you the same." Elyse told her. She embraced Maria in a brief hug that surprised her, but Maria was grateful to have someone that seemed to understand. Maria felt the tears sliding down her face as she brushed them away.

"Thank you again, Elyse. I appreciate all your work to get this information for me." Maria waved as she left her office. As she got into her car, she could feel her mother's presence that she hadn't felt in so long. "You did the right thing, Maria. Now you know and you need to tell him the truth."

"No, I don't mom! It would hurt him too much! He already said he doesn't want to know!" Maria yelled in frustration back at her. "I'm not telling him!"

"Then how are you going to explain being at the police station? He knows that you went there. He followed you." Her mother's voice came back at her. She wanted to scream at her, but she was right. What was she going to tell him? Maybe he thought she was ratting out Stanley and his agreement for his business. Then an idea came to her that would solve the problem; for the moment anyway. She would tell William that she had met with Elyse to make a statement about the rape, and that they were looking for Dan Ahearn.

"I have it figured out, mom." Maria said out loud. There was no response, but she knew that her mother could hear her. She was tired of her mother's advice. So far, it had ended in heartbreak and nothing had changed except that now her husband was accusing her of having an affair, then apparently followed her to the police station that she would now have to explain.

William

When Maria's car finally pulled into the driveway at 7:00, he felt relief, followed by anger. Why hadn't she called him? And what was she doing at the police station? He tried to calm himself before she walked in the door, but he couldn't help but feel his anger boiling over. He'd managed to make hamburgers and some frozen fries for dinner for himself and Krista had eaten already at his mother's so she was upstairs playing. He was grateful for small things at this point. "Where have you been?" He tried to keep his tone even and calm, although he wanted to yell at her because he knew that she hadn't been at an appointment with Dr. Sanchez.

She managed to compose herself on the drive home. "No, I wasn't. I was at the police station. I didn't want to tell you about it, because I didn't want to tell you that I was talking with the sex crimes investigator." Maria told him, but he could tell that she was shaking and close to tears.

"About what? About the rape that happened over 5 years ago?" William hated the words as soon as they came out of his mouth. But what he didn't understand was what she was trying to achieve. He knew about Dan Ahearn and what happened. He'd thought they'd moved past it. But obviously not.

"Yes. She knew when it happened and I was just providing information for her. That's all. I'm not having an affair and I wasn't there to talk about your deal with Stanley Ahearn, Bill! You know that I would never do that!" Maria insisted and sat down on the couch, sobbing into her hands. William immediately was at her side and put his arm around her. "Maria, I'm so sorry for accusing you of an affair. I didn't really think you were, but you've been secretive. You have to admit that." William backed down with his accusations.

"I'm sorry that I didn't talk to you about this, but I really didn't want you to know. It was just something that I needed to do. So someone else doesn't get hurt by this monster. At least I can help in that way." Maria told him. "I'm really ready to move on. I'm trying, Bill." He could hear the pleading in her words, so he decided to let it go. There was only so much he could do for her. In the end, it really was up to her to be happy.

"Okay, honey. Let's just put this past us and look forward to our vacation next month." William wanted to remind her of the fun trip in hopes that she would refocus on their marriage and Krista. "You must be hungry. Want a burger and some fries? They're fresh from the freezer but when they're heated up, they're not bad for a real estate agent." He tried to joke.

She smiled weakly. "I am kind of hungry. Thanks, Bill." She sat quietly at the table while he fixed her a plate. She picked at the food, barely eating anything and then robotically got up and dumped the remains in the trash, rinsed the plate off. "I think I'll say good night to Kris and go to bed myself. It's been a long day." She gave him a hug and headed upstairs.

"Maria, it's only 7:30!" He reminded her, but she just shook her head. "It feels like midnight to me." Her voice faded as she reached Krista's room.

William wasn't sure what to do anymore. He believed that she wasn't having an affair, but this interest in helping the police investigate Dan Ahearn about a rape that happened more than 5 years ago was concerning. It wasn't healthy for her to be so involved as she claimed to be. He was suddenly hit with a thought that was so out of left field that he almost dismissed it immediately. 'Maybe she's trying to find out if Dan is the twin's father.' He told himself he was being paranoid now, but the thought lingered with him. It would explain her going out more than usual to see Dr. Sanchez, and Maria made it sound as if she'd gone to speak with the sex crimes investigator more than once. He knew that now wasn't the time to inquire. He'd give her a few weeks. But if things didn't improve with her overall mental health and behavior, he wasn't going to avoid this question any longer. He needed to ask what was going on, but he feared he already knew. It was just a matter of asking her and hoping she'd tell him the truth.

Maria

She vowed to spend more time with Krista after finding out that Bill wasn't her father. Maria knew she'd made the wrong decision about finding out because it changed the way she looked at her husband and her daughter. As she engaged in a 'tea party' with Krista, she couldn't get over how much her personality was like William's, fun-loving, outgoing and happy much of the time. From what she could remember about Dan, he'd been controlling, and arrogant. Which is why she'd only dated him for a few months until William swept her off her feet. But now she knew and there wasn't any turning back from it. She smiled as she watched Krista laugh and play, wishing that things had turned out so differently. "Mommy, it's your turn to pour the tea!" Krista said insistently.

"Oh, I'm sorry!" Maria grabbed the tiny tea pot and pretended to pour it for one of Krista's dolls. "Don't forget to pour it for Kawyn. She wants you to do it for her." Krista said, pointing to the empty chair with a tea cup set in front of it.

Maria froze for a moment. "Is she right there, Kris?" She pointed to the empty chair.

"Yes, mommy. She's ready for some tea. She wants you to pour it, mommy." Krista insisted. Maria nodded, an eerie sensation coming over her. She could feel Karen's presence and she pretended to pour the 'cup of tea'. "Do you want cream and sugar, Karen?" She asked. She was actually hoping that she could hear Karen answer, but she didn't. But Krista apparently could. Or at least was pretending, Maria wasn't quite sure.

"She says, yes, mommy. She told me she misses you and wishes you weren't so sad." Krista told her.

Maria's eyes filled with tears that she held back from spilling over. "Well, you tell her that I miss her very much and I am sad but I'll be okay." Maria managed to tell Krista with her voice cracking slightly.

Krista just nodded her head. "She heard you, Mommy. She says she'll come talk to you soon."

Maria reached over to hug Krista. "I hope so, sweetheart. But I'm glad that you talk to her and keep her company. "

Krista looked thoughtful. "She tells me she misses me and you and daddy. She told me soon she won't be able to talk to me. I'll miss her, mommy." Krista looked sad as she said the words. Fat tears started sliding down her smooth cheeks as she went to her for a hug. Maria hugged her tightly, fighting back the urge to sob.

"Krista, your sister will always be with you, even if you can't see or talk to her anymore. Remember that necklace that your dad got both of you?" Krista pointed to hers that she never took off. "Where did Kawyn's go?" She asked.

"I have it and one day, I'll give it back to you when you can put it in a safe place. Right now, you have lots of things to do; go to school, make friends and when you're older, it will be yours to keep." Maria promised her.

"Promise, mommy?" Krista asked.

"I promise. I know Karen would want you to have it. Right now, you have yours to take care of." She pointed to her neck. Krista was very attached to it and didn't like to take it off, even to take a bath. Maria insisted that she take it off in the bath, but Krista always wanted it back on immediately after.

After Maria put Krista to bed, she wandered downstairs. William was sitting watching TV and sipping a beer. She suddenly knew that she needed to talk to him about what she'd done. No more secrets. "Bill, I need to tell you something." She knew that he hadn't wanted to know, but she went ahead and found out anyway. Now it was only fair that he did know.

"Come sit down, Maria. Sit with me." He patted the couch cushion next to him and she suddenly felt warning bells going off as she sat down. He knew. He was just waiting for her to tell him, she realized.

He turned off the TV and faced her. "Maria, I know what you're going to tell me; you had paternity testing done, didn't you?" His voice was calm and matter of fact. He didn't seem angry and it took her by surprise.

"Bill, I thought I needed to know. I really did. But I wish I hadn't." Maria said softly. She was afraid, but she reached for his hand and hoping he didn't pull it away. He didn't. He grasped her hand and turned to give her a hug. "I know. I'm not happy about it, but I know that you felt like you had to."

"He is the father as far as the DNA results are, but you're their father, Bill. I just wish that I'd told you what happened to me earlier."

Maria was crying softly, as she said the words. She'd never planned to tell him, but she also didn't want to hide anything from him.

"Maria, I didn't want to know, because I knew there was a chance. But I don't blame you for wanting to know. I'm not angry with you, I just want you to be able to come to terms with Karen's death. It's hard for me too, you know. I don't know what I'd do without you and Krista in my life. I really don't. I just want you to promise me that you won't tell Krista about this paternity test. I *am* her father. She doesn't need to know." William told her.

"Bill, you are their father in every sense of the word. I would never tell her that. She doesn't need to know." Maria agreed with him.

They hugged and spent the rest of the night just curled up together until they fell asleep. It was probably one of the best nights they'd had together as a married couple since the accident.

Maria found herself alone in a thick fog in what seemed the middle of nowhere. She could hear a child's voice calling for her "Mommy, where are you?" Maria felt frantic, knowing that it was Karen. "Where are you? I'm coming!" She ran through the soaking wet grass until she reached a cliff that led straight down. She stopped just in time as she saw the frothing white caps and waves churning 100 feet below. "Mommy! I can't see you, where are you?" Karen's voice seemed to be coming from out in the ocean. "Please come find me!" Maria looked down at the cliff and at the threatening rocks and ocean below. She lifted one wet muddy bare foot off the side of the cliff, but pulled it back in fear. Was she ready to go with her?

"Mommy! Please, I need your help!" Karen's voice called again, pleading with her. Maria took a deep breath and was ready to step off the cliff when someone was shaking her.

"Maria! Maria!" She suddenly woke up to William shaking her shoulders. "What? What happened?" She found herself standing at the sliding glass door out to the patio and William was staring at her as though he'd seen a ghost.

"You were sleepwalking, Maria. You were talking to someone, then got up, opened the sliding door and were walking around outside. Thank god there isn't any snow on the ground!" William told her. She looked down at her muddy wet bare feet. "I woke up just as you were headed outside and tried to get you to wake up, but you just stared straight ahead as if you were still dreaming." William told her, as he grabbed the blanket from the couch and wrapped it around her.

"I was just dreaming, Bill. I'm fine. I'm sorry to scare you!" Maria was shaken but she wasn't about to tell him about hearing Karen's voice. He'd have her put back in a psychiatric hospital in the morning!

"Well, come upstairs and get into a hot shower. It's 35 degrees out there and you're still shivering." William practically pushed her up the stairs with the blanket over her shoulders and turned on the shower for her. "Thanks, I'm okay now, Bill. I can get in the shower by myself." She told him, annoyed that he was standing by the shower, watching her every move.

"Sorry. It just scared me, honey. I'll go to bed and wait for you there." He went back in the bedroom while she stood under the warm spray, remembering every part of that dream as if she were living it. She was ready to follow her now. She didn't need a psychic or anyone else telling her what that meant.

She finished her shower and got ready for bed, then hugged her husband close to her. She'd miss these moments. She glanced over at the nightstand with the picture of her, Krista and Karen at the beach. She needed to remember to take it with her.

William

It was almost 50 degrees outside, very warm for a Rhode Island January morning and he was happy for some better weather as he headed out to work at 7:30am. Somehow he didn't mind the early mornings and late days since starting the business. He felt energized, eager to keep what success he had going and building up the clientele. Maria's news last night about Dan being the biological father didn't surprise him. Especially since she'd told him about the rape around the time she found out she was pregnant. He felt more let down that she hadn't told him she was going to do the testing. He knew damn well Dan would never come looking to try and be the father to Krista. If he ever did, he'd have to kill him to take her from him and Maria.

She'd been sleeping when he left. Her sleepwalking episode had been scary last night. She'd been sound asleep when he got up, so he'd gotten Kris up and ready for school, then dropped her off. He called his mother as soon as he got to the office. "Can you check on Maria later this morning? She didn't get much sleep last night and I want to make sure she's okay. I'm busy with clients all day.

"Sure. I'll call her later this morning. If she's busy and can't pick Kris up from school, then I'll pick her up and bring her over here for a few hours. Krista and I are working on planting an herb garden. She loves it!" Sara told him.

"Great. Let me know if there's any problem." William was so grateful for his mother. She'd always been his rock throughout his life but especially now.

The day went by quickly. He was getting calls all day long about properties and Shane had been booked solid for showing houses for the next several weeks, so he'd taken on several calls that had come in that day. Callie was struggling to keep up with all the paperwork coming in and told him so. It was after 5:00 and Callie knocked on his door that was open, but she was always polite and professional.

"Hi, Callie, is everything okay?" William was just finishing up with a phone call.

"Mr. Carson, I'm not sure I can keep up with all this paperwork. I'm behind on my schoolwork because I've been working late every night." Callie admitted.

William had been so busy getting the business up and running, that he'd forgotten how much work it'd be for Callie. After all, she was part-time and in school. "I'm sorry, Callie. Go ahead and head out. I'm going to hire someone soon to help you out. In the meantime, just stick to your scheduled hours. I'll figure it out, school is important!" He told her. She was a great employee and hard-working. He didn't want to stress her out and lose her so he immediately put out an ad for another assistant to help Callie out.

"Thank you, Mr. Carson. I hope you get to go home soon. It's getting kind of late." She pointed to the clock. It was now 6:00.

"Wow, the time flew by. Thanks, Callie! Have a good night, I'll see you tomorrow." William told her. It was dark outside now and he hadn't heard from his mother or Maria all day. He called Maria to let her know he was on his way but there was no answer. He tried several times, hoping she was just in the bathroom or dealing with Krista. Still no answer. He tried his mother. She picked up on the second ring.

"William! I was just going to call you! Maria's not home. I tried calling her later this morning, and no answer, so I picked Krista up from school. I went over an hour ago and she still wasn't home." Sara sounded panicked.

"Don't worry, mom. I'm sure she's just out seeing one of her friends or had a doctor's appointment." William tried to smooth things over, despite the fact that he was concerned. She didn't have any doctor appointments as far as he knew and she had always told him if she was going out to meet friends which was very rare. "I'm leaving work now. I'll be at your house in about 20 minutes." He grabbed his jacket and keys and made sure to lock up before running to his car. When he arrived at his mother's house, Krista had just finished dinner and was reading a story to his mother's cat, Beatrice.

"Hi, daddy!" Krista left the couch as he walked in and ran to him to give him a hug.

"Hi, sweetheart! How was your day?" William tried to keep his voice from sounding upset as he hugged his daughter. "Any word from Maria?" He asked his mother quietly.

Sara shook her head. "No, I've tried at least three more times. I almost wanted to go over and see if her car was there, but I didn't want Krista to think anything was wrong."

William nodded. "Good thinking. Knowing Krista, she'd want to know why she wasn't home." Krista was exceptionally observant and seemed to know when something wasn't right.

Sara seemed worried as well. "Maybe you should go over to the house first. I'll keep Krista here and entertained. Just so you can find out what's going on." She said in a low voice so that Krista couldn't hear her.

"Kris, honey, daddy's going to go check on some things and I'll be right back. You stay here with grandma." William gave her a hug.

"What things, daddy?" Krista always required details.

"Mommy had some errands to run today, so I'm just going to check and see if she's done." William hoped that this would answer his 4- year -old daughter's line of questioning.

He left after giving Krista another hug and jumped into his car. His house wasn't far, and soon he pulled up into their driveway. Maria's car wasn't there and there weren't any lights on in the house. His heart started pounding as he unlocked the door. 'That's a good sign, at least it's locked.' He thought to himself. He turned on the lights and started looking around the house, calling out her name. He wasn't sure why; after all her car was gone. "Maria?" He ran upstairs to their bedroom and discovered that some of the drawers had been left open and some of her clothes from the closet were gone. "Maria? Are you here? Are you okay?" He was starting to panic. He looked over at the nightstand where the picture of Maria and the girls had been. It was gone.

He went downstairs and called his mother. "Maria's not here. She's gone. I don't know where she went but she's gone!" He was almost yelling into the phone. "Mom, I'm worried. There's no sign of a break in, but some of her clothes and this picture that she had on the nightstand is gone. I'm going to call the police. I don't know what else to do!"

" Maybe she's just out for the day. " Sara advised. "Of course I'll keep Krista here. Don't worry about her. Call me and let me know!"

William called the South Kingstown police and let them know about the situation. "Maybe she's just out with friends." He got the initial response that he'd expected from them.

"No, really, she doesn't go out without letting me know where she is! I'm telling you, something's wrong!" William was getting upset. The dispatcher told him she'd have an officer at his house soon. She sounded like a bored teenager that they'd hired to manage the phones, but he had no choice but to wait for them.

He called his mom back and let her know that he had no idea where Maria was. "I'm worried that she's gone off the deep end and just took off. That would explain the missing luggage and clothes. I just called the police, so they're going to send someone out eventually."

"I'll keep Kris here with me. I have some of her clothes here that I washed and didn't send back with her. Just keep me posted." His mother assured him. She'd been his rock so many times in his life, he couldn't even begin to count.

"Thank you, mom! Just tell Krista that I had to go back to work or something. I'm sure I'll hear from her soon." William told her, although he wasn't so sure. Maria had her quirks in the past, but she'd never taken off like this. He had a bad feeling about this. He continued to look around for other signs of where she might have gone or other things that were missing. He was looking around in their bedroom when he noticed that her jewelry box that had belonged to her mother was also gone. That had been one thing she treasured most. His heart sank and he knew that she'd left them. She was gone. And she'd left on her own. He was sure of it.

Officer Spencer showed up about an hour later and talked with him. He told him about the entire day's events and what he'd noticed missing. William could tell that Spencer was fairly new to the job as he would go from one room to another, forget to take pictures, then go back. Afterwards, he sat down at the kitchen table with him. "Have you had a fight with your wife recently?" Spencer asked him. He was on the heavy side. He was visibly sweating after going up and down the stairs.

"No. I mean we had a disagreement, but it wasn't significant. We went to bed on good terms." William said honestly. He didn't feel as though Maria's jaunt through the yard sleepwalking was important.

"Disagreement?" Officer Spencer wrote that down, thinking he had something. William tried not to roll his eyes. This guy was clearly the latest hire, rookie and just sent out to investigate something they didn't think was worth their time.

"Yes, it happens. We're married. We have a child. We have disagreements!" William was starting to get irritated with the line of questioning. "But we always talk out our problems. She's been especially depressed since the death of our daughter recently. I'm concerned for her safety. That she might have left because she intends to harm herself." William told him.

"Ok, Mr. Carson. I understand. I just need to ask these questions, they're pretty standard." Rookie cop Spencer recited probably from his handbook. "I just need us to look outside to see if anything looks out of place to you." He advised.

"Really? It's dark out there, what do you think you're going to find?" William asked. "I don't mind taking you out there, but there's nothing out there that's going to help you find my wife."

Spencer insisted so they went out the sliding glass door to look around. The outside lights provided some assistance, but only for about 15 feet, then they were out in darkness. They'd just crossed the deck to the stairs when Spencer stopped. "There's some blood here. Did any of you come out here with a cut recently?"

William groaned inwardly. It was likely that Maria had a cut on her toe or something from wandering around outside last night while she was sleepwalking. Now he was going to have to talk about that incident which he felt was irrelevant. Spencer took a picture of it, then dabbed it with a tissue and placed it in a baggie.

He began to explain the incident as they went back inside while Spencer was scribbling in his notebook. After he finished telling him, Spencer informed him that he'd give out the information and put out a 'be on the lookout (BOLO)' for Maria's car and license plate. "That was all I wanted in the first place. I want to know where she went, that's she's safe!" William was more than frustrated by now. Spencer just nodded and continued his report.

As he was leaving, Spencer told him to 'not take any trips out of state in the next few days, so we can be in contact." William didn't like the sound of that. It sounded like because he found a spot of blood outside, that he was now going to be suspected of his wife's disappearance. It was now 11:30 at night and he got on the phone with his mother.

"Mom? I'm sorry to call so late. An officer was here which took a long time. He went through the house, took pictures, then told me they'd put a look out for her vehicle." William was emotionally exhausted by this time.

"William, just go to bed and get your rest. Krista is asleep, she's fine. You can't do anything when you're too tired. Get something to eat and get to bed. Call me in the morning." Sara was giving him her best mom advice. But there was no way he could eat anything right now, and sleeping was going to be non-existent. He had no idea how he'd get to sleep. He headed for the bottle of Jack Daniels that had been sitting months in the kitchen and poured himself a glass with more than 2 shots worth, trying to figure out what he could do to find her!

Maria

She'd woken up that morning, later than she'd wanted. It was already 9:30! She'd hoped to be gone by now, but William had taken Krista to school so she had a small window in which she could get herself together. She had already made a plan for what she was taking with her; the jewelry box with her treasures. She'd written a poem last week that she added to the box, along with the picture of her and the twins. She hid the frame in the closet. Maybe he wouldn't notice it was gone until much later.

She packed a suitcase with some warm clothing and took a quick shower. Maria felt a twinge of pain as the water hit her left foot. She looked down to see a cut on the top of her left big toe. 'Where did that come from?' She wondered, then shrugged it off. It wasn't serious and she needed to move forward with her plan before she lost her nerve.

She could hear Karen's voice as she went into what was her bedroom for the last time. "Mommy, where are you? Are you coming?"

"Yes, I am." Maria said out loud. She stepped into Krista's room, sat on her bed and wrote her a note on a piece of her construction paper. "*I love you, love mommy.*" She picked up one of Krista's favorite books, 'Raggedy Ann and the Cookie Snatcher' and put the piece of paper inside it. She would find it eventually, Maria hoped. She loved Krista so much, but she felt as though she couldn't keep up this constant pain, the reminders, the dreams and Karen's voice that she was hearing.

She went through the bedroom that she and William had shared, put her hand on the down-filled lilac comforter and ran it down to the pillows that they'd slept on last night. She placed a note under the pillow that read 'I love you always.' She didn't want to say goodbye. If she did, she'd just lose her nerve and just make this worse than it would be later on. As she walked through the rest of the house, it was almost as if she were in a dream now. One last look around.

She got into her car and drove away, brushing back her tears. She wanted to make one last trip to her parent's graves in Vermont and maybe see what Aunt Sylvia was doing. Maybe she'd changed and maybe her scumbag cousin had left the house. She knew that she couldn't stay here now. She felt as though she'd betrayed William, Krista and his family because she now knew the truth about the twin's father. Even though William had said it didn't matter, she knew that she'd hurt him by having the testing done and her reaction to it. She was thankful that it was warm enough that it wasn't going to snow today, unless the weather in Vermont was different which was a significant possibility. She'd stashed some money aside every month in her own separate account that she'd had since she was a teenager, so there was enough to get by for a little while. She'd figure it out.

As the miles went by, she was finally able to relax a little and enjoyed the ride as she went through New Hampshire and crossed into Vermont. It didn't take long for the memories of her childhood to come flooding back. The trips to Lake Champlain and taking the ferry over to New York, the fishing trips with her father on Silver Lake in

Barnard, and the skiing trips to Okemo in Ludlow. She could hear her mother's voice again. "Welcome back home. I'm proud of you for being honest with him."

"I was honest and look what I've done. I can't be with them anymore. Now, I've nowhere to go." Maria felt lost. The only hope was that Aunt Sylvia had changed her ways and would welcome her; at least until she could get back on her feet.

It was after 3:30 when she pulled up in front of her aunt's home in Middlebury. The house looked almost the same, but clearly her aunt hadn't been keeping it up. The porch was missing part of the railing and the yellow paint was peeling off the exterior of the house. She didn't bother to call, because she couldn't remember the number. Besides, this surprise visit would tell Maria all she needed to know about her aunt. It didn't give her time to give an illusion that she gave a shit about anyone, as she'd done with her parents so long ago prior to their death.

Maria suddenly felt nervous as she walked up the porch stairs that also needed some attention. The stairs themselves were starting to rot and she was almost afraid she might fall through one of them. She took a deep breath and rang the doorbell. There was no answer at first. She went to ring it again, when a thin woman with stringy grey hair and wearing a shapeless nightgown came to the door. 'Do I have the wrong house? Maybe she moved.' Maria thought.

"Yes? Can I help you?" The woman asked in a weak, strained voice. Beyond the obvious differences in her appearance, Maria suddenly realized it was her aunt. "Aunt Sylvia? It's me, Maria!" The woman peered closer at her. "Maria? Is that really you?" She smiled and Maria was horrified to see that she was missing her front tooth.

"It is, Aunt Sylvia." Maria smiled at her, suddenly feeling sorry for her. She looked horribly frail and sick. As her aunt invited her in, she noticed how thin she was. Aunt Sylvia had never been overweight; just a larger frame that made her seem larger than she actually was. Now, she looked almost emaciated.

Surprisingly, her aunt gave her a hug as she came in. "It's so good to see you again, Maria. You're looking as beautiful as always." It was as if the aunt that she'd left behind had been replaced by another person! Who was this woman now? She brought her into the kitchen, which looked the same as when Maria had left. She had the same old silver tea kettle on the stove and Maria nodded when she asked if Maria wanted some tea.

"Thank you Aunt Sylvia. I hope you're doing.....well." The last part of her sentence trailed off. It was obvious that she wasn't and suddenly she felt awkward.

"I wish that were the case. Unfortunately, as you can probably tell, I'm not doing so well physically. I was diagnosed with pancreatic cancer just a few weeks ago." Sylvia told her.

"I'm so sorry, Aunt Sylvia." Maria felt tears coming to her eyes, despite how her aunt had treated her in the past.

"I'm sorry, Maria. For the way I treated you when you lived with me. I was being greedy and selfish and didn't think about you; just how upset I was that your mother was gone." There were tears in her eyes now as she spoke. "But you haven't said why you're here now. Why is it that you've decided to visit me again?"

Maria told her about her marriage and the twins and what happened to Karen. She didn't mention the rape or the fact that the twins weren't her husbands. In the end, she told her that she needed to find herself again. As she said the words, she realized that it was true. She'd basically run away from her home in Rhode Island to find anything that would make her feel better, less depressed and no more reminders of the accident.

Sylvia advised her that she was in hospice care now, because she didn't want to do any treatment. "I did a couple of weeks after the initial diagnosis and it was brutal." Sylvia told her about the nausea and hair loss and the hospital stays. "I've decided that I'm going to live whatever time I have left without the added agony of treatment that won't save me anyway." Now *that* sounded like the Sylvia she remembered.

"Where are you planning to go from here now?" Her aunt asked after they'd had tea and a light dinner of Caesar salad that her aunt had prepared earlier in the day.

"I'm not sure to be honest." Maria admitted. "Probably check into a hotel tonight and see where I go from there."

"Nonsense! You won't stay in a hotel when I have plenty of room here with me!" Sylvia insisted. Maria suddenly got a look on her face, remembering Lucas. It was as if Sylvia could read her mind as she said, "Don't worry, my dear, I kicked Lucas out years ago. After I found out how he was acting, he's been on his own. The last I heard, he was hanging out with some drug dealers in New Jersey. You're safe from him here." Sylvia came over to Maria and gave her a hug. "I'm very sorry that I didn't believe you then. You were right."

Maria hugged her aunt back then. It was as if she'd gotten her mother back suddenly with her aunt having a change of heart. "In that case, I'd like to stay tonight. Thank you."

Later, she settled down into bed, a different room than before; she was consumed by guilt and worry about William and Krista. She even considered driving back tomorrow, but she knew that she couldn't go back there again, no matter how much she missed them.

William

The sun was peering through the living room and William woke up suddenly; sitting straight up. He must have fallen asleep on the couch. "Maria?" He called out in hopes that maybe she'd decided to come back from wherever it was that she went and got up, when he became dizzy and had to sit back down. Then he noticed the almost empty glass of whiskey that was on the coffee table. "Now I know why I stopped drinking that!" He said out loud. He must have had at least two drinks because his head was throbbing, but he managed to get up, get to the bathroom and take several aspirin. He glanced up at the clock in the kitchen as he went to make some strong coffee. It was only 7:30, but he was usually at his office by this time. Callie was usually there by 8:00 so he'd call her and let her know he'd be in late that day.

He poured himself a strong cup of black coffee as he wandered back upstairs to the empty rooms. He stopped at Karen's room and sat down on her bed. Maria had left everything the way it had been since she died. "Where's your mom, Karen? Please watch over her." He pleaded out loud. Before seeing that psychic Janice, he'd never believed in ghosts but now he wasn't so sure. Now he would take any help he could get from his daughter, his father or Gram Laura. When there was no response, he felt like a fool but at least no one was here to listen to him.

The phone rang and he grabbed it from the master bedroom phone. It was his mother. "Any word from Maria or the police?" Sara asked.

"No, mom. How's Krista?" He asked.

"She's asking questions, of course. You know her! I've been dodging them, but unless something changes soon, we'll have to tell her something." His mother sounded upset and stressed.

"I know mom. I'm going to check in with the police when I hang up and we'll go from there. Thank you again for taking care of her." He truly appreciated his mother. She really was there for him when he needed her.

"Anytime. I love having her here with me." His mother admitted. "She's good company and a distraction that I need right now with everything going on."

After he hung up with his mother, the phone rang again. This time it was the South Kingstown police. "William, this is Detective Sumner. Has there been any word from your wife?"

"No, I'm afraid not." He told the detective.

"I'd like to come out and meet with you in about an hour at your home. Does that work for you?" Detective Sumner asked him. William got a better vibe from this man on the phone, the complete opposite of the rookie cop from last night.

"Absolutely. You can come anytime." William obliged.

"Great. I'll be there in about 30 minutes." Detective Sumer told him.

William hung up and jumped into the shower. The last thing he wanted was to look like a complete hungover slob when the police showed up. He cleaned up and put on his usual suit attire for the office. He quickly picked up the bottle of Jack Daniels still sitting on the counter and put it away, along with straightening out the couch and putting his glass in the dishwasher. He called the office and Callie picked up immediately. "Callie, I won't be in until later today. I've had some things that I need to take care of here at home. Do I have any scheduled appointments or showings today?"

"You have one appointment at 2:00, Mr. Carson. Should I reschedule them?" Callie asked.

William thought for a moment, but knew that he wasn't sure he could do the appointment. "See if Shane has time to do the appointment and if he doesn't then please reschedule. Thank you, Callie, I'll be in touch." William decided quickly. For the first time since he'd started this business, his mind wasn't focused on it. Just finding his wife.

A few minutes later, the detective was at the door. Detective Sumner was around his age with dark hair. He was exceptionally tall with a chiseled face that most women would find handsome. "Mr. Carson, may I come in?" His demeanor was a far cry from the officer from last night. He put William at ease with his questions; last time he saw her, her moods lately, her depression and the death of their daughter. William felt as though he really listened. "There's the question about the blood outside that Spencer found last night." Sumner mentioned.

"My wife had been sleepwalking the night before. She wasn't wearing shoes so the only thing I can think of is that she must have cut herself or something." William told him.

"Officer Spencer didn't mention that in his report. I'll have to check on that." Sumner said.

"I'm not surprised. He seemed to think that I had something to do with her disappearing." William couldn't help but commenting. "He took a sample of it and I know that I told him what had happened the night before. Honestly detective, I just want to find my wife! She could be out there hurt or run into some people that would hurt her! I just lost one of my daughters less than six months ago. I just want the police to be looking for her!" William felt a sob in the back of his throat and tried to hold back from breaking down, but tears were pouring down his cheeks despite his struggle.

"Mr. Carson.." Sumner began.

"William, please. No need for formalities." William insisted.

"William, I apologize if Officer Spencer's behaviors last night were offensive or unprofessional. I can assure you that I'm going to take over your case in order to find your wife. That being said, do you have any idea where she might have gone?" Sumner's empathy was only fueling William's emotional break-down that he was struggling to keep in check. He reached for a box of tissues near the sink and blew his nose before answering.

"She's from Vermont, but she has only an aunt and a few cousins that I've never met. She isn't close to them. Her parents both died in a car accident when she was young and she was an only child. She has only a handful of friends; one of them she's fairly close with is Stephanie Martin. I didn't even think to check with her." William couldn't believe it hadn't occurred to him to call Stephanie, but then again,

Maria didn't leave the house very often. And she'd used that excuse to do the paternity testing behind his back. Sumner took down Stephanie's number as well as some of the neighbors that Maria nor William really spoke with on a regular basis, but he wanted to check with them anyway.

"Do you think I should contact her aunt in Vermont? That she might have some idea of where she might be?" Sumner asked.

"I've never met her, detective. And from what I've heard from Maria, she hasn't talked to her since she left her home after she graduated from high school. I don't know how to get in touch with her and actually don't know her last name." William believed it was the last place his wife would have gone.

"Well, if you can find a last name or a phone number for her Aunt Sylvia, I'd like to check it out. Do you know the town in Vermont?" Sumner asked.

"It was a small town- Middle something. Middlebury! That's it! Maria's maiden name is Evans so maybe her aunt had the same last name. I know that Maria grew up in a town called Orwell outside of Middlebury." William was desperate now. He had very little doubt that Maria had gone back to what she had referred to as a 'house from hell' to have a visit with her aunt. But then, she hadn't been herself since Karen had died. "It couldn't hurt to check out her Vermont family." William agreed with Sumner.

Sumner agreed to check it out as well as put out a press release for a missing person's report on Maria. "We'll do all we can. In the meantime, make sure you answer the phone if you're home and have your answering machine on when you're not. Let me know if you hear anything from her."

"I just need to know if anyone is suspecting that I had anything to do with this." William hated to bring it up, but after last night with Officer Spencer, it was reality.

"From what I've seen and what you've told me, I would say no. Just be aware that sometimes the media will speculate and rumors may surface. If they do, don't react, just give me a call. If you react, it will only cause more rumors and you don't need that. This is hard enough for you." Sumner advised him.

"I won't." William promised, but he didn't realize how hard that promise would be to keep.

For the next several months, William felt as though he was living in a nightmare. First, the police continued to view him as a 'person of interest' even though there was no evidence, besides the spot of blood outside that was found. The police had issued a warrant to search his house and literally tore his home apart looking for evidence and found none. They still continued to post surveillance on his house every night for over a week, but when they had nothing to go on, they finally stopped wasting their time.

Detective Sumner had put out an article in the Providence Journal the week after Maria disappeared giving the details and to contact the police if they had any information. Krista who had started to break away from talking about Karen as if she were there, began spending most of her time talking out loud to her again. Even his mother who had been his main source of support was starting to be concerned.

"William, she really needs to see someone again. I'm worried about her."

William agreed. He'd contacted Dr. Welch who saw Krista right after Karen's death. This time was different. He explained what had been going on to Dr. Welch prior to her seeing Krista. "She's been talking to her at school instead of talking to classmates, her teacher has mentioned that it's been a distraction in the class. I don't know what to do anymore." William was exhausted. Between working to keep his business going and being a single parent, while still looking for his missing wife, it was taking a toll on him.

Dr. Welch worked with Krista to help her understand that her mother's disappearance wasn't the same as Karen being gone. "Mr. Carson, she's just creating her sister's persona as a self-soothing mechanism now that she's missing her mother. You said that her grandmother spends a great deal of time with her?"

"Yes. She spends a lot of time with her." William agreed. It was true.

"Perhaps Krista could join a group at school that might help her to get acquainted with other girls her age and maybe do something she likes." William took her advice to heart and to his surprise, Krista wanted to do gymnastics. William enrolled her and was glad that she enjoyed herself and was starting to make friends. She started mentioning Karen less often, although sometimes she would still ask about her mother. "When's mommy coming home?' She would ask.

"I'm not sure, sweetheart. But I hope it's soon." It was the same thing he said to himself every day since she left. "But no matter what, I'll always be here."

Maria

It had been an exhausting four months since Maria had left William and Krista. She'd found a purpose for now, helping her Aunt Sylvia while she slowly deteriorated from pancreatic cancer. Her aunt was grateful for her help and one day while they were sitting outside on her rickety porch taking in the nicer weather at the beginning of May, Aunt Sylvia said "You remind me so much of your mother, you know. She always looked out for other people, more so than herself. She also had that special connection with people who've passed."

Maria knew that now, but had to ask. "When did you find that out?"

"Our mother, Janet, died when we were fairly young. Your mother was probably only 15 and I was 17. I can remember the night she died. She had a heart condition of sorts that was never diagnosed and died in her sleep. Our father woke up in the middle of the night and called the ambulance, but there was nothing they could do. Margo and I still shared a room at the time and she woke me up talking to someone. But I couldn't see anyone. I asked her who she was talking to, and she told me "It's mom. She's here in the room. She's telling us goodbye. She died." I sat straight up in bed and looked around the room and saw no one. I thought she was making it up. She insisted and we both got up to find our mother being wheeled out of the house with a sheet over her head and my father crying. I remember from that day on I was angry with her."

"Angry, why?" Maria asked her. She'd never heard much about her grandmother that she'd never met.

"I wasn't sure at the time. But we were never close after that. And when you came to stay with me after Margo died, I believe I took my anger out on you that I had toward her. But now, I know why. Because she was able to see her and say goodbye to her. I never had that ability that she had, that you have. It's a gift, you know." Sylvia turned toward her. "A gift not many people have."

Maria pondered what she'd said. "I suppose it is, but it's not helped me with Karen's death. I think being blind to this 'gift' only made it harder for me. I am glad that I reconnected with you." She smiled at her aunt and put out her hand, grasping Sylvia's thin shriveled hand in hers and closing Sylvia's arthritic ridden fingers around hers. "Thank you for telling me that. I never knew much about my grandmother."

Aunt Sylvia continued to get weaker and weaker. The hospice nurses had let Maria know that it would be soon and as much as she tried to prepare for her death, when it came exactly two weeks later, she found herself unable to handle it. She carried through what Aunt Sylvia had requested; cremation and burial with a simple ceremony. There were very few people present, and unfortunately, one of them was her son, Lucas that she hadn't seen since she'd left that morning for URI almost 6 years ago. He'd come up to her with the creepy face that was now covered in lesions from years of drug use.

"Hey, what are you doing here? How' bout you come back to my place?" He was clearly on some kind of drugs or alcohol, as he slurred his words. Maria gave him her best 'eat shit' look and said "Absolutely not!" She turned and left the reception then. There wasn't anything else for her to do here and she didn't want to stick around. Aunt Sylvia had her will intact and her attorney was handling her estate. She packed up and headed out for the one place she knew she wanted to visit. Block Island.

She packed up her few belongings and got in her car, heading back toward Rhode Island. At least she didn't need to worry about the weather now. It was the middle of May and warmer than usual for this time of year. As she pulled out of the driveway, she could hear her aunt's voice telling her that it would be okay. "There's nothing to fear on the other side. I'm not in pain and hoping to see Margo soon." Her voice faded away as quickly as it had come. Maria knew that she had crossed quickly. She had been ready, unlike her parents, Gram Laura and Karen.

Maria could feel the wave of depression coming on with a vengeance. She'd been so occupied with helping her aunt over the past few months, that she didn't have time to recognize how desperately sad she really was. She missed William and Krista. She missed Sara and her life with them. She missed Karen most of all. She should've been able to save her and help her and she'd failed. Over the past four months, Karen had come to her often in her dreams and asked her to come visit, but she'd been needed then. Now, she was free.

William and Krista had hopefully moved on from her leaving and now she could go. Tears filled her eyes as she crossed over into Rhode Island several hours later. As she drove closer to the exit for their house in South Kingstown, she decided she needed to see the house one more time. Her heart pounded as she drove down the familiar street and in front of their house, William was just getting out of the car and getting

Krista out of her car seat. She looked beautiful and William was more handsome than he'd ever been. She was tempted to stop but what would she say now? There was nothing to say. She'd left them and served a purpose. They didn't need her any longer. She didn't belong there.

She got back on the highway and headed to Point Judith to catch the 3:30 ferry to Block Island. She managed to get to the dock just in time as it was boarding. She sat in the enclosed area, glad to have some space to herself although it was still off season. She'd only brought her small duffel bag with her treasured jewelry box and few items of clothing and her notebook.

She could hear Karen's voice in her head, stronger now. "You're getting closer." She headed upstairs to look at the bluffs that she would soon be standing on. She was despondent that she was leaving behind the persons that meant the world to her. This time forever. Her tears mixed with the spray from the salt water, as the ferry sped along.

After docking, Maria followed the other passengers in her black hoodie sweatshirt in order to mingle with the crowd. Today was not the day to be noticed. Not that she ever wanted to be. She headed toward the Mohegan Bluffs that she'd remembered from the family trip. She stopped at a local liquor store and bought a bottle of wine. She needed some liquid courage now. She began walking toward the house on Mohegan bluffs and glad that she had left early while it was still light out in order to find it. She sipped slowly on the wine as she walked along until she'd finally arrived.

It was Gram Laura's estate that they'd come to last year before Karen had died. She could see lights on in the huge house and a No

Trespassing sign was posted at the circular driveway, but it was past 6:30 now and the sun was starting to set. Surely no one would see her now. She crept across the lawn behind the trees and made her way to the same spot where there was a slight path. She remembered that William had told her about where they used to play the game of chicken.

"Karen, I'm here." Maria said out loud. She was feeling tired and buzzed from the wine. She glanced over at her duffel bag and pulled out the jewelry box. She noticed a tree that was slightly off the cliff. She looked through the box and pulled out the picture of her and her girls; the treasure that mean the most to her and put it in her sweatshirt pocket. "You're coming with me." She said as she shut the box and scooped up the dirt under the roots of the tree near the cliff and covered it up. She didn't want her treasures to be found now. Krista would go on to be a beautiful young woman and William would eventually remarry. It was what she wanted for them.

She could hear Karen's voice coming closer. "Mommy, where are you?" She took a final sip of her bottle of wine and stepped closer to the edge. "I can hear you. I'm coming." She dropped the thermos off the edge of the cliff and took a deep breath. "I'm coming." She stepped off the ledge and felt as though she were flying for a few seconds before she hit the water below and suddenly everything went dark.

Stanley

Stanley Ahearn had been on vacation at his Block Island home when he was outside on the porch, having his glass of bourbon and smoking a cigar. He noticed a blonde woman in a black sweatshirt sitting on the cliff on his property. He walked toward her and noticed that she'd taken a drink out of a wine bottle and then stood up. He moved closer toward her, hoping that he wasn't going to have to deal with a drunk homeless person on his property and kick them out when she suddenly jumped off the cliff!

He started to run and saw that she had missed the rocks and hit the water. "Call 911!" He shouted out to the housekeeper that was outside cleaning up after him and headed down the stairs, that he'd built since he bought the property, to reach her.

She was unconscious and floating face down in shallow water when he reached her, her wet long blonde strands stretched out like a web around her head. He immediately pulled her face out of the water and brought her to the shoreline. He felt for a pulse on her neck and was relieved that he felt one. Her hair was tinted red from the blood and he could see a deep gash on her head that was bleeding profusely. He tried to wake her, "Ma'am are you okay? What's your name?" When there was no response, he knew he had to get her help. He hoisted her petite frame onto his back and prepared to bring her up the steps. He managed to hang on to her hands, as her limp neck and head was right near to his face. He trudged through the sandy beach to the steps and managed to get up to the top, just as the ambulance arrived.

By the time he set her gently on the ground, his shirt was covered in her blood. She definitely wasn't a homeless woman. Although she was dressed in a black sweatshirt and jeans, he could tell that she took good care of herself. Her nails were nicely painted and her skin was clear and unlined. Despite the blood, he could tell that she was a beautiful woman and looked somehow familiar to him, although he couldn't imagine where he'd seen her before.

The EMT's rushed over to the woman just as Stanley reached the top and two of them put her still unconscious onto a stretcher. "Do you know this woman, Mr. Ahearn?"

"No! I just happened to be outside when she was on the cliff." Stanley told them, noticing that they were eyeing his blood-covered t-shirt. "I happened to see her when I was on the porch. I noticed her sitting on the edge of the cliff, drinking from a wine bottle when she suddenly stood up and jumped."

"She's got a serious head wound that needs attention immediately", The lead EMT got on the radio. "We're going to need a life-flight out here on Block Island. Mohegan Bluffs Drive." He paused for a moment. "Mr. Ahearn, do we have permission to land a helicopter on your property?"

"Whatever it takes to save her." Stanley told them. Just then the housekeeper came running across the lawn after his two young daughters. Stanley was divorced, but had his two girls with him this week on vacation. "Please excuse me for a moment." He ran toward his daughters. "Amanda! Jane! Get back in the house NOW! This is adult business here!" He ushered them back toward the house and called for Loretta, the nanny that he'd hired to help him out with the girls while they were at the house.

"Loretta, please keep the girls in the house. There's been an accident on the cliff and I don't want them sneaking around out there." Stanley gave the young woman instructions. Loretta nodded. "Of course, Mr. Ahearn! I hope everything will be okay." She quickly engaged the girls in a game inside the house. Amanda was 7 years old and Jane was 6, but they might as well be teenagers, because that's how they behaved. He hated how their mother spoiled them. She made them believe that they were princesses and he had to deal with their behaviors now.

"Me too." He said. He usually tried not to get involved with other people outside his normal circle of friends in Hollywood. His success as a director had led to his lack of trust with people that knew who he was and just wanted to use him to get noticed.

He headed back outside to the EMT's that were working on the woman. They had her in the ambulance now, so he couldn't see her, but he wanted to know how she was. "Mr. Ahearn, we're stabilizing her. The life-flight helicopter is on the way." Stanley felt restless so he went back down the stairs and reached the beach where her found her. It was close to being dark, but he spied something on the sand right near the water's edge. It was a picture of a woman and two young girls that looked like twins. The background looked familiar, as if it were taken right in this area. The woman in the picture was clearly the same that jumped off the cliff and he dried it off quickly and put it in his pocket. He was sure that she would want it back someday if she recovered.

He could hear the sound of the helicopters from a distance and made his way back up the stairs. "Can you let me know how she's doing?" Stanley felt responsible now. Not just because she'd jumped on his property but because he wanted to know about this woman that was so beautiful and yet her life was so tragic that she would want to end it.

Days later, Stanley got a call from South County hospital. "There's a young woman here that was brought in from Block Island. She wants to talk to the person that helped her. Would you like to come in and speak with her?"

Stanley felt suddenly excited to meet with her again. "Of course. I can come right away." He suddenly felt strangely nervous about meeting this woman again now that she was awake.

"Mr. Ahearn, I just need to let you know that she doesn't have any recollection of anything of that day, or in fact anything that happened prior to the accident. She's had significant head trauma and some post-traumatic amnesia. She doesn't even recall her name right now. We're having a hard time with identifying this woman."

Stanley grabbed the picture that he'd hung up to dry off and brought it with him. Maybe that would help her remember something. He contacted his usual captain that he'd hired for trips to the mainland and they were on their way in an hour. He had a car waiting for him to take him to South County hospital and soon he was making his way to this woman's room. The nurse at the desk was waiting for him. "I'll take you in, Mr. Ahearn. Follow me."

There she was, prettier than he could ever imagine. Despite the bandages around her head, her beautiful blonde hair and her vibrant blue eyes were so captivating he was speechless for a moment. "Mr. Ahearn, I just wanted to thank you for all you did for me." The nameless young woman told him.

"It was my pleasure. I'm glad to see you doing much better." Stanley told her. He felt strange that he couldn't address her by her name. "Do you remember anything? What's your name?" Stanley asked, as the nurse in the room suddenly shook her head.

The beautiful woman on the bed shook her head. "I don't know. It's so frustrating. It's strange. I can remember other things like your name and where I am right now, but I can't remember who I am." He could see her eyes welling up with tears.

"Well, I'm glad that you're feeling and definitely looking better than you were a few days ago." Stanley said, finding it strange that he couldn't call her by a name. "If you could pick a name, what would you want your name to be?" He suddenly asked her without thinking. The nurse standing at the door was shaking her head, but the young woman in the bed looked intrigued.

"I never thought about it before. But since you mentioned it, I've always liked the name 'Caroline'. I used to watch 'Little House on the Prairie' when I was younger and I guess that's maybe where I heard it." She told him.

"Then, may I call you 'Caroline' from now on? I find it strange not to refer to you with a name." Stanley asked her.

"I'd like that." She told him and smiled. There was something about her that made him want to get to know her better and Stanley kept coming back week after week until she was finally able to be discharged. She'd kept her name as Caroline, and when it was time for her to leave, Stanley wanted to be there and help her out. He'd shown her the picture that he'd found, but she still had no recollection of what had happened or who the girls were in the picture. "They must have been related to me, but I honestly don't remember, Stan." She'd told him several times.

The day she was discharged from the hospital, Stanley picked her up in his limo and offered to put her up in a guesthouse at his Block Island estate. Initially, she declined. "Thank you so much for helping me but that's too much right now." She told him, although she wasn't sure where she would go.

"Caroline, you don't have any family that you can remember. I can't just drop you off at a hotel and not worry. I have a guest house that has everything you need; you can stay as long as necessary to get back on your feet." Stanley insisted. He wasn't sure what had come over him. Normally, he wouldn't be this concerned, but over the past few weeks with her, he'd found himself wanting to be around her more. He didn't want to lose contact with her and he didn't want her to be homeless as he thought she was when he first saw her on his property.

She was quiet for a moment. "I do need a place to stay. I'm not sure how I deserve someone to offer this, but I promise, I'll do housework around your property, whatever you need, Stanley." She was grateful because she did not have anywhere to go. She couldn't remember the girls in the picture. The only reason she knew that it was relevant to her life was that she was in the picture. It made her sad and she wished that someday she could remember these little girls. They must have been important enough for this picture to be taken.

"You don't need to do anything except continue to improve. I'll arrange for your physical and mental health therapy to come to you." Stanley assured her. He knew that he needed to be back in California within a few weeks to start a new movie project, so he made it his mission to get her trust before he left. He didn't want her to leave him now.

She made the choice to go and stay in his guesthouse. It was as if she were starting over. Although she wished that she could remember what she had left behind. She was tired from the ride but just before she fell asleep, she could hear a voice that was familiar. "I'm still here, mommy. I'm still waiting."

Over the next few months, Stanley had read the newspaper and seen clips on the news in search for Maria Evans Carson who fit Caroline's description, but now he had a choice to make. No wonder she looked familiar If in fact she was Maria, she'd leave him. He didn't want her to go. And he wasn't sure that she would believe him anyway. He deliberately kept the papers away from her and she didn't really watch TV. Still he knew that someday, she might remember and he'd have to deal with it. He couldn't help but feel guilty when he saw clips of William Carson on the news still looking for his wife. Once she was feeling better physically, she felt ready to leave the guesthouse. Stanley had begged to her stay. He confessed that he was in love with her and asked her to marry him.

She'd needed some time. She still had no recollection of her life before the accident, and needed some time to think. "I need some time, Stan." She'd told him, but they'd grown close and he could sense that she had the same feelings for him. His two young daughters were another factor because their mother had always been upset about the divorce and had gone out of her way to make it difficult for Stan to have another relationship.

In the end, Stanley had convinced her that no matter what, they could not let his children ruin their chance for happiness. He still had them visit over the years, but did his best to limit their interaction with Caroline. He took her everywhere around the world but kept her away from the press. The only thing that he worried about was that she kept seeing a little girl walking along the cliffs and disappearing. It would get her upset and then she would hibernate in their master suite for the rest of the day. The picture that he'd retrieved for her of the woman and the two little girls sat framed on their nightstand. From time to time, he would find her studying it, as if she were putting together the pieces of a puzzle. He tried to talk her into removing the picture and putting it somewhere else, but she wouldn't budge. "It's part of my past. I need it here with me."

It was the one thing he wouldn't take away from her. Stanley had convinced himself that he would protect her and to him that meant keeping her away from anything that would trigger memories of her past.

Epilogue

It had been almost 20 years since Stanley had found her in the water below the cliffs. It was a beautiful day for the beginning of May and Caroline had been sitting out on the deck looking out over the cliffs to the water. She caught another glimpse of the little girl that she'd seen for years near the cliff. She was a tiny blonde girl that looked very much like herself. Then she disappeared. Caroline shivered and went back inside.

Her memory had slowly begun returning about 10 years ago in bits and pieces. Through dreams, and other little things such as the sound of a little girl laughing, a gold necklace or just looking down at the beach from the cliffs began to spark flashbacks of what her life had been before she'd made that decision to jump. Stan's twin brother Dan's recent death in a car accident in California had also triggered the memory of the rape and finding out that he was the twins' father. It was one thing that she'd kept from Stanley. It was something she wanted to forget. Now she knew about her little girls and her marriage to William, as well as her name had been Maria. She thought about changing her name back, but now the name was foreign to her and she knew Stanley would be upset.

Stanley knew that she was regaining her memory, but she hid just how much recollection she had. She knew that he was worried that she'd leave him and go back to her life before him, despite her reassurance that she wouldn't. Caroline had even gone back to the mainland a few times and driven past where she and William had lived and waited to catch a glimpse of them. She had been disappointed when a young family appeared that was not William and Krista. They must have moved and she had no idea how to find them. Until she saw a picture in the society section of the paper one day that caught her attention. It was an engagement picture of Krista and her fiancé, Chad Burton. Below was the announcement; "William Carson, owner of Carson Realty announces the engagement of his daughter Krista Marie Carson to Chad Burton." Apparently, Chad was a real estate agent with William's company and Krista was a counselor at a high school in Johnston, a town outside of Providence.

Caroline's eyes filled with tears as she gazed at the picture of her daughter. Krista had grown up to be a beautiful young woman with her long blonde hair and blue eyes that were so like her own. She had the same dimples in each cheek and was smiling as if she were the happiest girl in the world. Caroline desperately wished she could be a 'hidden guest' at the ceremony, but the announcement stated that the wedding was taking place in St. Thomas in the Caribbean. Besides, she didn't want to put herself through that. Maybe someday, she'd be able to be part of her life again.

She continued to follow the occasional articles in the paper about Carson Realty. She was glad that William had built a successful realty business and when Chad was featured on an advertisement as an agent, she had an idea. Stanley had mentioned selling the Block Island property several times and she wasn't opposed to it, especially since the sightings of the little girl that she now knew was her daughter Karen were becoming more frequent.

She approached him one morning at breakfast before he was headed back to Hollywood, California to direct another movie. "I've got an idea. Why don't I have a real estate agent here in the Rhode Island area come out here and help us list this place? You keep talking about wanting to sell and honestly, this little girl I keep seeing is making me nervous. You'll be back and forth the whole time, so just let me know the asking price and I can contact an agent." Caroline hoped that he'd go for it and he did. She and Stanley had a good relationship, but he was often gone on business and it wasn't unusual for her to take care of house projects.

Stanley looked at her in amazement. "You really are okay with selling? I thought you were against it!"

Caroline shook her head. "I've thought about it. I think you're right about selling." Stanley looked more than happy. "Sweetheart, that's the best news I've heard from you in a long time. Absolutely." He agreed and gave her the listing price that he wanted. He looked at his watch as the limousine pulled up to the house. "I've got to run, the car's here. Call me when you've listed it. Love you and call you when I get there." He gave her a quick kiss on the cheek and then he was out the door.

Caroline went to the phone and dialed the number to Carson Realty. "Chad Burton, please." She was a step closer to knowing her son-in-law, even if he didn't realize it. Hopefully, it would lead her to Krista again. She stepped outside on the deck and could see the little blonde girl in the distance on the cliffs. The little girl suddenly waved to her, as if she knew. Caroline waved back and the little girl smiled at her before disappearing.